MW00627505

To
Repay
A
Debt

Enjoy!

Nancy Feldkul

Other books by Nancy Feldbush…
To Rebuild A Life

To
Repay
A
Debt

Nancy Feldbush

Moose Run
Productions
Clinton Township, Michigan

Published by...
Moose Run Productions
22010 Highview • Clinton Township, Michigan 48036
moose-run.com

© 2000, 2005 by Nancy Feldbush. All rights reserved.

Publishing History...
First Edition—Originally published as *Walking in the Midst*,
    © 2000, original ISBN: 1-893162-26-5
Second Edition—Expanded, © 2005

Manufactured in the United States of America

ISBN-13: 978-0-9766315-0-7
ISBN-10: 0-9766315-0-4

Library of Congress Control Number: 2005931015

Cover design by Nancy Feldbush
Printed in Michigan on recycled paper

No part of this book may be reproduced or transmitted in any form or by any means, electronic or mechanical, including photocopying, recording, or by any information storage and retrieval system—except by a reviewer who may quote brief passages in a review to be printed in a magazine, newspaper, or on the Web—without the written permission of the publisher.

This book is dedicated to…

Jesus, my Lord
You gave me the inspiration and courage to start this book.
Then Your guidance and love enabled me to finish it.
Thank you.

Mom and Liz
You allowed me to drag you all across Michigan because of my research.
I valued your company and assistance.
Thank you.

Ann, Colleen, Diane, Eloise, Jim, Julie, and Matt
Your input, support, encouragement, and prayers were appreciated
more than you will ever know.
You helped keep my head above the water.
Thank you.

Preface

A steady rain pelted Travis Perryn in the face and turned the summer-dry riverbed of the South Pine into a slippery muck that pulled at his boots. Stumbling over what he hoped was a root, Travis raised the glowing lantern in his hand, and as he watched the incessant drops strike the glass chimney, his resolve started to dampen. It was still a good plan, he reassured himself, even with the unexpected storm. The riverbed was still the best route to the railroad—and the only one that would keep him far from Sandorville's gaslit streets, where, even before daybreak, betraying eyes might see him making his escape. And, he silently added, by the time they figured out that he had chosen this exit, he would safely arrive at the railroad tracks.

As Travis studied the swaying trees lining the banks, his footing faltered once again, and he tottered to a stop. This had to be it. The trees were sparser than before—it had to be the Manvil farm. Pulling himself up the steep riverbank and out of the thickening mud, Travis surveyed the area. With a sigh, he nodded. Yes, it was Manvil's, but the wet darkness had altered the farm's appearance, making it almost...

Suddenly, a crack from the trees behind him sent a shiver through his body, and holding his breath, Travis paused as the rain splattered around him. He usually liked the sound of a storm—but now, it only made listening for pursuers more difficult. No, he told himself, it wasn't them. It was just an old branch breaking in the wind. With a deep exhale, Travis nodded and continued onward, following the bank of the river—all the while ignoring the familiar fear that quickened his pace. Then, in the flickering glimpses of dawn, he saw the swelling river curve to the south and he smiled—his final landmark would soon greet him.

Almost as if his thought had willed it into existence, a hollow, looming image emerged from the shadows just ahead of him, which slowly transformed into a massive boulder as he neared. And, soon, an outline of willow trees appeared behind the rock, their feathery boughs dripping into the South Pine River. Travis sighed again. It had been worth the effort to make a practice escape, mapping out the landmarks in his head. His only mistake was doing the test in the daylight, instead of the murky uncertainty of daybreak.

Reaching the mammoth boulder, Travis lifted his lantern and scanned the area. He was almost free. The unfurling forest would camouflage the remainder of his getaway—and in fifteen minutes he would exit the woods onto the railroad. But he had to hurry…sunup was approaching quickly.

"Ain't a very good mornin' for a stroll—is it, Perryn?"

As the words reached him and ripped through his body, his lantern crashed to the waterlogged ground, which immediately drowned the flame. Then a stocky, barrel-chested silhouette appeared from behind the rock and moved toward him. But he didn't need the lantern light to show him who was approaching—he knew it was Quentin Fetch.

"What a surprise meetin' you out here," Fetch said, his voice as chilly as the rain.

Surprise? Travis thought. No, it wasn't a surprise. Somehow, Fetch knew. Somehow, the man knew—and Travis slumped under the realization that he had told one too many about his plan. And, as his mind raced, trying to figure out whom he should not have trusted, two other well-known faces appeared, causing Travis to take a nervous swallow. Leland Bryce and Frank Hallam—of course. Fetch didn't go anywhere without his left and right hands.

"Now, Perryn, you didn't have to sneak out like this. You can leave anytime you want—as long as you pay me what you owe me."

The statement ignited a bitter anger inside Travis. "You know I can't pay you."

"Well, then you shouldn't be leavin' town, should you?"

"But I've got nothin' left to give. You've taken everything I have!"

"Not everything," Fetch murmured, tilting his head toward the dark-haired man on his left.

Leland Bryce raised a heavy piece of wood into the breaking daylight. It was the table leg Travis had begun to carve the day before—and the threat was extremely clear. "You'll never get your money if you kill me."

"That's true...so get back to the factory, and work a little harder, then you'll be able to pay me."

Travis couldn't stop himself from shaking—nor could he tell if the shivering was caused by the rain or the ice in Fetch's voice. "Harder? I can't, Fetch, and you know it." All emotion drained from Quentin Fetch's countenance and Travis bowed his head—he knew the lifeless expression all too well. "Sir," he added between clenched teeth, "I'm just too tired."

Fetch's lips spread wide with a smug grin. "Oh, I think you could put in a few more hours, if you really tried."

The words sucked away Travis' remaining strength, and he sank to his knees. In the past five months, he had worked harder than he ever had in his life. And now, they wanted more. He just couldn't waste the rest of 1888 sweating under the same tyranny, and as he stared at Fetch, Travis' thoughts drifted to the railroad tracks that were so very close. If only he could...

It was then that Travis noticed the glimmer of sunrise along the horizon—and his desperate mind became alert. Yes, he could make it. In the gaining light and with the cover of the woods, he could make it.

Pushing himself up and forward, Travis shoved Fetch backward into Bryce, causing both men to lose their balance. Then, swinging a wild fist at Frank Hallam, Travis sprinted into the rain-drenched forest and blindly maneuvered his way through the branches as they whipped at his face. Run...just run, he told himself. Run and don't look back—but he did…and fear grabbed his heart. They were gaining.

Then Travis tripped.

It was Hallam who first reached him and kept him pinned to the ground. Fetch was nearing fast, and Bryce, still carrying the table leg, was directly behind his barrel-chested leader. Using what strength he had left, Travis tried one last effort to free himself, but as his three breathless opponents surrounded him, he lost all hope. And, in that instant, Travis understood what was going to happen, and he wished he had gotten to know God a little bit better.

⇥ One ⇤

Peter Leighton stepped back from the brick building in front of him and studied the carved name above the front doors. *Rheinhardt Furniture.* The inscribed-marble nameplate, which separated the first and second floors, spanned the entire front and gave the structure a truly grand appearance. As he continued to examine the embellishment—and calculated the cost—Peter whistled quietly, then, with a shake of his head, he moved to the ornately decorated doors and pushed the right-hand side open. Instantly, an overhead bell announced his entrance, and just as instantly, a stooped man appeared at his side.

"Yes Sir, how can I help you?" the hunched man rattled out.

After giving the door a slight shove with his elbow, Peter removed his top hat and held out a card. "Mr. Rheinhardt is expecting me."

The man snatched the card from Peter's grasp and studied it. "Peter Leighton. Yes, yes, of course," the man happily announced.

"Is Mr. Rheinhardt in?"

The bowed man bobbed his head fervently and darted through a wide velvet curtain without a word.

Grinning at the man's gerbil-like mannerisms, Peter hung his hat on the stand near the door, then, circling, he surveyed the furniture showroom while savoring the sweet smell of freshly cut wood. The walls, which were unfinished and unclad, were in complete contradiction to the various pieces of furniture—mostly tables and chairs—that waited in polished anticipation for a buyer. Then, suddenly, a chill trembled through him as his attention fixed on an elegant table that sat upon a display platform in the back of the room. Staring at the skillfully carved legs and edges of the table, Peter's jaw clenched—the piece practically eclipsed the more modest items surrounding it.

"Peter! Peter, my boy, it's so good to see you!"

Pulling himself from his trance, Peter turned and nodded at the brisk little man, who had returned and who was now followed by an older, taller figure. Immediately, Peter's expression lightened as he recognized the second man. "Mr. Rheinhardt, it's good to see you too."

"I'll have none of that," the older man returned as he reached Peter. "It's Karl now."

Shaking Karl Rheinhardt's hand, Peter forced a casual grin. "All right... Karl," he replied, feeling immensely awkward about being so informal with his father's friend.

It had been two years since Peter had last seen Karl Rheinhardt, but as he examined the man's leathered face, it looked more like ten. Karl's hair had turned a silvery white, and creases of time and sadness had dug themselves into the man's face, hiding the strong features that Peter remembered.

"It's wonderful to see that handsome face of yours again," the older man went on, smiling broadly. "It's been a long time."

"Yes Sir, it has."

"Peter, I'd like to introduce Adelbert Franz," Karl said as he settled a hand on the hunched shoulder of the quick little man next to him. "Del is the best bookkeeper and purchasing clerk in Michigan."

"It's very nice to meet you," Peter offered, shaking Del's extended hand.

"And you," Del returned. "Peter Leighton...your name is so familiar to me...I know I've heard Karl use it—even before he decided to hire you as his assistant."

"No, I'm sure you're just—"

Snapping his fingers, Del nodded as if his head were on a spring. "Now, I remember...you're the gentleman who's been sending us all those wonderful pieces," he exclaimed, pointing a stubby finger toward the elevated carved table in the back of the showroom.

Peter moistened his suddenly dry lips. "Yes...I am."

"Are you the cabinetmaker?"

"No...no."

"Peter's stepbrother is the woodworker," Karl put in. "He's quite remarkable for being so young."

His jaw muscles tightening, Peter flinched at Karl's reply, especially the word 'stepbrother.' It was true—he had gained a stepbrother from his mother's second marriage—but he never thought of his sibling as anything less than a true brother.

"You must be very proud of your stepbrother," Del offered.

"I am...my brother's talent is definitely amazing."

"Amazing? It's heaven-sent," Karl chuckled. "And, if I didn't care for the boy so much, I'd be jealous of him."

"Is he here in Sandorville with you?" Del asked. "I'd like to meet this marvel."

Wanting to distance their conversation from his brother, Peter shook his head and forced a wide smile onto his face. "No, he's home working on another project."

"Ah, that's unfortunate," Del returned as he rocked back on his heels and folded his arms. Then, unfolding them, he dug in his waistcoat pocket and consulted his watch. "Well, it's been a pleasure...I look forward to working with you," he said, twitching a good-bye.

After watching the clerk dash through the velvet curtain, Peter raised his eyebrows and glanced at Karl.

"I know," the older man laughed, shaking his head. "You would kill Del if you asked him to stand still for five minutes. Sometimes, I have to catch my breath just from watching him."

Peter half-smiled in return.

"I haven't seen that little smirk of yours in years," Karl announced, his face beaming. "It's your father's, you know...you favor him very much."

With a deep sigh, Peter bobbed his head in agreement. His father's traits were becoming stronger and stronger with the years, which Peter had little objection to—except for the premature gray that was creeping into his charcoal-colored hair and mustache. Most everyone told him that the sprinkling of gray enhanced his appearance, but still, he wasn't quite ready to accept the change.

"Did you find your hotel to be adequate?" Karl asked as he began to roam through the showroom, shifting the positions of a few select chairs.

"Yes, it's excellent."

"I was hoping that the Besyrwan would have been finished by now...it's going to be a splendid hotel when it's done."

"My place is just fine. I noticed that there's a lot of building going on in town."

"Indeed there is! My brother-in-law is even moving his wagon business to Sandorville."

"Really? That'll be great having him so close."

"It won't be for awhile though...his factory is still being constructed. We'll have to take a carriage ride out to see it."

"It must be nice to see all this growth."

Karl nodded. "It is, but it's made for quite a mess trying to get around... that's why I wish you had let me meet you at the depot or at least send my coach for you."

"There was no need," Peter replied with a wave of his hand. "I'm used to finding my own way...besides, the driver knew exactly where to go."

"I just don't know how you can stand to ride in those hackney carriages," Karl murmured, sliding a small, armless chair closer to its matching table.

"Oh, I don't mind them...and actually, I prefer walking."

"Walking? There are faster—and more advanced—ways of getting around, my boy."

"You wouldn't say that if you saw how crammed the streets were earlier."

Karl chuckled.

"Plus, walking usually clears my head and helps me think."

"Still…any of my carriages are at your disposal."

With a smile, Peter shook his head. "Thank you, but as I said, I can find my own way…and pay for my own hotel room."

"Nonsense! I explained that to you in my letter, young man," Karl returned, shaking his index finger at Peter. "I asked you to come here and help me. And I insist on paying your expenses—all of them. Now, not another word."

Peter finally yielded. "Yes Sir—and thank you."

Examining his alterations to the room's layout, Karl breathed in deeply, then he glanced up at Peter and grinned. "Why, this is the first chance you've had to see the new offices and showroom, isn't it?"

"Yes, it is…why did you choose to build the showroom here?"

"It was my son's idea—'improvement and movement' he always said. Because of the distance between the factory and the depot, buyers would just stay on the train and continue to Grand Rapids…so Marcus wanted an impressive showroom here in town and closer to the depot—to give the buyers a reason to get off the train."

"Sounds like a good idea…but has it caused any management problems having the offices so far from the factory?" Peter asked.

Karl pushed his shoulders back and lost his smile. "It's not that far—it's only a short carriage ride to the factory from here," he snapped. "My son had considered the distance, and he said it wouldn't matter."

Realizing that he had stumbled close to an edge—one that he had hoped to avoid—Peter blew out a long breath and rubbed his temple. No one could ever question the actions of the Rheinhardt children—no one. They were their father's only blindness, and in Karl's eyes, they could do no wrong.

"I was just wondering," Peter said quietly. "Then you haven't had any trouble?"

Karl relaxed slightly. "No. When my son was foreman, I never had to worry."

"And now?"

Grief swept over Karl and he didn't answer.

Peter silently cursed. He had backed away from one edge, only to fall off another. The subject of Marcus Rheinhardt's death was the second issue he had wanted to stay far away from—for as long as possible.

Karl aimlessly wandered toward a chair and nudged it a few inches to the left. "There," he said as if the ten degrees improved the chair's appearance. "And now, I still don't have to worry," the older man added, finally acknowledging Peter's question. "I promoted one of my men—Quentin Fetch—to take over as foreman. He's been a great help, and he has everything running so smoothly that I haven't had to set foot in the factory for months…I couldn't have gotten through these past three years without him."

Peter swallowed hard as he considered the repercussions of Karl's inaction—especially if Quentin Fetch was not an honorable man. "When will I be able to meet Mr. Fetch?"

"Right after lunch."

"Good," Peter returned. And, trying to lighten Karl's somber mood, he added, "Once the walls are finished, this showroom will be outstanding."

Pride sparkled in the older man's eyes. "And we can fit so many more samples in here than we could in the factory's showroom. It seems the more we show, the more orders we get. And the one-of-a-kinds sell just as fast—especially your stepbrother's," Karl said, motioning to the elevated table. "But come, I want to show you the offices upstairs."

His energy noticeably renewed, Karl gestured for Peter, and the two passed through the velvet-curtained doorway that Del had disappeared into. Once inside the back room, Peter paused to get his bearings—and his jaw dropped in dread and puzzlement. To his right, a rough-hewn, banisterless staircase turned and rose to the second floor. To his left, Del leaned over a makeshift desk full of papers, frantically scribbling figures into a ledger. And straight ahead stood the room's only light source—two large battered doors that were propped open with buckets. It was more than clear that all efforts to complete the showroom had died with Marcus Rheinhardt.

"Peter?"

As he pulled himself from his reverie, Peter glanced upward and realized that Karl had continued up the stairs without him, and now, his host stood impatiently on the top landing. Rushing up, two steps at a time, Peter emerged into a large anteroom stuffed with more Rheinhardt Factory-made tables and chairs. Karl then opened the first of the three doors adjoining the waiting room and motioned Peter inside. As he entered the office, Peter's attention was immediately drawn to two floor-to-ceiling windows, which displayed a stunning view of the North Pine River.

"I never mind coming into work when I have that landscape to marvel at," Karl commented.

"Neither would I," Peter murmured as he surveyed the rest of his surroundings. Unlike the rooms downstairs, Karl's office was decorated as superbly as the scene outside the windows. In fact, it was almost a showroom in itself, stocked with samples of the best hand-carved furniture Peter had ever seen—then, as he recognized three of the pieces, he frowned.

"What's wrong, Peter?"

"You have some of my brother's furniture in here...I don't want you to think that you still have to take care of us."

Karl's face crinkled with bewilderment.

"You bought these to—"

"Now, just a minute, young man," Karl said, holding up his hand to silence Peter. "I love well-made furniture. And every piece in here is from a carver that I respect very much—the reason your stepbrother's creations are here is because I wanted them here."

Peter grunted quietly but said nothing.

"Sit down, Peter," Karl urged as he lowered himself onto a velvet-upholstered chair facing one of the picture windows.

Following the example, Peter sank onto an identical seat next to Karl.

"During the war," the older man continued, "your father and I promised to watch over each other's family—in case something happened to either one of us."

"I know," Peter nodded. "He told me about your pact."

"So I was pleased that I could help out before. It was a way to fulfill that promise. But, concerning your stepbrother's pieces, I would have bought the furniture—regardless. Being able to give you two the money was a bonus."

"I apologize, Mr. Rheinhardt...sometimes my mouth has a mind of its own."

"It's forgotten—and it's Karl."

Peter half-smiled. "Karl."

"While we are on the subject, how are you and David faring?"

"Daven," Peter corrected as his grin faded.

Confusion etched its way onto Karl's face. "What?"

"My brother's name is not David...it's Daven," Peter replied, both surprised and puzzled. That was something he wasn't used to—Karl Rheinhardt making mistakes, especially when it came to the fine details.

"Yes...yes...of course," Karl stuttered with a wave of his hand. "So are the two of you doing all right—financially?"

"Basically...things were pretty good for awhile—we stopped taking in boarders, and I went back to just one job...then it all soured again when the Miller Factory closed and Daven's income disappeared. That's why I'm grateful you agreed to put his pieces in your showroom and sell them for us."

"I'm the grateful one...I have many carvers sending me one-of-a-kinds, but my customers are always drawn to Davis' work. Sometimes his things sell faster than my own."

As he winced at the second name error, Peter's trust in Karl's wit involuntarily slipped down one notch, and he began to sense that he was going to have scores...and scores...of unexpected obstacles to hurdle during his mission. Carefully forming his words, Peter leaned forward and whispered, "Daven has a very distinct style…if he does any amount of carving in your factory, someone could recognize his work."

Karl shook his head. "No, that won't happen. I appreciate elaborate pieces like this," he said, sweeping his arm in a wide arc, "and my father acquired quite a fortune making them. But I want people to be able to afford my furniture—so it's much plainer and simpler. Davis won't be carving anything that would show off his full talents."

"I'm just concerned because, when we were talking with Del, you mentioned how good Daven is—and how young he is…that description could trigger a connection for Del when Daven applies for work in the factory."

"I told you, your stepbrother won't be carving anything elaborate…and Del is very trustworthy."

"I'm sure he is, but he could still, inadvertently, reveal Daven's identity."

"That's not going to happen…Del rarely goes over to the factory. I'm sure he and Daven won't ever cross paths."

With a long, unsatisfied exhale, Peter sat back in his chair.

"Peter, no one, not even Del, knows anything about why I brought you and your stepbrother here."

"It's just that anonymity is vital for our plan to work—and for my brother's safety…when Del said he recognized my name, I—"

Karl sighed. "Just like your father. Worry, worry, worry. Daven Ashby will be a stranger to everyone—I'm the only one who will know that he's your stepbrother…and as he said, Del recognized your name from the furniture you've sent me. He knows you're the son of an old friend and that I've hired you as my assistant. That's all anyone knows."

Peter bobbed his head somewhat relieved.

Pushing himself from his seat, Karl ambled over to the window and leaned against the carved sill. "I can't tell you how much I appreciate you and your stepbrother coming here to help me—you both gave up a lot."

"Not that much."

"Come on, Peter, I know how far you had worked your way up in that printing company."

"Yes Sir, but our debt to you was more important."

"But you don't owe me anything anymore."

"Yes, we do…our thanks."

"Well, for whatever reason—I'm glad you're finally here. It's been pretty lonely since…" Karl mumbled as he drifted into thought.

In the stillness, Peter studied Karl Rheinhardt's countenance. There was no doubt as to what was causing the older man's melancholy. Karl had lost all three of his sons—leaving him with only one child, his daughter, Lorelei. Each time a son died, a part of Karl had dimmed. But, apparently, the loss of Marcus, the favorite son, had extinguished a great deal of the older man's spirit.

"I miss him," Karl began, returning from his memories.

Peter nodded.

"I know the accident happened over three years ago," Karl sighed, "but sometimes, it feels like yesterday."

"I wish I had been able to attend the funeral."

"No, my boy, that's all right…with having just lost your mother and dealing with your work and the boarding house, I really didn't plan on you coming," the older man replied. Then he took a deep breath and shook his head. "I appreciate that you're here, now, so much more."

"Thank you, Sir."

"I just can't believe that you're finally here…how long has it been? Five…six years?"

Consternation rippled down Peter's back, and he rose and walked over to Karl. "No Sir. You came up to Bradlee about two years ago…when we settled my debt…and you also came when Mum died…don't you remember?"

Again the older man waved away his forgetfulness. "Yes. Yes, of course," he muttered, then, strolling to his desk, Karl pulled out a large winged-back chair and slumped onto the cushioned seat. "So are you and Daven still butting heads?"

Karl's effort to change the subject was obvious, but deciding that it was best to just bypass the faulty recollections, Peter replied with a shrug, "Sometimes…I do hope the move here will improve the situation though."

"He's still young, Peter…give him a chance to be youthful."

"I know he's young, but it's still time that he learned how to commit to something worthwhile—and stay with it…he just doesn't seem to have…to have any concerns."

"And you, young man, have too many."

Peter responded by gazing out the window. He agreed, but unfortunately, the truth didn't help with one basic fact…he had no choice—there was no one volunteering to take any of his concerns away.

"You have to understand," Karl added, "Daven doesn't have your head for numbers and answers and such."

Meeting the older man's stare, Peter's eyes narrowed. "And we know who to blame for that, don't we?"

Karl's expression hardened. "Isn't that grudge getting a little heavy to keep carrying around?"

The question stabbed a nerve and Peter's jaw stiffened. Yes, his grudge was weather-beaten and weighty, but it was also completely valid. Swallowing the retort that sat on the tip of his tongue, Peter walked over to the desk and perched himself on the ornate wooden chair opposite Karl. "I know Daven's not a business man," he offered, hopefully steering the conversation in a new direction. "And I can't make him one—I know, I've tried…but we've actually been talking about combining our talents and starting our own business."

"Doing what?"

"Doing what Daven does best—making furniture."

"Giving me a little competition, are you?"

Peter's mouth dropped open—it probably was not the right time to mention to his employer that he planned to start his own furniture business. "I, um…we won't be able to do that for some time…and, uh, it won't be here."

"It's all right," the older man chuckled. "I think it's wonderful that you two will finally be working together."

"Well, we're not absolutely sure if we can overcome our differences and be business partners...that's why this time in your company is going to be so good for us—it should show us if we can work together," he explained, being careful to remain silent about the fact that he and Daven also intended to use their current incomes as the capital for their venture.

"I'm glad to hear it...but I must admit, I was praying that...that you'd take a different route," Karl said as he rose from his seat and shuffled over to Peter.

"What do you mean?"

"I...I wanted to...to offer you..."

"What?"

"A part...well, let me show you. Come," Karl proclaimed, pulling Peter up by the arm. His face now beaming, the older man guided Peter back into the anteroom and pointed toward the last of the three adjacent doors. "That's Victor's office," he explained.

"Victor?"

"My salesman. He's on a selling trip right now...and this," the older man whispered, moving to the middle door, "is...was Marcus' office." Slowly, Karl unlatched the door and tiptoed inside, as if he didn't want to disturb his absent son.

As he entered the obviously prized chamber, Peter was immediately choked by the confined, stale air that hung from the ceiling. Although smaller than Karl's office, Marcus Rheinhardt's room projected more elegance. Its matched, walnut furnishings and intricate, hand-carved trimmings and massive, multi-paned picture window added a richness that could be felt as well as seen.

"This is quite an office," Peter offered, gazing at the window and its glorious view of the wooded riverbed.

"I made every piece of furniture in here for Marcus," Karl explained as he stepped over to the window. Then, as he pushed a long, vertical pane outward, he added, "I'll have Del air the room out and clean it up a bit so you'll be more comfortable."

"Me?"

"This will be your office while you're here."

"Are you sure?" Peter asked, uneasy that the seal to Marcus' shrine had been broken just for him.

"Absolutely, I wouldn't consider letting anyone use this office—but you...I, uh, I also hoped it would influence you to stay."

"Stay?" Peter questioned as a slight summer wind stirred the room's frosting of dust.

"Yes...you see, Peter, I'd like you to stay on here—even after you find out what's going on in the factory...I don't want to interfere with your plans for your own business, but I would like you to consider becoming my partner."

"Partner?" The proposal caught in Peter's throat, smothering any response he could think of. He had just finished remapping his future, finally overcoming the disaster that had erased it before—now, with a few unexpected words, Karl was asking him to rewrite it again.

"I had always thought your father and I would end up as partners," the older man went on sadly, "but that thief's bullet killed that hope."

"It killed a lot more than that," Peter put in softly, bowing his head.

"Yes, but at least God gave you a stepfather to fill that void...you must be grateful for that."

Immediately, Peter's head jerked up and he glared at Karl. "Grateful?! How can I be grateful after the mess he made?!"

"But you still had someone who cared for you," Karl countered, the lines on his face intensifying. "Your stepfather was far from perfect, but he was there for you—and you were blessed enough to get a stepbrother out of the deal...you weren't left alone after your father died."

As anguish and loneliness washed over the older man, Peter finally realized that Marcus' death had burned a hole clear through Karl's soul.

"So you're in here!"

Startled by the voice, Peter pivoted on his heel and watched as a radiant young woman breezed into the office, obviously not caring if she was an intrusion or not. A feathery hat hid most of the woman's dark, uplifted hair—except for the few strands carefully pulled down to frame her porcelain face—and a gilt-edged lavender silk suit hugged her small figure and cascaded, in layers and folds, over her bustle to the floor. Pausing for a moment at Peter's side, she smiled coyly, then brushed by and continued over to Karl—all the while bathing the dusty, stagnant air with the scent of roses.

"Father, did you forget that you promised to take me to the Vanya for our afternoon-dinner?" she asked with a pout, tapping his chest lightly with the handle of her parasol.

The years had erased Lorelei Rheinhardt's features from Peter's memory, and he stared at her as though looking at a stranger. There had been a time when the Rheinhardt and Leighton families had visited each other almost every month. But that tradition died when John Leighton was laid to rest—it was as if his father had been the only glue that held the two clans together. And, because of that lost connection, Karl stopped bringing his wife and children when he visited. Now, seeing Lori after nine years, Peter silently confessed that she had blossomed into a mesmerizing woman. Yet a remembrance of disliking her still resounded in his head...

"And who is this dashing young gentleman," Lori questioned as she waltzed over to Peter.

"Lorelei, you remember Peter Leighton...I told you that he was coming to work for me."

"Of course. It's so kind of you to help Father," she purred. Then, slipping closer to Peter, she added in a sugared tone, "And to be able to get away from your store to come here and...oh, that's right, you had to close your little mercantile shop for good, didn't you?"

Peter's jaw clenched. The comment instantly brought back the reason he had disliked Lorelei—she loved to scratch at people's wounds. "Yes, it's closed," he replied.

"And then Father said you went to work making ink or something…"

"It was a printing company," Peter corrected.

"Obviously that didn't work out either, since you're here," she chirped with a sly smile.

Peter searched Karl's face for recognition of Lori's taunting—but there was none. To her father, Lorelei would always be the sweet girl she pretended to be, and Peter had learned, long ago, to never challenge that image. Then, as he reconsidered Karl's proposed partnership, Peter shuddered—Lorelei's proximity was definitely making him lean toward the answer 'no.'

"I'm here because your father needed me," he returned, struggling to control his simmering temper.

Suddenly, a sharp rap sounded at the office door, and all eyes fell on Del, who was standing over the threshold. "Karl, a moment please?"

As the older man excused himself and joined his clerk, Lori spun around to face Peter. "Why are you in Marcus' office?" she demanded in a sharp whisper.

"Your father is letting me use this room while I'm here," Peter replied, also keeping his voice quiet.

A flash of rage crossed Lori's face, marring her delicate features. "One day here and already you've squirmed your way into my brother's office!"

"Squirmed? It was your father's idea."

"I'm sure it was," Lori seethed with a sarcastic lilt. "Don't you dare think about taking advantage of my father's grief."

"I have no intention of—"

"And, if you have any designs to further yourself in our company, you should take them and leave!" she hissed.

"Look," Peter fumed through clenched teeth, "I'm here to help your father, not to…" Catching a slight movement out of the corner of his eye, Peter let his response drift into oblivion—Karl's conversation with Del had ended, and the older man was once again within hearing distance.

"And how are my two favorite youngsters getting along?" Karl inquired, his eyes twinkling as if he had just wound an old plan into motion.

Lori's mock charm returned instantly. "Peter's wonderful, Father…it seems as if only a month has passed since I last saw him—instead of almost a decade."

Peter found it harder to overcome his indignation, yet he pushed himself to sound calm. "That's true…the more Lori and I talked, the more I realized that things haven't changed."

Obviously enraged by the comment, Lori's eyes narrowed—but she remained silent.

"Good, good," Karl declared. "Now, Daughter, I have business to discuss with Peter."

"But Father—our afternoon-dinner."

"I did not forget about lunch. You're early…why don't you have the coachman drive you to that millinery you like so much. Peter and I will be ready for lunch in an hour."

A pout answered him.

"Lorelei…"

"Oh, all right," she brooded. Then, whipping Peter a last look of suspicion, she stomped out of the office.

Holding his index finger up to his lips, Karl waited voicelessly until he heard Lori's heels clack on the wooden stairs, then he turned to Peter and sighed. "She exhausts me sometimes…whenever Victor's out on a selling trip, she just doesn't know what to do with herself."

"Victor? As in Victor your salesman? They're courting?"

Karl nodded with an uneasy grimace. "She has bounced from one romance to another and decided that Victor Kilian would be her next conquest."

"You don't approve?"

"It's not a matter of approval…I like Victor very much. He wouldn't work for me if I didn't…he's just not the caliber of man I want for my daughter. She always seems to pick…to pick the wrong kind of fellow," Karl grumbled in exasperation. "I want her to find a beau of a higher quality…such as…such as you."

The invitation shot through Peter like a lightning bolt—he had no desire to ever get that close to Lorelei's claws. "Mr. Rheinhardt, we should probably go over the letter before lunch."

"Karl," the older man corrected as he placed a fatherly arm around Peter's shoulders and led him back into the anteroom. "It's so good to have you back."

"Back?"

Karl chuckled nervously and lowered his arm. "I meant here."

As they reentered the older man's office, Karl immediately headed over to his desk, then, after motioning for Peter to sit, he pulled out the top drawer and began to sift through the papers inside.

With a long exhale, Peter unbuttoned his frock coat and, once again, settled onto the seat opposite his host. He was both puzzled and bothered by the older man's recent words, and as he absently fingered the deep, carved grooves in his chair's arm, the morning's conversation replayed inside his head—then his thoughts drifted to Lori's accusations.

"Mr. Rhein…Karl?"

"Don't worry. I'll find it…the letter's here somewhere," Karl mumbled, trying a different drawer.

"How does Lori feel about me being here?" Peter's eyes suddenly widened at his poorly phrased question. "I mean, what have you told Lori about my being here?"

"That you're my new assistant," Karl returned, his attention on his search.

"You haven't told her about the letter?"

Glancing up, Karl shook his head. "This is a man's business. Neither my wife nor my daughter has any need to know what goes on here."

Not quite convinced, Peter chuckled silently as he mulled over the idea of asking Lori if she felt the same way.

"Ah, here it is," Karl exclaimed, yanking a folded paper from the bottom drawer. "Besides," he went on, "my daughter's only concern about Rheinhardt Furniture is that it keeps her in new hats."

Doubting the statement, Peter rubbed his temple. Lori's fiery whispers revealed that she had more than just that one concern. "Then you haven't told her anything about Daven being here?"

"I told you," Karl replied sharply, slamming the drawer shut, "Lori has no desire to give input to this company—and it wouldn't be allowed if she did."

With an inward smile, Peter nodded. Maybe now, he could consider Karl's partnership offer without being swayed by Lorelei's presence. "I'm just concerned that Lori will somehow reveal who Daven really is."

Karl perched himself on the edge of the desk and handed the folded page to Peter. "Now, you seem to be the one forgetting," the older man said, irritation stiffening the lines on his face. "Lori never even met your stepfather—let alone Daven. She couldn't possibly recognize him."

"I know she can't recognize him by sight," Peter persisted, ignoring the fact that his search for a satisfying answer was agitating Karl, "but she does know that Daven Ashby is the name of my stepbrother...if she goes near the factory, she—"

"Peter, please. It'll be fine. Even when Marcus was...when Marcus was alive, Lori refused to go near my 'dirty little factory.'"

"I don't know...maybe I should have him use an alias," Peter murmured, more to himself than to Karl.

"How many times do we have to go over this? I said it'll be fine...if you're so worried about Daven's safety, just forget that part of the plan. I've told you it's not necessary."

Peter's jaw muscles tensed, and he shifted positions in his chair. "I disagree...if your employees are misusing the factory's supplies, Daven can find out a lot more than I ever could from my position here."

"I still say it's unnecessary. It's not any of my employees...the trouble is outside the factory and that proves it," Karl returned as he pointed toward the paper.

The gesture reminded Peter of the letter in his hand, and he unfolded the reason he had come to Sandorville...

April 1, 1888

My Dearest Sir,

I write to congratulate you on the magnificent piece of furniture that the Rheinhardt Factory crafted. This newest gift from my dear husband is truly a treasure. I commend your skill and the skills of those in your employ. This grand cabinet displays my most precious memories.

The fanciful carvings equal those on my other pieces of fine furniture purchased from you. Your mark of excellence deserves to be applauded. We shall only buy furniture with the engraved Rheinhardt "R" of distinction. My husband will soon contact your salesman to order my long-awaited, mahogany ladies' writing desk.

Yours, with all sincerity,

Mr. and Mrs. Brinton Hopewell

Crestfield, Michigan

Refolding the letter, Peter looked up at Karl and stuffed the paper inside his breast pocket. "It's clear that she believes her cabinet came from your factory."

Karl leaned forward, supporting himself on the desk. "Well, it didn't."

"You can't be sure of that…maybe someone's using your supplies to—"

"I told you, Peter," Karl cut in, "my factory makes simple, affordable pieces—tables, chairs, an occasional bookcase—we haven't turned out anything even close to what this woman is describing. Plus, I checked my books…I have no record of any 'Hopewell' customer."

"Do you think she's mistaking it for a piece from someone else? Maybe a one-of-a-kind that you had in your showroom?"

Karl shook his head. "No. You read where she talks about the engraved 'R'—every piece of my furniture gets branded with that mark…there's only one answer…some other company is using my name and reputation to sell their furniture."

Gazing at Karl Rheinhardt, Peter gritted his teeth. Why was Karl ignoring the obvious? "Possibly...but more likely, someone is—"

"What?!"

Peter bowed his head, searching for the words that would open Karl's eyes. "More likely, someone is using your factory's supplies or tools to make some furniture on the side, then he's selling the pieces as his own—and keeping the profits."

Slowly and without a reply, Karl rose from the desk and withdrew to the window.

Unsure if the older man had accepted his point, Peter stood and added, "Mrs. Hopewell fully believes that her furniture came from your factory here in Sandorville. That's why I want Daven in there, just in case something is going on that you don't know about."

"Don't you think I'd know if hand-carved furniture was being made at my factory?"

Peter realized that he was, once again, approaching the unapproachable— and that he needed to tread lightly. "When Marcus was alive, yes, you would have. But now, with your...your detachment from the factory, someone could be working on the side, and you might not know it."

Karl circled to face Peter, outrage flushing his face. "You're wrong, Peter. My employees have been with me for years. They're loyal—not thieves. This is all just a matter of another company using my name!"

With an impatient grunt, Peter marched over to the window and stared into Karl's defiant eyes. "Maybe it is another company—maybe not. That's what I intend to find out," he stated firmly. "Isn't that why you asked me to come here? Because I'd be objective?"

"Yes, Peter, but—"

"Then you have to let me investigate every possibility, Mr. Rheinhardt...Karl. If I'm wrong, I'll be the first one to admit it...but if you're wrong, I need you to be able to accept it." Crossing his arms, Peter released a long, disconcerted breath—after so many years of looking up to and admiring Karl Rheinhardt, he was finding it very difficult to be the one giving orders.

"Brazen as your father," Karl returned, his countenance softening. "One of his traits I never liked."

"It comes with his gray hair," Peter returned as he unfolded his arms. Then, trying to heal the situation, he put in, "As I said, sometimes my mouth has a mind of its own."

Turning back toward the window, Karl sighed. "It's difficult to believe that someone here could…could be stealing from me."

Grasping the older man's forearm, Peter gently moved him so they were once again face-to-face. "Before we start making any conclusions, I want to speak with the Hopewells."

"Why? Isn't that only going to alarm them?"

"No…no, I won't bring up why I'm really there…I'll just…I'll just tell them that I'm auditing our procedures and that I want their input. That way, I can ask about their furniture and the salesman that calls on them without frightening anyone…then, maybe, I can determine if our problem originates outside—or inside—the factory."

"Just be careful…don't upset them—that would be terrible for our reputation."

Peter couldn't stop a wide smile from parting his lips. "No. I won't upset them…I'm usually very diplomatic."

Karl chuckled in return. "I know you are…Marcus and I used to have our share of altercations too…when were you planning on seeing the Hopewells?"

"Soon…the sooner the better. I'm meeting Daven's train at three o'clock today…when I do, I'll check the schedule south, then telegraph the Hopewells to make an appointment."

"Ah, that reminds me," Karl declared, stepping over to his desk. "I had these printed up just a few days ago…you'll need them if you go see the Hopewells," he explained as he picked up a stack of cards and held them out.

Taking the bundle, Peter examined the ornate calling cards bearing his name. "Karl, I do have cards of my own."

"I know, but this way the Hopewells will definitely know you're from Rheinhardt Furniture...how long do you think the interview will take?"

Peter shrugged. "It'll depend on the Hopewells, but I shouldn't be gone more than a couple of days."

Lounging on a bench outside the Sandorville Depot, Peter Leighton straightened the newspaper he was holding and started to reread the same article for the fourth time. After skimming just the first two lines, he groaned, folded the paper, and laid it on the bench—the lifeless story didn't deserve even a first read. With a shake of his head, Peter slowly slid his watch from his waistcoat pocket, and although he knew it would do nothing to quicken the tardy train's arrival, he checked the time once again. Why was he so bothered by an overdue train? he wondered. Then, as he reviewed the day's events in his head—the disturbing and distressful conversations with Karl...the exhausting and exasperating confrontation with Lorelei...the unsettling and uncomfortable meeting with Karl's foreman, Quentin Fetch—Peter realized that it wasn't the train that was worrying him...it was the growing list of obstacles to overcome.

Tired of brooding over his uneasiness, Peter grabbed the newspaper and stood, then he strolled to the edge of the platform and looked down the tracks— nothing. Tapping his leg with the folded paper, Peter circled back and noticed that he had lost his place on the bench to a woman with two young boys—and after considering the woman's lack of control over the youths, he chose to amble among the others waiting for the belated train.

As he neared the far end of the platform, Peter's eyes focused on a young woman who was chatting with a husky bearded man standing next to her. Golden hair showed at the edges of the girl's bonnet, and a blue-striped jacket, over more layers of blue dress, highlighted her tall, slim figure. And, even though her parasol shaded most of her creamy features, he was still drawn to the gentle beauty he saw. Without warning, the young woman's conversation abruptly stopped, and she turned and met his gaze. Caught in mid-stare, Peter swallowed hard and tipped his hat in apology. The girl blushed slightly and answered him with a sparkling smile.

The sudden, sharp blare of the train's whistle jostled him from his muse, and while the crowd pressed forward to meet the slowing parade of cars, Peter retreated to the depot. Thankfully, the woman and her two unruly children had disappeared, giving him back his perfect vantage point. Leaning against the depot wall and next to his previously occupied bench, he waited while the train crept to a stop and belched out a last groan of steam. Then, as the station bloated with exiting passengers, he carefully perused the faces of the congregation on the platform—returning, quite often, to the golden-haired, blue-clad woman.

Finally, he found what he was searching for—a sandy-haired, shabbily attired youth carrying a tattered satchel and a handled wooden box. Watching as his young brother talked with a gaunt, hollowed-eyed man, Peter rolled his eyes—he had asked Daven to do only one thing before leaving Bradlee—just one...

Sighing in frustration, Peter glanced away from his rebellious brother and again stared in the direction of the pretty girl in blue. At first, he saw only the young woman's bearded companion, who was shaking the hand of a curly-headed man. Then he spotted his beauty—hugging a slightly older duplication of herself.

"You are here to help Karl," he murmured, trying to keep his mind on his task.

As if she had heard the comment, the girl peered into his eyes and whispered to her sister, who turned to inspect him. Caught ogling once again, Peter quickly opened his newspaper, hoping to escape from his indiscretion.

"Hey," came a whispered call as a shadow moved across his paper.

Adjusting the newspaper to shield his face from the increasing throng, Peter nodded in return as he scrutinized his brother's unpressed trousers, ill-fitting jacket, worn derby hat—and shoulder-length hair.

"What's the matter?" his brother muttered, placing his luggage on the bench.

"Daven, I thought I told you to get your hair cut," Peter replied under his breath.

"You suggested it," came the quiet answer.

"Then why is it still at your shoulders?"

"You only suggested it."

Peter's jaw instantly clenched—typical Daven. "It was the only thing that I asked you to do before you left home...the only thing," he whispered, his voice steeped with irritation.

No reply.

"Daven, you have to get hired at the factory—our plan depends upon it."

"I'll get the job."

"No, you won't—not if you go there looking like a guttersnipe."

Silence.

"Did you hear me?" Peter asked as he moved the newspaper to get a better view of his brother. "Daven, did you hear?"

"Yes," his brother hissed, giving him a harsh stare.

Peter instantly recognized the scowl. "That doesn't work with me," he murmured. But, unfortunately, it did. Daven had inherited his father's piercing pale-blue eyes, and a long, icy stare from those eyes unnerved most people. And, as much as Peter hated to admit it, he was included in that group.

Eventually, Daven averted his gaze and fingered the handle of his valise. "All right...I'll get it—"

A sudden commotion stopped the brothers' discussion, and they, along with everyone else in the crowd, turned to see a stone-faced woman loudly protesting the railroad's destruction of her trunk. While all eyes were pulled in the woman's direction, Peter refolded the newspaper and lightly tapped his brother's shoulder.

"We better finish up—before people realize that we're together...I want you to meet me tonight so we can finalize our strategy."

"Where...here?"

"No...I'm staying at the Vanya Inn on the corner of Second and Park Streets. There's a garden behind the hotel with a lot of nooks where we can talk in peace."

"What time?"

"Seven-thirty…now, you're going to need a place to stay. Karl gave me some names of the more reputable boarding—"

"I have a name of a boarding house."

"How?" Peter asked, his brow furrowing.

"From a man I met on the train…he even said I could use him as a reference."

Peter nodded, remembering the hollow-eyed gentleman who had been talking with his brother earlier. "All right. I'll see you tonight…don't be late."

A sly smile spread across Daven's face. "You can't blame me for this one—the train was late—not me."

Peter half-smiled at the cheerful tease, then, as he continued to study his young brother's countenance, his newfound uneasiness about their mission escalated, and his grin slowly faded. He never thought Daven would be in harm's way while working in the factory—now, he wasn't so sure.

"What?!" Daven demanded. "Why are you starin' at me?!"

"Quiet!" Peter countered, surveying the people wandering nearby. "You better get going."

Daven snatched his satchel and box off the bench, then glared at his brother. "I told you, my hair will get cut."

"Daven, that's not what I was—"

Without listening to the rest of his brother's explanation, Daven stomped back into the crowd, heading, he hoped, southward. But, as the depot grew smaller and smaller, a hollowness started to overtake him—as it always did after a confrontation with his brother—and Daven set his luggage down on the wooden sidewalk. He loved and respected his brother very much, but Peter's domineering nature constantly tried to push him down paths he didn't want to go. And trying to relay that message always proved fruitless. Words were ignored, and actions—such as keeping his long hair—were regarded as rebellious.

Digging in his vest pocket, Daven removed the calling card he had received from his acquaintance on the train, and as he examined the roughly scrawled map on the back, he released a long breath—the boarding house was practically on the other side of town. Suddenly, a yell drew his attention to the street exiting the depot, where the driver of a horsecar shouted to a wagon to clear the tracks. As the car's horses strained to pull their load along the rails embedded in the brick road, Daven considered hailing the driver—until he noticed the overstuffed car and full back platform. Choosing to walk over cramming himself onto the horsecar, he watched it rumble by, then, picking up his cases, he continued toward the Tadman Boarding House.

Glancing at the various buildings and businesses as he trudged along the walkway paralleling Second Street, Daven tried to distract himself, but uncontrollably, his thoughts drifted back to Peter—and a twinge of resentment wriggled down his back.

"'Our' strategy," he mumbled to himself. "Since when was it ever 'our' strategy."

His brother's dictate to work for Karl Rheinhardt had irked him from the beginning, and all efforts and prayers to sway the decision bounced off Peter's granite determination. He knew he would end up in Sandorville, even as his brother was still proposing the idea—but to have been asked or included in the decision, would have made it much more agreeable. Instead, Peter had chosen to guilt him into complying, and although he had no real ills against Karl Rheinhardt, the name still hammered on the wedge that had developed between him and his brother.

Head down and immersed in thought, Daven suddenly realized that he had wandered into a cross street—and the bellowed condemnations from a teamster confirmed it. Shaken from his trance, Daven froze and quickly backed up, then, dropping his baggage on the timbered sidewalk, he surveyed his surroundings. He had finally reached the intersection of the bricked Second Street and the unremarkable Park Street. Probably once neatly paved with wooden blocks, Park Street had rotted into a lumpy disgrace, and as Daven watched the teamster's overloaded wagon stagger by, he tipped his hat in apology.

The bearded driver scowled at him in return and hollered a few more curses as he passed.

Half-smiling at the response, Daven waved and couldn't resist calling cheerfully, "Good to see you again, Friend."

Immediately, the teamster turned in his seat—confusion, worry, and regret covering his face.

With a chuckle, Daven waved again...his little prank never failed to douse a temper.

Then the significance of the name 'Park Street' finally grasped him—he had also reached the hotel where Peter was staying, the Vanya Inn, which stood across the street. Colorful flags collared the building between the third and top floors, and people swarmed the walkway in front of the large double doors, hurrying to and from carriages. With a shudder, Daven shook his head—the thought of living so close to the crushing crowds dampened his spirit...but Peter wouldn't have it any other way. Pulling out his hand-drawn map once again, Daven blew out a small sigh. Thankfully, his route turned down the lesser Park Street and away from the bustle of town.

As his journey continued through a grid of rutted roads, each shuffle of Daven's boots caused his wooden toolbox and heavy valise to pull harder and harder on his arms. Eventually, exhaustion washed over him, and he wished that a horsecar, even one gorged with passengers, would pass by, but that was as unlikely as hearing an apology from Peter. It would be a very long time before rails ever made it to the meager roads he was following. Stopping to get his breath, Daven circled and studied the houses around him...he knew he should be getting close...

Suddenly, a green corner house caught his attention and he smiled. It had to be the Tadman Boarding House...it perfectly matched the description given to him—right down to the roses engulfing the porch. Quickening his pace, Daven entered the boarding house's yard and headed over to a plump woman hanging linen on a line. "Hello! Are you Mrs. Tadman?"

The round-faced woman peeked around the sheet she was holding and frowned. "I've got nothing for you. Don't beg here."

Setting his luggage down, Daven stretched his aching arms, then lifted his hat in greeting. "I'm not begging, Ma'am. My name is Daven Ashby. Your boarding house was recommended to me."

Mrs. Tadman's frown deepened, causing her eyes to almost disappear in the wrinkled scowl. "Recommended? By whom?" she questioned, slowly edging her way over to Daven.

"Hugh Relanger," Daven answered as he handed her the now tattered calling card.

The woman studied the name on the card, then scrutinized Daven from head to boot. "How do you know Mr. Relanger?" she asked.

"We met on the train. After we talked for awhile, he suggested that I come to you for a room."

Suspicion remained in Mrs. Tadman's eyes, and although he would never admit it to his brother, Daven began to regret his roguish-looking appearance.

"Fifty cents a day," she snipped, searching Daven's face for a reaction to the fee. "That's for a room and three meals—whether you eat them or not. I'll wash, but that's extra."

"That's more than agreeable."

"I usually don't take on new boarders midweek," Mrs. Tadman continued sternly. "I like to spend time with them on Sunday and get to know them, before I let them into my home."

"I understand," Daven returned. And, still sensing the woman's apprehension, he added, "I do apologize for my rough dress. I've been out of work for some time and I suppose it shows. If you'd prefer that I not stay, just tell me, and I'll find another place."

Mrs. Tadman shook her head and held up the card. "No. I trust Mr. Relanger. He wouldn't send just anybody," she returned, her features finally softening. "What did you say your name was?"

"Daven Ashby," he replied with an automatic tip of his hat.

"Mr. Ashby, you said you've been out of work…you do have a job here in Sandorville, don't you?"

"Yes and no. Tomorrow, I'm going to see about an opening for a carver at the Rheinhardt Furniture Factory."

"Then you don't have a job yet?" she asked, her eyes narrowing.

"Not yet, but I'm quite sure I'll get the job at the factory," he tried.

Putting her hands on her hips, Mrs. Tadman grumbled under her breath. "Well, you can stay through Sunday night, and we'll see how things work out… come on, I'll show you to your room."

"Thank you," Daven sighed, and grabbing his cases, he followed her toward the house.

"Anna, come look at this dress."

Anna Spreyer glanced toward the far end of the porch, where her four sisters flocked around the newest issue of *Harper's Bazar*. She usually enjoyed perusing the magazine with her mother—studying the fashions that she probably would never wear. But, with her sisters, it was different. They truly believed it was their duty to find fault with every dress, and after hours and hours of their clucking and criticism, Anna was bored.

"This one would look darling on you, Anna. Much better than that old thing you have on."

"Marion is right," Gretchen chimed in. "You need to rejuvenate your wardrobe."

Anna sighed. She knew her blue-striped outfit would never be featured in a magazine, but she liked it—and so did her silent admirer at the train depot. And, as she recalled the gentleman's voiceless compliments, she couldn't help but smile.

"I'll be there in a moment," Anna called, resuming her task of pouring lemonade for her brothers-in-law and father. "Would you like more ice, Papa?"

"Nein, I'm fine," he answered. Then, leaning in close, he grasped her hand and added in a whisper, "I think even Hans would find it a challenge to deal with those four today."

Anna nodded in agreement and gently squeezed her father's fingers. Normally, she could tolerate Wednesdays—the day three of her four sisters came to perch themselves on the veranda and chatter about nothing. But now, with her sister Marion's arrival in town, a family reunion had been called. The four of them were together again, brooding over her as they always did—and the only one who could make them shoo, her brother Hans, was miles away.

"Why don't you see if Mama needs help," her father offered loud enough for everyone to hear.

A smile brightened Anna's face, and murmuring a thank-you, she circled and headed toward the front door.

"Anna, this will only take a moment," her sister Elsa clucked as she waved the *Harper's Bazar* in the air.

Instantly, Anna's grip on the lemonade pitcher tightened, and she reluctantly joined her sisters' gaggle. "It's very nice," she said as she viewed the dress.

"Oh, girls, we have been so thoughtless," Marion declared with mock tenderness. "She won't be able to wear anything so beautiful while she's in nursing school."

Anna stiffened. The visit had barely begun, and Marion had already resumed her role as a thorn. "I told you," Anna flared, angered by the goading. "I haven't decided yet."

"But you'd make a fine nurse," Gretchen said.

"I'm not disputing that…I mean, I know I could be a good nurse—I could even be a good doctor…I just haven't—"

"Of course you'd make a good nurse," the usually silent Ida added. "You've always enjoyed helping Papa's patients."

"Yes, because I enjoy helping Papa…but I may want to do something else with my life."

"Like what?" Marion prodded.

Anna's shoulders slumped as if a heavy yoke had been placed over her head. She didn't plan on having the developing conversation so soon—especially with all four sisters at the same time. "I…I've been thinking of going to Belding to work in the new silk mill." Then, as she surveyed her sisters' disgusted expressions and listened to their screeching, she regretted even venturing onto the subject.

"That's ridiculous!"

"You will do no such thing!"

"A daughter of a doctor working in a factory?! Never!"

Anna shook her head in frustration. "It's not your decision to—"

"And who will take care of Mama if you run off and do such a foolish thing?" Ida put in, wiping her handkerchief at nonexistent tears.

"We would get someone in to help while I would be away…just as we planned to do if I left for nursing school," Anna explained.

"Of all the backward…" Gretchen moaned.

"If you are going to be that way about it," Marion seethed, "we will pay you for taking care of Mama."

"It's not about money," Anna puffed. Then, before she could stop herself, she stomped her foot—her sisters could always reduce her to the child they treated her as. "It's about following my own path."

"I won't listen to this nonsense any longer," Ida sniffed.

"Neither will I," Elsa returned, slamming the magazine onto the table next to her. "The only way I will allow a stranger to come into this house to care for Mama is if you go to school."

"All right then," Anna said, her voice shaking with defeat, "I'll stay in Sandorville and work in the millinery."

"It's not where you work…the problem is your working in the first place."

"Why?"

Not one sister offered an answer.

"Mama and I have already discussed it," she tried. "She is the one who said I should go to Belding."

"I doubt that," Marion snipped, her nose in the air.

Anna released a quivering breath and shook her head at her sisters' incessant pecking. "She did…she wants me to have the same opportunities as you all did."

"The same opportunities?" Elsa shrieked. "If any one of us ever had the opportunity to shame ourselves and disgrace this family by leaving our poor mother without a caretaker, I assure you, we would not have taken it."

"Why don't you want to take care of Mama?" Gretchen demanded.

Angered by her sister's guilt-laced accusation, Anna constricted her fist around the lemonade pitcher's handle until her nails dug into her palm. "Me? Why don't you want to take care of Mama?! We shouldn't have to hire anyone—even if I go to school…you four should be the ones who take over for me…in fact, you should be helping out even now!"

"Anna, we have families of our own to take care of," Elsa returned, pointing toward the children at play in the yard.

Anna rolled her eyes in disbelief. "And what are you going to use as an excuse when I get married?"

"Is that what this is all about?" Marion cackled. "Anna Helene, you are such a naive romantic…I'm sure many women have already set their caps for your gentleman."

A cold shiver of panic twittered through Anna, and she cradled the pitcher with both hands to hide her sudden uneasiness. "Marion, I asked you not to say anything about—"

"Who?" Gretchen prompted excitedly.

"Oh, just a man we saw at the depot today," Marion teased as she fluttered her fan under her chin.

"Marion, don't you dare—"

"What about him?" Elsa chimed in, scooting to the edge of her seat.

"Well, he's going to be Anna's husband," Marion giggled.

Wincing at the painful reminder of why Marion could never be trusted as a confidant, Anna closed her eyes against her forming tears. "Marion, you promised that you wouldn't—"

"What are you talking about?" Ida asked, both astonished and amused. "How do you know that?"

"Because God told her."

"What?"

"Marion, please!" Anna begged, but it was too late. Her sisters were already bathing themselves in her agony and embarrassment.

"That's right, God told our dear sister that this stranger at the train station would eventually be her husband."

The four sisters laughed in unison.

"Really?" Gretchen snickered. "So what does our new brother-in-law look like?"

"Tall…well-muscled…and oh, so handsome," Marion returned, taking obvious delight in Anna's humiliation. "But too sophisticated and manly for our baby sister."

Anna knew she was powerless to stop the intensifying chatter between her sisters, and any denial from her would only send them into full flight. Swirling the last of the lemonade inside the pitcher, Anna glared at Marion. Her sister had promised to keep her revelation private—now, it was feed for her sisters' needling. Suddenly, the thought of soaking Marion's curls was too inviting to resist, and Anna raised the pitcher, then, realizing that their father now stood behind her, she slowly—and reluctantly—lowered the container.

"You girls have had enough fun—now quiet!"

"But, Papa," Marion offered, "it's all so silly. Anna can't possibly know—"

"I said enough!" the doctor bellowed. "Anna, go and help Mama."

Wiping away her tears, Anna slid past her tormentors, and as she raced down the side porch toward the back of the house, she took some comfort in hearing her father's roaring chastisement of her sisters. Finally rounding the back corner of the veranda, she ran to the kitchen's screen door and yanked it open. Once inside the warm, cinnamon-scented kitchen, she limped to the table, sank onto a chair, and allowed her mortified and outraged tears to fall—her sisters would cluck about this for months.

"Liebchen, what's wrong?"

Immediately, the tears faded as her mother's delicate hands caressed her shoulders.

Looking up, Anna breathed in deeply, then, realizing that she was still holding the near-empty lemonade pitcher, she shoved the container onto the table and answered, "Your daughters…that's what's wrong."

"You spoke to them about going to Belding?" her mother asked, easing onto the chair next to her daughter.

Anna scowled in confusion—humiliation had chased the original discussion from her thoughts. "Oh…yes, I did," she returned, recalling how the whole mess had started. "I don't understand them, Mama. They keep pushing me to go to school…they won't even listen to what I have to say."

"That is not their decision to make, Liebchen."

"I know…but they said that nursing school would be the only reason they'd allow someone else in the house to take care of you…why can't they help?"

"Because they can't," her mother whispered.

"You mean won't."

"No, they can't."

Finally, understanding nudged itself into Anna's thoughts. Illness after illness had ravaged her mother's health, and now, tuberculosis was destroying it completely. Anna knew her mother's life was fading, but her sisters worked very hard to blind themselves to that awful truth. "No, I guess they can't," she agreed, wiping the moisture from her cheeks.

"It doesn't matter if your sisters don't want someone else brought in…it's not their choice to make."

"Maybe they're right, Mama. It's not fair to you."

"You don't know who the Lord will bring to us. That person may need us more than we need—" her mother said before being cut off by a hard cough. "Besides, I was the one who suggested to Papa that we hire someone—even if you remain here in Sandorville."

"But I don't mind helping you, Mama."

"Liebchen, I know," her mother said, grasping her hand. "But Papa and I want to be fair to you—to give you the same chances your sisters had…without worrying about me. I want it that way."

Anna studied her mother, who spoke with a fire and independence that her affliction usually dampened. "Are you sure, Mama?"

"Don't let them put that kind of doubt into your head."

Her sisters' merciless teasing slid back into Anna's memory. "They're good at that."

"You have to stand up to them—and without Hans."

Anna nodded. "But how? They always have something to use against me—and this time, I handed it to them on a platter."

"I don't understand," her mother answered, followed by another bout of coughing.

"Do you remember what I told you about that gentleman at the depot? Well, I made the mistake of telling Marion how I felt when we met her and Michael at the train…now, she just told the other three, and they are having a marvelous laugh about it."

"Liebchen!" Mrs. Spreyer exclaimed. "That's how you'll be able to stand up to them."

Anna shook her head in bewilderment. "Now, I don't understand."

"You said the Lord pointed out this man to you…all the girls' needling can't change what God's put into motion. Eventually, they'll have to admit they were wrong."

Anna blushed and gently squeezed her mother's hand. "I hope 'eventually' comes very soon."

"Daven!"

As his name shot through the twilight, Daven stopped and examined the dusky perimeter of the hotel's garden. Finally, he spotted Peter in a far corner, leaning against a large red pine tree. Trotting over to the secluded hideout, Daven smiled, then, as he noticed a familiar habit, his grin vanished and he slowed his pace—Peter's temple massaging was never a good sign.

"You got a headache?" Daven asked as he reached his brother.

"Yes," came the muffled answer. "And you're late."

Daven frowned and pulled his pocketwatch from his vest. "Nah, I can't be. I know I figured right," he mumbled as he clicked open the watch's cover. "Ten after eleven," he said. And, after a few moments of silent arithmetic, he added, "That makes it seven-thirty."

"It's eight o'clock," Peter growled—and somewhere in the distance, a chiming clock confirmed the statement. "Daven, we are involved in something serious…you have to stop being so careless."

Tensing at the accusation, Daven slowly returned his watch to the safety of his waistcoat. "I was careful…I just have to fix my formula."

Peter rubbed the back of his neck as he let out a low, grumbling exhale. "Your games for making that watch tell time never work—just get rid of it."

Instantly, Daven's dander soared upward. His brother's chronic disparagements regarding his pocketwatch were irksome enough, but he knew, deep in his heart, that they were also camouflaged barbs against his father—and he was growing very weary of receiving the continual jabs. "I don't want to start this argument again, Peter."

"Fine…just be on time from now on, okay? I want to be able to rely on you."

"Yes Sir!" Daven snapped, still simmering.

Peter rubbed his eyes, then glowered at his brother. "Don't start…not tonight…now, where are you staying?"

Daven breathed in deeply, cooling his temper—fighting was never productive when his brother had one of his headaches. "The Tadman House on Severns."

"Is it a decent place?"

"So far," Daven replied with a shrug.

"Listen, I have to go to Crestfield to see a customer, so you're going to be on your own for a few days," Peter offered as he surveyed Daven's appearance—including his uncut hair.

The examination instantly refreshed the memory—and unpleasantness—of their earlier altercation at the train depot. "I'm old enough to take care of myself," Daven returned, "and to know when my hair needs cutting."

Peter's jaw clenched, but he remained mute.

"I'm a man out of work and looking for a job, Peter…I can't very well dress like you."

"I suppose," Peter murmured, averting his eyes.

Daven knew the response was as close to a concession as he was going to get—which fueled his annoyance.

"You are planning to go to the factory tomorrow, aren't you?" Peter inquired, massaging his neck muscles again.

"Yeah."

"Good…I want to meet when I get back, so you can let me know if you got the job or not."

"I'll get the job."

"I still want to meet…it's important that we keep in touch throughout this whole thing."

"So where do you wanna meet? Here?"

"'Want to' meet," Peter corrected softly.

Daven rolled his eyes—even a headache couldn't stop his brother from badgering him about his speech. "Do you wish to meet here again, Sir?" he quipped with a smirk.

Peter's jaw muscles visibly tightened. "No…Karl said that the farmers bring in their produce to sell on Saturdays, and they set up in the empty lots just south of the depot…meet me there at three o'clock."

"And what if I'm still working at three? I wouldn't want to be late," Daven pushed, knowing full well that he was gnawing on his brother's patience.

"You won't be," came the reply between clenched teeth. "Karl says he pays the men on Saturday and lets them go at noon." Then, as he started to rub his right temple, Peter put in quietly, "And I hope your attitude will improve by our next meeting."

Stepping closer to his brother, Daven laughed incredulously. "My attitude?"

"Lower your voice," Peter snapped as he surveyed the area for listening ears. "Yes, your attitude…ever since we decided to help Karl Rheinhardt, you have been impossible."

"We? No, no, no. You decided," Daven returned, using his finger to jab every syllable into his brother's shoulder. "You never asked for my opinion on the matter."

"We had no choice, Daven. We had to repay our debt."

"It wasn't my fault that—"

"It wasn't mine either," Peter cut in sharply as he grabbed Daven's forearm and pulled him in so close that they were nose-to-nose. "If you'll remember, Karl had to bail us out after your father lost everything for us!"

The words sent a chill through Daven, and yanking his arm free, he backed up a step.

Peter's features immediately filled with alarm. "Oh, Dave, I didn't mean that," he offered, moving toward his brother.

"Apology accepted," Daven replied, battling against the hurt and shame that Peter had dumped on his shoulders. "The problem is—you did mean it... you just didn't mean to say it." Then, as grief grasped him around the throat, he choked out, "Why? Why can't you forgive him? My father gave up every-thing...everything he loved to stay and run that blasted store...and you cared less about his death than you did about losing your precious business."

"No, Dave...that's not true."

As he blinked hard to clear the tears from his eyes, Daven shoved Peter back against the pine. "When this is over," he fumed, "my father's mistakes will be paid for...don't ever use them to force me into anything—ever again." Then, piv-oting on his heel—and ignoring the whispered pleas from his brother—Daven elbowed his way through a gap in the bushes surrounding the hotel's garden.

Silently chastising himself, Peter followed Daven to the shrubs, then, deciding to abandon the pursuit, he let his brother disappear into the fading light. Why? he yelled silently. Why couldn't he have held his tongue? Now, he and Daven had parted, once again, on a bitter note. And, even worse, he didn't get the chance to tell his brother to use an alias when applying for the job at the factory. With a disgusted sigh, Peter returned to the pine, stretched out his arm, and leaned on the tree. He had specifically dropped the issue of Daven's uncut mane to avoid the fight he didn't want to have—and instead, he blundered into a deeper rift.

Pushing himself upright, Peter absently stared at the hedge where Daven had passed through. His brother, unfortunately, was right about one thing...he couldn't forgive Tait Ashby. His stepfather was responsible for the backward spin that had ruined his life, and he couldn't find forgiveness—not yet. But that, he inwardly chastised himself, was no excuse for making Daven share the blame—and for guilting his brother into submission. Shaking his head in remorse, Peter sighed. He definitely had to stop using that tactic—it left a sour taste in everyone's mouth...his own included.

"I'm sorry, Daven," he offered to the uncaring bushes.

⊷ Two ⊶

Lounging on top of his toolbox and using the rail fence surrounding the Rheinhardt Factory as a back rest, Daven absently gazed at two men who were unloading a pile of board lumber from a wagon. Then, as he continued to watch the duo inharmoniously stack the boards to dry, apprehension began to chip away at his spirit. The last thing he wanted was to work in another factory, but no matter what his brother thought, it wasn't the labor that he dreaded—it was losing the chance to create what was in his heart. His father had taught him many, many things—yet the lesson he remembered the most was also the simplest…

'Furniture should be crafted by quality, not quota.'

As he stretched out his legs, Daven wiped at the sweat dripping down his neck and returned his attention to the two workers struggling in the baking heat. The one, a small, wiry gentleman, constantly voiced the same grievance over and over in German, and the other, a much taller black man, either didn't understand or care, and the two forged ahead with their teamless effort to move the boards.

"He's saying that you keep knocking him off balance," Daven called, hoping to improve the situation.

The black man turned a weary face toward Daven. "What?"

"He's just asking that you don't push so hard. He doesn't have your height or strength."

Only a scowl answered him, but Daven did notice a slight change in the tall man's technique—and so did the German, who nodded his thanks. Glancing back at the factory, Daven sighed. He always prided himself on his ability to wait, but he was quickly losing that capability—to the fault of Mr. Quentin Fetch. It really didn't matter that he was told to return at one o'clock to see the foreman, but what did matter was the hour that had passed since that time. It was obvious that the unpunctual Mr. Fetch didn't respect him or his time—which agitated him to the bone. Then a deeper realization struck him, and Daven began to understand the message his own tardiness kept sending to Peter.

Removing his hat, Daven rested the back of his head against the fence, immersing his face in the afternoon sun. He knew, in his heart, that he was partially to blame for the skirmish the night before and that he shouldn't have prodded his headache-plagued brother so hard. Still, neither he nor his father deserved Peter's rebuke. He prayed endlessly that his brother would just forgive, yet that was unlikely—not even one grain of Peter's bitterness had evaporated in six years.

As his thoughts drifted into the past, Daven closed his eyes. Everything would have been so much easier if only his father and Peter had gotten along, but the two men constantly crossed swords. And any chance of conciliation ended when Peter had to lock the doors of Leighton's General Store forever—that horrible closure pushed the battle into a permanent war for his brother.

A hard kick to his boot jerked Daven from his reflection, and he jumped up to face three men. Two of them, Frank Hallam and Leland Bryce, he recognized from his first attempt to see the foreman, and the third—a big man with muscular arms and a wide chest—Daven assumed was Quentin Fetch himself.

"Are you the foreman?"

The man nodded as he chewed on a cigar clamped between his teeth.

"I was told you're the man I need to talk to about the carver's position," Daven began.

Removing his cigar and using it to point at Daven's face, Fetch offered, "Those're real fancy lookin' eyes…color's a bit watered down though, huh?"

Uncontrollably, a strong dislike for the foreman sprouted up inside Daven. He had heard every snide remark possible regarding his eyes, and they had all staled over the years. "Perhaps," he returned blandly.

Fetch chuckled. "So you're a carver, huh? Kinda young, ain't ya?"

Both Bryce and Hallam snickered at the big man's comment.

"Your advertisement didn't say that age was an issue. It also said you needed a carver and would pay twenty-five cents an hour for one."

The foreman's expression tensed and he stroked the stubble on his chin. "You'll have to prove you're worth twenty-five cents."

"I'm worth more…but I'll work for that."

Grunting skeptically, the big man stuffed the cigar back between his teeth. "So where'd you apprentice to become this great carver?"

Fetch's patronizing tone ate at what little patience Daven had left. "My father taught me."

"All right, so where'd he work?"

Daven shrugged. "Everywhere."

"Everywhere? What kinda answer is that? Prob'ly couldn't keep a job," Fetch chuckled, then, as if cued, his two assistants joined him in a long laugh.

Daven sighed and shook his head, growing bored with the ribbing. "My father was an itinerant cabinetmaker…he liked to move around, so we'd do what people needed and then move on."

As a cloud nudged itself over the sun, a deep gloom spread over the big man's face, transforming him into a menacing behemoth. "You expect me to hire you as a carver with a history like that?" he snarled. "I need a factory man."

"That was an earlier time," Daven quickly added, realizing that his cockiness was damaging his chances of being hired. "I spent three years at the Miller Furniture Factory."

Quentin Fetch maneuvered his cigar to the opposite side of his mouth while surveying Daven from hat to boot. "Never heard of it," he growled, then he glanced to his right and left. "Hallam, Bryce, you ever heard of Miller Furniture?"

Both replied with shakes of their heads.

"It was in Bradlee…up North. They went out of business about a year ago."

"You worked as a carver for them?"

"I started as a lugger and ended as a carver."

Fetch grunted. "You got a name?"

Smothering the sarcastic reply that had formed in his head, Daven nodded and pasted a wide smile onto his face. "Daven Ashby." And, sensing that the interview was not going in his favor, he added, "I know I don't look as if I can do the job—but I'm sure my work will convince you that I can...it did for Mr. Miller."

"Those your tools?" the big man asked as he motioned toward the wooden box.

Daven nodded.

"Hallam will take ya up to the assembly room," Fetch said, poking his thumb at the blonde-haired man to his right. "Make me a sample...ya got an hour."

"An hour?"

"Yeah, an hour...you need longer than that Mr. Master Carver?"

Daven considered responding that if Fetch hadn't kept him waiting so long there would have been plenty of time to create a sample, but after studying the big man's stern expression, Daven figured a more yielding answer would be wiser. "No, that's fine."

"If I like what ya do, then we'll talk more."

Grabbing his toolbox, Daven followed the three men as they headed toward the factory, and as he passed by the duo still unloading the lumber, he offered a few words of encouragement to the wiry German. The little man cast a watchful look toward Fetch, nodded, and then continued his work.

"You speak German?" Bryce asked.

With every fiber of his body now fixed on the building in front of him, Daven barely heard the question and only nodded in return. Then, as he stepped up onto the high platform used for loading the furniture for transport and peered through the vast doorway, a familiar bleakness settled upon him. When he had finally been freed from Miller Furniture, he had vowed to never leave another footprint in a factory—now, not only was he about to set down many unwanted imprints, but he was doing it voluntarily...well, somewhat voluntarily.

Once inside the building, Daven's stomach soured—the scene duplicated his memory of the Miller Factory. Large and frequent windows dotted the long factory walls, letting in some—but not enough—daylight. The multipaned windows also alternated with the workers' lockers, which were built into the walls. And above, a few gas lights glowed, filling the spots where the afternoon sun could no longer reach. Then two other memories, long subdued in his thoughts, clearly resurfaced with the screaming saws—the incessant noise and the smothering sawdust.

A tug on his sleeve interrupted Daven's reverie, and he peered through the dusty air at Hallam, who, obviously irked by the dawdling, rudely motioned for him to follow. Trailing behind the blonde-haired man, Daven worked his way through the maze of machines while keeping his distance from the unprotected leather power belts that whipped from the overhead shafts, down to the machines, and back up again. With his eyes on the rotating bands, Daven didn't see the boy pushing a cartload of furniture pieces—until he bumped into him. Hollering his apologies, Daven watched the young lugger drive the pieces to their next station and he grinned slightly—thankfully, his days in that position had passed. Then, spotting Hallam lingering at the bottom of a staircase, he quickened his efforts to get through the factory. Finally joining the blonde-haired man, Daven heard him yell something, but the din of the machines muffled the words as soon as they were spoken. Positive that it was a reprimand, Daven just smiled and followed Hallam up the stairs.

The second floor, which served as both the assembly and finishing rooms, also used oversize windows for most of its light. A large opening in the middle of the floor allowed a platform to be raised and lowered, enabling the rough pieces to be hoisted up for completion. Although cleaner and quieter than downstairs, the upper floor—and the employees working on it—suffered from a heavy, stagnant heat and the pungent odors of varnish and glue.

"Go over there," Hallam ordered, pointing to a window. "I'll be back in a minute with some wood."

As he sauntered over to the empty spot, Daven became greatly aware of the odd glances he was receiving from the other men on the floor. Not looks of curiosity or jealousy, but of sympathy—which troubled him to the core. Placing his toolbox on the carver's bench under the window, Daven flipped open the latches and pushed back the lid.

For a moment, all his anxieties faded as he gazed at the small carved picture nailed to the inside of the cover. The detailed carving was the only piece of his father's handiwork that he was able to save from Peter's frantic attempts to raise money. And, to prevent his brother or anyone else from ever finding it, he kept the picture concealed in the only sanctuary he had—his toolbox. Removing a few chisels and gouges from the box, Daven lightly caressed the engraved picture as he always did before he began any carvings of his own.

"You carve that?"

Daven jumped, not realizing that the blonde-haired Hallam had returned. "No, this is my father's work."

"What's it a picture of?"

"My father's home in Sweden," Daven answered as he closed the toolbox, once again hiding his valued treasure from sight.

"Here," Hallam said, handing Daven a scrap piece of maple wood. "Now, it's time for you to do some carvin'—but if you're even half as good as your pa, Mr. Fetch will definitely want ya here."

Quentin Fetch heard his office door open, then close. Moving the paper he had been studying to the side, he slowly lifted his gaze. "Is he any good?" he asked, mumbling around the cigar clenched in his teeth.

Frank Hallam approached the foreman's desk and handed him a piece of maple. "Look at that!" the blonde-haired man exclaimed. "Compared to this kid, Travis Perryn scratched out his carvings with his fingernails."

Fetch examined the unfinished but well-crafted carving in the wood, then he began to chuckle. Finally, they had found the talent they so badly needed.

Pushing himself from his chair, Leland Bryce stepped behind the foreman and studied the carving. "He's good, all right."

"That ain't all," Hallam added. "I got him talkin'…he knows more than just German."

Fetch glanced up at his assistant.

"When he traveled 'round with his pa, he did most of the talkin'…the old man had a hard time with English, so it was up to the kid to talk business."

"So?"

"So he picks up a little of everything—Swedish, German, Polish…"

"You know," Bryce remarked, "he might be able to help us get through to all these foreigners…and just think how many more of them we could persuade to work here if we had the kid on our side."

Fetch nodded in agreement—at last his deputies were grasping the concept of long-range planning. "Yeah, looks like our advertisement did real good this time—but let's just work on gettin' him in here first…with a talent like this," the foreman continued, holding up the carved piece of maple, "we just might make our deadline…where is he?"

Hallam tilted his head toward the door. "Outside."

"Good. After I'm sure that the kid can do the job, I want ya to go out to our lumberyard and get the mahogany—and get back as fast as you can."

"That will still take a day or so," Hallam returned.

"I know, but we'll need that time to get young Ashby right where we want him."

"Why not just hire him the regular way?" the blonde-haired man asked. "With Peter Leighton around, it might not be a good idea to give the kid the treatment."

Fetch slammed his fist on his desk—he had grown very tired of Hallam's newfound jumpiness. Why couldn't his men understand—or believe—that he would never allow Peter Leighton to take away what he had worked years to achieve? "Stop worryin' about Leighton…he can meet with an accident as easily as anybody else."

"Prob'ly even easier," Bryce finished with a wicked laugh.

Fetch nodded and smiled. "Well, Hallam, why don't you call in our new carver."

Daven rested against the Rheinhardt Factory's office wall, once again waiting for Quentin Fetch. Then, remembering his purpose for being in the factory, he closely scrutinized the interior of the building for anything peculiar. As in the Miller Factory, the saws and machines stood in lines the length of the building—each reaching up to a shaft above it with a leather belt. And those shafts—and endless others—joined to form an overhead web of belts and pulleys, lacing the machines to the steam engine hidden in another part of the factory.

With a sigh, Daven started to massage his left palm with his right-hand thumb, suddenly becoming very aware of the sympathetic stares that followed his every move. Disconcerted by the workers' gawking, Daven shifted his attention to the factory's office. Set in the southeast corner, the room was an obvious addition to the first floor's layout. And, although it appeared harmless with its single door and crude construction, it still emitted a menacing essence—especially since nary a flutter of sound had emerged since Hallam entered the fortress.

As if he had heard his name, the blonde-haired man opened the door and motioned for Daven. Reluctantly, he stepped inside the ominous office and faced Quentin Fetch, who sat behind a desk that looked as though unskilled hands had assembled it from three different pieces of furniture. As he wondered how a furnituremaker could work at such an embarrassment, Daven's gaze slowly moved upward, where he met the cold, charcoal-eyed stare of Leland Bryce. Standing behind his employer, the dark-haired Bryce smiled humorlessly and lifted his foot onto the only other chair in the office, leaving Daven no choice but to stand opposite the foreman's splintered desk.

"Your carving could use some improvement," Fetch began.

The remark instantly ignited Daven's parental defense for his work. "Well, I think it's rather good…for the time I had."

"And where's your pattern?" the foreman demanded. "Any decent carver marks out a pattern first."

"My patterns are up here," Daven returned as he tapped his forehead.

Fetch chuckled, then motioned for Hallam and Bryce, and as the three men held a quiet conversation, Daven continued to survey the office. Frowning in puzzlement, he once again scrutinized the walls, floor, and ceiling—the inside was so cramped...and yet the room seemed so huge from the outside...

Ignoring his mounting uneasiness, Daven set his now heavy tools at his feet and peered straight ahead, where another door, this one leading to the outside, stood closed behind Fetch's desk. And two windows, one on each side of the door, were propped open, letting in light and fresh air—both of which the office craved.

Finally, the private meeting concluded, and without a word, Hallam left the office, using the door behind his boss and Bryce.

"If you want the job, it's yours," Fetch remarked, then he held up his hand to silence any answer. "You'll work Monday through Saturday, six-thirty to five—sometimes later—with a half hour lunch at noon. And you'll get paid on Saturdays—at five o'clock."

As Daven listened to the typical and energy-draining factory hours, an alarm rang in his head. "Saturday has the same hours?"

"That's what I said."

Wiping at the perspiration rolling down his temple, Daven tried to hide his confusion. Peter had told him that the factory quit at noon on Saturdays—his brother wouldn't have made a mistake like that.

"You got a gripe about working on Saturday?" the foreman inquired with a growl.

How could he tell the barrel-chested man that Peter Leighton had told him otherwise? "No...no, I...uh, I...we only worked until noon at the Miller Factory."

"Well, this ain't the Miller Factory...you want the job?"

Although his head and heart were screaming 'no,' Daven knew what he had to answer. "Yes...yes, I do."

"Good…now, let's talk about your pay."

Daven's brow furrowed. "We already talked about that…it's twenty-five cents an hour."

"Why don't you have a seat," Fetch said with uncommon cordiality.

Staring at the chair that Bryce was using as an ottoman, Daven shrugged. "Where?"

"Bryce!" the foreman bellowed.

With a grunt—and using his raised foot—Leland Bryce shoved the chair toward Daven. "All yours," he sneered, then, bending over, the dark-haired man whispered in Fetch's ear.

Misgiving spread through Daven, and trying to overcome the concern, he sat and returned to his inspection of the office, this time concentrating on the unconventional windows, which were surrounded by thick wooden shutters—on the inside. How odd, he thought…then he noticed it. The quiet. He couldn't even hear the screech of the saws. And, with that realization, he knew just about anything could happen in the room—and no one from the factory would be aware of it.

"Need a place to stay?" Fetch asked.

Daven shook his head, not quite sure how they derailed from the money issue. "No, I have a place."

"I know of some good boarding houses close to the factory," the foreman pressed.

"Thank you, but I'm fairly close now—Severns and Market."

"The Tadman House?"

Daven nodded.

Slowly, a wicked smile formed on Fetch's face, and he pitched his dead cigar stub into a spittoon next to his desk. "The carver's job pays ten cents an hour."

Daven laughed at the apparent joke, then stopped as he studied Fetch's glacial expression. "Ten? Your ad said twenty-five, and I've proven I'm worth that."

"You've proven you're worth thirty—but you're bein' offered ten."

Sitting in stunned silence, Daven's jaw dropped open. He had to get the job—Peter's plan depended on it—but he couldn't accept such an insult. Even a day laborer deserved more, and Fetch knew it. "Never."

"Tomorrow it'll be nine cents."

Indignation burned within Daven, and he stood and grabbed his toolbox. "I don't know what you're playing at, Mr. Fetch, or why you'd think I would ever come back—tomorrow or any other day."

The foreman rose, and pushing back his chair, he leaned on his rough-hewn desk. "Because, Ashby, you'll soon be in desperate need for money and a job."

As anger and apprehension fought to gain control of him, Daven looked from Fetch, to Bryce, then back again. "There are lots of jobs in town."

"Just try findin' one," Bryce replied, spitting a wad of tobacco juice on the floor.

Daven shook his head again as the reason for all the workers' looks of sympathy and sadness became vividly clear, and circling, he stomped to the door and yanked it open. Instantly, he was blasted by the cacophony in the factory, which forced him to abandon his final and precisely worded rebuke. Slamming the door behind him, Daven took a deep breath of the sawdust-filled air, finally relieved to be free from Fetch's disturbing presence. Then, as he trudged through the factory toward the security of the outside, a new nagging began to gnaw at him—how was he going to tell Peter that he refused the job?

Quentin Fetch smiled at his closed office door, then, biting at the end of a new cigar, he tilted his head and looked at Bryce. "You better get started. I want that kid crawlin' back here by tomorrow."

The words brought a roguish smirk to the dark-haired man's face. "I'm gunna need to use Patrolman Elsbee."

"Fine...just tell him same deal as last time."

"I'm also gunna need—"

"Bryce, use whoever and whatever you want...just make it good."

Spitting out a wad of tobacco juice, Leland Bryce headed to the door behind Fetch and grabbed the latch. "Don't worry, Boss…by the time I'm done, it'll be like Ashby's got the plague."

Arms folded behind his neck, Daven lay on his bed, watching the rising sun while it peeked through his window. And, even though he could hear the clink of dishes as Mrs. Tadman and her daughter Sally prepared breakfast, he still didn't budge from his warm covers—since there wasn't a job to go to, there wasn't really a reason to hurry down to the meal. Then, as it had throughout the night, his meeting with Fetch once again repeated itself inside his head.

When? he pondered. When did Fetch gain the advantage? Where did the conversation change? And why?

Giving up on trying to find an answer, Daven breathed in deeply as the morning light filled his room, erasing any remaining darkness. How was he going to tell Peter about his failure? He dreaded the look of disapproval he knew he'd receive, and yet he didn't—he never would have believed it…he actually missed his big brother's firm and protective presence. As he chuckled at his own inconsistency, a warm breeze billowed the curtains inward, causing one side to catch on an open dresser drawer. Not quite sure why it bothered him, Daven studied the bureau, then his concern crystallized…the other drawers were also ajar—as well as the wardrobe.

"Oh, no…"

Bolting from his bed, he found most of his clothes on the floor and the rest carelessly flung over the furniture. Then, as his pulse raced, he quickly searched through the debris and found his wallet—and opening it, he confirmed the worst.

"How could you have slept through this?" he chastised himself.

The thief had rummaged through every pocket and pigeonhole—and even managed to find the few coins he kept inside his dressing case. Every asset was gone…

Suddenly, a cold chill whipped through him, and he spun back toward the bed. Spotting his watch still hanging on the bed post, Daven exhaled in thanksgiving.

"Praise God for that habit," he murmured, then, sinking to his knees, he peered under the bed. "And for that one," he added, relieved that his tools were also undisturbed. "Why?" he moaned as he pushed himself from the floor and scanned his ravished room. "Why?"

As if answering his question, Quentin Fetch's words crept back into his thoughts...

'You'll soon be in desperate need for money and a job.'

Slumping onto the bed, Daven closed his eyes, finally recognizing the moment when everything changed between him and Fetch.

Their meeting in the foreman's office was for one purpose only—to find out where he lived. And this was why. Fetch's control reached much further than his box of an office—much further...

As Daven slowly massaged his left palm with his right-hand thumb and mourned his losses, the voices from the dining room below wafted upstairs and spawned a new hope in his heart. Maybe—just maybe—it wasn't Fetch.

Yanking off his nightshirt, he snatched his clothes from the floor and hastily dressed. Then, after darting down the stairs and into the dining room, he stopped short, completely devastated by the commonplace scene in front of him. His fellow boarders, with forks and knives in hand, were busy devouring their breakfasts, and Mrs. Tadman, who stood near the buffet, watched them as if she were a mother hen guarding her chicks. If anyone else had been robbed, they were hiding it very well. And, realizing that his suspicions about Fetch were most likely correct, Daven's desperation exploded.

"I was robbed last night!" he hollered.

Only silence answered him.

"I said I was robbed...was anyone else?"

Only grunts and shrugs came from the boarders.

"No one's said anything," Mrs. Tadman returned, shaking her head.

The statement crushed Daven's lingering hope that it was all a coincidence. "You'll soon be in desperate need for money and a job," he murmured, swallowing hard. Gazing blankly at the other boarders, he added, half to himself, half to them, "So I was the only one...how could this have happened?"

"Don't look at me," one of the boarders returned through a mouthful of food. "I didn't do it."

The other four at the table scowled at Daven and also voiced their innocence.

"Don't you be blaming my boarders, Mr. Ashby," Mrs. Tadman snapped as she shook her index finger at him.

"No, I didn't mean—"

"I don't need you causin' trouble," she interrupted. "I'm sorry it happened, but don't be puttin' the blame on none of us."

Incredulous, Daven shook his head—in less than a minute, he had gone from victim to villain. "No," he tried again. "I'm not blaming you, I just meant—"

Without warning, Sally Tadman entered the room with a plateful of steaming flapjacks, replacing Daven as the main attraction.

"Do you think talking to a patrolman will do any good?" he asked anyone who would listen.

Mrs. Tadman just shrugged—and immediately, the weight of his predicament settled on his shoulders.

Daven exited the clockmaker's shop, and as he slowly descended the few steps to the sidewalk, he exhaled in disappointment. Why? he silently wondered. Why wouldn't the clocksmith hire him? He would have cherished creating the wooden cases and frames for the clockmaker's timepieces—and for awhile, he thought that opportunity was very possible. He had made quite an impression as he explained his ideas, and a mutual Scandinavian background endeared him even more to the craftsman. Then...then he introduced himself. And, as with all the other merchants, the offer of employment was quickly retracted. With a sigh, Daven shrugged his shoulders. Perhaps it was best that he didn't get the job, since he and Peter would be starting their own business—but it sure would have improved his current financial difficulties.

Looking back at the shop over his shoulder, Daven stared at the sign in the window begging for help. Why wouldn't anyone hire him? People needed his help—and wanted it—but at the mention of his name, they always paled and sent him on his way. Why? Trudging along the wooden walkway, Daven bowed his head and tried to push the daylong list of rejections from his thoughts. *What does it matter?* he reasoned. *You don't really need any of these jobs—Peter will be back soon and make the whole nightmare go away.* Yet, despite his convincing argument, a few bothersome facts still chewed at his soul. Quentin Fetch was maneuvering him around as if he were a figurine on a chessboard, and until his brother's return, he was on his own—without a cent...he had no choice, but to play the game.

Abruptly, all Daven's concerns refocused as he collided with a young woman leaving a dry goods store. For a moment, he stood motionless—as did the girl.

Realizing what had happened, Daven knelt and picked up the neatly tied bundle he had caused her to drop. "I'm terribly sorry," he offered, handing the young woman her package. "I'll gladly pay for any damaged goods." As he heard the words leave his mouth, Daven's eyes instantly widened—he didn't have the money to pay for anything.

"No harm done," she returned with a smile.

Although he was captivated by the golden-haired beauty and wanted to talk with her more, he knew he couldn't—the Rheinhardt Factory and its foreman were, unfortunately, waiting for him.

"Again, I apologize," he said with a tip of his hat, then, stuffing his hands into his pockets, he started the inevitable walk to see Quentin Fetch.

With dread weighting his every step, Daven entered the factory's yard. *If only there were another option,* he silently groaned...but there wasn't and he shuffled over to Bryce, who was loudly barking orders to three men trying to load some crates onto a wagon. Nearing the confusion-dazed workers, Daven instantly recognized the spry German that he had helped the day before, and out of pity for the man and his coworkers, he translated Bryce's directions.

Smiling and obviously relieved to finally understand, the men waved and announced their thanks in German.

Bryce grinned upon seeing Daven. "He's been waitin' for ya…go around to his office, but use the back door."

As Daven ambled toward the office, he fought an overwhelming desire to just keep walking. He had suffered for three years in the Miller Factory before it closed, and even though his position there brought in some much-needed money, he was still delighted to step away from that misery. Now, he felt an even greater entrapment and aloneness overcoming him. And, as much as he hated to admit it, he wanted—and needed—Peter back within reachable distance.

Arriving at the office door, Daven closed his eyes and offered up a voiceless prayer for courage, then, with a deep breath, he knocked on the heavy wooden door.

Finally, after what seemed like an eternity, the door swung open, and Fetch appeared at the threshold. "You want somethin', Ashby?"

"The carver's job."

A smirk formed on the big man's face. "You've lost a bit of your fire, Kid… what happened?"

Frowning at the remark, Daven smothered the anger flaming up inside him. "Seems that I'm in desperate need for money and a job," he replied with as much calmness as he could muster. "Last night, I was robbed of every cent I had."

Fetch leaned against the door frame. "Huh."

The foreman's noticeable enjoyment of the situation ate away at what little patience Daven had left. "May I have the job?"

"Why come here? I thought you said there were lots of jobs in town," Fetch returned, his sarcasm chilling the summer air.

"Seems nobody wants me."

"Really?"

"What kind of rumors did you spread about me?"

A wide smile parted the foreman's lips.

Massaging his palm with his thumb, Daven shivered even though the hot July sun showered him with warmth—he was being routed right into Fetch's snare, and there was no way out. "May I have the job?"

"Of course...for nine cents an hour."

"You offered ten."

"No, you turned that down...I said if ya came back today it would be nine."

Daven shook his head in frustration. "Well, maybe I'll go to Mr. Rheinhardt and see what he has to say about it."

Fetch shrugged. "Go ahead...but all you'll end up doin' is makin' him mad, then he'll give ya even less...in fact, I'll save him the trouble and make it eight cents right now."

"But—"

"You want it to be seven?"

"No, I..." Daven started, but confusion fogged his thoughts. Was this the way Karl Rheinhardt ran his business?

Karl had occasionally visited their home in Bradlee, but since his brother was the primary reason for the stopovers, he was never given the opportunity to know anything about the furnituremaker. It wasn't likely that Peter would uproot them both to help someone so devious, but Daven still reminded himself to question his brother about why they were supporting the older man and his intimidating business practices.

As Daven peered into the foreman's dark eyes, desperation and helplessness hacked away at his composure. "I'm sure the authorities would be very interested in how you and Mr. Rheinhardt are treating your workers," he tried, his voice quivering with gloom.

Quentin Fetch let out a loud belly-laugh. "Go ahead and tell somebody... but just remember, you'll never know if you're talkin' to a friend of mine—or not. And, I can tell ya right now, it'll be very painful for you if I find out that you've been tellin' tales about us...so are you takin' the job? Or are ya gunna stay in town and live on nothin'?"

"Well…well, maybe I'll…I'll just leave town then," Daven answered, crumbling under Fetch's threats and smugness.

"Maybe ya will…maybe ya won't…but it's gunna take money no matter what ya decide."

Daven swallowed hard. He knew he had lost the skirmish and any more fighting on his part would only benefit Fetch. "I'll…I'll take the job."

"Good. I think we're finally beginnin' to understand each other—huh, Ashby?" the big man snickered. "See ya at six-thirty tomorrow."

"Marion, please…it's time to go," Anna pleaded, yanking on her sister's sleeve, but once again, the gesture was shrugged off.

Sighing in annoyance, Anna leaned against the dry goods store's counter and fingered the string tied around her package. Time and distance had erased the memory of how exasperating it was to shop with her sister, but Anna was soon reminded when Marion spent most of their hour in the store circulating and creating gossip with two other women. Then, catching a few strands of the conversation—and realizing that she was now the center of the discussion—Anna started to tremble.

"Marion, it was bad enough that you told the family, please don't—" she begged, but a light tittering from the others quelled her efforts. Her anger mounting, Anna grabbed her purchase from the counter and marched from the store—only to have the bundle jostled from her grasp by a young man plodding down the sidewalk.

Instantly, Anna's irritation vanished as the sandy-haired young man smiled and offered her the package and his apologies. She knew she had never seen him—or his crystal-blue eyes—before, but he still seemed so familiar…so fraternal…so much like family. And, trying to discern what she was sensing about the young man, Anna could not stop her gaze from following his tall, broad-shouldered frame as he continued along the walkway.

"Now that's the kind of handsome you only get to read about," Marion announced from behind her. "A woman could get lost wading through that mane of his."

Pivoting on her heel, Anna faced her sister, who was watching the stranger— a little too intensely. "Marion, you are shameless."

"Oh, please, you know you were thinking the same thing...you should go after him, dear sister...that's a man definitely worth setting your cap for."

"Why?"

"Why? Just look at him."

"Marion, I need to know someone before I set my cap for him."

"Oh, really? And what about your dear husband at the train depot? You have yourself married to him, and you haven't even said 'hello' to each other!" Marion replied with her usual biting taunt.

"That's not what I said...I told you that it was as though I had seen a sign telling me he was the one...but no matter what, I would still want to get to know him first."

"Uh ha," Marion snickered.

Both sisters glared at each other, then, simultaneously, they raised their parasols and strolled wordlessly down the sidewalk. Sighing in both disappointment and frustration, Anna gritted her teeth—she always regretted that the sister closest to her in age was also the one with whom she had the worst rapport. As long as she could remember, it had been Marion's mission to cause her endless annoyance and embarrassment. And, usually, she accepted the teasing without causing too much of a ruckus—but her sister's attitude about the stranger at the depot nudged Anna beyond her customary silence.

"Marion, I do not appreciate your telling everyone what I said at the train station."

"I suppose not, but it is rather silly...I'm sure God has more important things to do than to go around pointing out future husbands."

"What have you got against this man? You haven't even met him."

"And, remember, neither have you, Dear...he's just not right for you."

"But the young gentleman we just saw is right for me?"

"Well, yes."

Anna swung her package by its string, mulling over Marion's words. And, as she carefully considered the differences between the two men in question, Anna suddenly saw a reason for her sister's baiting. "You're worried."

"That you're going to choose the wrong man for a husband—of course, I'm concerned."

Anna nodded, and still in thought, she hardly heard her sister's words. "You'd rather see me with a young man just starting out—one who needs to stay in Sandorville while he makes a name for himself."

As they approached Main Street, the sisters slowed, letting a carriage speed by before they crossed, then Anna noticed a distinct acceleration in her sister's pace. "Marion, why are you in such a hurry?"

"Because of your dawdling," her sister returned as they neared the park where their father and Marion's husband waited.

"No, that's not why you're rushing," Anna returned, pulling on her sister's sleeve so that Marion had to lessen her gait or tear her dress. "You're rushing because you realize that I've figured out why you've been badgering me...you're trying your best to make me too embarrassed to speak to the gentleman at the depot—if I ever see him again."

"That is absolutely ridiculous!"

"No, it isn't...you're worried that I am meant to be with him...and you're even more worried that he's established enough to whisk me away from Sandorville—forever...because then you and the girls would have to deal with Mama's tuberculosis."

Marion stopped abruptly, a scowl emerging on her face. "Stop calling it that."

Indignation began to boil inside Anna and she faced her sister. "That's what Papa says it is...do you think calling it consumption makes it more romantic... or less deadly?" As she watched the horror spread across Marion's face, Anna's mood cooled—she had no idea that her words would slap her sister so hard. "Marion, I'm sorry...I know you and the girls don't want to face Mama's illness, but you will have to—eventually," she offered, gently taking her sister's hand. "Especially, if I go to nursing school as you girls are pushing me to do."

Yanking her arm away, Marion lifted her nose in the air and twirled her parasol handle. "If you do end up marrying the stranger from the train station, my dear Anna," she announced as if the last few lines of their conversation had never been spoken, "don't expect a wedding gift from me."

Anna's jaw dropped open in disbelief—her sister was perfectly happy to wear blinders, even if that meant ignoring their mother along with her illness. "Well, when I do marry him, my dear Marion," Anna replied, pushing her shoulders back, "all I'll expect from you is an apology."

Marion snorted in reply, then, catching sight of their father and her husband relaxing on a park bench, she pointed and exclaimed, "There's Papa and Michael!"

As she watched her sister scurry toward their waiting escorts, Anna sighed. At least the mystery of Marion's incessant teasing about the gentleman at the depot had been solved—that left only one puzzle…why did her sisters want her to go to school when they were so afraid of being left alone to care for their ailing mother?

Suddenly, as a warm breeze tickled her face, she thought of her brother—and finally began to understand her sisters' logic. If she went to nursing school, she would become completely immersed in her studies, leaving little chance to be swept away by a dark-haired stranger, and school would be easy enough to walk away from—if her mother became gravely ill. Either way, none of her siblings would ever have to fill the role of caretaker.

As they strolled through the open-air market grounds, Anna Spreyer looped her gloved hand around her father's bent elbow and snuggled close to him—nothing comforted her more than her father's strong presence and the sweet, musty aroma of medicinal herbs that scented his clothes. Of all her activities during the warm summer months, she longed for and appreciated her Saturdays at the market the most—the food, laughter, music, and friends were always a joy, but it was the time with her father that she truly cherished. Breathing in deeply, Anna grinned, inwardly thanking God for another pleasant Saturday.

"It's a beautiful day," she offered in a whisper, not wanting to disturb the tranquility that surrounded her.

"Ja," Doctor Spreyer agreed as he glanced upward. "Even more so since the weather's cleared."

Anna nodded as she, too, looked up at the azure canopy above them. The morning's somber rain clouds had been completely chased away by a cool wind, which now frolicked around the poplar and willow trees, sending their leaves into a silvery dance.

"I'm sorry that my calls took so long today, Liebchen," the doctor continued. "I'm afraid that you have missed most of the activities."

As the gentle breeze played with the lace on her parasol, Anna reached over and lightly kissed her father on the cheek. "As long as I'm here with you, that's all that matters."

"That…and getting Mama's cherries."

Anna giggled, knowing her father's insatiable appetite for the fruit. "Ah, that's right. We wouldn't want to forget Mama's cherries," she teased lightheartedly. "And, maybe, we should get some extras…just in case someone else would like one…or two."

Doctor Spreyer chuckled nonchalantly, but his eyes danced with merriment over the ribbing. "Ja, maybe we should."

"I just hope Mr. Parker hasn't left yet," she returned, searching the area for the merchant.

"So do I…maybe you should have come this morning with your sisters—instead of helping me with my calls."

Anna gazed at her father in disbelief, then, seeing the humor in his eyes, she laughed. "Believe me, Papa…I would much rather deal with your patients than with your daughters…you do remember last year's family outing at the market, don't you?"

"I remember," Doctor Spreyer returned, giving his daughter's arm a slight squeeze.

Anna smiled at the even-tempered response—although her father spoke calmly, she knew how much he was still bothered by the disastrous excursion. "Oh, look!" Anna announced, grateful that she could change the subject. "There's Mr. Parker!"

"Hello, Thomas!" Doctor Spreyer called as he motioned to the fruit farmer.

As Anna and her father approached, Thomas Parker waved in return, then tossed a large, empty crate onto his wagon.

"Hello, Thomas," the doctor repeated as they reached the vendor. "I hope that empty carton doesn't mean you're out of cherries."

The farmer smiled wide, revealing a large gap between his front teeth. "Doctor Spreyer...Miss Anna, it's good to see you," he offered with a tip of his frayed hat.

"Thank you and it's good to see you," Anna returned. "Has it been a good day for you?"

"Very...seems everybody wanted cherries today."

"Then you don't have any left?" Anna asked as her father's smile transformed into a crestfallen smirk.

Thomas winked and chortled out a mirthful laugh. "I thought you might be coming by," he said as he knelt by his wagon and slid a small basket from under the bed, "so I saved you some."

"Oh, bless you, Mr. Parker!" Anna exclaimed.

Pushing himself to his feet, Thomas Parker held the container out and offered a gap-toothed grin as the doctor plucked a cherry from the basket and popped it into his mouth. "Thank you, Thomas...my wife will be very pleased."

As he set the container on his makeshift counter, the farmer chuckled and winked at Anna again. "I think your father will be pleased too...don't you?"

Anna clasped her father's hand and twirled her parasol. "Yes, I think Papa will be very pleased. In fact, he'll...oh, Papa! I almost forgot! Mama asked me to pick up some honey."

"I think Mrs. Keen's gone," the farmer offered with a shake of his head. "Oh, dear."

"Why don't you go and make sure," Doctor Spreyer put in, grabbing another cherry. "I need to discuss something with Thomas anyway."

Anna nodded, and slightly raising her skirt with her left hand, she circled and quickly headed toward the honey vendor's usual place—yet even from a distance, she could see that Mrs. Keen had departed. Disappointed for her mother, Anna stopped, but the light wind at her back urged her to continue, and she ambled through the market grounds, visiting the few merchants still remaining. As the evening sun shimmered through the trees, blanketing the ground with long shadows, Anna closed her parasol and let the sun's soft glow touch her face. Immersed in the peaceful quiet, Anna slowed her pace and nodded to a young couple who meandered by arm in arm.

Without warning, a large bouquet of wildflowers appeared from behind her, held by a strong, sturdy hand. Startled, Anna turned—positive that the courier was mistaken and that the wonderful gift was meant for someone else. Then, as her breath caught in her throat, she looked up into the softest brown eyes she had ever seen. For days her mysterious admirer's memory had walked through her thoughts—now...now, the genuine person stood in front of her.

"I...I don't know if you remember me," he started with a smile—which added a youthful warmth to his countenance. "We met, rather informally, at the depot the other day."

Instantly, a rush of heat washed over her, and Anna condemned the blush that she knew was coloring her face—it would betray any other answer but the truth. "Yes, I remember," she returned, completely mesmerized by her admirer's rugged features and the slight dusting of gray in his hair and mustache.

"I couldn't believe it when I saw you arrive," he said. "I was expecting to see someone else—and there you were...again. Now, I'm glad that my br...that my associate didn't show up...because it gives me the chance for a proper introduction...my name is Peter Leighton," he continued as he tipped his hat and held out the wildflowers. "And these are for you, Miss..." Then his cheerful grin disappeared. "Or is it Mrs.?"

"No, it's Miss," she murmured, taking the bouquet. "Miss Anna Spreyer."

Gently, Peter Leighton took her gloved hand, and lifting it to his lips, he gave her a light kiss.

Feeling her blush deepen, Anna cleared her suddenly tense throat. "You, uh…you said you were expecting someone else?" As she heard the question come out of her mouth, Anna inwardly moaned…couldn't she think of anything better to say?

He nodded. "Yes…a business acquaintance. We were supposed to meet here, but he's long overdue."

Delight instantly bubbled up inside Anna, and a wide smile spread on her face as she realized that the Lord had mapped out the perfect meeting—if the day had unfolded as planned for either her or her admirer, their paths would have remained parallel, instead of finally crossing.

"Miss Spreyer, would you allow me to call on you sometime?"

"If my father approves."

"If I approve of what?"

Her father's booming voice echoed through the market grounds, and Anna spun around—and faced an expression she had never seen before. "Papa? Is everything all right?" she inquired as her excited and nervous stranglehold on the flowers tightened even more.

"I began to worry when you didn't return, Liebchen," the doctor announced, his eyes fixed on Peter Leighton.

"I apologize, Sir," Peter offered with an extended hand. "I'm the one responsible for your daughter's delay…my name is Peter Leighton."

The doctor hesitated for a moment, then, with a long exhale, he set his basket of cherries on the ground and shook Peter's hand. "Doctor Otto Spreyer…now, what must I approve of?"

"Of me calling on your daughter, Sir."

Doctor Spreyer grunted and looked from Peter, to Anna, then to the flowers she held in her hand. "Possibly…I don't remember seeing you around here before, Herr Leighton."

"No Sir, I just arrived in Sandorville a few days ago."

"I would like to talk with you further—before I make my decision."

"Of course."

"Unfortunately, it will have to be another time...I have a patient to see."

Anna considered her father's words, unsure if they had been spoken in fact or as a refusal. "Perhaps Mr. Leighton could join us for church tomorrow," she tried, but her elation weakened when she noticed Peter wince at her suggestion.

The doctor nodded. "We could have our talk after the service, if that's agreeable, Herr Leighton."

"That would be fine," Peter returned. "Just tell me when and where."

"Nine o'clock, at Trinity Lutheran Church on the corner of Maple Road and East Lane," Doctor Spreyer answered. Then, for the first time since meeting Peter, the doctor's features mellowed. "The service will be in German though."

Peter smiled and replied with a shrug, "I don't know German—but I don't mind."

Anna's pulse quickened at the sight of his grin, and feeling herself flush once again, she offered, "Would you like us to give you a map to the church?"

"That won't be necessary...I know exactly where it is. I remember passing it on the way to the factory."

"Which factory?" Doctor Spreyer demanded as the sternness returned to his countenance.

"The Rheinhardt Furniture Factory...you have to take East Lane to get to the factory."

"Yes, I'm very aware of how to reach the Rheinhardt Factory."

Glancing at Anna, then back at the doctor, Peter's brow furrowed. "Is something wrong?"

"Were...were you applying for a job at the factory?" Anna asked as she took her father's hand.

"No, I already work for the company...I'm Mr. Rheinhardt's new assistant."

A chill quivered through Anna, cooling the blush on her face. Everything had started out so perfectly, she silently lamented. How? How did it end up so wrong?

There were very few people in Sandorville who knew the truth about the Rheinhardt Factory and how its workers were really treated—but she was thoroughly aware of the brutal management methods, having helped her father clean the wounds of those methods many times. Over and over, her father urged the men to talk to the authorities, yet they never did—they were too afraid of losing their homes...and their families...and their lives. And, since she and her father could not betray the workers' confidence to voice their accusations, all remained the same.

"You must not know Mr. Rheinhardt very well," Anna tried, still hoping that Peter did not agree with his employer's tactics.

"I've known him all my life," he returned, his frown deepening.

"Well, I hope you don't share his principles," Doctor Spreyer declared.

"I...I don't understand...Mr. Rheinhardt's a kind and generous man, and I respect him very much."

Disillusioned, Anna bowed her head, trying to hide the tears that were flooding her eyes.

"Then you are not going to challenge his ethics?" the doctor charged.

"I don't appreciate his passive approach to management...but I haven't found anything wrong with his ethics...Sir."

Anna's heart sank. Why? Why would God pair her with someone who sided with such a wicked man? Did she misunderstand what the Lord had told her at the depot? Had her sisters been right all along? She wouldn't...she couldn't be with this man now—knowing what he represented. Nor could she understand why God would want her to be.

"I am sure that Mr. Travis Perryn would have disagreed with you," Anna put in, her disappointment causing a quiver in her voice. "If that's where you stand, Mr. Leighton, you needn't bother to ask my father's permission to call on me—because the answer is no."

Peter stood speechless. The shift in the Spreyers' mood completely bewildered him. He didn't know why he had suddenly become the enemy—all he knew was he didn't want things to end with Anna's emphatic 'no.' "I merely meant—"

"Herr Leighton, I believe my daughter has made her position quite clear... and if you force the issue, I'll make it even clearer," Doctor Spreyer announced, his German accent emphasizing every word. Then, after picking up his basket of cherries, the doctor grasped his daughter's hand, and the two turned and walked away.

Taking hope in the fact that Anna was still clutching his flowers, Peter followed after them—until he spotted Daven just a few yards away. Reluctantly, he stopped. His brother's timing, as usual, was lousy. And, as if answering the thought, Daven consulted his pocketwatch for the time—which ignited Peter's already fatigued temper. He hated that watch. It was a constant reminder of his late stepfather's failures—and of the hardships his family endured because of them.

Finally, his brother looked in his direction, and Peter motioned for Daven to follow him. Knowing that he had to calm his temper, Peter wandered toward a nearby willow tree and concentrated on the task of finding a place where they could meet unnoticed. Then he found it—a weathered bench mostly obscured by the willow's drooping branches. As he reached the hideaway, Peter nodded—the tree's ground-scraping limbs would definitely hide them from the few vendors and townsfolk that remained in the area.

Leaning on the back of the bench, Peter gazed numbly at some distant figures playing and watching a base ball game at the far end of the grounds—then his thoughts drifted to a different contest…his encounter with Anna Spreyer. Even though she had unquestionably expressed her feelings about him and his position with Rheinhardt Furniture, he was still too intrigued to give up. Somehow, he had to figure out where he went wrong—and how he could mend the situation. Suddenly, the willow's branches parted and Daven entered their sanctuary. Not quite ready to deal with his brother, Peter lingered on the memory of Anna Spreyer…and her sweet face…and her golden hair…and her…

"I said I'm sorry."

The words poked at Peter and renewed his irritation. Pulling himself from his reverie, he deliberately slid his watch from his waistcoat pocket and checked the time. "I was ready to leave after half an hour, but then I wondered just how long it would take you to get here…it's been over three and a half hours, Daven. Three and a half," he stated, his outrage fully refueled. "I swear I'm going to take that watch of yours and—"

"It has nothing to do with my pa's watch…I was working," Daven replied as he plopped onto the bench.

"Don't add lies to the problem."

Daven slowly turned and glared at Peter. "I have never lied to you…and you know it."

Stepping around the bench, Peter surveyed their surroundings through the veil of willow leaves, and seeing no curious eyes in the vicinity, he sat next to his brother. "So why are you late?" he asked, trying to sound more puzzled than perturbed. "Karl told me everyone gets to leave at noon on Saturday."

"Well, we don't…we work until five. And, believe me, if you're not there at precisely five o'clock—you don't get paid," Daven answered as he removed his hat and absently brushed the sawdust from his hair. "Why are we on Rheinhardt's side anyway?" he went on, replacing his derby. "We should be on the side of those who really need us."

Peter frowned. His brother's tone and implications equaled those of Anna Spreyer and her father. "What do you mean?"

Leaning forward, Daven rested his elbows on his knees, and it was then that Peter noticed it—Daven's massaging of his left hand. That said more than words ever could. Peter hadn't seen his brother's nervous habit since Tait Ashby's burial, where the quirk had driven Daven to thumb his palm raw. His anger now melted, Peter gently pried his brother's hands apart and asked, "Daven, what's going on?"

No answer.

Peter grasped his brother's shoulder and slowly pressed him upright. "What happened while I was out of town?"

Tension instantly enveloped Daven's features. "What happened? What happened?" he repeated, his voice rising. "I was robbed, manipulated, cheated—"

"Robbed?" Peter echoed, grabbing his brother's arm. "Are you all right? Were you hurt?"

Daven shook his head. "It was just part of his grand strategy."

"Whose strategy?"

"Your friend's."

Confusion wove its way onto Peter's face. "Are you trying to tell me that Karl had something to do with you being robbed?"

"I'm not trying to tell you—I am telling you...then he had some kind of rumor about me spread all over town, so I couldn't get a job anywhere—except from him...for eight cents an hour."

Peter tried to form a response, but bewilderment choked any efforts he made—he knew his brother was sincere, but the words still didn't make any sense. The picture of Karl Rheinhardt that he was being shown was not the man he was acquainted with. "Dave, just start with Wednesday night and tell me everything."

As Daven sketched out his experiences and tragedies, guilt began to nag at Peter for allowing Fetch and his men to take advantage of his brother. Inwardly, he admitted that he sometimes did the same—but to have someone else treat his little brother that badly was unacceptable.

"I...I don't know...maybe I shouldn't have turned the job down the first time...what...what do you think?" Daven asked as he started to rub his palm again.

The question pierced through Peter's concentration—he never really thought his opinions mattered to his brother. "No, you made the right choice about that," he replied. "If you had accepted Fetch right off, he would have become suspicious."

Standing, Peter peered at the evening-lit market grounds. Sometime, during their discussion, the base ball game had ended and all concerned had departed, leaving the entire area deserted. What, exactly, did he get himself—and his brother—into? Peter wondered. And how was he going to solve the unfolding Rheinhardt Factory mystery without causing Daven any more hardships?

"Karl's not the mastermind," Peter murmured as he continued to ponder the situation.

Bolting from his seat, Daven clutched Peter's forearm and spun him around. "Haven't you heard anything I've told you?!" he demanded. "I'm not making this—"

"Yes, Daven, I heard you," Peter cut in, trying to quiet his brother. "And I believe you…but you have to believe me…Karl wouldn't treat you like that…he knows you're my brother."

"Well, that doesn't seem to matter to him."

Placing his hands on his brother's shoulders, Peter held back his next exposition until Daven looked him in the eyes. "Karl wouldn't do it…he told me, just a few days ago, that if he didn't care for you so much, he'd be jealous of your talent…he wouldn't humiliate and exploit you," he went on. "But Fetch would."

Still visibly frustrated, Daven opened his mouth to interrupt, but Peter barreled over the attempt and continued with his argument. "Think about it, Daven…it would be to Fetch's advantage to let you believe that Karl is the tyrant—because then you would never go to him for help."

"But I'm not the only one…I overheard some of the other men, and they think it's Rheinhardt too."

"That's exactly what I'm talking about, Daven. The workers aren't about to approach Karl for a remedy if they're convinced that he's the one making all the policies—that leaves Fetch open to do exactly what he wants."

Suddenly, something clicked into place in Peter's thoughts, and releasing his brother, he ambled back toward the bench. Maybe, Doctor Spreyer and Anna believed the same as the factory men—at least that would explain their reaction to him being associated with Karl Rheinhardt.

"I suppose," Daven offered with a resigned shrug.

"And, if Fetch threatened the other men into silence as he did you, then no one—not even Karl—will know that there's a problem to fix."

"I have to tell you, Peter," Daven said as he returned to his seat on the weather-beaten bench, "Fetch worries me."

"He worries me too. But, if it's any consolation, I think I worry him…he wasn't exactly happy when I met him on Wednesday and told him I would be reviewing his books."

"So now what?"

"So now we…" Letting his words drift into the evening-saturated heavens, Peter shook his head and sank onto the bench next to his brother. How could he ask Daven to continue? Especially when their opponents kept growing in number and in strength. "When Karl first contacted me," he said, more to himself than to Daven, "I just thought it was some of his employees using his supplies to make their own furniture…now…now, it's turning into quite a…a situation."

"What're you saying, Peter?"

"I think Fetch is up to a lot more than we've discovered so far…a lot more. And, with Karl being so removed from…from everything, I want you out of this whole thing."

"What?"

Peter nodded—now that the words had been spoken, he agreed with them completely. "Fetch has already put you through enough…I don't want you involved anymore."

Daven smiled wide, then his merriment faded into uncertainty. "The past few days have been…have been awful…even though I knew my problems weren't permanent…I…I still couldn't stop thinking about what would happen if you didn't come back."

"Dave, I would have never left you here."

"I know…I know…that's not what I'm trying to say," Daven returned as he pulled his hat from his head.

Sliding sideways on the bench, Peter stared at his brother—who usually didn't have any difficulty in speaking his mind. "Then what—"

"I want out, Peter."

"I know. I said—"

"I want out…but I'm gunna stay."

Opening his mouth to correct his brother's enunciation, Peter immediately checked himself—why would he want to dampen such a profound declaration with such a petty detail? "I…I don't know, Daven."

"If I leave, Fetch is just gunna trap somebody else…maybe, somebody who doesn't have a big brother to help him."

Smiling at the unselfish statement, Peter reached over and tousled his brother's sandy-colored mane. "I…I'm proud of you."

Daven instantly beamed. "Can we…can we really stop Fetch?"

"Yes," he returned firmly—although, in his heart, he wasn't quite as sure. "I know you just started, Daven, but have you noticed anything odd in the factory?"

"Not yet, but then again, I just loaded and delivered the last of a table order today," he replied. "That's why I was so late—I didn't get back to the factory until six...missed getting paid too."

"What?"

"Yeah...seems Fetch was very serious when he told me I'd get paid at five."

"This is ridiculous! How can Karl not know Fetch is doing things like this?" Peter muttered as he dug in his other waistcoat pocket and pulled out some coins. "Here," he offered, holding them out to his brother.

"I can't."

"You need some money, Daven."

"No."

"You said you only paid Mrs. Tadman through tomorrow night. You're going to need some money to pay her for another week...so take these."

Daven shook his head. "Fetch knows I don't have a cent—I can't just suddenly show up with money."

Slowly, Peter repocketed the coins, once again impressed with his brother's maturity and insight.

"I'll talk to Mrs. Tadman," Daven added, "and see if she'll let me stay a few days on credit...and I guess...I guess I'll have to ask Fetch for an advance."

Pushing himself from the bench, Peter gazed at the curtain of willow branches in front of him, then at the crimson sun hugging the horizon. He realized that he couldn't help Daven without jeopardizing their purpose, yet he hated to send his brother back into Fetch's grasp with nothing. "I suppose you'll have to," he finally conceded. Then, turning around to face his brother, he asked, "Have you heard the name Travis Perryn at the factory?"

Daven thought for a moment, then shook his head.

"Try to find out who he is and let me know."

"I'll try...if I can get anybody to talk to me."

"And I want to know what Fetch says about the advance—if he doesn't give it to you...well, I'll think of something."

Daven nodded.

"We're going to have to meet more often—to keep on top of things…not much can happen between now and Monday, so how about Monday night?"

"Where?"

"Where…" Peter sighed as he considered their dilemma. "How about here—it's out of the way yet close enough for both of us."

"Same time?"

"No…make it…make it ten…no, that's no good…seven. I don't want you out after dark."

Daven stood and crossed his arms. "I'm not a child, Peter," he declared. "I can be out after—"

Holding up his hand to silence his brother, Peter went on, "We don't know what kind of rumors they've circulated about you…it'll just be better if you're at the boarding house when it gets dark."

"I guess," Daven murmured as he grabbed his hat from the bench's ragged slats. "So Monday night at seven?"

"Yeah…and—"

"I know—don't be late."

The corners of Peter's mouth turned upward. "I was going to say be careful."

"Oh," Daven returned with a cheerful grin, "and then you were going to say 'don't be late,' right?" he kidded, giving Peter a departing pat on the shoulder.

Chuckling at both the remark and his own predictability, Peter fingered the coins in his pocket as he watched his brother saunter out into the dimming sunlight. They had never gotten along as well as they had tonight—and yet he was relieved to see Daven's playful nature resurface. As much as he wanted his brother to develop a serious disposition, Peter found himself admitting that it just wouldn't be Daven without the annoying free-spiritedness.

⊶ Three ⊷

As her thoughts wandered once again to Peter Leighton, Anna stopped singing and just listened to the words of the hymn as it resounded throughout the church. Why couldn't she put him out of her mind? she wondered. She was so disenchanted by Peter's association with Karl Rheinhardt—and yet she was still so attracted to him. Did Peter really revere the heartless furnituremaker? Or was he fooled by the man's benevolent facade—as most of Sandorville was? Did Peter have an honorable spirit? Or a cold and treacherous one? And her mother's simple comment on the matter only added to Anna's questions…

'You'll know what is in Mr. Leighton's heart by the fruit that he bears.'

How could she get to know him now, when her temper had pushed him away? Was it too late? Or would God give her another chance?

Feeling a tug on her skirt, Anna looked up and realized that the service had ended. Trying to ignore the cackles from her sisters, she moved into the aisle and clasped her father's hand. Then, as the congregation leisurely shuffled toward the door, she caught a glimpse of Peter's tall frame standing in the back of the church—and her father stiffened as he did the same. Biting her lip, Anna tried to hide her excitement. The Lord had arranged another meeting for them…she had another chance. But, as her pulse quickened and a blush flooded her face, she reminded herself to be cautious. She needed to know Peter Leighton's heart first—because he could yet be the kind of man she prayed he wasn't.

As they emerged from the church, Anna felt her father's grip immediately tighten—perhaps because they were approaching the steps that badly needed repair…or perhaps because Peter Leighton was waiting for them at the bottom of the stoop.

"Doctor Spreyer…Miss Spreyer," Peter offered with a tip of his hat as they descended.

The doctor grunted and turned away. Although he knew it was wrong—especially after such a stirring sermon—he purposefully ignored the cordial salutation from Peter Leighton and guided Anna toward their waiting carriage.

"Doctor Spreyer, wait…please," Peter called as he followed after them.

The doctor growled, then, glancing at the chapel, he reluctantly stopped. Leighton, just as any of God's children, deserved some mercy. "Herr Leighton… what do you want?"

"Just a moment of your time, Sir…to explain," Peter said, removing his top hat. "I know you're upset that I work for Mr. Rheinhardt. He has always been very kind to me, but I—"

"Of course, he would be. The devil takes care of his own," the doctor cut in. "And, as long as you agree with his way of running that factory, I don't want—"

"But I don't…I don't agree with it at all," Peter interrupted, and after surveying the area, he pointed to a gnarled oak tree near the entrance of the church's cemetery. "Is it all right if we talk over there?"

Still suspicious but even more curious, the doctor nodded and released his daughter's hand. Anna had already witnessed one of his uncharitable outbursts at the market. If the mysterious Peter Leighton angered him beyond control again, she didn't need to see another. Then, as he considered his daughter's infatuation with the charcoal-haired stranger, the doctor stretched out his arm and took her hand once more. If Leighton proved to be a scoundrel, Anna needed to hear it firsthand—that way she would not doubt the man's unsuitability as a beau. "Herr Leighton, I do not appreciate all this secretiveness," he announced as he escorted Anna to the ancient tree.

"I understand, Doctor Spreyer, but there is good reason for it," Peter remarked, reaching the oak. "I'm very aware that there is something wrong at the factory."

Not quite sure if he should trust the cryptic young man or not, the doctor exhaled deeply but remained silent.

"I can't tell you everything, Sir, but I want you to know that I am working to put an end to the injustice."

"Herr Leighton, I want to believe you..."

"But you don't."

"No...you are Herr Rheinhardt's assistant...to get that kind of position, you must agree with his...his tactics."

"Doctor, the miseries at the factory are not Karl's...Mr. Rheinhardt's doing."

"I have been told, Herr Leighton, that the barbaric conditions at the factory are a result of his—"

"They're not, Sir. Karl's not aware of what is going on...that's part of the problem."

Doctor Spreyer grunted as he studied Peter Leighton. He wanted to trust the young man and give him a chance to prove himself—and the sparkle in Anna's eye and her ever-tightening grip said she wanted to do the same. "But what if you find out that it is Herr Rheinhardt's fault?"

"I'll still put a stop to it, Sir."

With a reluctant nod, the doctor allowed the interrogation to end. He knew Peter wasn't being one-hundred-percent truthful, but he somehow believed the young stranger nonetheless. "Herr Leighton, my daughters and their families are planning to go on a picnic this afternoon. If you would like to join them, I will allow you to accompany Anna," he offered, ignoring his daughter's expression of surprise and concern. If Peter could survive a day with his four eldest daughters— and their prying—he would accept the gentleman as a possible suitor for Anna.

"Thank you, Doctor. I'd be honored."

"But Papa, I—"

The doctor patted Anna's forearm. "Your mother and I will enjoy the peace for a few hours," he replied, and putting his daughter in the Lord's care, he hesitantly let Peter take her hand.

As the doctor watched Anna and Peter head, arm in arm, toward the waiting surreys, a cloud descended upon him—the same thunderhead that appeared whenever a young man started wooing one of his daughters. And, even though this was the last cloud he would have to endure...it was going to be the hardest.

Keeping her mother's words in mind, Anna studied Peter as he talked politics with her brothers-in-law, played catch with the children, and suffered through her sisters' endless questions. And the more she watched, the more she found her heart yearning for him. He emanated such a strong, staunch gentleness, and a tender confidence, which could be heard in every sentence he uttered, added to his charm. Even her sisters appeared to be taken with him, and he, in return, was faring quite well with them. He had successfully dodged the girls' most prying inquiries—which, unfortunately, included the ones about his family background—and thankfully, he didn't seem very interested in their melodramatic stories about her many foolish blunders. Then, as Marion began another tale, Anna shivered...she couldn't bear to have Peter know about the feelings she had at the depot.

"Marion, I'm sure Mr. Leighton is tired of hearing all these boring stories," she announced, purposefully cutting off her sister's narrative.

Obviously miffed by the interruption, Marion turned and glared at her. "No, he isn't."

Ignoring the sneer and comment, Anna stood and straightened her lace overskirt. "I think I'll take a walk."

"Fine," Marion snipped. "That will give us girls a good chance to really talk with Mr. Leighton."

"Marion, I thought I'd show Mr. Leighton the path by the creek," she replied as she grasped the handle of her parasol.

Instantly, Peter grabbed his top hat and jumped up from his place on the picnic blanket. "Ladies, if you'll please excuse me," he said, donning his hat and giving it a small tip all at the same time. "Your sister shouldn't go for a walk unescorted."

With a triumphant smile, Anna popped open her parasol, then looped her right hand through Peter's waiting arm. "Up ahead, there's a trail that leads to the creek and follows it for awhile…it's a rather long walk—but very quiet."

"Sounds wonderful," he replied with a grin as they headed for the grassy pathway.

For a few, cozy moments they strolled silently along, meandering, as the path did, in and out of a stand of trees, then Peter began to chuckle. "You have quite a family."

Anna laughed at the audible relief in his voice. "They can sometimes be…a challenge. But you handled them very well…do you come from a large family?"

"No," he responded with a shake of his head.

Anna waited, hoping for more details—but none came. Again, he was skirting the questions about his family, just as he had with her sisters. "And this isn't even all of us," she continued, breaking the awkward silence that had suddenly materialized. "We're missing my brother, Hans. He's in Ann Arbor…doing his best to become a doctor."

Peter's eyes focused on the path and his jaw clenched. "Your brother's very lucky to be in college," he said as he reached down and grabbed a small, dry stick from the ground.

Hearing a twinge of bitterness in her escort's voice, Anna looked up and studied his rugged, pained features. "Hans doesn't always think so," she offered, wondering why Peter's mood had changed so abruptly.

"It's too bad that your parents weren't able to join us," he put in as he snapped off inch-size pieces of the twig and tossed them to the side. "I would have liked the opportunity to talk to your father some more."

"Mama just wasn't up to it today…I think having everyone around is draining what strength she has."

"Your mother's not well?"

"No...she has tuberculosis."

Peter's brow wrinkled in thought. "I don't think I know..."

Anna shook her head. "I'm sorry...Papa prefers to call it that. She has consumption."

"I'm very sorry," he returned. "That must be very difficult for you."

"Sometimes—but I try to appreciate every day I have with her," Anna said as she watched Peter fling the small bits of wood to the ground. "What about your parents?" she tried, hoping he couldn't one-word his way out of an answer. "Do they live in the area?"

Peter broke the last of the stick in half and let it fall from his hands. "No... not anymore...all of them are deceased."

"All of them?"

He half chuckled, then, peering into her eyes, he replied, "It's a long story."

"There's plenty of time," she returned as she gestured toward the path, which now imitated the bends and twists of the small brook that it bordered. "We've just now reached the creek...the trail goes on for at least a mile from here."

"This is a nice walk," he offered, gazing at the stream as it rushed over the rocks and branches in its way. "It's quite a change from all the bustle in town."

Anna nodded. Although disappointed in the conversation's new course, she still took hope in the fact that Peter was continuing along the pathway. "If you'd rather not talk about your family, I'll understand."

"No, I wouldn't...thank you."

Not prepared for such an unwilling response, Anna's jaw dropped open, and she glanced up at her reluctant escort—only to find him looking at her with a boyish grin and a mischievous glint in his eye. Immediately, a blush washed over her, and Anna smiled at the jesting. "Is that a hint that I'm prying too much?" she returned, matching his lighthearted manner.

"No, no," he replied with a laugh. "Forgive me...it's just that...well, it's just not very interesting."

"It is to me," Anna said, then she waited for him to continue—which, unfortunately, he didn't. Although her family did grieve her at times, she had never experienced any trauma that was too horrible to talk about, and as she wondered what wickedness her reserved suitor had witnessed, she began to regret the memories that she had dredged up. "I'm so sorry, Mr. Leighton. I didn't mean to bring up bad mem—"

"No, you didn't. My thoughts just wandered to my br...uh, to something else," he responded, patting her hand. "And I apologize for being so mysterious...after my father was killed, my mother remarried, and I had a stepfather for awhile—that's what I meant by 'all of them.'"

"Killed? Did...did your father have an accident?" she asked softly, beginning to understand why he was so closemouthed.

"No," Peter murmured as he snatched up another stick and started the methodical snapping once again. "We, uh, we owned a general store in Bradlee, up North...my dad was...working late one night...and two men broke in to rob the store...my father was shot."

"Oh, Peter, uh, Mr. Leighton, I'm so sorry," Anna said, praying that he didn't hear her impropriety. "Were you and your father close?"

"Yes."

"What was his name?"

"John...he grew up in Bradlee—back when it was just a couple of buildings...all he ever wanted to do was open a store and help his town to grow...after the war, that's just what he did."

Anna smiled and squeezed Peter's arm tenderly, trying to hide her surprise and delight—it was the first time he offered up his past without being nudged. "It sounds as if he was a very determined man."

"Yes, he was," Peter returned as he continued to break his newest twig into bits.

"And is his son anything like him?"

"Sometimes too much."

"You said your mother remarried after your—" Anna started, but as they made a sharp turn toward the creek, she stopped in mid-sentence and mid-stride. "Oh, my!" she exclaimed, staring at the massive, broken willow limb in front of her and at the crushed little bridge that used to span the fast-moving brook. "It wasn't like this last week."

"Is there any other way across?" he asked, throwing his stick into the water.

"No," she moaned in reply, saddened that their walk had to end. "This side gets quite marshy from here...that's why the city aldermen had the bridge built."

"I guess that means we have to go back...unless you want to rest here for awhile."

Anna nodded gleefully and pulled her parasol closed. "That would be nice."

Heading over to the willow tree, Peter surveyed the fallen branch, then tested its stability. Satisfied that the downed limb was solidly lying on the ground, he removed his frock coat and laid it over the rough bark. "Miss Spreyer," he called, extending his arm, "your throne awaits."

"Why, thank you, Sir," she giggled as she grasped his hand and settled onto the shaded branch.

Lowering himself onto the ground, Peter leaned against the willow's bough, and as he listened to the water gurgle over the rocks, he looked up at his beautiful, golden-haired companion. He had wooed many women over the years, but none of them ever made him feel so at ease...so warm...and so peaceful.

"Please continue...you were telling me about your mother."

Peter chuckled at the statement—quite amazed at how quickly Anna had piloted the conversation back to his parents. "Well," he sighed, resigning himself to the inevitable, "Mum had a very difficult time being alone...a little over a year after my dad's death, she remarried."

"Was your stepfather cruel to you?"

"Tait?" Peter replied with a laugh. "No. Actually he was a very warmhearted man."

"Why do you dislike him so much?"

Removing his top hat, Peter tilted his head and studied Anna. "How do you know that?"

"It shows...on your face and in your voice."

Fingering one of the many willow twigs that lay under the fallen limb, Peter considered the comment and wondered just how large a dent his grudge had made in his appearance. "My stepfather and I worked together in the store for awhile, then he took over when I left for college...about ten months later, Tait's heart just gave out and he died...unfortunately, during the time he was in charge, he...he made some...some rather poor business decisions. He left us in a lot of debt, and I was forced to close the store...everything changed after that...I had to quit college and try to rebuild what my stepfather had destroyed."

"I'm terribly sorry," she said as she gently placed her hand on his shoulder. "That must have been very hard...but I, for one, am glad that the store closed."

"What?!" Peter exclaimed, pulling away. "Why would you say something like that? That store was my future...and Tait lost it for me...and he destroyed my father's dream."

"I'm sorry, Peter...Mr. Leighton. I...I didn't say that right," she returned, wringing her gloved hands. "If your stepfather had been a good business man, where would you be now?"

Still annoyed at Anna's comment and not wanting to continue with their current discourse, Peter just shrugged.

"Where would you be?" she persisted.

With an agitated sigh, he shrugged again. "I don't know." Then, after pondering her question for a few moments, he offered, "I guess I'd be done with college and back in Bradlee...maybe running the store...maybe opening another."

"Maybe...but you wouldn't be here in Sandorville...and you wouldn't be helping those poor men in the factory...and you wouldn't be sitting here with me now...that's why I said that I was glad the store closed...maybe, it was the only way the Lord could make you go where He needed you to go."

Peter frowned and rose to his feet. There had been too many disappointments, too many setbacks, to believe that God was shepherding his movements.

His bumpy life's path had taught him one thing—to rely on only himself. And he had persevered through all the difficulties on his own—without any help from above. Or had he? Had the Lord guided him all these years with him not knowing it? Was there really a purpose for all the misery he had gone through?

"Mr. Leighton?"

The question pierced his rumination, and he peered into Anna's dazzling hazel eyes. "You honestly believe that Tait ruined my business so I would end up in Sandorville?"

With a shy shrug and an embarrassed grin, Anna replied, "I just know that you wouldn't be here otherwise...when...when we're crossing through dark seas, it's difficult to imagine that any good can come out of all the storms we meet...we just have to trust that the Lord is navigating our steps to a...to a bountiful harbor."

Rolling his watch chain between his fingers, Peter shook his head. The reasoning sounded fair, yet he just couldn't accept it—God had given up on him a long time ago, and he, in return, had given up on God. That's the way it was...and that's the way it would stay. "I just don't believe it works like that...not anymore."

"Don't give up, Mr. Leighton...it's when we turn our backs on God's course that we truly get lost."

Chuckling at Anna's persistence to save his soul, Peter shook his head again. Even though he didn't agree with her philosophy, he still found himself enamored with her compassion and resolve. No other woman he had called on before compared to the young woman sitting in front of him. Her alluring figure...her dovelike voice...even her stubbornness had captivated him from the start. And, as he peered at her fine features—now glowing with a blush—he was, admittedly, content to be in Sandorville. Then, with that thought, he smiled...maybe, just maybe, he could finally abandon his grudge against his stepfather.

"We should be going," Peter announced as he leaned over and held out his hand. "Your family will be wondering if we walked all the way back to town."

"Oh...yes, I suppose you're right," she murmured softly, clutching her parasol. Then, placing her fingers into his palm, she stood, using his grip to steady herself. "I...I apologize for my...my sermon."

Bending to grab his hat and frock coat, Peter chuckled. "That's all right...I guess I had one coming, since I really didn't get much out of the German one this morning."

"It's too bad you had to sit through that," she offered as they started strolling along the curved trail once again. "We keep trying to get the minister to have at least one service in English, but he's...he's not willing to change."

With a half-smile, Peter tilted his head and gazed at Anna, trying to determine if her last statement was just an innocent comment or the punctuation to their previous discussion. And, as he continued to focus on her golden hair and sparkling smile...and her slender figure, wrapped in yellow and lace...and her creamy, lightly flushed features...the urge to kiss her bubbled up inside him.

"What?" she asked, peering into his eyes.

"May I call on you again?"

Her smile widening, Anna nodded vehemently. "Would you like to come for supper tomorrow? You could meet Mama."

"That sounds won—" Peter began, then he cut himself off, remembering his meeting with Daven—that was something he couldn't miss, no matter how much he wanted to see Anna. "I can't...I have a late appointment."

"Oh."

Bolstered by the disappointment in her voice, he reconsidered his answer. "Perhaps I could stop by after my meeting...say about eight?"

"That would be very nice," she returned as she tightened her grip around his arm.

"I still wish you'd let me help you out...just take this dollar, all right?" Hugh Relanger offered, holding up a silver coin.

"No...I can't," Daven returned as he ambled along the rough plank walkway, his friend at his side.

As they reached the sidewalk, both men stopped, then Daven glanced back at the hollow-eyed man's small but warm house. "I want you to know how obliged I am for all you've done."

"My simple invitation to church and dinner doesn't deserve that kind of praise," Hugh replied.

Shifting his attention to his friend, Daven smiled sadly. "I'm grateful for those things, but I'm more grateful for the way you've accepted me...you're the only person in this town who hasn't treated me as if I were carrying some deadly fever."

Hugh shrugged. "Well, I don't listen to gossip—I form my own opinions about people...and I liked you the minute I started talking with you on the train."

"And, for that, I thank God."

"Unfortunately," Hugh added, "there are many people in Sandorville who enjoy listening to gossip—and stretching it even further out of shape."

Daven nodded in agreement.

"So, please, let me give you some money...I don't want you to be without."

"I appreciate the offer, Hugh, but I...I can't."

With a dejected sigh, Hugh Relanger repocketed his coin. "I just feel responsible, in a way, for you getting robbed, since I recommended the Tadman House to you in the first place."

"Please don't blame yourself...no one could have guessed the outcome," Daven replied mournfully. He wanted to explain the real reason for the robbery, but a grain of uncertainty forced him to remain silent—and so did the memory of Quentin Fetch's recent well-worded warning...

'You'll never know if you're talkin' to a friend of mine—or not.'

"Thank you again," Daven put in as he shook Hugh's hand. Then, as he peered into his friend's deep, hollow eyes—and remembered Fetch's malevolence—he realized that he had no choice but to remain closemouthed...for his protection and, perhaps, for Hugh's also.

"If you need anything, Daven, just let me know."

With a bolstered grin, Daven patted his friend's shoulder, then turned and started the hike back to the Tadman Boarding House—his feet dragging with every step. He dreaded the all-too-quickly-coming Monday and wondered, if he walked slowly enough, could he delay its arrival? Laughing at his own foolishness, Daven gazed up at the pink-tinted clouds and descending sun. At least, he reasoned, in twenty-four hours, he would be able to talk to Peter—whom he craved to see.

Despite his procrastinating pace, Daven eventually entered the Tadman's yard. Then, climbing the few porch steps, he circled, crossed his arms, leaned against the right-hand support post, and watched the ever-changing color of the evening clouds. His father had always told him to appreciate the wonder of God's artistry, and as he closed his eyes, he could still hear the gentle Swedish voice telling him to learn his craft from the Master's hand. Smiling at the reminiscence, Daven sighed, wishing that he could touch his father's talented and loving hands once more…

Suddenly, as the memories flooded back into his head, he jerked alert and tried to push away the reflections before…

But it was too late—the one recollection of his father he wanted to forget still flashed through his thoughts. And he prayed that he could someday erase the memory of his beloved father's crumpled, lifeless body lying on the ground outside their home.

"Mr. Ashby?"

Pulling himself from the past, Daven wiped his eyes with his sleeve, then turned to face Mrs. Tadman, who stood on the porch just outside the doorway. "Yes Ma'am?" he greeted, pasting on a cheerful grin.

"Mr. Ashby, I…I've been waiting for you…I need to speak with you," she said, wringing a dish towel over and over in her hands.

"I'm sorry, I should have told you that I was going to spend the day with the Relangers," Daven returned. "But I'm glad you want to talk…because I need to ask you something about my room."

"That's what...what I wanted to...to speak to you about," Mrs. Tadman began, fumbling over her words. "I'm...I'm expecting a previous boarder to return tomorrow."

"You've waited to tell me that?"

"This man's an old and dear friend," she went on, her face sagging with fear.

"And..." he prompted as a burning lump formed in his gut.

"And he...he usually stays in your room...so you'll have to...to pack your things and leave at first light."

Daven closed his eyes, then slowly opened them as hopelessness settled on his shoulders. "I'll be willing to sleep on the floor...or anywhere...I need a place to stay, Ma'am."

Mrs. Tadman twisted the towel tighter. "I'm...I'm sorry, but I've been told that, um, that...I'm sorry, but you just have to go."

Realizing that the gossips had finally whispered their rumors in Mrs. Tadman's ear, Daven shook his head. "Whatever you've heard about me—it's not true," he tried. "I've lived in your house for days...you've got to know by now that I'm not a bad person."

Tears flooded her eyes, and she brushed them away with her mangled dish towel. "You'll still have to go."

"But no one will want me if they've heard the same humbug as you have... please let me stay," Daven begged, moving toward her.

The color faded from Mrs. Tadman's usually rosy face. "No, Mr. Ashby," she announced as she backed up a step, "you have to leave."

In the fading sunlight, Daven clearly saw the apprehension in Mrs. Tadman's eyes, and he knew it would be futile to pursue the issue. "You did tell me that we would wait and see how things worked out between us...I guess they didn't, huh?"

Slowly, Mrs. Tadman relaxed her hold on the coiled towel. "I...I'm sorry, Mr. Ashby...I, uh, guess you can stay through breakfast, but then you must leave."

While he watched Mrs. Tadman reenter the boarding house, Daven began to rub his palm with his thumb. Now, not only did he need to ask Fetch for an advance—and get it—but he also had to find another boarding place that would accept him. Then, as he stood on the twilight-soaked veranda, his brother's words surrounded him…

'Not much can happen between now and Monday.'

The ironic statement echoed through his thoughts, jeering at them both for underestimating Fetch's reach.

Ten chimes resounded in the office from a tall, thin clock that sat in the farthest corner of the room. Glancing at the timepiece's ornate hands, Peter growled under his breath and shoved away the open book in front of him. Eleven o'clock, he inwardly grumbled. Eleven o'clock and no sign of Karl—no wonder the man lost the reins of his company to Quentin Fetch. With a discouraged sigh, Peter slowly pushed himself from his chair and stretched his stiff back and shoulder muscles. Then, carefully stepping around the neat stacks of papers and books on the floor, he walked to the opposite side of the desk, reached up to the chandelier, and rotated the gas valves, extinguishing the now unneeded light.

"It's only Monday…leave some work for the rest of the week."

At the sound of the voice, Peter frowned and turned toward the door. "Karl, I expected you much earlier than this," he said with little effort to disguise his impatience.

Leaning on the doorjamb, the older man scowled in confusion. "Why?"

"Why?!" Peter exclaimed. "Because there's work to do."

Karl shrugged. "I knew you'd take care of things."

Instantly, Peter's dander raised—as did a feeling of being taken advantage of.

"What's going on here?" the older man asked as he waved his finger at the paper-filled desk and floor.

"I wanted to start going over your books as soon as I could."

"As soon as you could…it looks as though you've been here all night."

Peter nodded, scanning the office. "Since four this morning to be exact."

"Four? I've always said that you're too much of a workhorse, Marc…uh, Peter."

Recognizing the error, Peter shook his head. He knew Marcus would always dominate Karl's thoughts, but as he stared at the older man's dreamy, wonder-struck features, a new and disturbing realization hit him full force—in Karl's eyes, he was Marcus.

"I need to discuss some things with you," Peter said as he rubbed his aching neck muscles. "Do you have a moment?"

His eyes lighting up, the older man nodded and passed over the threshold.

"Karl," Peter called, motioning toward the open door, "will you close that please?"

The older man glanced over his shoulder, grunted, and continued into the room. "It'll be fine," he replied as he settled onto one of the two velvet-uphol-stered chairs opposite the desk.

Peter's jaw clenched, and moving toward the doorway, he swept his hand against the back of the door and pushed it closed with a loud clack—somehow, he had to convince Karl that secrecy was a critical element of their plan.

"So how was your trip, Son?" Karl asked.

As he returned to his desk, Peter tried to calm his developing apprehension and anger. Normally, he wouldn't have been bothered by the fatherly gestures and references, but Karl's occasional lack of lucidity made them very worrisome. But, at least now, Peter silently remarked, he knew the reason the older man wanted him to become a partner so badly.

"The trip was informative," Peter answered as he once again avoided the mounds of paper on the floor and lowered himself onto his chair. "The Hopewells have some beautiful pieces of furniture."

"And..."

"And they were made by your company."

"You mean by the company using my name."

"Karl, every piece had your 'R' branded on it."

"Someone could have copied my mark, Peter...it's just an 'R.'"

Peter shook his head and started sketching the letter on a piece of paper. "No...the same iron that's used in your factory was used to burn those marks into the Hopewells' furniture."

The older man scowled. "You can't be sure of that."

Taking a deep breath, Peter finished his drawing and pushed it toward his reluctant boss. "Yes, I can…that is the mark that was on all of the Hopewells' pieces," he explained, pointing to his sketch. "It had a chip in the serif."

Karl leaned forward and slowly picked up the paper. "And my 'R' has the same chip?" he asked as he studied the drawing.

With a small smile of triumph, Peter nodded. "I checked all the furniture here in the showroom…every 'R' has the chip."

"Maybe this other company copied the chip too."

Instantly, Peter's grin disappeared. "That's doubtful, Karl."

"Hmm."

Tiring of the older man's skepticism, Peter pointed at the sketch. "Did you know about the chip?" he inquired. Then, without waiting for a reply, he went on, "You can see the flaw when you're looking for it, but it's not that noticeable."

"You saw it."

"Yes, after hours of studying the Hopewells' furniture," Peter countered. "But that's not the only connection…I also saw the bills of sale for their pieces. They were written on exactly the same paper as we use…the only difference is that we have no record of the sales."

"Peter!" Karl hollered as if he were yelling at an errant child. "I said I didn't want to alarm the Hopewells…asking for the bills of sale was—"

"I didn't ask to see the bills…I told the Hopewells that, as one of our best customers, we wanted their evaluation of Rheinhardt Furniture—from ordering to delivery. They were more than happy to show me everything…the bills of sale…their furniture…their home…photographs of their family…believe me, they were not alarmed."

Karl shifted his gaze to a painting on the wall. "This only proves what I have been saying all along…someone is just using my name and reputation."

"I fully agree…and that someone is in your company."

"So you say."

Placing his elbows on the desk, Peter interlaced his fingers and studied Karl. "Why are you fighting me so much on this? Why won't you even consider that it is someone in your employ?"

Karl stood and meandered over to the painting he had been examining. "Because it's just impossible…how could these fine pieces of furniture get made without Quentin noticing?"

Peter's face lost all expression, and he slowly rose from his chair. "Without him noticing?" he asked as he walked over to the older man. "Quentin Fetch is the reason these pieces are getting made."

Karl whipped Peter a fierce look. "That is ridiculous, Peter. I told you before how much Quentin has helped me since my son's accident…I trust him as much as I trust you…he wouldn't do this."

Suddenly, a chill raced up Peter's back—partly from a breeze that wafted through the open window, but mostly from the doubt that Karl's statement had planted in his thoughts. "Have you told Quentin Fetch about my real purpose here? Or Daven's?"

The older man sighed loudly and returned to his seat. "As I said before—no, I haven't told anyone—even though I disagree with the request."

Sighing in relief, Peter crossed his arms, leaned against the wall next to the picture, and studied his employer. If only he could deal with the Karl Rheinhardt he had known years ago. "Sir, if I'm going to succeed at finding our culprit or culprits, it's crucial that we keep my mission a secret."

"You're wrong about Quentin, Peter. He's a devoted employee…why are you so insistent in accusing him?"

"Because of what Daven has already told me," Peter returned. Then, wandering toward the window, he repeated the story of his brother's recent maltreatment—and as he did, both guilt and regret reminded him that he was the one who involved Daven in the first place.

"That is all nonsense," Karl mumbled as Peter finished the narrative.

"Fetch manages your business like a dictator and makes it look as if you're doing it—and you call it nonsense?"

"Your stepbrother has to be exaggerating."

A sudden rage fumed through Peter, and he stomped over to the desk. "I'm not going to stand here and let you call my brother a liar."

"But it's all right for you to call Quentin a criminal?!" Karl exclaimed, jumping up from his seat. "You just met the man on Wednesday...I've known him for years...I know what he was, and I know what he is now—and I trust him completely."

Again, an icy worry trembled through Peter. "What do you mean, you 'know what he was'?"

Perching himself on the edge of the desk, Karl's features wrinkled with determination. "Quentin told me this in confidence, and I'm only telling you because I want you to see how much he has changed...I don't want you to use it against him."

His jaw clenched in apprehension, Peter lowered himself onto his chair, knowing that he probably wouldn't like what he was about to hear. "All right..."

"Do you remember how bad things were when the panic hit in '73?"

"Yes, Dad barely held onto the store."

"Well, Quentin's father lost everything...and the man killed himself because of it," Karl said as he pushed himself from the desk and started roaming through the office. "Quentin was just a lad, and it was up to him to provide for his family...he admitted to me that he resorted to...to illegal means to make money."

"What kind of illegal means?"

"That doesn't matter, Peter."

"Yes, it does, Karl...stealing is one thing and extortion is another."

"Quentin just told me that he did 'anything' he had to...but he also said that he left that kind of lifestyle when he came to work for Rheinhardt Furniture."

"Just like that."

"Yes...just like that," the older man snapped as he ceased his pacing. "Don't you believe people can change?"

Taking a deep breath, Peter nodded. He was beginning to believe that very much—especially since his creek-side chat with Anna Spreyer. Never before had he entertained the thought of forgiving his stepfather, but now, after

Anna's a-reason-for-everything explanation, he found his own heart melting. "Yes, I think they can," he admitted aloud. "But, according to Daven, Fetch hasn't altered any of his methods."

"Well, your stepbrother is wrong...he must have misunderstood," Karl returned, his hands on his hips. "Quentin said that his friendship with Marcus changed him—that he wanted to leave his unlawful life behind because of the goodness he saw in Marcus."

While stroking his mustache, Peter digested Karl's statement and recalled the few times he had met Marcus—although somewhat arrogant, the young Rheinhardt seemed to be a decent fellow—and a good judge of people. "Fetch and your son were friends?"

"Yes, Quentin told me at the...at the funeral...that they had become very good friends."

"Fetch told you? Then Marcus never mentioned the friendship?" Peter inquired as the cold chill, once again, ran down his spine.

"No...Quentin said Marcus didn't want the other men to feel slighted or think that he was giving special treatment to a friend...it was then that I decided to make Quentin the foreman."

Peter grunted at Karl's grief-stricken naivete and at Quentin Fetch's self-serving cunningness. Fetch obviously spotted the older man's vulnerability—and took full advantage of it. "Karl, did you ever think that...that Fetch might have invented the friendship to get you to promote him?"

"No!" the older man replied sharply.

"If you would just objectively look at—"

"You listen to me, young man," Karl snapped, jabbing his finger at Peter. "Quentin himself told me, when I promoted him, that he wasn't the right person to be foreman...when I asked him why, he told me about his past and how it might cause problems," the older man went on as he ambled toward the window. "Quentin was worried that the other men in the factory might start telling tales about him...that's when I told him that I trusted Marcus' judgment and that I would take any complaints with a grain of salt."

With a long, heavy exhale, Peter slouched back in his chair. At least now, he knew how Fetch had manipulated his way into the company's management and Karl's heart...and how the foreman's reign had continued unchecked. Now... now, all that had to be done was to peel back the older man's unseeing adoration and defeat his paralysis regarding the whole matter.

Pushing himself from his chair, Peter joined Karl at the window and searched for the words that would affect his employer without alienating him.

"The wind's picking up," Karl absently announced.

As he glanced out the opened pane, Peter nodded. Outside the trees swayed back and forth over the North Pine River as if being stroked by an invisible hand, and two young boys, playing at the bank, loudly expressed their glee when the wind made their small boats dance on the water. "And it looks as if it might be bringing in some clouds," Peter added as they watched the relaxed scene below.

The older man bobbed his head in return.

"Karl, do you trust me?"

"You know I do."

"I understand how you feel about Fetch, but—"

"Don't call him that...his name is Quentin."

Peter's jaw clenched as he gazed at the ring of clouds hugging the horizon. "All right...I'll stop referring to him as Fetch, if you stop calling Daven my stepbrother."

"But he is your—"

"He's my brother—plain and simple."

"All right."

"As I was saying," Peter continued, "I understand how you feel about Quentin, but after what Daven told me, I believe that he...that he's taken advantage of you and your grief."

Suddenly, a light rustling from the desk caused a ripple of panic to crawl through the hairs on the back of Peter's neck, and he circled, hoping to find no one else in the office. Then, as a strong breeze wafted by him and shuffled through the piles of papers, he breathed out in relief. Pulling the window closed,

Peter looked at his employer and finished his accusation. "I think Fetch... Quentin is the one using your factory for his own gain."

"If you had told me that it was anyone else—I'd believe you," the older man replied, meeting Peter's stare. "But Quentin has kept my factory—and me—from withering away...if you want me to believe that he's guilty—you'll have to prove it...beyond any doubt."

"I understand...but I need you to...to stop fighting me so much and to keep an open mind."

"And I need you to do the same," Karl murmured, then, turning from the window, he approached the documents and books spread around the office. "What have you found out from these?"

Peter leaned against the windowsill and crossed his arms. "I found out that Del is a meticulous bookkeeper...listen, Karl, I apologize for spouting off, I—"

With a quick flip of his hand, the older man cut Peter off. "We are not always going to agree—Marcus and I didn't...now, what else have you discovered?"

"From what I can see, all your books are fine...but I still want to continue checking things over...I'm more interested, though, in the books that Fet...Quentin keeps at the factory—especially the payroll...you should have kept more of a hand in that." As he heard the condemnation emerge from his mouth, Peter's jaw muscles instantly tensed. Even though Karl had given Fetch far too much authority, he didn't want to start another debate over the subject—not yet anyway.

The older man shrugged absently. "Marcus handled the payroll...when Quentin replaced him, I just let..."

Noticing that sorrow had enveloped his employer once again, Peter knew he needed to steer the conversation away from the absent Marcus. "I also want to check over the inventory at the factory...if there are additional pieces being made, the wood and those pieces have to be kept somewhere."

Karl sighed with a nod, then began to peruse the documents on the desk. "There's just one thing I don't understand."

Quickly curbing the sarcastic reply that had surfaced in his thoughts, Peter offered, "What's that, Sir?"

"I understand how this...this counterfeit furniture can get made and shipped without me knowing about it, but how in Sam Hill do the orders get to the factory in the first place?"

Peter smiled slightly in triumph—perhaps, at last, he had pounded some doubt into his employer's head. "I believe Quentin has a partner out there working as his salesman—I just have to find out who it is."

"You don't think it's my salesman, do you?"

"I don't know if Victor's involved or not...the Hopewells refer to their salesman as 'Samuel Kelly'...Victor could be playing both parts."

Karl's face wilted and he slowly sagged onto Peter's chair.

"Or maybe he isn't," Peter added, trying to revive the older man's eroding hopes. "That was the one thing I couldn't ask the Hopewells—what Samuel Kelly looked like."

"Why?"

Leaving the window, Peter sauntered over to the desk while rubbing the back of his neck—coping with his employer's absentmindedness was definitely going to teach him the art of being patient. "Because I didn't want to alarm them, Sir...they think Samuel Kelly is our salesman...I didn't think it would sit very well if I asked the Hopewells what my own salesman looked like."

Karl chuckled and tapped his forehead. "That's my Peter...always thinking...and I'll bet that you've already come up with an idea of how to find out what this man looks like, haven't you?"

Peter grinned in mild exasperation—if only his employer would stop pendulating between comprehension and confusion. "Yes Sir, I have...and I've already put the plan into motion," he announced as he walked over to the chairs opposite the desk and settled onto one of the upholstered seats. "Do you remember reading in Mrs. Hopewell's letter that she was planning to contact your salesman soon?" he asked as he placed his elbows on his knees and leaned forward.

Karl nodded. "For a mahogany writing desk."

"Right," Peter returned, elated that the older man had remembered. "Well, she told me they had already placed the order for the desk with Mr. Kelly...and what's more, it's supposed to be delivered a week from today."

"But there's no Samuel Kelly here...there never was," Karl muttered as he rubbed his eyes.

"I know," Peter soothed, sensing his employer's angst. "But, with Mrs. Hopewell bringing up the subject, I was able to ask her how she liked working with Mr. Kelly."

"And?"

"She said he was wonderful, but that communicating with him was rather cumbersome...seems Kelly made it mandatory that he be contacted only by mail—not telegraph or telephone."

"Ah, that makes sense," Karl proclaimed, sitting up straight. "Since the correspondence is sent to another address, we never know about it."

Overjoyed and relieved by Karl's sudden acuity, Peter stood and leaned on the back of his chair. "That's what I thought too...but it's not."

"It's not what?"

"It's not sent to another address...it took some very carefully worded questions, but I found out that Mrs. Hopewell writes to Mr. Kelly at this address."

"But that's impossible...how could—"

"The letter you have from Mrs. Hopewell," Peter cut in as his mind clicked on a thought, "who was it addressed to?"

"Me."

As the situation—and the solution—crystallized in his head, Peter snapped his fingers. "That's it," he murmured, not even realizing that he said the statement aloud.

"Would you care to enlighten me?"

"Mrs. Hopewell wrote to Samuel Kelly, at this address, and asked him to come to Crestfield so she could place her order."

"Well, now we're right back where we started...we never received her request."

"Right, that's because it was addressed to Mr. Kelly...just think, if she had sent her letter of praise to him instead of you—you would have never gotten it," Peter reasoned. Then he added silently, *and Quentin Fetch would have continued using you and your factory without anyone being the wiser.*

"Thank God for Mrs. Hopewell," Karl mumbled.

Peter nodded but barely heard as another piece snapped into place. "Who usually picks up the mail from the post office?" he asked, peering into his employer's eyes.

"Del or myself…oh, no you don't," the older man declared as he slowly rose from his chair. "I don't want you even remotely thinking that Del's involved in this scheme."

"No…no, I don't think it's Del," Peter murmured, stroking his mustache. "But whoever it is—we'll find out soon enough."

"How?"

"You told me Victor was on a selling trip…when do you expect him back?" Peter asked as he started to pace aimlessly through the office.

"You didn't answer my question."

"I will in a moment…when do you expect him back?"

"This Friday…sometime in the afternoon."

"You're sure?"

Karl released a long and loud exhale, then settled onto Peter's chair once again. "Very…he'll be back in plenty of time for Lori's birthday reception… she'll have his head if he misses it."

"Good. I need you to ask him to stay in town until the following Wednesday…say you want him to help me with the inventory or something."

"Why? Peter, what are you planning?"

"While I was in Crestfield, I sent a letter to Mr. Samuel Kelly in care of Rheinhardt Furniture and called myself Joseph Leander…I wrote that I had heard about him and his company from the Hopewells and that I wanted to discuss ordering a very ornately carved dining set."

"You still haven't answered my question, young man."

"Well, I told Mr. Kelly that I wanted to surprise my wife…and if he was interested in the order, I could only see him on Tuesday, July thirty-first."

Karl smiled as the plot obviously unraveled in his head. "So, if Victor says he has to leave town on Tuesday…"

"Most likely, it'll be to go to Crestfield…but no matter what Victor says, I'm going to be at that depot next Tuesday to see who gets off the train and tries to find Joseph Leander."

"Think it'll work?"

"Oh, I'm sure it will tell us something."

"I'll speak to Victor the first chance I get," Karl said. Then, after a few moments of watching Peter meander throughout the room, the older man cleared his throat and added, "Speaking of the reception…you are coming, aren't you?"

Peter nodded absently, his mind preoccupied with analyzing Fetch's operation.

"Lorelei's been looking forward to seeing you again…I think you made quite an impression upon her."

Instantly, Karl's words yanked Peter from his thoughts, and he stopped in mid-stride. If Lorelei Rheinhardt had any interest in him, it was only a fabrication to please her father. "Oh, I don't think she was that pleased to see me."

"Yes…yes, she was…she talked about you all that evening…asking all kinds of questions about you."

As he fingered the chain on his pocketwatch, Peter shook his head. After his last encounter with Lori, he had no desire to ever see the girl again. But, obviously, Karl had a different agenda—and the glint in the older man's eyes made his motives more than clear. Knowing that he had to squelch Karl's matchmaking efforts immediately, Peter searched furiously for the right words to say. He just couldn't allow himself to be cornered into a relationship with the two-faced Lori Rheinhardt.

As he stared out the window and watched the trees sway over the North Pine River, his outing with Anna Spreyer wafted back into his thoughts, and the perfect response instantly formed. "She did? Well, then I look forward to giving her my best on her birthday…you don't mind if I invite someone to come with me, do you?"

"Oh…no…that's fine," the older man returned, his gaze drifting to the floor.

That is, Peter put in voicelessly, *if I can persuade her to set foot in your home.*

⊰ Four ⊱

"Mister Fetch, may I see you now?" Daven called from the doorway of the foreman's office.

Quentin Fetch looked up from the ledger in front of him, and biting down on his cigar, he smiled humorlessly. Then the big man motioned with his arm and returned his attention to the ledger.

As he stepped into the room, an uneasiness landed on Daven's shoulders, which only intensified as he closed the door and entombed himself with the foreman.

"Sit," Fetch ordered while scribbling in the book.

Moving to the chair in front of Fetch's desk, Daven sat and tried to calm the nervousness swelling inside him. "Mr. Fetch?" As he waited for the foreman to acknowledge him, Daven checked his surroundings, still amazed that the little room could lock out the blaring sounds and bustling activity from the factory just outside its walls. Looking past the foreman and through the open door, Daven peered at a band of clouds as it washed over the sky, and he wished he had the freedom to get up and run away.

"What do you want?" Fetch demanded as he closed the ledger.

"I was wondering if I could get an advance on my wages."

"An advance? Whatd'ya need an advance for?"

"If you'll remember," Daven answered, trying to sound as pleasant as he could, "I told you that I was robbed and that I didn't have any money."

"So?"

"So, since you refused to pay me on Saturday, I still don't have any."

"I didn't refuse, Ashby…you were told the rules—be here at five or don't get paid."

"But I couldn't be here…I was delivering furniture for you."

A shrug was the foreman's only response.

Daven sighed resignedly—he knew the missed pay route was hopeless, but he had to try. "So can I get an advance?"

"You've been here only two days…how do I know that you won't just run off when you get the money?"

"Because I'm telling you I won't," Daven returned as his features tightened and he started to rub his left hand. "All I want is to find a place to stay and get something to eat."

"A place to stay? I thought ya said ya had a room at the Tadman House," Fetch said with a sly grin.

Instantly, resentment swept through Daven—he hated being the source of Fetch's amusement. "I did…but one of Mrs. Tadman's old boarders returned and she needed my room."

Fetch leaned back in his chair and took a puff on his cigar. "Pity…you've just had the worst luck, haven't you?"

"I suppose."

The foreman chuckled. "And it ain't gettin' any better—no advances…but I don't think the money would help you anyway."

"Why?"

"Well, I just happen to know that it'll be as difficult findin' yourself a new boarding house as it was findin' a job in town."

Daven sat in stunned silence as Fetch's statement—and its meaning—resounded in his head.

"Looks like I made my point."

Swallowing hard, Daven nodded. "So what do I do now?" he prayed out loud.

The big man smiled broadly as if Daven had stepped into his snare. "I know of a boardin' house where you could stay...a lot of our men use it. You interested?"

Daven suddenly felt the trap spring shut. "Do I have a choice?"

Fetch's face turned to granite and he removed his cigar. "No, Ashby, you don't...but I do. The room ain't available no more...you can just sleep on the street tonight...now, get out of my office," the foreman growled as a gust of wind blew into the office and retreated back through the door—slamming it shut.

Slowly, Daven stood, holding onto the chair for balance. Why didn't you just keep your mouth shut? he asked himself. Now, because of his careless, flippant remark, Fetch was right—he would have to sleep on the street. Or, instead, he could just go to Peter and tell him the mission was over...of course, then the foreman would never be stopped. "Mr. Fetch?" he murmured, fighting the indignation and dread churning within him.

"I said leave!"

"I'm sorry, Mr. Fetch...I didn't mean to be so...so disrespectful...may I have the room?"

The foreman's eyes narrowed and he stabbed at the air with his cigar as he spoke. "The only way someone gets one of these rooms is by my say so...if I were you, Kid, I'd button my lip."

Daven breathed in deeply. "You're right, Mr. Fetch...I've been told that I can be a smart aleck at times...what will I have to do for the room?"

"Well, to start, I'd like to hear the word 'Sir' when you talk to me and my men."

Instantly, Daven's dander stood on end—the thought of giving his enemies so much verbal respect grated against his nerves. But, knowing that he had been corralled into a corner, he pasted a faint grin onto his face and tried to hide his irritation. "Yes...Sir."

With a wide smile, Fetch fitted his cigar stump between his teeth and drew in a deep puff as though rewarding himself for his victory. "That's much better...your room's at Everly's Boarding House...ask Hallam—he'll tell ya how to

get there. I'll be at Everly's at six tonight...if you want the room, you'd better
be too."

"All right...but will they let me stay on credit?"

"Oh, that won't matter none...you see, the owners and me are kinda partners...so you'll be paying me, not them."

Daven's heart quickened—Fetch had now taken control of yet another
aspect of his life. "Okay...and how much will I be paying you?" he questioned,
not being able to conceal the dismay in his voice.

"We'll work that out tonight...now, get back to work."

Shaking his head in defeat, Daven turned and shuffled toward the door,
then, as he grabbed the latch, Fetch called to him. "Yes...Sir."

"You and Averill are gunna be workin' on a special project...see Hallam
when you get out there."

Daven nodded and left the office as the confrontation with Fetch swirled
inside his head—then it abruptly stopped. "Six..." he moaned. "Six o'clock." He
was supposed to meet Peter at seven. Now, he would most likely be late for his
meeting—if he could make it at all. Suddenly, his heart sank, and he blinked
back a forming tear. He needed to see his brother...he needed to hear Peter's
deep, reassuring voice...he needed to know that he wasn't alone.

Shaking away his heartache and uneasiness, Daven scanned the factory's
interior for Frank Hallam, and he finally caught sight of the man's clownish
attempts to get his attention. Quelling the urge to laugh, Daven quickened his
pace and hurried toward the loading platform.

"When I call you," Hallam hollered as Daven joined him on the platform,
"I expect you to come—immediately!"

"Yes Sir."

The blonde-haired man laughed and grabbed Daven's arm. "I see the boss
talked to you 'bout your manners."

"Yes Sir, he did," Daven mumbled, trying to cool his simmering temper.
"He also said that I'd be working on a special project."

Hallam snickered again and shoved Daven toward the platform's edge. "That's right…now help Averill move that mahogany inside—fast."

Surveying the factory's yard, Daven spotted a wagon piled with dark red wood and the same tall black man who had unloaded last Thursday's lumber with the wiry German. Jumping down from the platform, Daven walked over to his new teammate and held out his hand. "Hello, I'm Daven Ashby…I don't know if you remember me, but—"

"I remember ya…Ol' Helpful," the man returned, then, with a tired sigh, he reluctantly shook Daven's hand. "Jaxson Averill."

"It's good to meet you Jaxson, I—"

"All right already," Hallam barked. "You two can have your tea party later… get that mahogany inside—now!"

As he moved toward the lumber, Daven's stomach growled out a complaint, and instantly, he remembered Fetch's order. "Mr. Hallam? Wait…Mr. Hallam?"

"What?!"

"I almost forgot…Mr. Fetch told me to ask you for directions to Everly's Boarding House."

Hallam whooped merrily and flipped his hand at Jaxson. "Averill can tell ya."

Tired of being passed around, Daven watched the blonde-haired man disappear into the factory, then he circled and studied Jaxson—who was, in return, studying him. Fatigue hung from the young black man's features, and inside his dispirited eyes, Daven saw—what was it—fear? No, it was pity. "Will you tell me how to get to this place?"

"You'd be better off someplace diff'rent."

"No place will take me."

"Ain't you got anybody to help ya get out of this?"

"No," Daven replied, his thoughts wandering again to Peter, who seemed so very far away.

"You don't know what you've done to yourself," Jaxson murmured, grasping an end of one of the mahogany boards.

"What do you mean?" Daven pleaded as a strange tingling crept up the back of his neck.

"You'll see soon enough," Jaxson returned with a shrug. "Now, quit your yakkin' and help me with this wood."

"Mr. Fetch!" Frank Hallam shouted as he burst into the foreman's office. "Mr. Fetch...that Leighton guy, he just walked into the factory," he finished, trying to catch his breath.

Quentin Fetch swore aloud, closed the ledger in front of him, and rose from his desk. "I knew he'd be trouble...I'd really like to know why the old man hired him anyway."

"Maybe...maybe, we can get him on our side."

Fetch shook his head. "He ain't the kind to be bought."

"So what are we going to do?! He'll be here any minute!"

"Quit your bellyachin'...I've just finished fixing the books," the foreman announced, stroking the ledger. "And everybody's workin' on a real job—'cept those two upstairs."

"And if Leighton tries to go up there?"

"Then, Hallam, you'd better make sure you get upstairs before him—and get that stuff under cover," Fetch snarled as he moved around his desk and headed toward the door.

"But what if—"

With a loud curse, the foreman cut Hallam off and stepped into the factory. "Where'd you go, Leighton?" he murmured, peering into the dust-filled air. Then, spotting the tall, charcoal-haired intruder, he dashed into the maze of machines. "Leighton," he bellowed, trying to be heard over the saws, "I'm surprised to see you."

"Why is that?" Peter called back.

Fetch pointed to his ear, then to the machines, and shaking his head, he motioned toward his office.

Peter nodded and followed the big man toward the rough-hewn corner room—all the while searching the interior of the factory for a glimpse of his brother.

"Can't hear a thing out there," Fetch growled as he shoved Peter inside the office and closed the door.

Removing his hat, Peter brushed the sawdust from his hair. "Don't push me, Mr. Fetch," he said, hoping the statement would be perceived as both a reprimand and a warning. And, as his words faded into the deathly quiet room, Peter glanced at the unfinished paneling around him. "Just how thick are these walls?"

"I don't like to be interrupted…by noise or anything else," Fetch returned, glaring at Peter.

"You said it was a surprise to see me. Why?"

"Like I said, I don't like interruptions."

"I told you last Wednesday that I'd be coming to check your books."

"Well, I figured you'd send word before comin'…I might've been out."

"That wouldn't have mattered…I came to look over the books—not to see you," Peter returned coolly. He knew his condescending manner was only heaping more wood on an already angry fire, but he couldn't even bring himself to act courteously—not after all the foreman had put Daven through.

Fetch's face stiffened and he removed his cigar. "Next time, you better let me know when you're coming."

"Part of my job is to monitor the factory…I'll be stopping in whenever I please."

"We'll see," Fetch sneered just loud enough to be heard. "Hallam here can get what you need…I've got things to do."

Peter was quite certain that Fetch would head straight for Karl to complain about the current situation—that was something that would probably happen very often. But he couldn't let it happen quite yet. He needed to review the books first—he had to find a sliver of proof before the foreman had a chance to maneuver Karl back into apathy. "I hope your 'things to do' are in the factory, Mr. Fetch…in case I have questions."

Fetch stomped over to the door and jerked it open, and as the office filled with the factory's din, the foreman circled back, his countenance ablaze with rage. "I'll be here," he shouted. And, with another yank on the door, Fetch was gone and the room was silent once again.

Feeling a momentary ripple of relief, Peter sighed and set his hat on the desk, and after making a quick study of the room, he turned to Hallam, who stood motionless and wide-eyed—obviously, not many people defied Fetch. "I'd like to start with the payroll," Peter announced as he settled onto Fetch's chair.

The blonde-haired man nodded and motioned to the ledger on the desk. "That's it there."

As he pulled the book toward him, Peter opened the cover—and was immediately hit with the odor of old cigar smoke. Coughing back his repulsion, he started to scan the entries and figures scribbled on the lines in the ledger. Then, as if it were a mist rising from the water, a strange stench emerged from the furniture and blotches of tobacco juice on the floor and began to surround him. With a sigh of disgust, Peter clenched his churning stomach and glanced over this shoulder—not even the cool breeze wafting through the windows could cleanse the office of its filthy scent. "Mr. Hallam, would you mind opening the door?"

Hallam snickered under his breath, walked over to the door, and yanked it open. "It ain't gunna help," he chuckled as he shoved a piece of wood under the top hinge.

In time, Peter had all of the foreman's books spread in front of him—each one more disappointing than the last. On the surface, the records didn't reveal any of Fetch's abuses—which was going to make it very difficult to convince Karl that the foreman was a thief. But a few entries were of interest—one in particular—the one that said Daven had gotten paid on Saturday…for five and a half hours of work…at twenty-five cents an hour. From that discovery, Peter guessed that the entire payroll book was fiction, but only Fetch and the men who were cheated knew the truth.

"Mr. Hallam?" Peter called, realizing the man had disappeared.

Frank Hallam appeared in the outside doorway, a wad of chewing tobacco now lumped inside his cheek. "Yes Sir, whatd'ya need?"

"Would you see if you can find Mr. Fetch? I have some questions."

The man spit on the ground and grinned. "I'm sure he'll enjoy hearin' that," he offered as he crossed through the office and exited into the factory.

Once alone, Peter stood and stretched. Although he was sure that Fetch didn't keep anything incriminating in the office, he quickly searched the desk and shelves anyway—just in case. As he had figured, he found nothing out of the ordinary—except a revolver hidden in the bottom desk drawer. Exhaling in exasperation, Peter turned and peered at the thick shutters on the inside of the windows—and his jaw automatically clenched. The foreman definitely had a lot of secrets—and only Daven had the facts to expose them. Suddenly, worry and consternation began to jab at Peter's temples and he rubbed his eyes. If Fetch ever found out who Daven really was...

Without warning, the words he had once spoken to his stepfather in an argument flooded back into his head...

'I can take care of Daven, better than you ever could—or have.'

Now, he wasn't so sure, and he wondered what the gentle and shy Tait Ashby would have said to him regarding Daven's involvement in their current situation. Moving to stand in the open doorway, Peter breathed in the fresh air as the wind circled around him and brushed a few strands of his hair onto his forehead...then he smiled. It had been years since he had thought about his stepfather—without bitterness. And it felt good.

"What now?!" Fetch bellowed as he stormed into the office.

Pulled from his musing, Peter circled and faced the steaming foreman. "I just wanted to talk with you...ask a few questions."

With his crossed arms, Fetch perched himself on the book-filled desk. "So ask."

"Your books are very interesting," Peter started, walking over to the ledgers.

The foreman laughed. "Well, maybe now, you'll leave us alone to do our work."

Ignoring the remark, Peter flipped through the pages of the book nearest to him. "How do you usually clock the men's hours?"

"Me, Hallam, or Bryce keep track."

"Then Mr. Rheinhardt gives you the money, and you pay the men according to those hours?"

"Yeah...why?"

Peter feigned nonchalance. "Any problems with the system?"

"Nope...you can even ask the men if you like," Fetch replied, chewing on his cigar.

Peter brushed his hair back into place and stared at the barrel-chested man in front of him. None of the workers would admit to being cheated—and the foreman knew it. "Things might run more smoothly if we purchased a time clock."

Fetch removed his cigar and stabbed at the air with it. "Go ahead...I don't think it'll make any difference."

Shaking his head at the arrogant answer, Peter fought the urge to throw the big man and his smelly cigar out the door. Then, not being able to resist doing a little prodding himself, he offered, "I think it will...if we install it at the showroom."

Fetch cursed. "You're wasting my time, Leighton...are we done?"

"No, Fetch, we are not done," Peter returned, thumbing through the payroll ledger. "Who is this?" he asked as he pointed to an entry.

Fetch leaned in to read the name under Peter's finger. "Travis Perryn...he was our carver."

"Was?"

"Yeah, he got killed...had an unfortunate accident with a runaway ice wagon," Fetch said, not attempting to hide a lofty smirk.

As he thumbed through a few more pages in the book, Peter noted the foreman's smugness, and after recalling Anna Spreyer's comments about Perryn, he knew the death was, most likely, not an accident. Stopping on the last written page in the payroll ledger, Peter tapped his finger on Daven's name. "And who is this?"

"Daven Ashby...the new carver."

"I'd like to meet him."

A bead of sweat rolled down Fetch's temple. "He's...he's out on a delivery right now."

Peter raised an eyebrow. "Delivery? He's a rather expensive delivery man, isn't he?"

Shoving his cigar back between his teeth, Fetch stood and crossed his arms. "I put Ashby to work where I needed him...I'm sure Mr. Rheinhardt would agree with my decision—he always has...any more questions?"

As uncertainty edged its way into his thoughts, Peter shook his head. His opponent was proving to be a very calculating man...could he and Daven, alone, put an end to the foreman's reign?

As he examined Everly's Boarding House, Daven tried to bolster his spirits, but they still plummeted. By the building's age and architecture, he figured it must have been one of the first hostelries in Sandorville and, in its time, had probably filled many eyes with awe. But now, decaying and collared by dying bushes, the two-story building sagged under its years and begged for someone to give it a dab of paint and care. Sighing in pity for the old hotel—and himself—Daven wrapped his fingers around the handle of his valise, tramped up the rotting porch steps, and tried the front door—but it wouldn't budge. He knocked...then pounded...then tried again...but nothing happened.

Rolling his eyes in frustration, Daven surveyed the empty yard, then his gaze drifted to the small, crumbling restaurant that sat in the boarding house's shadow. It, too, showed the faint glimmer of once being an elegant building, but neglect had sucked all the brilliance and dignity from the little eatery.

"Well, it's worth a try," he mumbled as his stomach loudly reminded him that he had not eaten since breakfast.

With his satchel clasped tightly in his hand, Daven took one last look around the yard, then descended the hostelry's steps and headed for the restaurant. Perhaps, he silently reasoned, he could persuade the cook to give him a handout of bread…or something. But, as he reached the front door, he hesitated. Attached to the lintel above him was a broken, weather-beaten sign reading 'Restau,' and next to that was the word 'Everly.' The boarding house and the eatery were both owned by Fetch—that couldn't be good.

Grabbing the broken latch, Daven tried to open the door again and again, then, finally, it yielded and scraped along a well-worn arc on the floor. Overhead, a rusted chime clinked out an announcement of his arrival, but no one listened to its message. As his appetite soured from a greasy film that hung in the air, Daven surveyed the restaurant's patrons. Everyone inside the eatery was from the factory—including Jaxson—and was either hunched over his plate cramming food into his mouth or hollering to do the same.

Suddenly, a door on the opposite wall flew open, and a girl bolted into the room, with three plates balanced on her arms. She was tiny but shapely, and a long flaxen braid hung down her back. Darting between the tables, she headed toward three men who sat with their forks raised, ready for shoveling.

"Hey, that was supposed to be mine!" a man sitting near Daven shouted to the girl.

"You just have to wait!" she yelled as she slid the plates in front of her three hungry customers.

"Come on, Girl!" the man called again, punctuating his words with a whack on the table.

"All right!" she shrieked. And, with a quick spin, she barreled right into Daven. "Sit down and get out of my—" the girl yelled, then, looking up at him, she stopped in mid-sentence.

"I'm sorry, Miss…I was wondering if…if I might get a bit of food…maybe… maybe in exchange for some chores?"

The girl didn't respond, but her intense stare embraced Daven's face, and her eyes never left his.

"Miss?"

"Looks like Ivy's found another beau," someone declared as the men began to snicker at her obvious attraction to Daven.

"Now, we're not gunna get any food from her," another announced.

"Or nothin' else," a third chimed in.

"Shut up!" she shouted over her shoulder. "If you wanna eat—just shut up!" Turning back toward Daven, her wrath instantly melted, and she smiled, causing long dimples to form on her cheeks. "Just sit anywhere," she purred. "I'll be right back to see what ya wanna eat."

"No, I'm not here for—" Daven offered, but she was gone before he could finish. With a shrug, he slipped onto a chair at a small, lopsided table near the door and shoved his bag by his feet.

Even though his coworkers, basically, kept to themselves, he had still gathered enough information, directly and indirectly, to know that he was not in the presence of the privileged factory workers—the ones who had become Fetch's allies to make life easier for themselves. Nor did he see any of those with families—they had different and much worse arrangements with the foreman. All he saw were the single men—broken, desperate, and like himself, trapped.

As if she were an actress making an entrance, the girl reentered the room with a flourish while holding a plate filled with gray mounds of food. Glancing at Daven, she smiled and winked, then she bounced over to the man who had clamored for his food and shoved the dish in front of him. Daven smiled inwardly at the flirting—and at the infatuation she didn't bother to hide.

"Hey, Handsome," the girl chirped as she approached Daven's table. "You gotta be new in town."

"Why's that?"

"Because you just picked one of the worst places to have a meal," she returned with a laugh.

"Thanks for the warning, but I'm not here for a meal."

"You came for…for the scenery?" she asked, motioning at the dingy room with a wide sweep of her arm.

Daven grinned. "Maybe," he offered, staring intently at her tanned features.

Immediately, a smile spread on her face and she stroked his shoulder. "Why, thank you…what's your name, Handsome?"

"Daven Ashby."

"Ah, that's definitely a name worth keeping," she cooed. "My name's Ivy… so, Daven, what does bring ya to our lovely restaurant?"

"I'm supposed to meet Mr. Fetch at the boarding house next door…he said he'd be here at six."

The girl's smile faded, as did the blush in her cheeks. "You're the new carver, aren't you?"

Daven frowned in dismay—once again a total stranger was pitying his situation. "Yeah."

"Mr. Fetch won't be here for at least two more hours…he likes to keep his new arrivals waiting."

Closing his eyes in disappointment, Daven shook his head. He should have known. Now, he would definitely miss the meeting with Peter—unless he wanted to forfeit his room…and he was just too tired to do that.

"You're hungry?" Ivy whispered, half as a question, half as a statement.

He nodded, then looked up at her sheepishly. "But I don't have any money."

Sympathy radiated from her face, and she gently petted his hair.

"Ivy! How about our food, Girl?" a worker roared from the other side of the restaurant. "Quit the sparkin' and feed us!"

"Don't get yourself in such a pucker, Smitty!" she shouted in return. Then, leaning closer, she purred in Daven's ear, "I'll see what I can find for you."

"Thank you," he called, and as he watched Ivy swivel through the maze of tables, he wondered if the extra sway in her hips was for him.

Pivoting in his chair, Daven rested the back of his head on the wall and surveyed his coworkers once again. Each man had, obviously, responded to Fetch's treatment in his own way—some becoming resigned, some rough, and some resilient—yet all of them shared one thing…the same bleak and sunken expression. Closing his eyes once again, Daven tried to push his predicament from his thoughts, but a wave of gloom and hunger still engulfed him. He had never felt so alone before. Even after his father's death, his emptiness had been appeased, somewhat, by Peter…faithful, dictatorial, protective Peter. But now…now, it seemed as if he were being dragged further and further away from his brother's watchful eye.

"All right, Smitty…here's your lousy supper."

At the sound of Ivy's voice, Daven's eyes fluttered open, and he watched the boisterous girl drop one of the two plates that she held in front of the man called Smitty.

"It's about time!" the man snarled.

Ignoring the remark, Ivy smiled at Daven and scurried over to his table. "It's just chicken and potatoes," she said, placing the dish in front of him. "It's all that's left."

"Thank you, Ivy," he murmured as he stared at the colorless meal. "But I can't…I can't pay for it."

"Don't worry about it…just eat."

Picking up his fork, Daven breathed in deep as the aroma of his meal encircled him—and reminded him of just how hungry he was. "Thanks, Ivy…I'll repay you—when I get the money."

The girl coughed out a sad laugh. "Sorry, Handsome, but I won't live that long."

"What do you mean by—" he tried, but he was cut off as another man called her away.

With a sigh, Daven shrugged his shoulders—he'd probably find out what she meant soon enough. Then, after thanking God, he followed the example of this coworkers and started shoveling his meal into his mouth. At any other time, he might have criticized the taste and quality of his chicken and potatoes, but tonight…tonight, it was the best food he had ever eaten.

As he continued to devour his supper, Daven surreptitiously watched the actions of his fellow workers. After finishing their meals, most of the men exited the eatery and disappeared into the boarding house, while the others just ambled aimlessly around the grounds.

"Here," Ivy announced as she approached Daven's table holding a frayed basket and a large mug. "I thought you might like some bread and coffee too."

"Yes…thank you."

Placing the basket and cup next to Daven's right arm, Ivy slipped onto the chair opposite him. "Land sakes," she declared, putting her elbow on the table and resting her chin on her hand, "you've got the most beautiful eyes I've ever seen."

Daven swallowed a mouthful of food, smiled, and offered, "And you have the most beautiful hair that I've ever seen."

Ivy pulled her thick flaxen braid over her shoulder, and while stroking it, she peered at Daven. "With my hair and your eyes…what pretty kids we'd have."

Coughing slightly, Daven grabbed his mug and downed a mouthful of his tepid coffee. "Um…how…how did you know that I was the new carver?" he asked, hoping to distract Ivy from her musing.

"Mr. Fetch said the new carver would be coming to stay with us soon."

With a grunt, Daven stuffed another forkful of potatoes into his mouth. He was still in the middle of Fetch's maze and could do nothing—except go where he was prodded.

"But he didn't say that you were even more handsome than Travis was."

"Travis?"

Ivy nodded, shifting her gaze downward. "Travis Perryn…the man you're replacing."

Daven repeated the name silently. He had heard it before, but where? Then he remembered—Peter had asked him about Perryn. "Did Travis quit?"

Laughing harshly, Ivy shook her head. "Nobody quits the factory."

Without warning, a bell clanged from somewhere outside.

"What's the bell for?" Daven asked through a mouthful of chicken.

Ivy remained silent but gazed out one of the grease-tinted windows.

Shifting his position to get a better view, Daven watched as his coworkers climbed into a large wagon. He had seen the dilapidated vehicle, many times, shuttling some of the men to and from the factory…but where was it taking them now?

"What was that bell for, Ivy? And where are they going?"

Ivy tossed her braid over her shoulder and slowly rose from the table. "Listen, you'd better finish up…we close at seven o'clock."

"Close? But—"

"You can wait for Mr. Fetch on the boarding house's stoop…he'll show up—sometime," she mumbled, then walked back into the kitchen.

As he watched the wagon waddle out of Everly's yard, Daven shook his head—Jaxson's warning was becoming more and more profound…

'You'd be better off someplace diff'rent.'

Quarter to eight. With a long, frustrated sigh, Peter snapped his watch shut and stuffed it back into his waistcoat. Quarter to eight—and no Daven. As worry and anger played tug-of-war inside his head, Peter scrutinized the deserted market grounds, hoping to glimpse his brother's tall, long-haired figure…but the image never appeared.

"Daven, where are you?" Peter called softly. He knew, if he wanted to arrive at Anna's on time, he had to leave—now. But, still, he didn't budge from his spot under the willow tree. Maybe, Daven thought the meeting was at eight…or maybe, it was just his brother's watch causing the delay. That's it, Peter silently stated with a nod. The faulty timepiece was to blame.

"Lord, please let it be the watch that's keeping him," he added quietly, then, raising an eyebrow, he grunted in disbelief. It had been a long time since he had asked God for anything—or had even spoken to Him. In fact, the only words he had offered up to Heaven in the last few years were curses.

Now, the chasm between him and the Lord didn't seem quite so deep. He finally understood, at least somewhat, why his life's journey had been allowed to twist from one disappointment to the next. Then, as clearly as if she were standing next to him, Anna's words repeated themselves…

'I just know that you wouldn't be here otherwise.'

That was true, Peter admitted. If his life had progressed as he had planned it, he would still be in Bradlee, running the family store. Never…never would he have chosen the heartbreaking and rugged path he had been forced to take—but having the chance to meet—and possibly court—the lovely Anna made the journey worthwhile…very worthwhile.

With a long sigh, Peter closed his eyes and shook his head. He had wasted so much time trying to restore his old life...a life that God, evidently, didn't want for him. And now, it really wasn't the life he wanted either. Maybe, he pondered voicelessly. Maybe, it was time to release his grudge against the Lord, along with the one against his stepfather.

Drawing out his watch once again, Peter squinted and moved the timepiece to and fro, trying to determine the positions of the hands in the dimming daylight. Eight o'clock. He was now officially late to meet Anna.

"Let it be the watch," he murmured as his thoughts strayed to all the alternative reasons for his brother's absence. Then, casting his eyes upward, he whispered, "Take care of him...please take care of him."

Clicking his watch open, Daven peered at the face and hands. Five after two. After a quick calculation, he moaned. "Eight o'clock...sorry, Peter," he mumbled as he perched himself on the railing encircling the boarding house's porch. If only he could hear his brother's voice—even if it was a rebuke for missing their meeting—then, maybe, he wouldn't feel so isolated. As exhaustion pulled at his eyelids, Daven slid his right leg onto the railing and leaned his head back against the hostelry's decaying front wall. All he wanted now was to sleep, and he began to wonder just how well the porch would serve as a mattress.

Suddenly, a voice rang out, but it wasn't the one he longed to hear. Pulling his aching body from the railing, Daven waited in the fading daylight as Fetch and his shadow Bryce climbed up the stoop and onto the porch.

"I was about to give up," Daven grumbled, trying to clear his sleep-clouded head.

Disapproval hung from Fetch's face and he sneered in return.

Remembering that his employer could turn around and leave him with nowhere to sleep, Daven gritted his teeth and added, "Sir."

Fetch's lips parted in a wide smile. "That's right...you were about to give up your only place to live."

"I apologize, Mr. Fetch, if I sounded rude," Daven offered as he reached for his satchel.

But, before he could grab the bag, Bryce pushed him aside. "Allow me," the dark-haired man said with mock civility. "This all you have?"

Daven nodded. "You suggested that my tools stay at the factory—remember?"

Bryce answered with a low, guttural laugh as he seized the valise.

"Well, shall we go in?" Fetch asked, then, with a wicked grin, he slowly searched through each of his pockets and finally pulled out a tarnished key from his vest—the last pocket investigated.

Irked by the teasing, Daven forced himself to smile—he was too close to having a room and a bed to ruin it all with a smart-alecky comment.

With grand sweeps of his arms, Fetch unlocked the boarding house's front door and shoved it open. "After you, Ashby."

As he stepped over the threshold, the odor of sweaty, hardworking men met Daven first. Then, after his eyes adjusted to the dim interior, he saw something even more pathetic than the smell. The battered hotel had been gutted—everything that had once decorated the stately old building's interior was gone. Instead, what faced Daven was a staircase and a hallway that had doors off either side—obviously the rooms. And, from the closeness of the doors, he guessed that they were very, very small rooms.

"Up!" Fetch ordered.

With uneasiness weighting his every step, Daven reluctantly ascended the stairs, still in the lead. Reaching the top, he moaned in despair. A hallway, similar to the one below, spanned to his left and right, but this passageway, if it was possible, was even more bleak and barren. Even the two large windows, which capped each end of the hall, and the twilight glimmer from the outside couldn't cheer the funereal corridor.

"That way," the big man commanded, pointing to the right. "All the way to the end...your room's on the left."

Forcing himself to turn in the dictated direction, Daven trudged down the spongy-floored hall until he reached his assigned room. An almost unreadable two-twelve was scratched into the battered door, and although he couldn't be sure in the faint light, he was still quite positive that he saw a large bug scurry over the sill and into the room.

"What's the matter, Ashby? Don't ya like the 'commodations?" Bryce chuckled.

Laughing at the taunt, Fetch twisted the latch, swung the door open, and pushed Daven inside.

Instantly, the room's stale air and incredible filth sucked the air from Daven's lungs. And, as he stared in front of him and focused on his abode's only window—whose glass had been replaced with wood—he gasped, trying to rid his nostrils of the stench. Rushing to the tiny wooden window, he tugged and tugged, but the warped frame refused to raise more than an inch—which was definitely not enough to ventilate the malodorous room.

Without warning, the chamber filled with darkness as Daven heard the door close with a loud clack.

"Afraid of the dark, Ashby?" Fetch needled as he struck a match and lit the wick of a candle stump that sat at a slight angle in its holder.

"No Sir," Daven replied. Then, in the scant light, he turned to face his tormentors while examining the room's furnishings. An old chamber set sat on a narrow table under the window, and a wardrobe stood next to that. Across from those were the bed and the door. That was all the room could hold. That and maybe one man—definitely not three.

Shoving Daven to the side, Fetch placed the candlestick on the little table and looked at the partially opened wooden window. "Since you're a bit skittish about the dark, we better make sure the wind won't blow out the candle," he teased and slammed the frame down. "All right," the big man continued, moving toward Daven, who now stood trapped between the wardrobe, the wall, the bed, and the foreman, "I only go through the rules once...so listen good."

Daven nodded, barely able to breathe.

"This opens the front and back doors," Fetch went on, holding a key between his index finger and thumb. "They are to be locked at all times, and don't let nobody else in."

"Yes Sir," Daven murmured as he grasped the latchkey.

"Just remember," Fetch sneered, "it can be taken away anytime I feel like it…understand?"

"Yes Sir," Daven repeated, understanding both the words and their meaning.

"You can leave anything you want to be cleaned outside your door, and Mrs. Everly will wash it. There's a room downstairs, just under this one, with a stove, pump, and washtub. The outhouse is in the back. A bell is rung at five-thirty in the morning. You get up and eat at the restaurant next door. A wagon leaves for the factory at quarter after six. Be on it—or walk. Mrs. Everly will fix you a lunch, and you'll get it—when you get off the wagon at the factory. You miss the wagon—you miss lunch. You'll take the wagon back here after work and have supper at the restaurant. Any questions?"

"How much?"

"Right down to business, huh, Ashby?" Fetch chuckled. "First we need to discuss the…the initiation fee."

Suddenly, the candle flickered, warping the big man's features.

"The what?" Daven asked, trying to calm his racing heart.

"Oh, did I forget to mention that?"

Fetch and Bryce both laughed.

"What's it for?"

"It's sort of my bonus for givin' you this fine room—so I'll be takin' any cash you have."

"I don't have anything…you know that."

"What about your tools?"

Daven's jaw tightened. "I need my tools."

"That's true," Fetch replied as he began searching through Daven's pockets.

"What are you doing?"

"Lookin' for somethin' as good as cash…what about this?" the foreman inquired, pulling the pocketwatch from Daven's vest.

"No!"

"No?"

Daven swallowed hard, and sweat streamed down his face as the room's stagnant, heavy air pushed against him. "It doesn't work…it's only a keepsake," he tried.

Fetch opened the watch and moved so he could see it clearly in the candle-light. "It's silver…it's worth something."

"You can't have it."

Clutching the timepiece, the foreman tilted his head at Bryce, who lifted Daven's valise up, then over, dumping the contents onto the bed.

"You have no right to—" Daven groaned, but it was too late—Bryce was already rummaging through his things.

"Just clothes…a dressing case…um, wait," the dark-haired man said, grab-bing a book from the pile of clothes.

"What is it?" the big man demanded.

With a grunt, Bryce showed the Bible's cover to Fetch, and after flipping through the pages, he tossed the book back onto bed. "That's it."

"Well, since you ain't got nothin' else to offer," Fetch sneered as he swung the pocketwatch by its chain, "I'll just have to take this."

"No!" Daven yelled, lunging for his watch.

As if he had practiced his part many times before, Fetch smiled and imme-diately yanked the timepiece away—it was then that Daven realized he had made a terrible mistake. His action, along with getting him only a handful of air, placed him dangerously close to the foreman—which was, obviously, what the big man wanted. Instantly, Fetch lashed out with his left hand, striking Daven across the face with a hard backhanded slap.

"Don't ever try anythin' like that again," the foreman hissed, moving closer to Daven.

Rubbing his stinging cheek and trying to escape the big man's advance, Daven took a step backward—and promptly found himself against the wall. "No Sir," he murmured.

"If you want this watch so bad, then pay me for it."

"Pay for my own property?!" Daven asked incredulously.

Fetch grinned. "It ain't yours no more—it's mine...you want it?"

Overwhelmed by both the foreman's crushing presence and the thought of losing his father's timepiece, Daven blinked away his forming tears. "You know I do."

"Then it's yours...for twenty dollars."

"But, I don't—"

The foreman's smile broadened as he once again held the pocketwatch up by its chain. "Let's just say you'll owe me the money."

Reaching for his property, Daven hesitated, expecting Fetch to pull the watch away, then he snatched the heirloom from the foreman's grasp and clutched it tightly in his hand. "Thank you," he prayed in a whisper, grateful that God had saved his father's legacy.

"You're welcome," Fetch replied with a triumphant smirk.

Angered by the foreman's audacity, Daven shook his head and tried to maneuver around the big man.

"Oh, no, you don't," Fetch announced as he grabbed Daven by the collar and pressed him against the wall. "We ain't done talkin' business."

Daven's eyes darted from Fetch, to Bryce, then back again. What was there left to talk about? he asked himself. He had walked into the boarding house penniless—and now, he was twenty dollars in debt.

"I never got the chance to tell ya how much the room was."

Immediately, Daven's shoulders slumped. With all the turmoil concerning the initiation fee, he had completely forgotten that he still had to pay Fetch for the room. "How much?"

"What you make at the factory."

The statement sent a shock through Daven as though he had been poked with a hot branding iron. "Everything?! You mean I'm not going to get anything for my work?"

Fetch feigned confusion. "You get this charmin' little room."

"I...I can't pay you for the initiation fee if you take all my money for the room," Daven reasoned, his voice quivering in desperation.

The foreman barked out a loud laugh, and releasing Daven, he removed a cigar from his coat and chewed off the end. "That's true," he declared as he walked over to the candle, lifted it to his face, and sucked at the cigar until it lit. "So I guess you're just gunna have to put in a little extra time at the factory…any more questions?"

Daven shook his head.

"It'd be easier if you just gave me the watch."

"No," Daven returned, his voice breaking.

Fetch snickered again. "You're the stubbornest—and stupidest—kid I've ever met…do you know how many extra hours you're gunna have to work to pay me twenty dollars?"

With a hard swallow, Daven shook his head again. His mind was too frustrated to think, but at eight cents an hour, he knew it would be a very, very long time.

"Two-hundred and fifty," Bryce announced with a chuckle.

Laughing at the number, the foreman removed his cigar and tipped his hat mockingly. "Enjoy the room, Ashby," he mumbled, then he turned and followed Bryce into the hall.

Unsure if he was going to be sick or not, Daven hurried back to the window and yanked at the frame as hard as he could, but the wood still didn't raise more than an inch. Groaning and desperate for air, he thrust the table aside, sank to his knees, and pushed his face up to the slight opening. Just go and tell Peter you're done with this whole thing, he voicelessly cried. Tell him that you don't deserve to be treated like this.

As he continued to breathe in the cool, fresh night air, he shook his head in defeat—at least now, he understood the reason for all the looks of pity that he had received. Wiping his tears away, Daven crawled onto the bed, grabbed his Bible, and nudged the door closed with his foot. Although he knew, in his heart, that his brother would soon put everything together and that he would be free once more, that knowledge didn't give him much solace…not when he felt so awful—and so alone.

Absently, he thumbed through the pages of the Bible, and as he reached the Psalms, the book fell open to a page as if by habit. Straining to see the words, Daven stretched out on the bed, lying on his stomach, and edged the Bible closer to the fluttering candlelight.

"Truly my soul waiteth upon God, from him cometh my salvation..."

It was his father's favorite Psalm. How many times had he heard the deep and gentle voice read the passage? How many times...

With a sad smile, Daven allowed his thoughts to stray to the man he had lost so long ago. His father had very rarely read aloud, having so much difficulty with the English language, but there were times that he did—and it was always to read the sixty-second Psalm. Even though Tait Ashby had been a cheerful man, a deep pain sometimes clouded his eyes, and when it did, he read the Bible as a balm for his sorrow. Only a few words had passed between father and son as to what caused that pain, but from those words, Daven surmised that his father's departure from Sweden had been by force—not choice.

As Daven continued to read, the wind wrestled with a tree branch outside his window, slapping it against the wood—and slowly, the noise began to sing him to sleep. Pushing his pile of clothes onto the floor, he kicked off his boots and struggled to stay awake to finish the Psalm.

"...for thou renderest to every man according to his work."

Suddenly, a gust of wind found its way through the window's narrow opening, and whipping around the candle, it doused the small flame. Not having enough energy to look for a match, Daven laid his head on the open Bible and closed his eyes.

"Jesus, You'll have to help..."

The prayer faded as sleep claimed victory.

With a glass of lemonade in her hand, Anna pushed the screen door open, stepped out onto the candlelit porch, and headed over to Peter, who sat on the porch swing. "We also have some cherry pie left...if you'd like a piece," she offered as she neared.

No reply.

"Mr. Leighton?"

Looking as if he were in a silent debate with himself, Peter still didn't answer.

"Mr. Leighton?"

"Hmm? Oh, thank you," he said, rising and taking the glass from her outstretched hand.

"We also have some cherry pie."

"No, thank you. I'm fine."

Subtly adjusting her bustle, Anna eased herself onto the swing, then, as the candles flickered inside their holders, she gazed up at her distracted gentleman caller. Peter had apologized over and over for his late arrival, but she knew, from his preoccupation, that he was still someplace else. "Is everything all right?"

"Hmm?" he grunted, coming out of another trance.

"Is everything all right?"

"Oh…yes," Peter returned as he sat back down next to her and took a sip of his lemonade. "I apologize…I haven't been very good company."

"If you're not feeling well and would rather not stay, I would underst—"

"No…I want to stay…very much."

Anna smiled at the statement—even with muddled thoughts, her suitor could still make her blush. "Did…did your meeting go well tonight?" she asked, hoping to pull him from wherever his thoughts kept taking him.

Silence.

"Mr. Leighton?"

"Hmm?"

"Did your meeting go well tonight?"

"No, it didn't go well at all," he murmured.

"Oh, I'm sorry to hear that," she whispered, guessing that she had found the root of his distraction.

As they continued to slowly rock back and forth in silence, a cat appeared on the parlor's windowsill, then, after a few moments of hesitation, it jumped onto Anna's lap. Grateful for the interruption from their voiceless impasse, she petted the cat and said, "This is Patience."

Peter reached out and scratched the cat's ear. "What happened to her foot?"

Anna shrugged. "We don't know. We found her on the porch one morning—half starved. Her foot was gone then...but she does fine with three."

The cat began to purr and moved her head so Peter could scratch the other ear.

"She likes you," Anna happily remarked. And inwardly she sighed—it was a good sign...the shy cat only accepted those with kind spirits.

Breathing deeply, Peter gazed at Anna. "I'm sorry that your mother doesn't like me."

"No, she does...she's just...not feeling well," Anna returned, but it was far from the truth. When her mother met Peter, it was with definite—and obvious—distaste.

"And I'm sure it didn't help that I couldn't understand her very well."

Anna smiled sympathetically. "Mama knows that her accent is quite pronounced...don't let it worry you."

"I had planned to send your parents a note today...but I just didn't get it done."

"A note?" she questioned.

"Yes, to thank them for allowing me to accompany you yesterday...I enjoyed the picnic very much."

"So did I," Anna replied. And wanting to keep their conversation going and Peter away from his sullen pondering, she furiously searched for something to say. "I, uh, I also enjoyed hearing about your family...I'd love to hear the rest of the story."

Peter grunted and began running his finger around the rim of his lemonade glass. "There's not much left to tell...Mum died a few years ago from pneumonia...after losing both my father and Tait, I think she just gave up."

With a loud 'meow,' the cat stepped closer to Peter and shoved her head underneath his hand.

Anna's grin—and delight—widened. "That's quite a compliment," she announced as Peter rubbed the cat's head. "Patience usually doesn't even come out for strangers, let alone ask to be petted by one…I'm glad you like cats…we have four."

"I had to get used to just about everything," Peter chuckled. "Tait used to bring every stray animal for miles into the house."

"So do you have other family? Brothers or sisters?"

"My parents didn't have any other children—none that lived past a few months anyway…but I do have a brother—a stepbrother. Tait already had a son when he married my mother."

"Older or younger?"

"Younger…much younger."

"I'd like to meet him…is he staying here in town with you?"

Averting his gaze, Peter rose from the swing and ambled to the edge of the porch. "No, he's not here right now…but he'll be joining me soon—I hope," he replied as he set his glass on the railing and looked out into the cloudy darkness.

As she stroked Patience, Anna wondered why Peter's sulking had returned. She knew talking about his family dismayed him—she had learned that from their walk by the creek—but the gloom that followed him this evening was relentless, as if it kept poking him with a sharp spear.

After a few quiet moments, Peter turned and peered at Anna, then a smile slowly brightened his face.

"What is it?" Anna asked, unable to discern why his mood had changed.

"You just look very pretty sitting there."

Not ready for such a marvelous answer, Anna lowered her gaze from his stare as a blush flooded her face.

"Miss Spreyer, I'd like to ask you something."

"Yes?" she prompted, looking up.

"But I'm almost sure that you're going to dismiss the question—and me—the moment I ask you," he murmured as he leaned against the porch railing.

"Why?" Anna inquired, puzzled by the cryptic preface.

"Because, I'd like to ask you to accompany me to a reception—on Friday."

Anna's heart quickened. "I'd love to—"

Peter immediately held up his hand to halt her enthusiasm. "It's at Karl Rheinhardt's house...his daughter is having a birthday reception."

"Oh."

"Please consider it...I'd like to show you the Karl that I know."

Anna shifted positions on the swing, causing the cat to jump from her lap. Now, she understood Peter's trepidation about his question, and he was right to worry about her answer. She had no desire to meet Karl Rheinhardt—she knew enough about him by the injuries he inflicted upon his workers. Then, as she studied Peter's hopeful expression, she bristled at the reminder that he was such a loyal advocate of the ruthless Rheinhardt. "No, I don't think so."

"Please, Anna...just think about it?"

Peter's informal—and compassionate—use of her first name dampened her temper, and Anna sighed in frustration. How could such an intelligent man be so blind to his employer's tactics? As she fought with her disillusionment and forced herself to consider the invitation, she noticed that Patience had jumped onto the railing next to Peter and was rubbing her head against his arm. The cat's approval was more than apparent.

"I'll think about it, Mr. Leighton," she announced as her irritation vanished, "if you'll answer one question for me."

Uncertainty flashed across Peter's face. "All right."

"When you, Papa, and I were talking at the open-air market, why did you cringe at my suggestion to join us for church?"

"Oh...that," Peter returned with a shrug. "It wasn't really anything...I just haven't been to church for quite awhile, and I was...I was a little worried that I'd be hit with a lightning bolt if I tried to enter."

Smiling at her suitor's levity and uneasiness, Anna scooted to the edge of the swing and leaned forward. "You never have to worry about that...we always have second chances with God...and third ones...and fourth ones."

"Then won't you give Karl a second chance?" he inquired as he pushed himself from the railing and rejoined Anna on the swing.

In the soft, warm candlelight, Anna stared into Peter's brown eyes, and she knew he was right. She needed to open her heart and give Karl Rheinhardt another chance...she needed to allow him the opportunity to explain why his men were treated so shamefully...she needed to get to know the man's soul. And, maybe, if persuaded or confronted, the furnituremaker would right his wrongs and ask for forgiveness.

And then there was the fact that Peter kept touting Karl's innocence. If the furnituremaker was truly blameless, she would be the one who needed to ask for forgiveness.

"If Mama and Papa say yes, I'll go with you."

Peter's lips parted with a boyish grin. "I can go ask them right now," he offered, starting to rise.

Grabbing his arm, Anna shook her head. "No. Let me—later."

"But I should be the—"

"I know, but still let me...I want to talk to Mama—alone."

He nodded and slid back onto the swing. "Ah, yes...that probably would be best."

Anna grinned sadly. Obviously, Peter had not been swayed by her earlier attempt to explain her mother's disfavor.

"May I see you tomorrow?" he asked. "You could give me your parents' answer then."

"No," Anna moaned with another shake of her head. "I work at the hospital on Tuesdays. I go in at noon and I'm there quite late."

"Until when?"

"I have to wait until Papa's ready...he doesn't like me going home alone."

"And he's quite right...but you wouldn't be alone—you'd be with me."

Anna smiled at her suitor's interest—and persistence. "I usually finish about six."

⊷ Five ⊶

"Mama?" Anna called as she peeked into each of the rooms upstairs.
"Mama?"

Catching a glimpse of an unfamiliar knickknack on the floor of her parents' morning-lit bedroom, Anna hurried into the chamber, where she found her mother seated on the floor, leaning against the heavy wooden chest at the foot of the bed.

"Mama, what's wrong. Are you all right?" Anna cried, rushing to her mother's side.

"I'm fine," Irene Spreyer returned with a bright smile. "Sit down, Liebchen. Here...look at this."

Taking the small framed daguerreotype from her mother, Anna studied the metallic-looking picture, then she smiled. "That's you and Papa—a long time ago...look how thin he was!"

Irene laughed. "It was a very, very long time ago...Papa had it taken when we were first courting. It has been packed away for so long that I forgot about it," she said as she sat upright and started rummaging through the cedar-lined trunk.

Confused but still gladdened to see her mother so alert and chipper, Anna glanced at the photograph once more, then she surveyed the bedroom. The usually immaculate room was in total disarray, and an assortment of keepsakes lay scattered on the floor—some of which Anna remembered...but most she didn't.
"Mama, what are you looking for?"

"When Papa and I came to this country, we already had your sisters…and between our belongings and Papa's supplies—we didn't have room for much…ah, here it is," her mother announced, lifting an old tattered sack from the chest. "But I managed to squeeze a few things into our trunks…this is one of them," she continued as she handed the muslin bag to Anna. "Open it."

"What is it?"

Irene laughed. "Open it and you'll see."

Anna hesitated, then carefully opened the sack and weeded through the papers that surrounded her mother's mysterious treasure. "Oh, Mama, it's lovely," she purred, pulling a light-pink brocaded silk from the bag.

"Hold it up for me, Liebchen…I want to see if the years have faded it."

Sliding the muslin sack to the side, Anna stood and unfurled the fabric, then she wrapped it around herself and draped one end over her shoulder. "Look how the threads sparkle! It's beautiful," she said, strolling around the room.

"There isn't much," Irene put in, "but I think we can add some tulle and make a beautiful evening dress for the reception."

Anna stopped and studied her mother's delicate countenance. "Then I can go?"

"Yes."

"But…but you said 'no' last night," Anna returned, while carefully unwrapping herself and loosely folding the brocade. "Why is it okay for me to go now?"

"I did not say 'no.' I said I wanted to pray about it…I did and you may go."

"Oh, thank you!" Anna exclaimed as she knelt on the floor and hugged her mother tightly. "But are you sure you want to use this fabric? You've kept it all this time…don't you want to use it for something special?"

"Yes, I want—" her mother began but was interrupted by an attack of coughing.

"Do you need some water, Mama?"

Irene patted Anna's hand and shook her head, then, as the choking finally subsided, she replied, "No, I'm all right…and yes, Liebchen, I want you to have the fabric…I may not be around to make your bridal dress—so I want this gown to be special."

Anna's eyes watered and she kissed her mother's cheek.

"No tears, Liebchen…we've always known that the Lord could call me at any time."

"I know," Anna answered, blinking back the tears. "But thinking about you not being here for my nuptials makes me…makes me…"

"Then let's not think about it," her mother offered as she grabbed the empty muslin sack. "Let's think about the beautiful dress we are going to make for the reception."

As her mother started returning the mementos to the chest, Anna rose from the floor and redraped the brocade over her chambray day suit. Then, as she studied her reflection in the long mirror that stood in the corner of the bedroom, she stroked the gold threads woven into the silk. The material would indeed make a beautiful evening dress, and she couldn't wait for her mother—and Peter—to see her in it.

"Mama?"

"Yes, Liebchen?"

"Why don't you like Mr. Leighton?" she asked as she peered at the reflection of her mother in the mirror. "Is it because of Mr. Rheinhardt?"

Only silence answered her.

Turning, Anna stared at her mother, who was still busy filling the chest.

"Mama, you told me that I would know Mr. Leighton's heart by the fruit that he bears…I don't like that he works for Karl Rheinhardt, but in the few days that I've known him, I've only seen him do good and kind things…why do you hate him?"

"I don't hate him, Liebchen," her mother replied, stifling a cough. "His strength goes very deep…and so does his courage."

"Then why don't you approve of him?"

"He is not being honest about something."

"How do you know that?"

"Just as you knew that God meant him for you—I know he is keeping something hidden from us."

Disheartened by the answer, Anna slid the fabric from around her waist and laid it on the bed. "So what should I do?"

"What you've been doing—watching and praying…Peter's spirit will reveal itself," her mother returned, closing the trunk. "Now, if we're going to get that dress done by Friday," she continued as she tried to pull herself up with the aid of the chest, "we'd better—"

As she saw her mother falter, Anna sprang up and hurried to her side. "You should be resting," Anna said, helping her mother to sit on the cedar chest.

"Don't you deny me this," Irene replied, lightly tapping Anna's forearm. "I've been looking forward to working on that fabric for a long time…now, go find that *Harper's Bazar* your sisters had on Wednesday…we'll see if there are any new dress designs that we like."

Hearing a drawer slam shut in Karl's office, Peter lifted his head from the ledger he was studying and looked at the clock. Ten-thirty. As aggravation gnawed at him, he shook his head and angrily shoved the book away. His employer's lax and passive attitude had made it so easy for Fetch to kidnap the factory…and was making it so difficult for him to rescue the company from the foreman's clutches.

As he stood and walked to Karl's office, Peter's thoughts once again wandered to his stepfather, and he wished he could ask forgiveness for the grief he had caused the man. Tait Ashby's mistakes had been many—and ruinous—but at least his stepfather never ceased trying to save their store. Reaching the doorway to Karl's chamber, Peter studied the older man—who sat at his desk, staring at the air. And, at least, Peter added silently, Tait never relinquished his authority to a domination-hungry foreman.

"Karl?" Peter called, knocking on the doorjamb. "Do you have a moment?"

"Good morning, my boy!" the older man exclaimed. "Did you get a chance to check Daven's story with Quentin's records?"

Peter's eyes widened in alarm. "Karl! Quiet!" he scolded as he quickly surveyed the upstairs anteroom for possible eavesdroppers.

"No one's here...Del went for the mail," Karl returned with a nonchalant wave.

Breathing out in aggravation, Peter entered the office and elbowed the door closed.

"We need to keep it open...to hear the bell if anyone comes in."

His patience withering, Peter grabbed the latch and pulled the door back open.

"I don't know why you're so worried, young man," Karl declared as he slouched down in his chair.

"Because Fetch...Quentin isn't going to let me shut down his little enterprise without a fight...and I don't want my brother in the middle of that battle."

"All right. I'll try to be more careful...so did you go over Quentin's books?"

Peter nodded and reluctantly settled onto the chair opposite Karl's desk. "His records look fine—on the surface—but I don't believe any of them are accurate."

"Why?"

"Because I know, positively, that some of the entries are lies...and I don't doubt that there are many other forgeries."

"Which entries are lies?"

"To start, the ones about Daven's time and pay," Peter explained as he fingered the carved grooves in the arm of his chair. "Quentin marked that Daven was paid for five and a half hours of work on Saturday."

"So?"

"So, according to Daven, he worked eleven hours—and didn't get paid at all."

"According to Daven," Karl echoed quietly.

Peter frowned and adjusted his position on the chair. "My brother has no reason to lie—nor is he exaggerating...I doubt that anyone's getting paid what he's supposed to."

Crossing his arms, Karl leaned forward and placed his elbows on the desk. "Then why haven't the men come to me with their complaints?"

"Maybe they're just too scared."

"Of what?"

"Of..." Peter began, but he let his reply drift into silence as a faint ringing sounded from downstairs.

"It's probably Del back from the post office."

Pushing himself from his chair, Peter headed for the doorway, then Del called from below, "It's just me, Karl."

"Now, you can close the door," Karl remarked with a condescending lilt.

Peter gritted his teeth and shoved the door closed with his foot.

Karl straightened up in his chair, and with impish amusement, he grunted. "That's enough of that, young man."

Knowing that his anger would not help the situation, Peter tried to cool his simmering temper with a deep breath. "You're right, Sir."

"Now, what else did you find out from Quentin's books?"

"Something very interesting," Peter answered, returning to his chair. "Just about all of your employees have been here three years or less."

"What?! That's impossible!"

"Three years," he went on, emphasizing the words by holding up three fingers. "That's also how long Quentin Fetch has been foreman."

Karl remained silent as he considered the statement, then he shook his head. "Some of my men were hired the day the factory opened...if they were unhappy, why didn't they come to me?"

Peter sighed—maybe now, he could nudge Karl from the oblivion the man had settled himself into. "Because, Fetch, I mean Quentin, made them believe that...that all the changes for the worse were your doing."

"They wouldn't have believed that...those men knew me."

"Knew you," Peter agreed with a nod and a voiceless cheer—finally, he had penetrated his employer's apathy. Now, he had to choose his next words as carefully as he could. "You have, um…changed since Marcus died…I'm sure Quentin used that against you."

"I just can't believe that Quent would do that to me," Karl whispered in despair.

"Maybe, if you went to the factory with me, you'd see—"

The older man rubbed his hand over his face. "I…I can't. The factory reminds me too much of Marcus," he croaked out as grief almost visibly crawled onto his shoulders.

As Peter watched his employer's alertness fade, it became very clear how Fetch had been able to seize command of the factory so easily. "I understand, Sir…we'll just have to rely on Daven's reports," he put in, hoping the change of subject would lighten his employer's mood.

"Yes…I suppose you're right…when will he be able to tell you more?"

"Very soon—I hope…I was supposed to meet him last night, but he never showed up."

"Oh?"

With a shrug, Peter shook his head. "I don't know why or whether to be angry about it or not…but I need to talk with him. I wish I could get him up here."

"I have an idea of how you can do that."

Peter raised an eyebrow. "Really?" he asked, relieved to see that Karl's thoughts were back on their task.

"Come over here…I want to show you something," Karl said, rising from his chair and heading toward a long table by the window.

Curious about his employer's sudden sense of purpose, Peter quickly stepped over to the table as the older man grabbed a stack of dusty papers and spread them out.

"These are sketches for a new pedestal table that my son had wanted to introduce into our line of furniture," Karl announced, smoothing out the yellowed sheets. "As you can see, it's much more elaborate than what we've been producing, but it's a fine piece...don't you agree?"

Shuffling through the papers, Peter studied the fastidious but not-quite-complete drawings. "It looks like the table in my office," he commented.

Karl nodded. "It is—for the most part. I've made a few modifications, so it'll be easier to produce."

"It is a fine table," Peter agreed. "But I thought you said—"

"I know," Karl interrupted, holding up his hand. "I said my factory only produces simple pieces. But Marcus always wanted to expand our line, and he had me start on some new designs—ones that were more elegant but would still be affordable. This was as far as I got when...well, since Marcus' accident, I just haven't had the heart to finish them...until now."

"But how is this going to help with Daven?"

"Quentin knows about these sketches. You can tell him that I want Daven to look them over, so he can make up a few samples."

Peter grinned and stroked his mustache. "It just might work."

The older man chuckled and patted Peter's shoulder. "Of course it will...I still know a few tricks."

"I'll go over to the factory about two o'clock—if that time is good for you—and bring Daven up here."

"That will be fine...and while he's here, I want him to take a look at these plans," Karl replied as he gathered the pages together and stacked them in the corner of the table. "After we get things cleared up, I'd like the factory to start making some pieces like this."

"That would be a nice new start for your company."

"It would indeed be a nice new start...if it were our company," the older man murmured, examining Peter with worn, tired eyes. "Have you thought about my partnership offer?"

"I've thought about it," Peter returned as he averted his gaze and moved over to the window. "I just don't know yet."

"With you as my partner and Daven carving our furniture, our business would surely thrive."

"Wait a minute, Karl," Peter announced, circling to face his employer. "I doubt if Daven would want to stay on at the factory. He hates it there...it's just not what we had planned to do."

"Plans change...people change."

Leaning against the windowsill, Peter laughed and shook his head. "No one knows that better than I do."

"Then talk to your brother about it, all right?"

"All right," Peter returned with a shrug. "After this mess is cleaned up, the three of us will talk about it."

The older man clapped his hands together. "That's all I ask," he declared as he walked toward the doorway. "Listen, since you're not going to see Daven until two, why don't you join us for lunch."

"Us?"

"Yes, Lori and I."

"Oh...well, I uh..."

"Can I open it now?" Karl inquired as he jabbed a thumb at the back of the door. "It's getting hot in here." Then, not waiting for an answer, the older man pulled on the latch. "Lori wanted to have lunch and discuss something or other for the reception...I'm sure she won't mind if you come along," he added with a glint in his eye.

Peter forced a grin. "Thank you, but I can't. I saw an advertisement for a boarding house in the Want Columns, and I'd like to go take a look at it today...I need someplace to stay that's more convenient than the hotel."

"Well, I have the solution to that problem too," Karl gleefully trumpeted.

"You do?"

"Yes! You can stay in my guest house. It's perfect...and you'd be closer to Lori that way."

Trying to keep his smile, Peter turned slightly and glanced out the window. The only person that would be happy if he moved into the guest house was Karl.

Besides, he silently reasoned, Lori Rheinhardt was not the woman he wanted to get closer to. "Well, I want to look at this other place anyway."

With his arms crossed, Peter stood on the loading platform outside the factory doors and watched as Frank Hallam disappeared into the building. Finally, Peter inwardly sighed. Finally, he would get the chance to see his brother—and, hopefully, to stop missing him so much. Laughing at his own melancholy, Peter shook his head. It wasn't that he and Daven had never been separated before—they had, many times—but always with the capability to correspond. Now...now, the absence of any communication was making their separation intolerable, and Peter found himself longing to see his brother's bright spirit... and uncut hair...and flippant attitude...and crystal-blue eyes...

"How dare you order my men around!" Fetch bellowed as he marched out onto the platform followed by the blonde-haired Hallam. "If you want to see the carver, then you ask me...you don't order Hallam to get 'im."

Peter glared at the barrel-chested foreman. He outranked the big man, plain and simple—and he looked forward to one day making that fact vividly clear in everyone's mind...especially Fetch's. But this wasn't that day...he wanted nothing to interfere with his chance to see Daven. "They are my men too, Mr. Fetch...may I meet the new carver please?"

"Why?!"

"Because, if you'll remember, I didn't get to meet him the last time I was here."

"You can meet him later," the foreman sneered as he chewed on his cigar. "He's busy now."

"No, I need to see him now," Peter replied, trying to sound just angry enough and just polite enough to be believable. "Mr. Rheinhardt asked me to bring Mr....uh, what is the carver's name?"

"Ashby."

"Right. Mr. Rheinhardt asked me to bring Mr. Ashby to the showroom."

"Why?!"

"Mr. Rheinhardt has some sketches for a new pedestal table, and he wants Mr. Ashby to look them over—so he can do some carving samples...if you have an issue with me taking Mr. Ashby away, you'll have to talk to Mr. Rheinhardt."

Growling under his breath, Fetch dropped his cigar stub on the platform, then twisted it into the boards with his heel. "Take 'im then...but you better not keep him long."

Not being able to resist aggravating Fetch further, Peter smiled politely and offered, "Why does it matter? We don't have any carved orders with immediate deadlines...nothing will be hindered by Mr. Ashby's absence."

Fetch bellowed out a loud curse and raised his fist, then, slowly and with a long exhale, he lowered his hand. "I got Ashby workin' where I need him, so get him back here—fast."

"Mr. Ashby will be back when Mr. Rheinhardt is finished showing him the sketches...now, will you get him? Or do you want to waste more time arguing about it?"

"Fine!" Fetch snapped, pivoting on his heel toward Hallam. Then a sly grin parted the foreman's lips, and he stepped over to his blonde-haired assistant and whispered into the man's ear.

Clearly bewildered, Hallam shrugged, nodded, and disappeared into the factory again.

As he and the foreman waited in uneasy silence, Peter studied his adversary—who still wore a smug smile. What had crept into Fetch's head to cause such sudden arrogance? Peter wondered. And what trouble was it going to cause him and his brother? Then, as Hallam, Daven, and a tall black man joined them on the platform, Peter's questions turned to relief.

"The new carver," Fetch announced as he motioned toward Daven.

"How do you do, Mr. Ashby? I'm Peter Leighton, Mr. Rheinhardt's new assistant," Peter said, extending his hand.

"It's a pleasure, Mr. Leighton."

As he felt his brother's strong handshake and stared into his light-blue eyes, an odd disorientation settled upon Peter. It was as if he were truly looking at a stranger—a grown-up, talented, independent stranger—and not his little brother.

"And this is Jaxson Averill," Fetch added.

"Mr. Averill."

"You'll need to take Averill with you…he's the apprentice carver."

Instantly, surprise enveloped everyone's face—except Fetch's.

Was this the idea that had sparked the foreman's self-satisfied simper? Peter voicelessly questioned. Did Fetch somehow know he wanted to get Daven alone? Or was Jaxson being sent along as a spy? Either way, the additional man complicated things and gave him very little time to come up with an alternate plan.

"Mr. Ashby, Mr. Averill," Peter declared, pointing at his waiting carriage, "we need you at the showroom…I'll explain on the ride there."

As Peter and the carvers climbed into the coach, Frank Hallam studied his boss's smoldering expression. "Why'd you send Averill?"

"Because I wanna know if Ashby says anything about our…our methods."

"But ain't you worried about Averill sayin' somethin'?"

"Him? Nah, he knows better…I think all the men know better since Perryn's little accident…except Ashby—he's too new…he might not keep his mouth shut."

"But how can sending Averill help if the kid starts talkin'?"

Fetch released a deep breath, slipped his hand inside his jacket, and pulled out a new cigar. "He'll tell us what Ashby said…then I'll think of somethin' to fix it."

"I dunno, Boss…those two've been workin' together pretty close on that desk," the blonde-haired man returned as the carriage shrank to a dot, then disappeared. "Averill might not snitch."

"Yeah, he will…he ain't gunna take any punches for Ashby…when those two get back, bring 'em to me—right away."

Hallam nodded and turned to leave, then, with a frown, he circled back and stared at the foreman—whose face was now etched with hatred. "I thought you were gunna talk to Rheinhardt and make him change his mind about hirin' Leighton."

Biting off the end of his cigar, the foreman glared at Hallam and spit the nub onto the platform. "I did talk to the old man…at lunch," he growled. "But it's gunna take a lot of convincin' to get him to get rid of Leighton."

"How come?"

"Turns out Leighton's the son of a friend, and Rheinhardt's just about got him adopted."

"So he's here for good?"

Fetch snorted, then pulled a match from his pocket. "Nope."

"But you just—"

"Quit bellyachin'…I'll get rid of Leighton—one way or another," Fetch declared as he scraped the end of the match with his thumbnail and lit his cigar.

Leaning against the windowsill, Peter watched as Karl presented the table designs to Daven and Jaxson. Then, as his brother started to question the older man about the sketches, the odd disorientation descended upon Peter once again, making him feel as if he were watching a play. His young brother was blessed with talent—he knew that. But now, looking at Daven as a stranger, he realized just how knowledgeable, charming, and blithe his brother really was—and he wished, although he would never admit it to anyone, that he could be as gladsome as Daven was. Shaking his head slightly, Peter refocused on the three men in front of him. Somehow, he had to get Daven alone.

"Karl, why don't I show Mr. Ashby the table in my office…he could get more of an idea of what you're looking for," Peter offered, hoping his employer would not suggest that they all go look at the table.

"Excellent idea!" Karl exclaimed. "That will give me time to adjust my drawings and implement the changes we've already discussed."

Peter released a deep and relieved breath. Karl's intoxication with the table sketches had been as difficult to deal with as the presence of Jaxson. From the moment the bell announced Daven and Jaxson's entrance into the showroom, Karl had attached himself to them both, and only now was Peter able to pry his brother away.

"Mr. Ashby, if you'll please follow me," Peter announced as he pushed himself from the window and headed toward the door, "I'll show you the table that Mr. Rheinhardt fashioned his sketches after."

As he entered the anteroom, Peter gestured for his brother to remain silent, then, after considering the proximity of his office to Karl's, he led Daven to the salesman's room instead. Quietly and while making sure no one was witnessing their detour, Peter released the third door's latch, motioned for his brother to enter, and clicked the door closed behind them.

"That was a lot more work than I thought it would be," Peter murmured, finally satisfied that they were safe from detection.

Expecting some kind of response...or apology...or snide remark, Peter waited, but his brother just stood with his back to him, looking out the window. Still unsure if he should be annoyed or alarmed at his brother's actions, Peter's patience gave way. "Well?!"

Daven exhaled deeply but didn't answer.

"Did you forget we were supposed to meet last night?"

"No."

"Then what happened?"

No response.

His brother's uncommon silence was deafening, but it did, at least, answer Peter's daylong question—now, he knew that he should be worried about Daven's absence the night before. Walking over to the window, Peter gently grasped his brother's shoulder. "What's wrong? Talk to me...please."

Daven wearily brushed his hand through his long waves, pulling the hair away from his face, and as he did, Peter noticed a bluish discoloration on his brother's cheek.

"What happened to you?" Peter asked, tilting Daven's head so he could view the bruise better. "Who did this?"

Again, no response.

"Fetch?! Did he hit you?!"

Daven twisted away. "Yeah. He took my watch…and I tried to take it back."

"Why did he take your watch?"

"Because he wanted it," Daven returned, thumbing his palm.

The habit didn't go unnoticed—nor did his brother's rumpled clothes and haggard appearance. "I'll get the watch back for you," Peter said, his voice and heart breaking with guilt. "I promise."

"No, you don't have to," Daven replied as he began to roam haphazardly through the office. "I bought it back from Fetch for twenty dollars."

"Bought it? Where did you get—"

"Is this your office?" his brother questioned, scanning the messy room.

"No, it's the salesman's.…where did you get the money to give to Fetch?"

Daven smirked and ran his finger through the dust on the desk. "I didn't think it was your office—not with all this clutter…so where's yours?"

"It's the one in the middle…where did you get the twenty dollars?"

Silence.

"Dave?"

Daven rubbed his eyes, then looked up at his brother. "I'm sorry. Whatd'ya wanna know?"

At any other time, Peter would have condemned his brother's sloppy language, but now, it only added to his concern. "What's wrong with you? Why do you keep…keep drifting in and out on me?"

"Because I'm tired, Peter…I'm tired," Daven answered and slumped onto an overstuffed, winged-back chair. "That stupid desk is taking everything I've got…I just hate working on it—even more than I hated working on Pa's grave marker."

Staring at his brother's fatigued countenance, Peter shook his head. He had always wanted Daven to commit to something, but this commitment, obviously, was not the right one—it was extinguishing his brother's lifeblood. And that was something he couldn't let happen.

Slowly, Peter walked over to Daven and sat on the ottoman in front of the chair. "You don't have to work on it anymore...I'm pulling you out of this mess."

"What?" Daven whispered, lifting his head.

Instantly, Peter's worry and determination deepened—the usual spark in his brother's bright-blue eyes had disappeared. "I'm pulling you out of this mess."

"But what...what about our obligation to Karl?"

Peter shrugged. "It's my obligation—not yours."

Daven's mouth fell open and bewilderment blanketed his face. "Since when?"

"Since now."

"I thought you needed my help to stop Fetch."

"I'll figure something else out," Peter returned, patting his brother's shoulder. "I don't want you getting sick or hurt because of this mission."

Taking a deep breath, Daven combed a hand through his hair, then offered a one-shouldered shrug. "Nah, I'll stick with it...how much longer do you think it'll take though?"

"No, you're not...I said you're out and I mean it."

"Stop tellin' me what to do, Peter!"

"Daven, I'm your guardian. I'm supposed to look out for—"

"Ask me, Peter. Ask me what I want...as you didn't do when you told me we were goin' to help Karl in the first place."

Chagrined by his brother's words, Peter stroked his mustache and considered the plea. As much as he tried, he could never get it right—he could never figure out when to be a brother...and when to be a parent...and when to be a friend. "Okay...what do you want to do?"

"I wanna finish this...there're a lot of good men stuck in that factory, and if we don't stop Fetch, he'll just keep on abusing them."

Peter smiled at the unexpected maturity in his brother's voice, and after considering the reasoning, he offered, "All right…but if it gets too bad for you, you're out of it."

Daven nodded with a half-smile. "Are we close to stoppin' Fetch?"

"Yes and no…Karl's been one of the worst obstacles. He doesn't believe that Fetch would betray him…but I think next Tuesday will open his eyes."

"Why? What's next Tuesday?"

"That's when I should find out who's been acting as Fetch's salesman," Peter explained, then, peering at the pendulating clock on the wall, he winced. He knew he needed to get Daven back to Karl's office before the older man revealed something he shouldn't—and definitely before Jaxson started wondering what was taking so long—but he just couldn't let go…not yet anyway. "Daven, how did you get your watch back from Fetch?"

"I gave him twenty dollars—which he loaned to me."

"So he agreed to give you an advance on your wages?"

"No."

"But you just said Fetch loaned you some money."

"Yeah, to buy back my watch…he said I could pay him by putting in extra hours at the factory."

Peter frowned. "So Fetch didn't advance you the money you needed for Mrs. Tadman?"

"No."

Creases of worry lined Peter's forehead, and a shiver trickled down his spine. He was sure that he already knew the answer to his next question, but he asked it nevertheless. "Did she let you stay on credit?"

Daven shook his head.

"Then where did you sleep last night?"

"Oh, Fetch took care of that for me," his brother said wryly. "You were wrong, Peter."

"About what?"

"You said not much could happen between Saturday night and Monday… you were wrong."

"What happened?" Peter murmured, alarmed by his brother's words.

As Daven summarized the events that had occurred since their last meeting, Peter closed his eyes—the obligation to Karl had mutated into an affliction for both him and his brother.

"I'm sorry I missed our meeting," Daven said, finishing the story. "Fetch kept me waiting until eight."

"It's all right," Peter offered, raising his head. The last thing he wanted now was an apology.

"Did you ever get a chance to look over Fetch's books?"

Peter nodded. "Yesterday. I looked for you, but he said you were out on a delivery."

"I was there—upstairs, working on the desk…didn't the books show anything?"

"Yes, they showed that Fetch covers his tracks very well…everything looked perfect—but I knew it was just fiction by what you told me…do you think any of the other men would admit that Fetch was cheating them on their wages?"

Daven laughed quietly. "No. I…I still haven't gotten them to talk to me that much, but I did find out that the men with families owe Fetch for their homes—and I think he's even blackmailing a couple of them…and the others out at Everly's are either in debt, like me, or Fetch has something he's using to hold them there."

"It seems that our foreman has quite a few methods for making his money," Peter commented between clenched teeth.

With a nod of agreement, Daven leaned forward, putting his elbows on his knees. "So many of the men are new to this country, Peter. They just don't know what to do…and the rest…well, their concerns are for their families or their lives…no one's going to take the chance to come up against Fetch—they could lose everything…everything."

"Then it's up to us…do you think if I did an inventory of the lumber—"

"Fetch doesn't keep his wood at the factory," Daven said, massaging his hand. "Hallam had to bring in the mahogany for the desk I'm carving from someplace else."

Suddenly, a piece of his puzzle fit perfectly into an empty spot and Peter snapped his fingers. "Mahogany? You're working on a mahogany desk?"

"Yeah. Jaxson's making it and I'm doing the carving."

"Is it a ladies' writing desk?"

"Yeah…"

"And do you have to get it done for next Monday's delivery?" he questioned, rising from the ottoman.

"Yeah, but—"

"This is great, Daven," Peter broke in, his mind ablaze with the new information. "That desk is for one of Fetch's customers—not Karl's. Just keep working on it—and maybe, just maybe, we can use it to incriminate Fetch." Smiling at his small triumph, Peter glanced once again at the wall clock, and this time, he gulped in alarm. "Man alive! We've got to get back to Karl's office."

"Hey, what's this business about that pedestal table anyway?" Daven asked, pushing himself from the winged-back chair. "Karl's talking as if they're gunna be made in the factory."

"I know…we had to have an excuse to get you up here—only Karl's forgotten that it's just an excuse," Peter replied, moving to the door. Then, with his hand on the latch, he looked back at Daven. "What about tomorrow? Do you think you can make it to the market grounds by seven-thirty, so we can talk some more?"

Daven shrugged. "I'll try."

"I'm going to stop at the factory tomorrow for an unannounced tour…I want to see what Fetch is going to say when I want to go upstairs…I'll make sure I see you—either nod or shake your head to let me know if you can make it, okay?"

Shuffling over to his brother, Daven nodded. "Okay," he offered, then his eyes widened, and he grabbed Peter's arm. "I almost forgot...you asked about Travis Perryn. He was the carver before me."

"I know," Peter murmured. "And he's dead. Fetch said he had an 'unfortunate accident with a runaway ice wagon.'"

Each brother offered the other a long look of apprehension, then Daven finally broke the silence. "Be careful around Fetch, Peter."

Not accustomed to receiving precautions, especially from his brother, Peter raised an eyebrow and offered with a half-smile, "You too."

"I mean it, Peter...Fetch can get awful mean."

As the statement rattled through him, Peter's grin faded. The bruise on his brother's face was only a sample of the foreman's meanness—and soon, Daven would be back within Fetch's reach. Why didn't he just ignore what Daven wanted and pull his brother out of this mess? Peter angrily questioned himself.

"I know he can get mean," Peter soothed as he reached out and gently placed his hand behind his brother's neck. "That's why I want you to be on guard every minute—particularly with your carving."

"Whatd'ya mean?"

"Fetch might recognize your work from the one-of-a-kind pieces that Karl's been selling for us...so watch your style...do things a little differently," he explained. Then, as he pulled his hand away, he grabbed onto Daven's hair, gave it a slight tug, and added with a resigned grin, "It's good to see you little brother."

Daven's face immediately stiffened. "Long hair and all?"

Inhaling deeply, Peter surveyed his brother from head to boot. He had never liked Daven's rakish appearance or cheeky attitude, but after being without them for what seemed like months, he now appreciated all of it. "Long hair and all," Peter whispered as he twisted the latch and yanked the door open. Then, signaling for Daven to be silent and to follow, Peter searched the anteroom, and seeing no one, he stepped out of the salesman's office and headed for Karl's room.

Without warning, the door to his employer's office started to swing open, and Peter froze. He knew he had only seconds to come up with an excuse for his and Daven's lengthy absence—not so much for Karl, but for Jaxson. As he glanced at the furniture in the anteroom, an idea rang out almost audibly, and in one swift motion, Peter grabbed his brother's sleeve and lunged for one of the tables. "So, if we were to add some carved ornaments or edging," he announced just as Karl and Jaxson walked through the doorway, "how much do you think that would affect production time?"

"I was wondering what was keeping you two," Karl declared, joining Peter and Daven.

"I'm sorry, Sir," Peter returned with an apologetic shake of his head. "Daven was so fascinated with all the pieces in my office that you made, we just lost track of the time."

"Yes, your work is remarkable," Daven put in. "And so inspiring that I was telling Mr. Leighton how easy it would be to add some carved accents to the tables your factory already produces."

Completely impressed with his brother's keenness and quick wit, Peter nodded. "I think Mr. Ashby has some good ideas. We should probably meet again, so we can figure out how to implement them."

Karl's eyes sparkled with merriment. "By all means—yes!" he exclaimed, patting Daven on the back. "I've enjoyed this meeting—very much. It's been a long time since I've had other carvers to talk to."

"And it's been a pleasure talking with you, Sir."

Karl chuckled and slapped Daven on the back once again. "I look forward to seeing your ideas for the pedestal table too…start working on those samples for me—both of you…all right?"

"We will," Daven replied as he and Jaxson moved toward the staircase and started down the steps.

Trying to convince himself that their ruse had worked—and that Daven would be all right in Fetch's custody—Peter started to follow after his brother, but Karl grasped his elbow.

"I'd like to have a word with you," the older man stated.

"But I need to drive them back to—"

"You two don't mind walking back to the factory, do you?" Karl called.

Both Daven and Jaxson stopped and shook their heads. "No Sir," Daven hollered in return. "I wouldn't mind at all."

At Daven's response, Karl lifted his nose in the air and motioned toward his office. "As I said, Peter, I'd like to have a word with you—now," he ordered, then turned and stepped back into his room.

Although curious—and a bit concerned—about the seriousness in his employer's voice, Peter still lingered at the top of the stairs, watching Daven and Jaxson descend. He just couldn't let his brother leave without some token of assurance. "Wait!" he shouted, rushing down the steps.

"Yes Sir?" Daven questioned. "Is there something wrong?"

Peter smiled and removed several coins from his waistcoat pocket, then, after fingering through them, he picked out a nickel and a dime and slipped the rest of the money back into his vest. "There's nothing wrong…I just wanted to give you a little something for the trouble of walking back," he explained, offering the nickel to Jaxson.

"No Sir," Jaxson spoke out immediately. "I don't want nothin'."

Instantly, the edges of Peter's grin plunged downward—he couldn't very well give Daven something and nothing to Jaxson. "Please, take it," he urged, "for the inconvenience."

Hesitating for a few moments more, Jaxson finally reached out and snatched the coin from Peter's fingers.

"And for you," Peter continued as he took Daven's hand and discreetly pressed the dime into his brother's palm—all the while hoping that Jaxson hadn't noticed the difference in denominations.

"Mr. Ashby, Mr. Averill, thank you both for coming," Peter said, then he turned and bounded up the stairs and into Karl's office.

"Where in Sam Hill did you go?!" the older man inquired as Peter closed the door. "I told you I wanted to talk to you."

"Yes Sir...I apologize. I, uh, I just wanted to thank them again for coming...did you like Daven's suggestions?"

Standing at his drawing table and leafing through the sketches, Karl bobbed his head. "Very much."

Feeling as though a chapter in a book had gone by without him reading it, Peter tramped over to his employer, wondering why the man's demeanor had turned so acerbic. "Daven also gave me some good news."

"Oh?"

"Yes...your foreman has him and that Jaxson working on the writing desk for the Hopewells."

"Daven told you it was for the Hopewells specifically?"

"No, he didn't use their name, but they're working on a carved, mahogany ladies' writing desk that must be finished for next Monday's delivery...who else could it be for?"

"That's exactly what I wanted to talk to you about, young man."

Peter's brow furrowed and a tingle of dread tickled the hairs on the back of his neck—he definitely did not like the direction their conversation was taking.

"Quentin doesn't deserve the harassment he's gotten—not when it's based on just hunches."

"Hunches?"

"Yes, hunches!" Karl exclaimed, holding up his drawings. "You have shown me no solid proof...you've only told me stories about a man that I've trusted for years."

Suddenly realizing what must have happened in the missing chapter, Peter rubbed his eyes and sighed wearily. "So when did Fetch get over here and offer you his thoughts?"

"He…he didn't…I've just been thinking that…that maybe you've been too hard on Quent."

"Too hard on him?" Peter echoed incredulously as he stared into this employer's clouded eyes.

"Yes. After you took Daven to your office, I asked the other one how he liked working at the factory—and he said everything was fine."

"Of course he's going to say that…Fetch has everyone believing that you condone his method of management."

Only silence answered him.

His jaw clenching with indignation and defeat, Peter pulled the drawings out of Karl's hands and glowered at his employer. "Fetch has made my brother destitute and forced him to work for free just to survive…and now, he has him working on a carved, mahogany writing desk…a desk that we have no record of anyone ordering…those are not hunches, Karl…those are facts."

Peter knew his employer had heard him, but the words just seemed to hit Karl's confused features and fall uselessly to the floor. Somehow, Fetch had maneuvered the older man back into a void of lies—and somehow…somehow, Karl had to be reconvinced of the truth. Shaking his head, Peter sighed. All his work had been torn apart. And yet he still found a speck of hope in the ruins. Fetch's interference revealed one important fact—the foreman was worried.

Three times on the walk back to the factory, Daven tried to strike up a conversation with the reclusive Jaxson, and as usual, he received just grunts and mumbles in return. Even while they worked together in the factory, Jaxson rarely spoke to him—and when the man did, finally, open his mouth, it was always preceded by a vinegary 'Hey, Helpful.' Although he knew the nickname was used to annoy him—Daven didn't mind hearing it…it was better than silence.

Giving up on his one-sided efforts to talk with his coworker, Daven's thoughts, instead, drifted to his brother—his strangely patient and accommodating brother. Usually, discussions with Peter evolved into a battle of wills, but today had been different. His brother had treated him as an equal. That was an answer to a long-standing prayer and made his suffering under Fetch almost worthwhile. Thankful for the change, Daven nodded toward Heaven and tightened his fingers around the coin still in his hand.

Then, as he and Jaxson entered the factory's front yard—and saw Hallam rushing toward them—Daven's bright mood rapidly dimmed.

"Mr. Fetch wants to see you two in his office. Now!" the blonde-haired man yelled while approaching.

Instantly, trepidation spread through Daven, and he looked at Jaxson, whose expression mirrored his own dread. No, Daven silently corrected himself. Having Peter treat him as an adult was not worth the pangs of worry now churning within his gut. "What'd we do now?" he murmured.

"Do they need a reason to yell at us?" Jaxson returned under his breath, raising his hand to his mouth.

"I reckon not."

"Come on, you two!" Hallam shouted as he reached them and shoved Daven toward the building. "He's waiting!"

Glancing once again at Jaxson, Daven noticed that the man was having trouble breathing—as if he had swallowed something that didn't go down quite right. "Are you all right, Jaxson?"

"For now," his coworker answered in a hoarse voice.

Daven nodded in sympathy, and as they followed Hallam up the platform steps and into the factory, he felt his own throat tightening. Maybe, he should have let Peter pull him out after all.

"Go straight on into his office," the blonde-haired man bellowed, trying to be heard over the screaming saws. "He's expectin' ya."

With a knot of dread in his stomach, Daven tramped over to the foreman's fortress, then pushed the heavy wooden door open and stepped inside. Fetch, as usual, was seated behind the desk, chewing on a cigar, and the dark-haired Bryce, who looked as if he were a wolf readying for a kill, stood near the open outside door.

Pushing both Daven and Jaxson closer to the desk, Hallam slammed the factory door shut, slid a bolt sideways to lock it, and in the quiet, clearly announced, "Here they are!"

Slowly, Fetch looked up from the papers on his desk and peered at Jaxson and Daven. "So whatd'ya boys talk about with Rheinhardt and Leighton?"

Moistening his suddenly parched lips, Daven tried his best to sound nonchalant. "Mr. Rheinhardt showed us some sketches of a carved pedestal table that he wants to start manufacturing."

"You talk to Leighton about anything else?"

Instantly, Daven's heart began to gallop inside his chest, and he clenched his fist tighter around the dime in his hand. "No Sir."

"Is that true, Averill?"

"Ever'body just talked about the sketches," Jaxson answered, his eyes focused on the foreman. "Until Leighton took Helpful, here, into another room...I dunno what they talked about in there."

Wincing at the unneeded commentary, Daven glanced sideward at Jaxson, who refused to meet his stare.

"Is that so?" Fetch muttered as he leaned back in his chair. "What did you talk about, Ashby?"

"The tables," Daven returned with an overemphasized shrug. "Mr. Rheinhardt wanted me to see the pedestal table that he drew his sketches from, so Mr. Leighton took me to his office...we talked about that table, then about introducing some carved accents on our current tables...that was all."

Fetch removed his cigar and knocked the ashes onto the floor. "That was all, huh? So you're tellin' me he didn't ask you any questions about me or the factory?"

Feigning a look of confusion, Daven shook his head. "No Sir."

"And I'm s'posed to believe that you didn't say nothin' to him about...about anything?"

"I said nothing, Sir," Daven lied, his pulse beating so loud that he was sure Fetch could hear it. "After everything that...that's happened, I thought it would be...well, wiser to keep silent."

With a snort, the foreman leaned over his desk and jabbed at the air with his cigar. "Well, that was pretty smart of ya, Ashby...but don't go thinkin' that Leighton's prying is gunna help ya—or anybody else...that meddler's not gunna be around for long...so you just better keep on bein' silent."

A fear he had never experienced before shot through Daven, and using his fist, he wiped at the perspiration rolling down his forehead. He knew his own safety was subject to Fetch's whims—but now, so was Peter's. What would he do if anything happened to his big brother? "Yes Sir," he choked out, barely able to catch his breath.

"What's in there?" Fetch demanded, using his cigar to point at Daven's closed hand.

"Huh? Oh, just a tip from Mr. Leighton," he croaked as he opened his fist.

"Wasn't that nice of him," the foreman said, signaling Hallam.

A wide smile immediately appeared on the blonde-haired man's face, and he walked over to Daven, snatched up the dime, and tossed it to Bryce.

"Well?!" Fetch barked, turning his attention to Jaxson. "Where's yours?"

"Leighton tried, but I said no," Jaxson replied, still peering straight ahead.

With a long but silent exhale, Daven cast his eyes downward. He wasn't mistaken—Jaxson did swallow something that didn't go down quite right...the nickel. Then, tilting his head, Daven studied his coworker, and a stab of betrayal suddenly hit him as he realized that Jaxson hadn't bothered to tell him to do the same.

"All right, Hallam," Fetch growled. "Let's see if Averill is tellin' the truth."

Pushing Daven aside, Hallam moved over to Jaxson and started searching through the man's pockets. "Nothing."

"Where is it, Averill?"

Still embittered over his coworker's previous actions and comments, Daven considered informing Fetch of the coin's location. But, as he noticed the drops of sweat trickling down Jaxson's temples, the urge instantly faded, and compassion took its place. It just wouldn't be right, in God's eyes, to blab, Daven told himself. He was not one of Fetch's disciples...he was one of the Lord's. "He's telling the truth," Daven offered quietly. "When Mr. Leighton offered him the money, he said he didn't want it."

Jaxson's brow furrowed, and for the first time since entering the office, he looked at Daven.

Grunting in reply, Fetch rose from his desk and walked over to Jaxson, then, with another grunt, he turned toward Daven. "But you took the money Leighton offered," the big man accused, standing so close to Daven that they were almost nose-to-nose.

"I didn't know that I shouldn't have accepted it."

The foreman smiled broadly. "It's not that you shouldn't accept it...it's just that you should have given it to me—immediately."

"Why?"

"Did you forget 'bout the money you owe me?"

"No, I haven't forgotten...but you said that I could pay you back by putting in more time here at the factory."

Jaxson shook his head and averted his gaze as Fetch and his two henchmen laughed at the statement.

"You!" the foreman growled, motioning at Jaxson, then at the open outside door. "Get back to work."

Flashing Daven a brief but unmistakable expression of pity, Jaxson rushed past Bryce and through the door without saying a word.

"You just don't seem to get what it means to borrow money from me, Ashby," the foreman announced as he started to meander around the office. "It means I get every penny you get—until I'm paid."

Vexed by the foreman's tactics, Daven's dander stood up on end, and he offered through clenched teeth, "Fine…then I'd like to start working those extra hours now—so I can pay you your twenty dollars."

Fetch threw his head back with a loud laugh. "Twenty? You owe me a sight more than that now."

A shiver instantly ripped through Daven. "What…what do you mean?" he gasped. "You're taking my wages for my room at Everly's…so I don't owe you for anything—except the lousy initiation fee."

"Not quite, Ashby," Fetch replied, rocking back on his heels and grinning smugly. "What about your supper at the restaurant last night? And your breakfast this mornin'? You also took a wagon ride and the lunch Mrs. Everly made."

The words knocked Daven off balance, and he shook his head, trying to force the foggy confusion from his brain. "Those're…those're all part of the room's price."

"Who told you that?!" Fetch exclaimed over Hallam's and Bryce's chuckles.

Crestfallen and fearing that he had stepped into yet another of Fetch's snares, Daven shook his head again and wiped his sweaty brow with the cuff of his shirt. "You…you did. When you listed the rules the other night, you told me about the meals at the restaurant and the wagon ride and the—"

Once again, laughter filled the room, cutting him off.

"Those were only the rules, Kid!" the foreman returned, chuckling. "The meals, Mrs. Everly's washin', towels for a bath, the wagon…they all cost money."

Panic immediately grabbed Daven around his neck. "You…you never said that!"

The foreman sucked on his cigar, then shrugged. "Oh, well."

"But…but every day I'll just get…get more and more in debt."

"He catches on fast, doesn't he?" Bryce scoffed and spit a wad of tobacco juice on the floor.

"You never said anything about extra costs," Daven moaned, sinking into despair.

"Good thing you can work those extra hours, huh?"

As he started to rub his left palm, Daven stared at the three men who were taking so much pleasure in his misery. It was no wonder, he silently surmised, that Jaxson and the other workers were so lifeless and callous—Fetch had taken away their dignity, their freedom, and even their hope of ever escaping their circumstances.

"After you finish supper," Fetch continued, "the wagon will bring you here at seven o'clock, then it'll take you back at eleven."

Hopelessness whirled inside Daven's head, and he tried to steady his wobbly legs—now, he knew where all his coworkers were going when they piled into the wagon and left Everly's.

"You look a little peaked," the foreman offered as he thrust his barrel-size chest outward. "You know you could make things a lot easier for yourself and just give me that watch of yours."

His desperate situation and the possibility of once again losing his father's watch flooded Daven with outrage, and his self-control withered. "You can't do this to me!" he hollered, glaring at his tormentors.

"No?"

"No! And I'm sure that Peter Leighton would be very interested in hearing about all of this!" Then, as he heard the words come out of his mouth, Daven's eyes widened in alarm. That was just plain stupid, he told himself. Stupid.

Fetch's face turned from tan to crimson to purple. "I thought I made it clear that you better keep your mouth shut!" the foreman bellowed as he moved back to his desk and nodded at Hallam, who stepped over to a shelf, grabbed a soot-covered lantern, and handed it to his boss.

At the same time and without being prompted, Bryce strode toward the windows and closed the thick inside shutters, leaving the door to the outside as the only source of light in the office.

Daven swallowed hard—he knew something horrible was going to happen...and it was going to happen to him. "You...you did make it...it clear, Sir," he stuttered. "I...I should have nev...never said that."

Bryce kicked at the outside door, and as it slowly closed and shut out the daylight, the dark-haired man snickered, "You're right about that."

Standing in the unnerving blackness, Daven waited...and waited...and waited. Then he heard the scrape of a match being lit, and in the sliver of light, he saw Bryce's fist—just inches from his face.

The blow landed on his left cheek and sent him to the floor.

"Ashby."

Daven looked up at the foreman, who was perched on the edge of his desk next to the now lit lantern.

"Do ya understand why it wouldn't be too healthy to talk to Leighton or anybody else?"

He nodded—grateful that his lesson was over.

"I don't think he understands yet, Mr. Fetch," Bryce countered, spitting out a glob of tobacco juice.

"Me neither," the blonde-haired Hallam added as he maneuvered his way behind Daven.

"Yes...yes, I do!" Daven shouted.

But it was too late—Hallam had already knelt on the floor and grasped Daven's shoulders, holding him steady as another punch came from Bryce. And another one. And another. Always to the left side.

Finally, the pummeling stopped, and Daven felt something glide across his face and drop to the floor. Unsure if it was sweat or blood, he glanced downward—and the red splatter told him all he needed to know.

"Remember this warning, Ashby," Fetch sneered, looming overhead.

"I...I will."

"I don't think he's gunna remember, Mr. Fetch," Bryce put in with a sly smile.

Daven's heart sank. Not again, he silently begged. Please, God, not again.

Fetch chuckled and, squatting, grabbed a handful of Daven's hair. "Well, maybe this will help ya remember," he said as he took his cigar and pressed the lit end closer and closer to Daven's face. "And, maybe, it'll put some color into those eyes too."

Feeling the heat of the menacing glow, Daven tried to pry himself free, but both Fetch and Hallam held him tight.

Grinning in obvious delight, the big foreman yanked the cigar away. "You're lucky I need ya to finish that desk."

With a sigh of relief, Daven ran his tongue over his lips—and tasted blood. Then he felt himself being hoisted up as Fetch moved to the outside door.

"Go to Everly's and get yourself cleaned up," the big man barked, pulling the thick wooden door open. "But be ready to come back to work on tonight's wagon."

Before Daven could reply, he was shoved into the blinding daylight, and, losing his balance, he fell to the ground.

"And keep your mouth shut, Ashby," the foreman growled, then slammed the door shut.

Slowly sitting up, Daven rubbed his swelling, aching face, trying to assess his injuries. A narrow gash above his left eye was most likely the source of the blood that now streamed across his face. Brushing away his soaked hair, he held his sleeve against the cut and tried to blink away his forming tears. Every inch of his soul wanted to run to Peter and tell his brother that he wanted out—that next Tuesday was just too far away. But he knew, in his heart, that he probably wouldn't make it to the showroom alive—and that he might endanger Peter if he did. Taking a deep breath, he pushed himself up and, with unsteady steps, started the very long trek to Everly's Boarding House.

As Daven trudged along and the hot July sun beat down on him, the blood on his face gelled, matting his hair against his forehead. He tried, more than once, to pull his long waves out of the gash, but he succeeded in only peeling off any clots that had formed. Suddenly, he started to hate the thick mane that had taken so much time to grow, and he wondered if Peter had been right all along—maybe, he should have gotten his hair cut before leaving Bradlee.

Shaking his head slightly, Daven struggled to keep his thoughts on his walk, but they kept drifting back to Peter. How would his brother react to this? he wondered. Normally, he was quite good at predicting Peter's actions, but after their recent meeting, he really didn't know what to expect. Then, as he massaged the left side of his face, trying to ease the throbbing, Fetch's remark came screaming back into his head...

'Don't go thinkin' that Leighton's prying is gunna help ya—or anybody else...that meddler's not gunna be around for long.'

As it did when the foreman first spoke the words, the statement rippled down Daven's spine. What would he ever do if he lost Peter? Shaking the notion from his head, he lifted his gaze upward and offered a silent prayer for his brother's safety. And, finishing his plea out loud, he whispered, "Please help us to get rid of Fetch and release everyone from his control...I just don't think we're gunna be able to do it—not without your support and guidance."

Finally reaching Everly's yard, Daven headed for the boarding house and staggered up the steps, all the while searching for his key inside his trouser pocket. Without warning, nausea washed over him, and holding onto the door frame, he rested his numb yet aching forehead against his arm.

"Daven?"

Uncertain if the voice was imagined or not, Daven ignored his name and slid the key from his pocket—then it fell from his grasp and hit the porch with a lifeless chinkle. Sighing mournfully, he bent down to retrieve it—and was immediately hit with a wave of light-headedness. Sitting down on the porch, before he keeled over, Daven leaned his head against the doorjamb and closed his eyes. And, as the pounding continued to beat against his temple, he couldn't help but wonder if this was how Peter felt during his migraine episodes. If it was,

Daven promised himself to never give his brother any grief during any headache ever again.

"Daven?"

This time he realized the voice was real—and whose it was. "Hey, Ivy," he mumbled, forcing his eyelids open.

Dropping her basketful of clothes on the porch, Ivy rushed to Daven's side and lightly stroked his face. "Oh, why'd they do this...your poor, handsome face!"

"Would you get my key, please?" he murmured. "I dropped it someplace."

Ivy picked up the fallen passkey and helped steady Daven as he pulled himself up. "Come to the wash room," she purred, wrapping her arm around him. "I'll put some water on to heat...maybe, you'll feel better when you get cleaned up."

He started to nod his head in agreement but stopped when the movement caused his head to swim. "And how much will this cost me?" he asked, thick with sarcasm.

With a humorless laugh, Ivy smirked. "I see you've finally learned all of Mr. Fetch's rules."

Titling his head slightly, Daven scrutinized Ivy's pouty expression. Evidently, she understood his predicament all too well. "Yeah...at least, I hope there aren't any more surprises."

She let out a small whimper in return and shoved the key into the lock. "Me too...but with Mr. Fetch, you just never know."

"Ivy?"

"Yeah?"

"Before I get cleaned up, I want you to do something for me."

"Anything."

"I want you to cut my hair."

"No, Daven, I love your hair," she cooed, caressing his sandy waves. "That's like askin' me to cut my own."

"Please? It's so hot and so heavy...I just want it gone."

"Okay...but you're makin' me feel like Delilah."

⇥ Six ⇤

Ivy groaned and picked her scissors up from the railing that bordered the back porch. "Are you sure?" she asked Daven, who sat on a crate with a sheet draped over his shoulders.

"I'm sure," he returned, holding an ice-filled towel to his battered face.

With a deep breath, Ivy ran her fingers through Daven's hair, then, pulling a handful upward, she sliced through it with the scissors. "Too late to change your mind," she murmured as she studied the severed lock in her hand.

"I'm not gunna change my mind…it probably should've been done long before this."

Opening her fist, Ivy started to let the sandy hairs fall from her fingers, but before they left her hand, her eyes lit up, and she stuffed them into her apron pocket instead. Then, as she combed her fingers once again through his thick mane and poised the scissors for another cut, she smiled giddily and tried to calm her pounding heart. No man, not even Travis Perryn, had ever kindled such passion and excitement within her. And she hoped that Daven felt the same about her—and that he was different than Travis…

Travis Perryn. He had promised her so much, then, just as every other man in her life, he used her and forsook her. After that betrayal, she had promised herself to never give her heart to anyone ever again. And she had kept that vow…until she saw Daven Ashby in the restaurant. Now, thoughts of Daven constantly whirled inside her head, prompting her imagination to etch out their future together—right down to the name of their third child.

"Why'd they hurt you?" she asked, brushing some of Daven's lose hair from his shoulders.

"Because I said something very stupid to Mr. Fetch."

Ivy laughed bitterly. "Well, he don't really need a reason to beat on somebody."

"So I've come to realize."

"Ain't you got anybody who can help you outta this?"

Daven released a deep exhale and lowered the iced towel. "I have a brother… but he can't help…at least not yet."

"No other kin?"

"My parents are dead," he returned with a shake of his head. "And, as for any other family, you could be a cousin, and I wouldn't even know it."

Ivy smirked and lightly slapped his shoulder. "Don't be funnin' me."

"I'm not…I don't know if I have any other kin."

"And how's that?" she prompted, unsure if he was teasing or being truthful.

"My father didn't talk much about his family…but he did tell me that he changed his name when he came to America."

"How come?"

"He didn't talk much about that either…I think he did something…or was accused of something…and was forced to leave Sweden…I'll never know."

Stepping around the crate, Ivy positioned herself in front of Daven to cut the last remaining waves of his long hair. "But what's that got to do with you and me bein' cousins maybe?" she asked, pressing her body close to him.

"Uh…well, he never told me what his name used to be…because of that, I have no idea if I have any aunts or uncles…or cousins."

"I don't think we'll have to worry," Ivy offered as she took a final snip with the scissors. "Unfortunately, I know all my kin…and there ain't a Swede in the bunch," she continued, then, backing onto the porch steps, she studied her barbering. Even with half his face red and swollen, Daven's muscular frame and handsome features were still a pleasure to look at. "What about your ma's family?"

He shrugged. "She died right after I was born...Pa didn't tell me very much about her side."

"I was wrong, my love," Ivy purred, leaning against the stoop's railing. "I like ya with short hair even better."

A wide smile parted Daven's lips, but a mournful cloud still cast a shadow over his countenance.

Returning to the porch, Ivy sauntered over to Daven and squeezed herself next to him on the crate. "Sounds like your pa had a pretty rough time of it."

"Yeah, he did...yet he was always so full of joy...even when he had to give up what he loved most—his traveling and carving—he still didn't complain."

"Why'd he have to give it up?"

Daven dropped the now dripping iced towel onto the porch's floorboards and started thumbing his left palm. "When Pa married my stepma, she wanted him to settle down and help run the general store that she and her son owned... so he did. He gave up his craft, and he put up with my stepbrother's badgering...all with a smile."

"Then why are you so sad?" she asked, grabbing Daven's hand and holding it tightly.

"I dunno...sometimes it's painful to...to remember."

"That's gotta hurt your pa."

Scowling, Daven shifted his position and peered into her eyes. "What do you mean?"

"I'm sure your pa's up there looking out for ya," she said, pointing up to the sky. "And it's gotta hurt him—knowin' that every time you think of him, you get sad."

Daven continued to study her face as his eyes filled with tears, then, tilting his head to the side, he wiped at them with the sheet. "Yeah, that would hurt him," he murmured, barely audible.

Gently and trying to avoid his bruises, Ivy grasped Daven's chin and lifted his head upward. "See?" she whispered as she stared at him and drifted away in his watery azure eyes. "There ain't no reason to be sad...about your pa anyway."

"That's right…thank you, Ivy," he added, and leaning toward her, he kissed her on the forehead.

The action wrenched Ivy from her daze, and before Daven could withdraw, she wrapped her arms around his neck and delicately kissed the welts on his face. Then, tightening her embrace, she pressed herself firmly to his lips, and as she continued to caress his mouth, Ivy felt Daven's strong hand clasp the back of her head and pull her even closer to him.

Clang. Clang. Clang.

The three-note message from the restaurant's bell pealed through the air, and Daven's embrace instantly slackened. Not wanting the thrill radiating inside her to end, Ivy dabbed a few more light kisses on his lips, then, regrettably, she drew back and sat up straight.

"What's the bell for this time?" Daven asked, pointing toward the restaurant.

"Huh?" Ivy returned absently, lost in the thought of being Mrs. Ivy Ashby.

"The bell…what's it for?"

"That's Mrs. Everly's signal…she prob'ly wants me to start gettin' things ready…the wagon'll be comin' in from the factory soon."

"You call her Mrs. Everly…you're not her daughter?"

Jumping up from the crate, Ivy faced Daven, her hands on her hips. "Sakes alive! No! Why'd you ever think that?"

"When I came yesterday, you called it 'our lovely restaurant.' I just assu—"

"That's insulting! If I was her daughter, I'd have run off years ago."

"Then why do you stay?"

Ivy averted her gaze, shrugged, and wrapped her arm around the porch post next to her. "Same reason you and everybody else stays."

Daven nodded his understanding. "Ain't you got anybody who can help you outta this?" he asked, echoing her own words back to her.

Ivy took a deep breath. Yes, she replied inwardly. She did have someone once—Travis Perryn. He had promised to take her along on his getaway, then he reneged. She had been so angry, so hurt, and so hopeful that he would send for her—then, after learning how Travis' escape had ended, her emotions melted into just sorrow. "Nah," she finally replied, "the closest kin I got is an uncle—and he ain't gunna help me outta this...not by a jugful."

Again, three clangs came from the bell.

"I better go," Ivy murmured, releasing the post. And, motioning at the boarding house, she put in, "The water's gotta be hot by now...you'd better hurry if you wanna get cleaned up before the others get here."

He nodded and pulled the sheet from around his shoulders. "Thank you."

Once more the bell sounded—and this time it didn't stop.

Ivy frowned, and looking as if she were heading for the gallows, she slowly descended the porch steps. "I'll come back soon and bring you your supper."

"You don't have to do that."

Reaching the bottom of the stoop, Ivy circled and gazed into Daven's sparkling blue eyes. "Yes, I do. It'll give you more time...and it'll annoy that woman to no end," she declared, jerking her head toward the incessant bell. And, blowing him a kiss, she hurried off toward the clanking.

Laying his Bible aside, Daven stretched out on his bed, closed his eyes, and tilted his head back against the warped headboard. Nothing, not even the Psalms' lyrical words, could stop the day's events from waging war inside his skull. Please make it go away, he silently begged—but he could barely hear his own prayer over the throbbing in his temples.

Suddenly, a quiet knock sounded on the door, and as uneasiness gripped his gut, Daven's eyelids snapped open. "Yeah?" he called quietly.

The door scarcely moved and a sliver of Jaxson appeared on the other side.

Relieved and surprised, Daven grunted. "You can come in—if you want to."

Jaxson pushed the door half open and popped his head inside the room. "I thought they killed ya," he whispered.

Daven smiled as much as his injured lips would let him. "No...not yet anyway...I have to finish the desk first...come on in."

Pulling back, Jaxson guardedly surveyed the hall, then, after a long hesitation, he entered and clicked the door shut. For a brief, awkward moment, neither spoke as Jaxson surveyed Daven's battered face. Then, finally, the dark-skinned man sighed and shook his head. "Man alive...you look awful."

"I know."

"They do that too?" Jaxson questioned with a nod of his head.

"What?"

"Your hair...they cut it?"

"No...I had Ivy do it."

Switching his weight from his right foot, to his left, and back again, Jaxson crossed his arms. "They havin' ya go back to work tonight?"

"Yep...I've finally joined the club," Daven returned, and encouraged by his coworker's uncommon willingness to talk, he slipped his watch off the bedpost and clicked it open. "We have some time before the wagon leaves," he offered, pointing to the foot of the bed. "Why don't you sit down?"

"Nah, I ain't gunna stay that long."

Exhaling in exasperation, Daven gestured once again to the bed. "Would you please sit? Starin' up at you is just makin' my head pound even harder." Then, as he moved his legs to the side, a tin plate sitting next to him clattered to the floor.

"Huh," Jaxson grunted as he stared at the fallen plate. "So that's why I didn't see ya downstairs...how'd you get supper up here?"

"Ivy."

Jaxson snickered and kicked at the dish. "She sure has set her cap for you."

"I suppose," Daven returned with a half-smile. It was true—Ivy's infatuation and, even more so, her intentions were quite obvious. But, after recalling her passionate kiss, Daven had to admit that he didn't mind being the object of her affections. "Have a seat," he offered again, motioning to the cleared place on the bed.

"I said I ain't gunna stay...I just came to...to just make sure you're still alive...and, uh, to thank you."

"Thank me?" Daven questioned happily—maybe some good was going to come out of his beating after all.

"Yeah…ya saved me from that," Jaxson said as he pointed to Daven's welts. "I dunno why ya did…but ya did…and I'm thankful."

"You're welcome."

"You knew I didn't care if ya got caught with your money, didn't ya?"

"Yep."

"But ya still didn't tell Fetch 'bout me swallowin' mine."

"Nope."

"Why? Why'd ya do that, Helpful?"

Daven shrugged. "I don't know…do unto others?"

Jaxson snorted, then glanced at the Bible lying next to Daven. "Yeah, I used to believe that…not no more."

"So I noticed…would you please sit down?"

"I told ya I ain't gunna stay," Jaxson replied with a shake of his head.

Daven smiled inwardly at his coworker's remark—especially since the man was making no effort to depart. Maybe he had finally broken through Jaxson's spiky husk.

"So why'd ya have Ivy cut your hair off?" Jaxson continued.

"It was just too hot."

"Well, by winter, you'll wish it was long again. There ain't no heat in here… you'll be glad to go to work just to get warm."

The statements rattled through Daven. Winter? he repeated silently as dismay and discouragement pressed down on him. He wasn't sure if he'd even make it to next week. Glancing up at his dark-skinned coworker, he asked, "How long have you been workin' for Rheinhardt Furniture?"

Jaxson peered at the ceiling for a moment, then shrugged. "About two years now."

"Two years?" Daven echoed, and as the thought shuddered through him, he grabbed his Bible and held it to his chest. He had just two sources of refuge— God and his brother…but at least he had those sources. If he didn't, he would be absolutely hopeless—just like Jaxson. Then, as he examined his coworker's sullen, desolate expression, he finally understood and forgave the man's apathetic spirit. "As long as you aren't going to stay, Jaxson…why don't you sit down?"

With a long exhale, Jaxson perched himself on the foot of the bed. "Yeah…I came north hopin' to find work—and got this…I was just a day laborer at first… that wasn't too bad. Then they hired me—that's when they started ropin' me in…it took about three months b'fore I knew I was trapped."

"Three months?" Daven murmured incredulously. "It took them less than a week with me."

"I know…they musta wanted you real bad."

"What do you mean?"

"They use different bait and traps for ever'body…but I never saw them pull in anybody as quick as they pulled you—"

A sudden, quick rap sounded on the door, silencing Jaxson in mid-sentence.

Frowning in bewilderment, Daven studied his coworker—who replied with his own puzzled expression.

"Who…who is it?" Daven called, his voice breaking with apprehension.

"Ivy…are ya decent?"

"Come on in, Ivy," he returned with a chuckle of relief.

"Mrs. Everly wants her plate back," she announced as she sashayed into the room, then, spotting Jaxson, Ivy stopped short, as if her foot had caught on a floorboard nail. "Why, hello, Jaxson! Payin' a house call?"

Gazing warily at the open door, Jaxson answered with a stiff shrug.

"Ya don't have to worry," Ivy teased with a grin. "Nobody's around." But, even as she was still speaking, she walked back toward the door and nudged it closed with her hip. Then, tousling Daven's hair, she smiled and cooed, "How are ya, Love?"

"Marvelous…can't you tell?"

"All I can tell is that you're gunna have quite a colorful face there…your eye's already turnin' purple."

Daven laughed mournfully and nudged himself toward the edge of the bed.

"Where do ya think you're going?" Ivy demanded.

"To get the plate for you," he replied as he pointed at the floor.

"You stay put," she ordered, squatting down and picking up the dish. "Did ya have enough to eat?"

"Yes. Thank you...I hope Mrs. Everly didn't give you too much of a tongue-lashing about bringing it up."

"She did...but you're worth it," Ivy chirped as she pulled an oily napkin from her apron. "I sneaked you some dessert," she continued, unwrapping the cloth to reveal a small piece of yellow-grayish cake.

"Thank you, Ivy!" Daven returned as he grabbed the crumbling dessert.

Draping the napkin over the tin plate, she smiled wide, causing her dimples to appear. "You take care of yourself tonight, okay? I don't wanna have any more bruises sullying up my beau's handsome face."

Although the movement pulled at his injuries, Daven still smiled and chuckled at Ivy—and her brassy comment. "Okay, I will."

"And you," she added, using the plate and napkin to point at Jaxson, "make sure he don't say any more stupid things to Mr. Fetch, okay?" Not waiting for a response, Ivy winked at Daven, grasped the door handle, and disappeared into the hall.

"What'd she mean?" Jaxson asked, tilting his head toward the back of the door.

Daven shrugged while breaking his lump of dessert in half. "Oh, I threatened to go to Peter Leighton about all of this," he said, holding out a piece of cake. "That's when they decided to row me up Salt River."

Peering at the cake, Jaxson grimaced and crossed his arms, then, warily, he reached out and plucked the gift from Daven's fingers. "That was a pretty stupid thing to say," he agreed with a slight laugh.

Immediately, Daven's eyes opened wide. It was the first time he had ever seen or heard even a glimmer of cheer coming from his coworker—Jaxson's shell was definitely cracking.

"Especially," Jaxson added after shoving a chunk of cake into his mouth, "when Fetch already hates your guts."

Startled by the remark, Daven sat up straight—suddenly feeling as if he were a bug trying to scurry away from Fetch's boot. "He what?"

"He hates ya…you can see it plain as mornin' every time he looks at ya."

"Why?" Daven questioned as he tried to calm his racing pulse.

"Well, first, 'cause you got more skill than he'll ever have."

"And second?"

Jaxson crammed the last of his dessert into his mouth, then tapped his temple. "Because ya got more up here."

Daven laughed. "I'm sitting here with fist marks on my face—and I'm the smart one?"

"Yeah, ya are…ya talk like a book sometimes…I've heard ya—and so has Fetch, and it puts him in a real pucker."

"Well, I'm not," Daven countered as he chewed on his cake. "If I were smart, I wouldn't be here."

"But ya talk like ya are."

"My brother's responsible for that…it's just the two of us now—so he's got no one to yap at but me…he said I was going to sound educated—whether I went to school or not. So I have to talk his way…or not at all."

Jaxson nodded slowly and lowered his gaze. "Least ya have somebody who cares enough to do that for ya."

"Cares?" Daven repeated, leaning back against the headboard. Was that why Peter continuously hounded him about his speech? Because his brother cared? That reasoning had never occurred to him, and Daven ruminated on it along with his dessert. He always figured that Peter's speech lessons were driven by control, not concern.

"Yeah, cares," Jaxson mumbled. "You're plumb lucky."

Staring at his coworker's dejected countenance, Daven shook his head. "Don't you have someone who cares?"

"Had a sister once," Jaxson returned with a shrug. "She's who taught me how to read—but her old man didn't think much of me. That's why I came north...and traded one hell for another."

"What if I teach you to talk better?"

"I don't want nothin' from ya, Helpful...there's no reason for it anyhow—talkin' good won't help me get outta here."

"Hasn't anyone ever tried to escape?"

"Sure...not too long ago, a fella named Travis Perryn tried sneakin' out one night."

"And?" Daven prompted, even though he already knew how the story ended.

"Fetch killed him—then made it look like ol' Travis got hit by an ice wagon."

"He must not have been very good at sneaking."

"Nah, that wasn't it. Travis had a pretty good plan, but he talked too much. It ain't safe talkin' to people around here...ever'thing ya say gets back to Fetch—somehow...I was plannin' on goin' with Travis, but then I didn't."

"How come?"

"Like I said, he talked too much...I knew he'd prob'ly end up tellin' the wrong person—and he did."

"What about going to someone for help...a patrolman or an alderman?"

Jaxson let out a cheerless laugh. "Just go ahead and try it—and you'll die. Fetch and Rheinhardt will find out...and they'll kill ya."

"Well, what about—"

"There ain't no way outta this mess," Jaxson cut in, shaking his head. "And your face is proof of that."

"Maybe," Daven replied. "Or maybe, you just have to believe that God's working on a plan to stop Fetch."

Although comforted by his own heartfelt statement, Daven realized that it did little to penetrate his friend's despair, and he wished he could tell Jaxson the truth—that within a few days Peter could turn everything upside down. But then his coworker's chilling warning crawled back into his thoughts…

'It ain't safe talkin' to people around here…ever'thing ya say gets back to Fetch—somehow.'

He knew, for Peter's safety and his own, that he needed to keep silent, yet he still wanted to give his friend a small taste of hope. "I think," Daven offered, carefully choosing his words, "that Mr. Leighton will make things right."

"Leighton's gotta be on their side."

"But what if he isn't?" Daven pressed.

"Doesn't matter…he can't do nothin'. He's alone—just like us."

"But we're not alone—the Lord's with us."

Jaxson frowned and rolled his eyes. "Jesus might be with you…but he ain't with me no more."

"Why do you say that?"

"After two years, you'll think the same thing…especially if He lets them take that away," Jaxson declared, motioning toward the Bible resting on Daven's chest. "I had one, but they took it…said a black man's got no business readin' anyhow."

Glancing at his Bible, Daven fingered the scarred leather cover and exhaled resignedly. In the past few days, he had come to hunger for God's Word—it was his only reminder that he wasn't alone. But now, after being allowed to look under Jaxson's flinty husk, he realized that his friend needed the reminder too. "Here," Daven said as he leaned forward and held out the Bible.

"I don't want it," Jaxson returned, pushing the book back toward Daven.

"It's just a gift from a friend."

"And I ain't your friend!" Jaxson yelled as he leaped from the bed and stomped to the door.

"Is that why you didn't tell me to swallow the money Mr. Leighton gave me?" Daven murmured, just loud enough to be heard.

As he reached for the door latch, Jaxson's shoulders instantly slumped. "I, uh, I reckon it is."

"It's all right, Jaxson...I underst—"

"No, it ain't all right," he cut in, shaking his head. "It's just that...that after you're in this place for awhile...you just get tired, Daven—too tired to care about anything...or anybody."

Clutching his Bible and swinging his legs off the bed, Daven stood and faced his coworker. "I understand—and it's okay...but you do realize, of course, that this means you have to take the Bible now," he announced, shoving the book at Jaxson.

"Why?!" the dark-skinned man demanded, bristling.

"Because...you just called me Daven, instead of Helpful...friend."

Half chuckling, half grunting in frustration, Jaxson peered into Daven's eyes. "You sure are a pain."

"Yep," Daven replied as he lifted Jaxson's arm and carefully placed the book in his friend's hand.

"But it's your Bible."

"And now it's yours."

"It's been a long time," Jaxson whispered as he carefully stroked the book's cover, "since I've even thought about God."

Bong.

For a moment, Daven stood motionless, trying to figure out the source of the odd sound that now resounded through his room, then the answer hit him—and his heart sank. "That's the bell, isn't it?" he moaned, sliding his watch into his vest pocket. "The one that means we have to go back to work."

"Yeah, we better get goin'," Jaxson mumbled. "Hey, Helpful?"

"Yeah?"

"I...I'm sorry...I should've told ya to hide your money."

Daven half-smiled and patted his friend on the shoulder. "It's okay," he offered cheerfully. But then, as he followed Jaxson out of the room and stepped onto the rotting floorboards in the hall, Daven's grin faded, and dread once again wrapped its arms around him.

Glancing upward, Daven sighed and rubbed the bruises on his face. Please God, he silently prayed, please don't forget about me…and please give me the strength to finish this mission…and please, please help us to rescue these poor souls from this nightmare.

Stopping just inside the hospital doors, Anna draped a shawl around her shoulders and adjusted the bodice of her worn, cotton work dress, then she sighed. When she agreed to meet Peter at the hospital, she had completely forgotten that it would be after hours and hours of work. Now, after knowing Peter Leighton for less than a week, he was about to see her at her drabbest.

"Oh, well," she murmured under her breath. "If he's going to be a suitor, he's going to have to accept you—even like this."

As she glanced out the window and caught sight of Peter leaning against a lamppost, Anna smiled and quivered in delight—until she spotted the twig in his hand, which he was carefully snapping into small bits. Recalling the quirk from their picnic, Anna wondered if she was the reason for his fidgeting…or was it one of the many subjects that kept him so distant? Swinging the door open, Anna took a deep breath and descended the few steps to the sidewalk.

"I guess it's my turn to be late," she called, heading toward the lamppost. "Please forgive me."

A boyish grin immediately formed on Peter's face, and he tipped his hat as she joined him. "That's quite all right," he returned. "My brother's given me more than enough practice at waiting."

"Has he arrived in town yet?"

Instantly, Peter's smile vanished, and he offered only a shake of his head as an answer.

Taking note of the sudden chill in her suitor's disposition and of the words that seemed to have caused the reversal, Anna lightly touched Peter's sleeve. "I hope you don't mind, but I told Papa that I would check on Mrs. Crawford—

one of his patients—on the way home…he said he could do it, but I thought I would save him the trip.”

“I don’t mind at all,” he replied as he extended his bent arm. “Shall we?”

With a pleased smile, Anna opened her parasol, then slipped her hand around Peter’s elbow. “It’s just down at the end of Third Street,” she said, gesturing toward the left.

As they strolled along the sidewalk, talking depthlessly about the weather, Anna noticed that Peter had returned to his methodical dissection of his twig. And, the more she observed the habit, the more it poked at her.

“What’s wrong, Peter?” she asked, then blushed at her own informality. She had been so used to calling him Peter in her thoughts that it automatically punctuated her question.

Dropping what was left of his stick, Peter patted her hand, but kept his eyes focused on the sidewalk in front of them. “I heard that,” he said with a teasing lilt. “I also heard it at the creek…and,” he added as he gave her a sideward glance, “I like it a lot better than Mr. Leighton.”

Anna felt the heat of a blush wash over her face, and she started to twirl her parasol to hide her nervousness. “So what’s wrong?” she asked, trying to move the discussion away from her impropriety.

“Nothing…I just have a few things on my mind,” he offered as he smiled and stroked her hand once again.

Although the facade appeared genuine, Anna still sensed a restlessness brewing inside her suitor. And, deciding that it was time to test her theory, she quietly asked, “Does it have something to do with your brother?”

Peter’s grip abruptly tightened around her hand, and deep lines of tension creased his forehead. “Why…why do you ask that?”

“Because you’re troubled.”

“What makes you think I’m troubled?” he questioned as he stopped and studied her.

“I know you better than you think, Peter Leighton,” she replied, “and I know that you’re troubled.”

"Fair enough…but why would you think that it has anything to do with my brother?"

"Because you become very distracted when you're reminded of him…why won't you be honest with me and tell me what's bothering you?" As her words floated away on the breeze, Anna's heart quickened and she bit her lip. Was now the right time to confront Peter about his secrets? And, if he finally did relinquish his silence, was she ready to hear them?

"Why…why won't I what?" he choked out.

Realizing that she couldn't retract her question even if she wanted to, Anna inhaled deeply and pressed onward. "Be honest with me…you've been keeping something from me—right from the start."

Immediately, Peter pulled away and refused to meet her gaze.

"I know you prefer to keep things hidden inside your heart," she began, "but you can trust me, Peter."

"It's not a matter of trusting you," he whispered, meeting her stare at last.

"Then what is it?"

Silence.

"I don't know if you think you're shielding me from something by not confiding in me," she tried, "but I feel useless as your…your…"

Exactly what was she to Peter? she questioned inwardly. She knew how she felt about him, but how did he feel about her?

"I feel useless as your friend if you don't allow me to help you," Anna continued, still unsure if she had chosen the correct moniker, "even if it's only to share what's troubling you."

As Peter peered into her eyes, all Anna could hear was his unsteady breaths and the faint ticking from the watch pinned to her lapel. He then gently embraced her hand and brought it to his lips for a light kiss.

"All right," he murmured, his jaw clenched with tension. "I just hope I'm not wrong in doing this…by telling you, I'm going to be placing my brother's life—and my own—into your care."

Anna swallowed hard as she steeled herself for Peter's revelation. Everything from 'my brother is wanted by the law' to 'I already have a wife and family' raced through her thoughts, and she wondered if she really was prepared to hear what he had to tell her.

"You see," he murmured, barely audible, "my brother is here in town…he's helping me—"

"Anna! Anna Spreyer!" a voice called from behind them.

Startled, Anna spun around—and frowned. Why now? she silently moaned. Of all the times and places, why did the approaching couple have to interrupt now? Trying to disguise her disappointment, Anna smiled and waved at the older couple crossing the street. "Mr. Keen, Mrs. Keen, how are you?" Anna greeted as the twosome joined them.

"Just fine," Mr. Keen replied with a tip of his hat.

"I'm so glad we caught up with you," his wife added as she eyed Peter.

Noticing the couple's interest in her suitor, Anna resigned herself to the intrusion and offered, "Mr. and Mrs. Keen, I'd like to introduce Mr. Peter Leighton…Mr. Leighton, this is Mr. and Mrs. Horace Keen."

After the three said their greetings, Mrs. Keen nodded slightly, then winked at Anna. "I'm terribly sorry for interrupting…but I just heard that you were looking for me at the open-air market, and I was wondering if anything was wrong."

"Oh, no," Anna returned. "Mama had wanted some honey, but Papa and I just arrived too late."

"Well, you can come to the house anytime for some, all right?"

Inwardly amused by Mrs. Keen's approving winks, Anna nodded with a grin. As much as she wanted to be upset with the Keens for intruding, she just couldn't be—it was the older woman's absence from the market that had set God's plan into motion…and allowed Peter's path to finally cross hers. "Thank you, Mrs. Keen…I will."

As the older couple said their good-byes and departed, Anna glanced at Peter, whose features were now clouded with apprehension. Was the moment broken?

she questioned voicelessly. Was her suitor going to retreat into silence once again? Unfortunately, there was only one way to find out. "Please, go on, Peter," she prompted, "you were saying that your brother is here in Sandorville?"

Peter's eyes darted from side to side, and he shook his head vehemently. "Not here, not now...there's too much of a chance to be overheard."

Taking hope in the fact that he didn't completely close the door to a conversation, Anna tried, "What if we walk to my house? We'll be off the main roads that way...and less likely to run into other people."

"I don't know..."

"That way you could stay for supper too."

Peter's jaw clamped down tighter, and he took a deep breath. "But you needed to stop at Mrs. Crawford's for your father."

"I'll go back and tell him I can't."

"No, I don't want you to have to—"

"It'll be fine," Anna cut in. Then, realizing that her suitor was on the verge of reconsidering his decision to confide in her, she added, "Please wait here...I'll be right back." And, before he could offer a reply, she turned and rushed back to the hospital.

Reaching the stoop she had descended just minutes ago, Anna closed her parasol, lifted her skirt slightly, and hurriedly stepped up to the hospital doors.

"Lord, what is he hiding?" she whispered as she entered. "What is grieving Peter so that he's afraid to talk about it?"

As Anna paused to catch her breath, the pungent odor that permeated every board in the hospital saturated her winded lungs. It had taken only a moment in the fresh air to erase the memory of the hospital from her senses. But now, standing once again within its staid, acrid interior, she was reminded of how downtrodden the soul could become, and she drooped under the weight of the trepidation that surrounded her—and Peter.

Wanting to return to her suitor and his struggles, Anna roamed through the wards of the hospital in search of her father. Half poorhouse, half infirmary, the Churches Cooperative Home and Hospital stored anyone and everyone, and as

Anna passed the sick, hurt, and destitute, her dread and dismay spread to every fiber within her.

"Liebchen?"

Relieved to hear her father's soothing baritone voice, Anna circled and hurried out onto the east-end porch.

"Oh, Papa, I'm so glad I found you," she said, giving him a hug.

"What's wrong, Liebchen? Didn't Herr Leighton come to meet you?"

Despite her cloak of worry, Anna still grinned at her father's question. She tried, over and over, to get him to use the English word 'Mister'—but he always refused...there were parts of Otto Spreyer's homeland that he just wouldn't give up. "Yes, he met me, Papa...but we've decided to walk home instead of visiting Mrs. Crawford. Is that all right?"

Doctor Spreyer studied his daughter and lightly caressed her cheek. "That's fine...what's happening?"

"I'm not sure, Papa, but I think Peter's finally going to unlock the door to his secrets."

As Anna and Peter strolled along in silence, the evening sun sprinkled the trees and houses with a warm glow and draped long shadows across the wooden planks of the sidewalk. At any other time, Anna would have credited her pounding heart to the slow-placed, romantic atmosphere and to the handsome man walking next to her, but tonight, she knew it was caused by something else—the anticipation of Peter's disclosure. Wanting to just grab her suitor and shake the truth out of him, Anna instead watched him absently roll his watch chain between his fingers and waited for him to offer the first words.

"I don't even know where to start, Anna."

"How about at the beginning?"

"The beginning? The beginning...I guess that would be the day my stepfather died...I never really knew how much financial trouble Tait had dug us into—until I started updating the books. We had debts up to here," Peter said, tapping the brim of his hat. "Poor Tait," he added with a grin, "bookkeeping was definitely not one of his skills."

Anna sighed contentedly and gazed up at her charcoal-haired suitor. The bitterness that had punctuated Peter's every word, just days ago, had melted from his voice. Now, listening to his deep and quiet tone, Anna tightened her grip around his arm and pulled herself closer to him.

"Eventually, all those we owed started asking for their money," he continued. "I tried everything to raise the funds...I closed the store and sold whatever I could get my hands on...we took in boarders, and I even started working an additional job...but none of it came close to what was needed."

"What about your brother? Couldn't he help you?"

"No. Daven's much younger than I am, and I wanted him to get an education...but trying to keep him in school was like trying to keep an eagle in a cage." With a deep breath, Peter paused, then shrugged. "That's when Karl Rheinhardt rescued us...as a favor to my late father, he loaned me enough money to clear up all our debts."

Sensing that it was as disheartening for Peter to tell the story as it was to live it and wanting to give him a brief reprieve, Anna quietly asked, "So were you able to keep your eagle in its cage?"

Peter chuckled and shook his head mournfully. "No...Daven tends to be a bit rebellious—all you have to do is look at the length of his hair to see that...I even tried giving him an ultimatum—either go to school or get a job."

"And?"

"And the next day, he became a lugger at a furniture factory...he'll never admit it, but I think he regretted that choice from the first day—until he was promoted to a carver's position."

"Is he a good carver?"

"I've never seen anyone who could match his work...give him a piece of wood and he's in his glory...but Daven needs to do things his way—just like Tait."

No longer concerned with the soft, disintegrating sun, Anna pulled her parasol closed and hung it on her arm. The maneuver also helped hide the smile that flashed across her face following Peter's remark, and she corrected him silently—*Daven needs to do things his way...just like his brother.* "Is that why you're here?" she prompted. "To pay Mr. Rheinhardt back?"

"Partly...it took a lot of years and Daven's—"

Curious as to why Peter had stopped in mid-sentence, Anna surveyed the area and spotted the cause—another arm in arm couple was slowly nearing them. "But what?" she tried, still not understanding the reason for his wariness.

Peter remained closemouthed until he and Anna exchanged greetings with the passing twosome. "This can't be very interesting for you," he offered with a shake of his head.

"Yes, it is," she returned, slowing to a stop. "Your past is a part of you, and I want to know it—so I can know you."

Peter said nothing. He just studied her with an expression Anna couldn't decipher and guided her toward a large maple tree, where he reached a hand around her waist, pulling her close.

As she gazed into her suitor's dark-brown eyes, Anna's heart began to flutter, and all her thoughts focused on him—and on the kiss she was sure was coming.

He stroked her hair and drew her even closer while tilting his head...then, without warning, a bicyclist sped by, bumping along the planked walkway, and Peter suddenly pulled back.

Anna released a deep breath of both disappointment and delight, and not wanting to let go of the moment...and maybe to persuade him to try again...she clasped his hand.

"We, uh, we should be going...I don't want to...to worry your mother by getting you home too late."

Trying to calm her racing heart, Anna nodded resignedly. "Yes, of course," she put in as they once again ambled down the walkway. "You, uh, you were saying?"

He let out a slight chuckle. "Um, where did we leave off?"

"You were talking about paying Mr. Rheinhardt back."

"Right, right…it took a lot of years and Daven's help, but I did, finally, pay Karl back—financially."

Although pleased to know the events that had shaped Peter's life, she was still puzzled by his somberness. "You've accomplished a lot."

"No, I haven't…I've done nothing but sail around in circles," he replied quietly.

"You don't give yourself enough credit," she tried. Then, remembering that Peter had stepped away from God, Anna realized that he had faced all his burdens by himself. He didn't have the comfort of knowing that he wasn't alone… and that, although difficult and laborious, his voyage did have a purpose. "Don't let all those things you suffered through tear you down, Peter—they built you into a strong person…and the Lord was guiding your sails, even though you don't think He was."

Peter just nodded.

"But I don't understand how any of what you've told me could place you or Daven in danger."

"No, that only set the stage for the favor we're doing for Karl now," he said as he halted and pivoted to face her. "Anna, what I'm going to tell you can't be told to anyone…well, I suppose your parents should know. I think they'd feel a little more comfortable about me if they knew…but please, please, don't let it go any further than that."

"All right," she gasped.

"You see," he went on in a whisper, "I owed Karl a lot more than money. He saved us from going to the poorhouse…he saved my family's name and dignity…he saved me from completely losing heart…and he continued to watch over us…when the factory in Bradlee closed and Daven lost his job, Karl agreed to sell some of my brother's carvings in his showroom. So, when he asked me for help, I couldn't say no."

"Help to do what?"

"To find out what's going on in his factory—and put a stop to it."

Forcing a smile, Anna averted her gaze. Although Peter had painted a pleasant depiction of Karl Rheinhardt, it was still difficult to picture the man as anything but a villain. "Are you sure that Mr. Rheinhardt isn't the source of the trouble?"

"He's not, Anna...trust me," Peter returned, embracing her hand. "The foreman, Quentin Fetch, is the one who's treating the men so badly...Karl isn't the source of the trouble, but he is to blame—in a way."

"What do you mean?"

"I keep telling him how Fetch is keeping the men's wages for himself and how he's created his own business using the factory's supplies. But Karl's so lost in grief that he just keeps turning a blind eye to any evidence that comes up."

"How...how do you know the foreman is keeping the men's wages?"

Peter took a deep breath and scanned the area for any passersby. "My brother's working in the factory and giving me the information I need to stop Fetch."

Anna froze, and twisting her hand out of Peter's grasp, she covered her mouth. "Oh, Peter! Daven is taking a big risk."

As his jaw muscles visibly tightened, Peter embraced her shoulders. "Don't you think I know that?" he asked in a hoarse whisper. "I'm the one responsible for putting Daven in there...if Fetch ever found out that he's my brother or that he's my witness to the goings-on in the factory, Daven could end up paying for it with his life...that's why you can't say anything...no one but Karl knows who Daven is or what he's doing—and no one can ever know."

Anna shook her head and a chill shivered through her. "But you could end up paying for it with your life too...I've seen some of the things that have happened to the factory workers...Mr. Fetch will do anything and everything to keep you from sharing the evidence you find." .

Peter released his hold on Anna's shoulders and stroked his mustache. "I never considered that."

"You never considered that you might get hurt?"

"I never considered that, by involving you, I might also be endangering you and your family...maybe we should stop seeing each other until this is over."

Stunned by the words, Anna's eyes began to water. The thought of not seeing Peter tore at her heart—and the thought of losing him to Quentin Fetch's brutality ripped it completely in half. "No, Peter, you are going to need allies that you can trust, even if it's just for spiritual support," she offered as she blinked back her tears.

"Your parents may feel differently."

"No, they won't...Papa knows some of what is going on in the factory already—he'll want to do whatever he can to help you."

Peter's brow furrowed. "How does he know?"

"Papa's treated the workers and their families...he's learned a lot from what they've told him—and what they haven't told him."

"Maybe he could persuade the men to come forth and—"

"He's tried, Peter, but they won't."

"Well, what if your father went to Karl and—"

"He can't," she cut in with a shake of her head. "He can't break his patients' trust."

As he blew out a long breath, Peter nodded. "And that's exactly why I need Daven in the factory...I need someone who knows exactly what's going on and who can tell me about it."

Realizing just how difficult and precarious Peter's dilemma really was, Anna sighed. "I understand." Then, seeing the agony of uncertainty on her suitor's face, she clutched his hands, not caring who might be witnessing the bold act. "God's in control—not Mr. Fetch. The Lord will guide you through this...trust Him."

Tightening his fingers around hers, Peter nodded again. "I have no choice but to trust Him...He's the only one who can keep my brother safe."

Carefully maneuvering between the machinery, Peter wandered through the factory, very aware that all eyes were on him—especially those of Quentin Fetch. And, through the haze of sawdust, which floated in the humid air and clung to the beads of perspiration on his face, he watched the wide leather power belts endlessly cycle from the overhead shafts, down to the machines, and then back up again. Finally, wielding his way to the bottom of the staircase, Peter continued to study the power belts and the exposed blades of the saws. So many naturally occurring dangers already loomed over the workers—proven by the missing fingers and mangled limbs of a few of the men—and having those hazards increased by Fetch's unnatural sovereignty more than explained the despondent atmosphere within the building. This needs to end, Peter told himself, and soon.

Turning toward the staircase, Peter grabbed the railing, then, out of the corner of his eye, he caught sight of a tan-colored blur heading directly for his face. Throwing himself against the wall, he felt the all-too-close breeze of a piece of lumber as it swung by, missing him by less than an inch.

"Sorry 'bout that, Mr. Leighton," the blonde-haired Hallam shouted as he tossed the board aside. "I didn't see ya...hope I didn't hit ya."

Gasping in relief and anger, Peter swallowed a mouthful of dusty air, and as he coughed his throat clear, he noticed that Fetch and Bryce were now standing, shoulder-to-shoulder, on the bottom step, blocking any access to the upstairs.

"Maybe you oughtta go back to your office," Fetch bellowed above the roar of the machinery. "You won't get your fool head knocked off there."

Knowing that he had just been given both a physical and a verbal warning, Peter shook his head. "I came to inspect the factory," he yelled, trying to project his voice over the screaming saws. "And I intend to do so—no matter what...now move, so I can go upstairs."

"No."

Peter raised an eyebrow. "No?"

Fetch's expression stiffened and he bit down hard on his cigar. "It's just the assembly room—nothin' up there worth seeing."

"I don't care...now move."

The foreman's features turned to granite, and he slowly raised his fist, then a devious grin formed on his face and he stepped aside. "Sure....go on up."

As Peter squeezed past Fetch and Bryce, a chill ran down his back along with several drops of sweat. He had learned to be very wary of Fetch's sly smirks, and he wondered what had caused the man's sudden turnabout.

With both the foreman and the dark-haired Bryce on his heels, Peter pulled himself up the last step, walked into the assembly room, and gratefully gulped in the cleaner but still humid air.

"I want ya to know that you're ruinin' a surprise for the Rheinhardts," Fetch announced as he and Bryce entered the room.

"How's that?" Peter returned, relieved that he could hear again without being shouted at.

"Well, since ya didn't like it when I had Ashby doin' deliveries, I put him to work on somethin' else...it was gunna be a surprise for Miss Rheinhardt's birthday," Fetch said as he pointed and chewed on his cigar.

Following the gesture, Peter looked to his left—and there it stood...what had to be the Hopewells' mahogany writing desk. Once again, the wily foreman had gained the advantage. "Where did you get the mahogany?" Peter asked, trying to appear unaffected by the desk or Fetch's smugness.

"Scraps from other projects."

His heart sinking in defeat, Peter forced himself to smile—the last thing he wanted was to give Fetch the chance to gloat over the win. Temporary win, Peter corrected himself. Although momentarily useless as a weapon against the foreman, the mahogany desk would, eventually, prove very helpful—especially after its arrival at the Hopewells' door. "I'm sure Miss Rheinhardt will appreciate the piece," he offered as he continued with his mock inspection and surveyed the upstairs.

"So are ya done wastin' our time?"

"If you two have things to do—please go right ahead," Peter replied. "I never asked for an escort in the first place."

"Maybe not…but we better just stay with ya," Bryce chimed in, pulling a pouch of tobacco from his shirt pocket. "Seein' as how you almost lost your head downstairs."

The foreman grunted in agreement and took a long puff on his cigar.

Tired of trading allusions and still not seeing his brother, Peter ambled over to the mahogany writing desk and nodded a greeting to Jaxson, who was busy attaching a piece of trim. Then, turning toward the carver's bench, Peter stared at the back of the man chiseling a piece of wood. He had finally found his brother…or had he? So much was familiar about the man at the window—and yet so much wasn't.

The worker was lean and broad-shouldered just like Daven…and he wore a shabby, mismatched suit identical to his brother's…and the man tilted his carving back and forth in the sunlight as Daven always did when he was checking his handiwork. But this worker had short hair and was stiff and lethargic—so very unlike his brother. Unsettled by the unfamiliar traits, Peter's jaw automatically clenched. Why would Daven cut his hair now? he wondered. Especially after their discussion that it was acceptable at shoulder length. And why wouldn't his brother turn around and give him the signal about meeting later at the market grounds?

"Mr. Ashby," Peter called loudly, hoping to grant Daven the opportunity to circle and show his face. "This desk isn't taking you away from the table samples that Mr. Rheinhardt wants, is it?"

At the sound of his name, Daven's shoulders instantly slumped, and setting his half-carved piece of wood on the bench, he moved to stand in front of Peter—all the while keeping his head bowed down. Then, as he straightened upright, he tapped his right temple. "No Sir, I'm working on them up here."

As Daven's features came into full view, Peter's heart dropped into his stomach. Somewhere beneath a layer of bruises was the left half of his brother's face.

Stop staring, Peter silently yelled at himself, knowing that he had to wipe the brotherly outrage from his expression. Stop staring before Fetch and the others begin to suspect.

"He didn't look like that yesterday," Peter announced, peering at the fore-man and jabbing his thumb toward Daven.

Fetch shrugged and chewed on his cigar. "What the mudsills do on their own time isn't my worry."

Peter's jaw clamped down tight at the remark, and he stuffed his hands into his pockets, hoping to hide the fury that trembled through them. "Mr. Ashby is an important part of this factory," he offered, trying his best to sound business-like. "And Mr. Rheinhardt is very impressed with his knowledge."

"So?" Bryce snorted as he pulled his pouch open and stuffed some of the tobacco into his mouth.

Angered by the snide interruption, Peter glared at Bryce—and at the scratches on the man's right-hand knuckles. Suddenly realizing that he was probably speaking to his brother's abuser, Peter's temper exploded, and he hissed between clenched teeth, "I wasn't speaking to you, Bootlicker!"

"What did you call me!" Bryce demanded, taking a step forward.

"Do you have a point to make, Leighton?" Fetch snarled as he grabbed his assistant and pulled him back. "Or do you just enjoy insultin' my men?"

Peter inwardly cursed himself for his uncontrolled outburst, and knowing that he had to curb his fury, he offered, "Yes...my point is simple, it will not help this company to lose Mr. Ashby or his skills, so I suggest you help him any way you can."

"Fine," the foreman growled. "Now, if ya don't mind, I'd like him to get back to work."

His jaw still constricted with rage, Peter nodded and reluctantly followed Fetch and Bryce toward the staircase. Then, pausing for a moment, he solemnly glanced back at his brother, who shook his head slightly in return. Peter nod-ded in understanding—although he had already surmised from the bruises that Daven wouldn't be able to meet with him that evening.

Leaning his chair backward, Fetch lifted his feet onto his desk and lit a fresh cigar. "We gotta get rid of Leighton—and soon," he declared, tossing the spent match at the spittoon.

"You got that right," Bryce mumbled as he rested against the sill of the window behind his boss. "And he sure didn't like seein' Ashby's face all beat up…you think he knows what's goin' on?"

Fetch nodded. "With him wantin' to check the books and always prowlin' around, I'm sure he's made some guesses—he ain't stupid…that's why he's gotta go…before he gets hold of any facts."

"I'll be glad to take care of that for ya," the dark-haired man muttered. "And I'll make sure he licks my boots before he dies."

The foreman grunted, then shook his head. "Not yet."

"But—"

"I said not yet…if Leighton was to die right now, I think the old man would lose his mind completely."

"So?"

"So, you idiot, he might do something stupid—like close the factory…you remember how loony he got after Junior died."

Bryce nodded. "Then what's the—" Without warning, the office door leading to the factory swung open, cutting him off. Then, as his blonde-haired counterpart entered the room, Bryce offered instead, "Well, it's about time!"

Hallam rolled his eyes and shoved the door closed.

"Maybe we should get somebody who ain't so slow, huh, Mr. Fetch?" Bryce teased under his breath.

"The job's all yours," Hallam snarled as he flung his coworker a vulgar gesture and walked over to the desk. "Of course, that'd mean you'd have to give up lollygaggin' around here all the time and actually work."

Eyeing Hallam from head to foot, Bryce chewed on his tobacco in silence, then, with a wicked grin, he spit out a wad of juice—which splattered onto the top of the blonde-haired man's left boot.

His eyes growing wide with rage, Hallam raised his arms and held his balled hands in front of his face. "Anytime, Bryce," he proclaimed.

With an impatient grunt, Fetch pulled his cigar from his mouth and knocked the ashes to the floor. Usually, he enjoyed watching his men play their daily game of baiting each other, but today was different. Today, the harassment grated on his already raw nerves. Today, he needed his men to direct their energies toward protecting the operation he had worked so hard to create. Today, he had to figure out how to stop Peter Leighton's meddling. "Enough! You two can finish when I don't need ya…now, what'd you find out, Hallam?" When no response came, Fetch slid his feet from the desk, causing his chair to bang upright. "Hallam!"

Casting Bryce a hostile sneer, Hallam lowered his hands and turned his attention toward Fetch. "Seems Ashby and Averill are becomin' pretty chummy," he replied as he used the desk leg closest to him to scrape the tobacco off his boot.

Fetch scratched at the stubble on his chin. "We'll have to put a stop to that…Averill's been actin' real ticklish lately…sorta like—"

"Like Perryn did right before he took off," Bryce cut in with a nod. "Yeah, I've seen it too."

"If Averill runs for it, he just might take the kid with him," Fetch continued, punctuating the words with his cigar. "And, as Leighton said, 'it will not help this company to lose Mr. Ashby or his skills.'"

Walking over to the spittoon, Bryce spewed out another glob of juice, then smiled wide. "You sayin' what I think you're sayin'?"

The foreman bobbed his head and stuffed the cigar between his teeth.

"But what about the Hopewells' desk?" Hallam asked as he lifted his stained boot onto the vacant chair opposite his employer and placed his elbows on his knee. "Can Ashby finish it alone?"

"If not, we'll just draft somebody else to help him…you find anything else out?"

Hallam snickered. "Ivy's set her sights on Ashby."

"That ain't news, Hallam," Bryce growled. "Everybody already knows that."

"Yeah? Well, does everybody already know that she went up to his room yesterday after supper?"

"She never gives up, does she?" Fetch chuckled, grateful that something had finally been said that brought a smile to his face. "You two better start figurin' out how you're gunna take care of Averill."

Bryce smiled and rocked back on his heels. "I already got that figured...and it'll work real good too...as long as Hallam gets better at swingin' a piece of wood."

His eyes narrowing, Hallam glared at his coworker. "Mr. Fetch said to scare Leighton, not hit him."

"I know," Bryce snorted. "Problem is, you almost did hit him...and speakin' of our favorite pest, whatd'ya wanna do about him, Mr. Fetch?"

"Don't touch him, Bryce...not yet. I'm gunna try and get the old man to fire him."

"And if that don't work?"

"Then he's all yours."

As he stepped into the post office and surveyed the gathering of people inside, Peter shook his head in frustration—obviously, he had picked the wrong time to question the postmaster. So now what? he inwardly questioned himself, glancing at the pendulating clock on the wall. Stay or go?

Knowing that he needed to fit more pieces into his ongoing puzzle, Peter sighed resignedly and worked his way to the opposite wall. They have to leave sometime, he reasoned. Yet, even though he agreed, he wondered which would dissipate first—the assembly or his fortitude.

"Why?" he chastised himself under his breath. "Why did you ever involve Daven in the first place?"

Not being able to find an acceptable answer, Peter tried to distract himself with the various postings tacked to the wall in front of him. But, no matter how hard he tried, the image of his brother's battered face kept drifting back into this thoughts.

"Oh, Lord, what have I done?" he whispered as he closed his eyes and rubbed his throbbing temple. "What have I done?"

"Why, Peter Leighton, this is a surprise!"

At the sound of the all-too-familiar voice, Peter's eyelids snapped open, and his mood sank even deeper. "Miss Rheinhardt," he said, turning to face her. "It is indeed a pleasure."

A wicked smile parted Lorelei's lips and she leaned forward. "You're such a liar, Peter," she hissed into his ear. Then, standing back upright, she tittered out a laugh, tapped his arm with her parasol handle, and stated in a much louder tone, "The pleasure's all mine, Sir."

Peter rolled his eyes—Lori couldn't even say a simple greeting without her usual theatrics. "I hope you're well," he offered, not being able to think of anything else to say.

"No, I'm not," she returned in a voice that only he could hear. "It's been a terrible day…I tore my dress on the carriage this morning, the reception decorations aren't ready yet, and I had to make that silly girl at the millinery redo my new hat…and now, to end this day of misfortune, I get to see you."

Peter frowned and massaged his forehead. "And I, you."

Pursing her lips in anger, Lori forced out a sweetened laugh, then pulled him to the far corner of the post office. "Father tells me that you're bringing someone with you to my reception," she said, making sure no one could overhear their conversation. "Is that true?"

"Yes, I am."

"Well, I hope the whore knows how to behave outside the bordello."

As a wave of pain shot through his temples, Peter's jaw clamped down tight. The last thing he needed was another animosity-filled battle—especially when the one with Fetch was still ringing in his ears. "It's nice to know," he replied, thick with sarcasm, "that your father didn't waste his money by sending you to that expensive finishing school…at least they taught you some manners."

Lori giggled at the censure, then her countenance hardened. "Speaking of wasting my father's money...why are you loitering around the post office when you should be at the showroom earning your money?"

"To tell you the truth, Lori," he wearily returned, "I don't really think that it's any of your business."

A savage sneer immediately formed on Lori's face, marring her delicate features, and she smacked her parasol handle against Peter's arm. "Well, you are wrong, Mister!" she seethed, hitting him again. "Everything that goes on at Rheinhardt Furniture is my business—especially when a persuasive scoundrel tries to worm his way into a partnership."

Grabbing the carved parasol handle before Lori could strike again, Peter stared into her smoldering, dark-green eyes—and he realized that he would always be at war with her. Although all the Rheinhardt children were adored by their father, Lori was unequal to her brothers in one very important area—the family business. And, because of that prejudiced but true fact, Peter knew her jealousy would constantly fight against anyone who became a son in Karl's eyes. "You know what, Lori?" Peter replied, pushing her and the parasol away. "I have no desire to become a partner in Rheinhardt Furniture...none at all."

"You are such a liar...you just want to steal my father's company so you can make up for the one you lost," she fumed, then, noticing that their conversation had attracted the attention of two women, Lori giggled and forced a coy smile onto her face. "I look forward to seeing you at the reception, Mr. Leighton," she declared with mock sweetness.

Grateful that their discussion had been interrupted, Peter genuinely grinned. "Goodbye, Miss Rheinhardt."

Wiggling her fingers at him, Lori offered, "Until Friday." She then hurried over to the women, grabbed their arms, and pulled them toward the door. "Sarah! Nadine! I was hoping to see you two...I just have to tell you what Mary plans to wear to my reception."

As he let out a deep breath of disgust, Peter scanned the inside of the post office. For the moment, it was empty—except for Lori and her companions.

Realizing that the respite would probably be short-lived, Peter approached the postmaster's counter and addressed the young clerk opposite him. But the boy didn't answer—he just leaned on the wooden counter with his head propped up on his hands, ogling Lori Rheinhardt.

"Excuse me," Peter tried again, tapping the boy on the forearm.

"Ain't she the prettiest thing you've ever seen?" the clerk mused with a dreamy simper.

Peter looked behind him and gazed at Lori. A lapeled and cuffed walking suit of emerald silk hugged her tightly at the waist. From there, the fabric split and flowed over a bustled, brocaded underskirt, and a matching, high-standing hat crowned her outfit. Between Lori's elegant ensemble and her stunning features and jet-black hair, she was, admittedly, a gorgeous woman...on the outside. But that picture was now marred by the ugliness that Peter had witnessed within her. "No," he returned quietly. "I know of someone even prettier."

As the three women started to leave, Lori flittered a wave to both Peter and the young clerk and disappeared.

Waving absently to the empty spot where Lori had stood, the boy slowly returned from his trance. "Yes Sir, how can I help you?"

"I would like to speak to the postmaster."

"He's not here right now, Sir. He's at the depot sending off a mailbag on the Kalamazoo route."

Peter rubbed his temple—all that time, waiting for no one. "When do you expect him to return?"

"Half hour or so...I'm Henry, his assistant...can I help you?"

Shrugging and not wanting his trip to be a complete waste, Peter nodded. "I hope you can...my name's Peter Leighton and I just started working for Rheinhardt Furniture."

"Boy, are you lucky," Henry sighed.

"How's that?"

"You get to see Miss Lori all the time...I'd give anything to trade places with ya."

"Yeah, I'm real lucky," Peter returned with a sarcastic laugh. "Anyway…if you had a letter come in for Rheinhardt Furniture, but it was addressed to a person that you didn't know—for example, me…what would happen to the letter?"

"We'd probably give it to them anyway…they'd return it if they didn't know who it was for."

"What if it was addressed to Samuel Kelly instead?" Peter asked, carefully watching for a reaction.

Henry squinted and started to snicker. "Those letters are different."

"Then you've had mail come through with his name?"

Chuckling again, the clerk shook his head. "No Sir, never have."

"But you said those letters were different…who told you they were different."

Henry's smile faded. "I just meant that he doesn't exist…okay?"

"But how would you know that he doesn't exist unless you—" Peter tried, but he cut his question off when a young farmer and his three children entered, followed by two businessmen. "Well, thank you, Henry…maybe I'll come back when the postmaster is here."

"Suit yourself…but he won't be able to tell ya anything."

As he circled and moved toward the door, Peter reflected on Henry's 'those letters are different' response. Could the boy be part of Fetch's ever-evolving enterprise? he wondered. He had to be, Peter silently answered himself—the young clerk's statements were just too odd for him to be completely innocent. Making a mental note to add requestioning Henry to his list of 'must dos,' Peter walked out of the post office, lowered himself onto the bench outside the building, and massaged his aching head.

It had only been a week—one very long week—since he had stepped over the threshold of the Rheinhardt Furniture Showroom. The plan had been so uncomplicated then…come to Sandorville, discover the thief in Karl's midst, then move on. He never believed the mission would be easy, but he never thought he would run into so many…so many complications either. He had never thought that Karl might close his ears to the truth and excuse every fact given to him…and he never thought that the chore of stopping Quentin Fetch would turn into a fight of life and death...and he never thought that he would meet such a beautiful and captivating woman as Anna Spreyer and that he'd want to stay in Sandorville to court her.

⇒ Seven ⇒

Peter paused, and glancing over his shoulder, he frowned. He had been walking for what seemed like hours and the post office was still visible behind him. Obviously, the pounding in his head was slowing down his physical capabilities along with the mental. Forcing himself to continue onward, he squinted blankly at the sunlit planks of Second Street's sidewalk as he passed over them, growing more and more nauseated with each step. Maybe, he should just go to the hotel instead of trying to return to the showroom, he reasoned. He could always send a messenger to tell Karl of his illness. Then, as he reached the corner of Second and Main and watched an overcrowded horsecar lumber along its rails, he sighed resignedly. Just like the poor horse, he also had to keep forging ahead. Daven was depending on him, and headache or no headache, he was not about to let his brother down again.

Stepping into the road, Peter waited for a clearing so he could cross. As he studied the traffic, he realized that the horsecar driver had no intention of yielding to anyone—including the vehicles already in the intersection. Suddenly, the other teamsters and drivers came to the same conclusion and moved their vehicles to avoid being hit by the heedless horsecar—which generated an immediate clog of horses, wagons, and carriages. Shaking his head, Peter dashed across the road and headed down Main Street, gladly leaving the tangled mess in the hands of the angry teamsters.

"Herr Leighton!"

At the sound of his name, Peter circled and noticed a small, covered black carriage trying to wiggle free from the traffic jam. Recognizing the husky bearded man holding the reins, Peter smiled and called, "Hello, Doctor!"

Finally managing to pull out of the congestion, Doctor Spreyer steered his buggy to the side of the road and reined his horse to a stop. "Where are you heading, Herr Leighton?"

"To the Rheinhardt Showroom."

The doctor nodded and slid over on the carriage seat. "Come...I'll be passing right by Oak Road."

Peter started to refuse, but the throbbing in his head forced him to agree, and stepping into the carriage, he squeezed himself next to the stocky doctor.

Edging slightly more to the side, Doctor Spreyer chuckled. "There used to be a lot more room in this rig."

Smiling at the comment, Peter bobbed his head. "Yes Sir...and I believe it's the smaller carriages that shrink the most."

With a laugh and a few German words, the doctor lightly tapped his horse with the reins and pulled the buggy back into the street. "I hope you don't mind," Doctor Spreyer began quietly, "but Anna told us about you...and your brother...and the task that you've both undertaken."

"No, I don't mind...I told Anna she could tell you and I'm glad she did."

"And don't worry, it'll remain only with us," the doctor added.

"Thank you."

"It's a very noble—and dangerous—thing that you're trying to do."

"And, I'm beginning to believe, hopeless," Peter murmured, bowing his head.

"Why?"

"Fetch's operation is like a hornet's nest—a huge, nasty hornet's nest that keeps getting bigger and nastier...when I agreed to help Karl, I thought it was just someone using his equipment and supplies for their own profit...now, I'm finding out that it's much, much more than that."

"Then why don't you go to the City Marshall?"

"Because I have no real proof—except what my brother's told me...and you know, as well as I do, that no one is going to corroborate his claims."

The doctor sighed deeply and nodded. "Ja."

"I'm even having trouble getting Karl to believe me," Peter added, removing his hat and rubbing his eyes. "If I could get his undivided trust, then I could probably talk to the Marshall."

"I don't understand," Doctor Spreyer replied as the buggy crossed over Third Street and rattled over the road's wooden-block paving. "Why won't Herr Rheinhardt believe you? That's what he asked you to do."

Squinting to shut out the bright sunlight, Peter glanced sideward at the doctor. "Karl's mind isn't...isn't what it used to be."

"Ah...that would be difficult," the doctor agreed while continuing to steer the horse and carriage along Main Street, whose surface had now become rutted and dirt-filled.

"And I have to keep reminding myself not to use his senility to my advantage."

The doctor's brow furrowed. "What do you mean?"

"Well, with a carefully worded phrase or two, I could probably get Karl to do anything I wanted...but I can't do that to him."

"That's because you are a kindhearted man."

"No, I'm not," Peter returned, once again rubbing his temples. "If I were truly kind, I would get rid of Fetch the easy way...so my brother and the other men would be free of him."

Doctor Spreyer's eyes narrowed and he stared at Peter. "And what would be 'the easy way,' young man?"

"Convince Karl to fire Fetch, then find someone trustworthy to take over as foreman."

"Why not do it that way?"

"Because that would be like just knocking the hornet's nest out of the tree—all it really would do is anger the hornets...Fetch would retaliate and Sandorville wouldn't be safe for Daven...or me...or An...uh, anyone else that I care for...we would have to leave town...and I don't...I don't want to do that."

"You're not making sense," the doctor put in, shaking his head. "Why would any of that make you an unkind man?"

Peter released a deep breath. How could he explain to the father of the woman he wanted to court that his motives were purely selfish.

With a discerning glint in his eye, the doctor studied Peter from head to boot, then, guiding the horse onto Oak Road, he reined the animal to a stop. "If this 'easy way' was really the best route to help the factory workers," he offered, speaking in a whisper, "you would take it—even if it forced you to leave town. I'm quite sure of that—because you are a kindhearted man…but deep in your spirit, you know it's not the right path, because Herr Fetch would still be free to manipulate and hurt whomever he pleased…only prison bars will stop that man…and you know that too."

Peter nodded at the doctor's lengthy but sound reasoning—reasoning that would have taken his headache-plagued mind hours to figure out. "I reckon so…I'm just not sure that I'm the right man for this mission anymore."

Shifting positions on the carriage's cramped seat, Doctor Spreyer patted Peter's forearm. "God's sure…that's why He brought you here, Pay-ter."

Peter grinned at the German pronunciation of his first name, then he glanced sideward, realizing that it was the first time the doctor had used it. "I hope you're right, because I'm not going to be able to do this without His help," he offered as he donned his hat and pushed himself from the carriage.

The doctor slid to the center of the seat, then leaned toward Peter. "The Lord didn't bring you this far to leave you."

Overcome by a sudden rush of nausea, Peter supported himself on the buggy's roof and rested his head on his arm.

"What's wrong, Son?" the doctor asked as he quickly alighted and moved next to Peter.

"It's a headache," he replied, massaging his temple. "One of the worst that I've had."

"Why don't you come to the hospital and let me look into it."

"No, that's okay…I get them all the time."

"That's even more of a reason to let me examine you."

Peter stood upright and shook his head slightly. "It won't do any good, Sir. I've seen lots of doctors, and they've all said the same thing—it's migraine and there's nothing that can be done to help."

"That is the general consensus, but I don't agree with it," Doctor Spreyer said with a deep exhale. "It's true—we don't know the cause or the cure, but I believe there's something, somewhere, that can help your symptoms...we just need to find it."

Completely dumbfounded, Peter stared at the doctor's gritty, determined countenance—no other doctor had ever given him even the slightest amount of hope or cared enough to want to search out a remedy. "Thank you, Sir...if everything works out and I get to stay in Sandorville, I'd like to take you up on your offer...but for now, I have to get back to work."

"Get in...I'll drive you."

"No Sir, it's not that far."

"Pay-ter..."

"I'll be fine, Sir."

"You're a very stubborn young man," Doctor Spreyer chuckled, patting Peter on the shoulder. "You'll fit into our family with no problem...and it's Otto—all my sons-in-law call me Otto."

Once again, the doctor's statement caught Peter off guard, and his brow crinkled in consternation. Ever since his father's death, he had stopped thinking of himself as a member of a family. He had become a patriarch...a protector...a provider...an outsider standing guard over a small household while never being a part of it. Nothing, not even Karl Rheinhardt's actions, could break through the estrangement—until now. With a few generous words, the doctor had blotted out the alienation and allowed him to feel whole again. "I, uh, I have to go," he croaked out, not being able to think of anything else to say.

"Will we see you at the party tonight?" the doctor inquired as he climbed back into the coach.

"What party?"

"To say good-bye to Marion and Michael—they're going home to Grand Rapids tomorrow...we'll understand if you're not up to coming."

Peter removed his hat and drew his sleeve across his sweaty forehead. He vaguely remembered being told about the gala during supper the night before, but the throbbing inside his head made the invitation a blur. "I'll come...for awhile."

"All right, see you then," Doctor Spreyer called as he steered the carriage in a wide arc and headed back toward Main Street.

Replacing his hat, Peter turned, and while the doctor's words replayed themselves in his head, he started trudging toward the showroom. Suddenly, his pained mind stopped on one phrase, and he repeated it over and over, trying to decipher its meaning. "'All my sons-in-law,'" he murmured aloud. Was Doctor Spreyer also giving him permission to court Anna? Still deep in thought, Peter shoved the showroom door open, and as the overhead bell sounded his entrance, he stopped—and so did Quentin Fetch, who was in a heated conversation with Karl.

As he eyed Peter, Fetch whispered a few more words to his employer, then he turned and strutted toward the door. "Leighton," the foreman growled as he passed.

"Fetch," Peter returned, echoing the big man's contempt.

"Peter, where have you been?!" Karl called from the far end of the showroom.

Snickering, Fetch pulled open the showroom door and said, "Seems the apple of Rheinhardt's eye just fell from the tree." And, before Peter could respond, the barrel-chested foreman stepped over the threshold and onto the sidewalk, chuckling all the while.

With a sigh of discouragement, Peter removed his hat and hung it on the stand next to the doorway. Then, gathering up all the perseverance that his headache would allow, he reluctantly walked over to his visibly upset employer.

"I've been doing what you hired me to do," Peter whispered as he joined Karl and sank onto a chair. "I've been investigating the irregularities in your company."

"Is that so," the older man returned, tapping his boot on the floor. "Lorelei came by earlier to inform me that you were loitering around the post office."

Too tired and too pained to be offended by the implied accusation, Peter nodded. "I was waiting to talk to the postmaster."

"Why?"

"Don't you remember? When I spoke to the Hopewells, they said that they contacted Samuel Kelly through only the mail—at this address...I just wanted to get an idea as to how Fetch winds up with Kelly's mail."

"And did you?"

"I have a suspicion that the clerk has something to do with it, but I'll need to ask a few more questions before I'm sure."

"And that took you all day?!"

Tiring of the wishy-washy interrogation, Peter scooted his chair backward slightly and rested his head against the wall. "No, I also visited some of your fellow businessmen."

"Now, why in Sam Hill would you do that?"

"I wanted to get their perspective of Rheinhardt Furniture."

Still thumping his boot on the floorboards, the older man placed his hands on his hips. "And?"

"They were very complimentary of you and your foreman...but they also wondered how your crew of 'thieving drunkards and unruly rogues' could produce such beautiful furniture."

"Well, I guess that shows what a great foreman Quentin really is."

Peter sat upright, shook his head, and retorted, "You mean what a great liar he is, don't you?" Then, lowering his voice, he added, "My brother has told me about your workers...the majority of them are immigrants and family men...the only rogues are Fetch and his henchmen."

"You just won't leave Quentin alone, will you?!"

"Is that what he was doing here? Complaining about me?"

Karl nodded. "He said that you are disrupting things at the factory."

Placing his elbows on the table in front of him, Peter propped his throbbing head on his hands and massaged his temples. "I wish I could," he murmured with a sarcastic lilt.

"And he said that you are very disrespectful of him."

"Anything else?"

"Yes…Quentin told me about the desk."

"And what, exactly, did he tell you?"

"That it was a surprise for Lorelei's birthday."

Slowly, Peter looked up and examined his employer's skeptical expression. "And you believe that? It's the desk that the Hopewells ordered."

"Quent wouldn't lie to me."

Peter shook his head incredulously—although he couldn't see it, somewhere, under the ruggedness, Fetch obviously possessed a very persuasive charm…a charm that enabled the man to manipulate Karl like a marionette.

"And he's right," the older man continued, lowering himself onto the chair next to Peter. "You shouldn't go over to the factory so much."

"Shouldn't go?!" Peter echoed as both shock and outrage fought inside him. "And what else did your puppeteer tell you to say to me?"

Karl's expression tensed and he pointed his finger at Peter. "Don't use that tone with me…I told you before—I trust Quentin."

"I thought you cared about making things right at the factory."

"I do care, but—"

"But what?" Peter interrupted. "Why did you ask me here if you weren't going to listen to me? Was it to solve the problem at the factory or to replace your son?" As he heard the question exit his mouth, Peter clenched his jaw shut. Once again, a migraine attack had loosened his tongue and caused him to speak without thinking. "Sir, I apologize…I never meant to—"

Karl reached out and motioned for Peter's silence. "Don't."

It was then, as the older man refused to hear the apology, that Peter knew his question held some truth.

Slipping his shaking hands into his pockets, Karl cleared his throat and offered, "I do want any wrongdoings at the factory stopped, but I want proof that Quentin is involved…proof—not words. You have told me things and Quentin has told me things…if you want me to believe you—show me that Quent is lying to me."

Kneading his temples, Peter tried to calm the hammering inside his head. "When I go back to Crestfield on Tuesday, I'm going to call on the Hopewells too…and if that same desk—the one my brother is working on and the one Fetch just told you is for Lori—is in their library, you'll have all the proof you need…but if you want me to show you the truth, you'll have to come with me."

"I'll go…I'll give you the same chances that I'm giving to Quent."

Peter studied his employer, and deep within the man's tired eyes, he saw a hint of the Karl he used to know. Prompted by that spark, he added, "But the only way you're going to know that it is the same desk is if you see it…while it's still in the factory."

Instantly, the spark melted away. "In the factory?"

"It's the only way."

Karl took a deep breath. "No, it isn't…I'll go to Crestfield with you and look at the desk that is delivered to the Hopewells…I'll know if Daven carved it or not."

Unsure if he should be wallowing in defeat or celebrating in victory, Peter peered at the older man and asked, "And what if it ends up being the same desk? Will you be willing to get the police involved then?"

The older man's shoulders sagged as he considered, maybe for the first time, the possibility that his cherished foreman had deluded him all along. "Yes."

"Even if it would result in Fetch going to jail?"

"Yes."

With a sigh, Daven set his elbow on the table, and placing his chin on his hand, he looked at his plateful of lumpy, semi-hot food, then at Jaxson who sat opposite him, then out the window. "Come on," he declared as he stood and grabbed his supper dish.

"Whatd'ya doin'?" Jaxson asked, alarmed.

"Going outside."

"But we're not s'posed to—"

Ignoring his friend's argument and the stares from his other coworkers, Daven moved to the warped restaurant door and pulled on the faulty latch. Immediately, as if it were tattling on his forbidden exit, the rusted overhead chime clinked out its call. For a moment, Daven stood motionless. Should he continue his trek to the sunny outdoors and possibly face a reprimand? he voicelessly asked himself. Or should he stay inside and slowly die from his greasy, tomblike surroundings? With a shake of his head, he laughed at himself—he was definitely working too hard if he had to think about that answer.

As he walked into the warm evening glow, Daven surveyed the front yard and headed over to a gnarled maple tree and the carpet of grass that lay under it. Muffling a groan, he lowered himself onto the ground and leaned against the tree. Finally, he could breathe again...and maybe now, he could stomach the gray mounds on his plate. Reluctantly, Daven lifted a forkful of beans to his mouth—and without warning, a shadow drifted over him. Dread immediately shot through him, and he slowly looked up, praying that he would not see Quentin Fetch's barrel-size chest or Leland Bryce's icy black eyes.

"Jaxson?!" he exclaimed, exhaling in relief and astonishment.

"You sure don't like bein' cooped up, do ya, Helpful?"

Daven inwardly smiled at Jaxson's continued use of the nickname 'Helpful'—at least now, it was spoken in friendship, instead of contempt. "Nope. Never have," he returned as his friend settled onto the grass next to him. "My father and I used to travel a lot...as a kid I never spent more than a month in one place. I guess it just stuck with me...sometimes, I think the day my pa had to give up being in the open was the day he started to die."

Shoving his now cold beans into his mouth, Daven chewed on both his supper and his last statement. Then his earlier conversation with Ivy slipped back into his thoughts, and he realized how much time and effort he had wasted on remembering his father's death—and how little he had spent on remembering the man's life. "But now," Daven finished, trying to imagine his father in the peace of Heaven, "my pa's free...he can go anywhere he wants to."

Laying his plate on the ground, Jaxson scanned the yard, then he raised his index finger to his lips and grinned. "Me too," he whispered, still examining the area for unwanted listeners.

"You too what?"

"I can go anywhere I want to…I'm gettin' outta here."

Daven chuckled at his friend's joke. "Right…can I come too?"

Jaxson shrugged. "I only got money to get me a train ticket…but after I get out and if I can get a real job—one that pays—I'll try to help ya."

Instantly, Daven stopped laughing and peered into his friend's blazing brown eyes. "You're not joking, are you?"

Jaxson shook his head.

"Where'd you get enough money for any kind of ticket?"

"Around…ya wouldn't believe how much money people drop and don't bother to pick up…sometimes, I don't come here for supper. I just stay in town and go around pickin' up all those coins for me."

"Doesn't Fetch or Bryce or Hallam wonder why you stay in town?" Daven asked as concern for his friend's safety began to tie his guts into knots.

"Nah…they followed me at first, but I pretended that I was goin' to the gospel church I used to go to…after that, they stopped carin' where I went."

"And Fetch has no idea that you have this money?"

"Nope…by swallowin' it, nobody knows…and when I 'ventually get it back, I keep it hid real safe," Jaxson returned, making another search for eavesdroppers. "That nickel I got yesterday finally gave me enough to go…so I'm goin'."

Daven swallowed hard and tossed his plateful of half-eaten food on top of Jaxson's dish. "You can't, Jax…they'll kill you, just like that Travis guy."

"No, they won't…b'cause I'm not gunna make the same mistakes as him… he had a big mouth. Me? I haven't told nobody about my plans, 'cept you…and Travis thought he could get away by just walkin' along the railroad tracks. Me? I might be walkin', but only as far as the next town…then I'm usin' my money and gettin' on a train."

"When…when are you planning to do this?" Daven croaked as fear gripped his throat.

"Friday...Fetch'll be at some party, so I'm goin' and nothin's gunna stop me...I ain't gunna miss the chance to get outta here."

"You can't go," Daven tried. "You just can't...they'll still find out and kill you."

"They ain't gunna find out...'less you tell 'em."

Daven sighed, trying to find the words that would keep his friend from making such a daring, dangerous, and—if Peter's timetable was correct—unnecessary escape. "I'm not going to tell anyone, Jax...but please, just wait...wait until next week...after Tuesday everything could be different."

"Why? What's gunna happen Tuesday?"

His eyes widening in horror, Daven shook his head. In his desperation to sway Jaxson, he had carelessly spilled some of his secret. Now, could he sponge up the mistake without his friend noticing? "I just meant that I think Mr. Leighton might be able to...to make things right again."

"Whatd'ya know, Helpful?"

"Nothing...I, uh, I just think he'll be able to make changes."

Staring deep into Daven's eyes—something most people couldn't do—Jaxson's countenance suddenly electrified. "You know him, don't you?!"

Daven shuddered—obviously, his efforts to clean up his earlier blunder only made it worse. "Who?"

"Leighton...you know him."

"No...no more than you do," he murmured, trying to hide the trembling in his voice.

A knowing smile gradually parted Jaxson's lips and he nodded. "Yeah, you do...at the showroom, after he took you to that other office to look at that table, he called you Daven."

"Well, that's my name."

"Yeah, but it was Mr. Ashby up 'til then...and he said the name real easy, as if he's said it before."

"That doesn't mean I know—"

"And he didn't have to give us that money, but he did—and he gave you more."

"Jaxson, it still doesn't—"

"Then, today, when he saw your bruises, he was—"

"He was surprised," Daven cut in, his heart racing. "That's all…I mean, he just saw me yesterday, and there weren't any bruises then."

"Nah, I got a good look at Leighton—better than Fetch or Bryce did—and what I saw on his face could only come from somebody who cares—really cares. Like…like kin." As he said the word, Jaxson's eyes widened and his mouth fell open. "He is kin, ain't he?! He's the brother you were tellin' me about."

Amazed by his friend's quick deductions, Daven sat dumbstruck, unable to think of even a denial. What was he going to do, he asked himself, now that his bucket of secrets had been overturned? Could he trust his newfound friend? Jaxson trusted him—the revelation of the man's upcoming escape was evidence of that. But could the trust be returned?

"You can't repeat that to anyone," Daven finally whispered as he glanced around, making sure he and Jaxson were still alone.

"You've been tellin' him stuff too, ain't ya? What do you two think you're gunna gain?"

"Freedom from our misery," Daven replied as he tilted his head toward the boarding house.

"You're both loony…it's Rheinhardt's factory—nothin's gunna change."

Daven sighed as he scrutinized Jaxson's unconvinced yet slightly uplifted countenance. Then, praying that Peter would understand, he decided to bring his friend into their alliance. "Mr. Rheinhardt doesn't know a thing about our treatment," he explained. "It's Fetch—all of it is Fetch."

"Uh huh…and Rheinhardt just walks around not knowin' about any of it."

With a smirk, Daven just nodded.

"If that don't beat all," Jaxson said, falling silent.

Suddenly, Daven's heart began to flutter, and he started to wonder if he had made a terrible mistake. Why did Jaxson reveal the details of his imminent getaway? Daven inwardly questioned. Was it really out of trust? Or was it all a hoax to spur him into dribbling out his secrets? He could still hear Peter stressing, over and over, to keep their plan confidential. Rubbing his left palm, Daven gritted his teeth as Travis Perryn—and the fact that someone had betrayed the poor man—wandered into his thoughts. Please God, Daven voicelessly pleaded, don't let Jaxson be the Judas here.

"So you really think the two of you are gunna beat Fetch?" his friend asked, finally pulling away from his reflections.

Daven licked his dry lips. "You said, a long time ago, that Peter couldn't do anything because he was alone…well, he's not alone."

"You and him, huh?" Jaxson laughed.

"Yep. And God…and…"

Jaxson's eyes narrowed. "And what?!"

"Well, if one can chase a thousand…and two can put ten thousand to flight…just think what we can do with three."

"We can fill three graves—that's what we can do," his friend hissed as he stood.

"Jax, we can use all the—"

"Shut up!" Jaxson cut in as he gestured to the approaching Ivy. "Your girlfriend's coming."

Glancing over his shoulder, Daven watched Ivy approach. "Maybe she's bringing us more cake."

Jaxson grunted, then offered under his breath, "Don't be includin' me in your plans, Helpful…if Fetch is goin' down, I want to live to see it happen."

"I still think that it's a wonderful idea, Otto."

With a long sigh, Doctor Spreyer dropped his meatless chicken leg onto his plate and wiped his hands on his napkin. "Michael, between my house calls, the hospital, and my office here, I don't have the time to start my own clinic."

"But that's exactly why you should…you wouldn't have to waste your time at that disgrace called a hospital or traveling miles to see a patient."

"I don't consider it a waste of time," the doctor returned gruffly. "Those people need my help."

Frowning, Anna peered at her brother-in-law. Michael Nealy was, most of the time, a pleasant enough man, but when he started one of his lectures about the joys of being moneyed, he became as boorish as his speeches. Throughout their evening meal, her brother-in-law kept trying to persuade her father to 'pursue the more upscale cases.' And, with every rejection, Michael fought harder to ram the suggestion down her father's throat. Luckily, within a couple of hours, the setting sun and darkening clouds would dissolve their outdoor party, and Michael's mission would come to an end—at least for this day.

"And you rarely get paid enough to feed your horses, Otto."

"That's my choice."

"If you don't start your own clinic," Michael pressed, "the other doctors are going to end up getting all the best patients."

"Best patients?" the doctor repeated, scowling. "I'm a doctor...my best patients are the ones who need me."

"The best patients are the ones who don't pay you with pumpkins and ears of corn!"

"Michael John Nealy," Doctor Spreyer shouted, smacking his hand on the table, "it is not the time to discuss my patients' finances."

Anna shook her head. Her brother-in-law's full name said it all—Michael had finally succeeded in making her father lose his temper. What would happen, she silently questioned, if Michael followed through with his earlier announcement and really did partner with his boss and open a jewelry store in Sandorville? How would her father cope with Michael around to pester him every day? And how would she cope with Marion constantly twittering and gossiping around town?

Hoping to distract Michael from his current tirade and herself from the impending jewelry store, Anna rose from the table and asked, "Would anyone like some lemonade?"

The joyful shouts from the children and the grateful nods from the adults made it more than clear that almost everyone was ready for something new.

"Would someone help me clear these dishes first?"

"I can help you, Anna dear."

"All you need," Michael persisted, oblivious to the interruptions, "is to buy that empty lot next door...it would be perfect for a clinic of your own."

Anna frowned once again. Not only did her diversion fail to quiet Michael, but it was Marion who had volunteered to help her with the dishes.

"Michael, Papa has a place of his own already," Anna tried.

"I'm talking about a real clinic—not a tiny room built onto the kitchen."

As her brother-in-law continued his crusade, Anna piled up most of the dishes from the tables and carried them into the house.

"Papa sure can be stubborn sometimes," Marion said, following Anna inside.

Rolling her eyes, Anna set her stack of plates in the right-hand washtub of the dry sink. "He's not the only one."

"Michael is only trying to help Papa keep pace with the other doctors, especially those in Grand Rapids."

"How can you say that, Marion? You know how hard Papa works to keep his knowledge above par."

"I'm not referring to his skills," Marion returned, sliding her three plates next to Anna's stack. "I'm referring to Papa's income…he should get paid for all he knows—and paid well."

"That's no one's business but his."

"Well, if he doesn't think about himself, he should think about Hans… and you."

Puzzled, Anna turned and faced her sister. "What are you talking about?"

"A clinic would be a wonderful place for Hans to start practicing medicine…and for you to be a nurse."

Tensing at the direction the conversation had taken, Anna moved over to the cupboards that lined the side wall, and opening the door to a tall, narrow compartment, she pulled out a large wooden tray and placed it on the counter. "Marion, Hans may have plans of his own—as I do," she offered, hoping to detour the conversation she saw barreling toward her.

"Do you mean that silly notion of going to Belding and working in a silk mill?"

"Maybe," Anna answered as she removed some glasses from the cupboard above her and set them on the tray.

"Or are you referring to your hopeless fantasy of marrying Peter Leighton?"

Anna winced and almost dropped the glass she was holding. She never considered, that by derailing one unpleasant discussion, she'd plow head-on into an even more dreaded discourse. Groaning at her own carelessness, Anna pulled out the drawer to her right, and as she hunted through the utensils for the ice pick, she waited—knowing that it wouldn't take Marion long to ask the inevitable question…

"So where is Mr. Leighton anyway? I though you said you invited him to come by tonight."

Anna paused in her search for the pick and considered the question—and her answer. She, too, was wondering why Peter hadn't arrived yet, but she knew she couldn't admit that to her sister—not after what Marion had put her through in the past week. "He'll get here when he gets here, Marion," she finally replied as she spotted the ice pick and slid it from the drawer. "Papa said that Peter wasn't feeling very well, perhaps he just went back to his hotel."

"So it's Peter now, huh? My, we've come a long way in a short time."

With the pick in her hand, Anna walked over to the icebox and replied truthfully, "Yes, I guess we have." Then, as she pushed the refrigerator's lid back and started to chip away at the block of ice inside, her thoughts drifted to the bouquet of flowers that Peter had surprised her with at the open-air market. Had it really been only five days since their paths had crossed? Even though her mind knew the answer was 'yes'—the devotion in her heart made it feel as if it had been five years.

Why did their romance bloom so fast? she wondered. Were she and Peter rushing things? As Anna continued to question herself, a stillness suddenly washed over her, and a theory she hadn't considered before drifted into her head. Maybe, it wasn't their doing, she surmised. Maybe, it was the Lord's. Maybe, God had quickened their relationship because He knew Peter needed the love and support of a family to press on with his mission.

"Fortunately, once Michael and I leave," Marion said, settling onto one of the kitchen chairs, "you can stop pretending that your little prophesy has come true."

Her anger rising at her sister's accusation, Anna stabbed at the ice block harder and harder, then she stopped, remembering her mother's words...

'All the girls' needling can't change what God's put into motion. Eventually, they'll have to admit they were wrong.'

Scraping the ice chips onto her apron, Anna circled and carried them to the tray, where she dropped the shards into the glasses. "Why don't you just admit that I was right about Peter?" she asked, wiping her hands on her now chilled apron.

"Right about what? That God told you that he was the one?" her sister giggled sarcastically. "Why don't you admit that you just made it all up—and that you're really a hypocrite."

"A what?!"

"A hypocrite...you always said that you wouldn't have anything to do with Mr. Rheinhardt or anyone that carried out his commands...now, you're going to a reception at the man's house—with his hand-picked assistant."

"You don't understand, Marion," Anna explained as she snatched up a pitcher of lemonade from the counter and slammed it onto the wooden tray.

"Oh, I think I—"

"First of all, dear sister," Anna cut in, barely controlling her outrage, "God did tell me that Peter was to be a part of my life, and that was long before I ever knew that he worked for Mr. Rheinhardt...secondly, Peter's working on getting—" Studying her sister's expression, Anna stopped in mid-sentence. Even if she went against Peter's wishes and told Marion about his mission, she realized that it wouldn't matter—her sister would believe only what she wanted to believe. And, knowing that, Anna's wrath melted into dispassion.

"Working on getting what?" Marion prompted.

Suddenly, a knock rattled on the front screen door and Anna sighed—even if it wasn't her suitor on the stoop, the interruption still came at the perfect time. "Why don't you take the lemonade outside," she said, closing the icebox. "And I'll see who's at the door."

"Anna, you shouldn't—"

Ignoring the rest of Marion's retort, Anna hurried toward the front door. Then, as she caught sight of Peter's tall, strapping frame on the other side of the screen, she smiled, and her concern about his absence evaporated. He hadn't forgotten…he was uninjured…all was well. Or was it?

"Peter?" Anna called quietly as she pushed the screen door open and saw his agony-ridden countenance. "Papa said you weren't feeling well…but you look awful." And, as her face turned crimson from her bluntness, she added, "I'm sorry, I didn't mean it that way."

Peter held up his hand and grinned weakly. "It's all right…I feel awful."

"Come on," she urged, grabbing his arm.

"Anna, I…I can't join the party…I just came to tell you that I—"

"I'm not taking you to the party," she interrupted. "I'm taking you to Papa's office so he can help you." And, before Peter could refuse, Anna pulled him over the threshold, down the hall, into the kitchen—and right into her sister's claws. "Marion!" she exclaimed at seeing her sister still dawdling at the kitchen table. "I told you to take the lemonade out to the others."

"I wanted to see who was at the door," her sister returned, lifting her chin upward. "Hello, Mr. Leighton."

"Hello, Mrs. Nealy…how are you?" Peter mumbled, then, without warning, he wavered and grabbed a chair to keep his balance.

"Ah, at least now, we know what caused your tardiness," Marion sniffed. "Exactly how many taverns did you visit before you decided to join us?"

Her eyes growing wide with embarrassment and infuriation, Anna stomped to the kitchen door and shoved it open. "Marion! The ice is melting…take the tray outside. Now!"

With a huff, her sister whipped around and snatched up the loaded tray. "And what should I tell the others?" she asked as she moved toward the outside door.

"You can tell them the truth—that Peter's ill and that Papa needs to come in and see him right away."

With an expression of regret—and a little suspicion—Marion glanced at Peter. "My apologies, Mr. Leighton," she murmured and exited with the lemonade.

"Anna, I didn't mean to cause any problems," Peter mumbled, rubbing his temple, "or dampen your sister's party…why don't I just go back to—"

"You're not going anywhere," Anna broke in as her concerns refocused on her suitor's well-being. "You can barely stand as it—"

"What's wrong, Liebchen?" Doctor Spreyer questioned, rushing breathlessly into the kitchen. Then, seeing Peter, he announced, "That headache's even worse…isn't it?"

Peter sighed and nodded slightly.

Stepping over to the doorway to his right, the doctor pointed into the adjoining room. "Come into my office, Pay-ter."

"I don't want to take you away from your guests, Sir."

Doctor Spreyer chuckled. "My boy, right now, I need the repose of my office as much as you do," he returned, once again motioning to the room.

Anna grinned at her father's remark, realizing that Michael must have continued with his bombardment after she and Marion had left the backyard.

"Liebchen, some water please."

"Yes, Papa," she announced as Peter, thankfully, yielded to the doctor's wishes and shuffled through the doorway.

"Sehr gut," Doctor Spreyer murmured, following his patient inside the office.

Hurrying to the cupboards, Anna grabbed a small cup, then, moving to the dry sink and washtubs, she furiously worked the pump's handle, filled the glass, and headed into the office.

"Do you need anything else, Papa?" she asked as she set the water in front of Peter—who was now leaning on her father's work table, barely able to hold his head up.

"Nein, that's fine," the doctor returned, stepping over to the first of three large glass-fronted cabinets. "At this point, Pay-ter," he continued as he scanned the assorted bottles and boxes on the shelves, "the only thing that will relieve your pain and let you sleep is a strong dose of laudanum."

Knowing full well what her father's next words would be, Anna turned and slid out the top drawer of the bureau opposite the work table. "This one should be fine," she declared, grabbing a striped nightshirt and handing it to Peter.

"What's this?"

"A nightshirt."

Peter's brow crinkled and he pushed the garment away. "I...I can't...what if...if Daven needs me?"

With a unconvinced grunt, Doctor Spreyer unlocked the cabinet's glass door and removed a small brown bottle from the bottom shelf. "After you take this laudanum, you'll be in no condition to do anything but sleep," the doctor declared as he walked to his work table, carefully measured out some of the liquid, and mixed it into the water. "Now, let Jesus take care of Daven—and let me take care of you...drink."

Reluctantly taking the glass, Peter swallowed the water and medication. "What if it doesn't work?" he questioned.

Doctor Spreyer chuckled again and gave Peter's arm a fatherly slap. "It will...now, both beds have clean linens, so take your pick, and I'll see you in the morning...Liebchen, are you coming?"

"I'll be out in a minute, Papa."

Grumbling under his breath, the doctor eyed Anna, then Peter. "Three minutes, young lady," he finally agreed, returning the bottle to the cabinet and locking the doors. "I will be on the back porch waiting for you."

Surprised and pleased that she had been given permission to remain with her beau—even if it was for only three minutes—Anna smiled and slowly slid the glass from Peter's hand. "I'll say a prayer for Daven tonight."

"Thanks," he murmured as he removed his hat and frock coat and tossed them onto the chair next to the first bed. "I...I'm worried about him...they hurt him."

At the sight of her suitor's muscular arms, which were now quite visible under his cotton shirt, Anna's heart began to rush. Then, realizing what he had said, she shook her head slightly and focused on Daven's plight. "I'm so sorry...was he taken to the hospital?"

"I...I don't know...I don't think so...they need him too much to hurt him that badly."

Setting the cup on the table, Anna moved closer to Peter and gently stroked his face. "I know how worried you are about Daven...I'll definitely keep him in my prayers," she soothed. "I...I have to admit, when you didn't show up for the party, I thought something had happened to you...or that you didn't want to come."

"These headaches can knock me down pretty fast...but I wasn't going to let anything stop me from seeing you," he returned, taking her hand and kissing her palm.

Her beau's touch sent an exciting yet comfortable quiver through her, and in return, Anna brushed her fingers through his thick dark hair. Slowly, Peter reached his hand behind her head and leaned forward. Then, as she felt the firm but gentle touch of his lips on hers, Anna wrapped her arms around him and closed her eyes, enjoying the warmth of his embrace.

"Liebchen!" her father's voice boomed from veranda. "It's time that we return to the party."

Reluctantly, Anna pulled back. "I have to go."

Peter bobbed his head imperceptibly and fingered the curls on the side of her face. "I wish..."

"What?" she whispered.

"I wish everything was over, and I could court you properly."

Anna wasn't sure if it was Peter or the laudanum speaking, but his words still sent a blush through her body. "This is proper enough for me."

Leaning in for another kiss, Peter's balance faltered, and he raised a hand to his forehead.

"You'd better lie down," Anna said as disappointment, concern, and elation all whirled within her. "I'll see you in the morning." Then, grabbing the empty water glass from the work table, she reluctantly exited the office and walked through the kitchen, stopping at the washtubs, where she deposited the cup. "Oh, Lord," she murmured, gazing absently out the window. "I know it's been just a few days, but I love him so much...please, help him through these battles."

⇥ Eight ⇤

Breathing in the crisp morning air while buttoning his waistcoat, Peter headed toward the doorway that led to the Spreyers' kitchen, then, as he rounded the half-open door and saw Anna and her parents sitting at the table, he paused and surveyed the peaceful scene. Platefuls of cold meat, cheese, hard-boiled eggs, and fruit-filled bread covered the breakfast table, and a large kettle of steaming coffee sat near Doctor Spreyer, who, between mouthfuls, was reading aloud from the Bible. Sitting next to her husband and nodding at his words was Mrs. Spreyer, and opposite her parents…was Anna.

Illuminated by the gas-powered lights and the glimmer of dawn peeking though the kitchen windows, Anna's youthfulness and innocence seemed to almost glow on her face. And her radiant long locks—which were usually hidden within a loop of silk netting that hung at the nape of her neck—now cascaded down her back like a golden waterfall. Holding onto the edge of the propped-open door, Peter smiled in contentment. He had never known anyone so beautiful, both inward and outward, and he longed to hold her and kiss her once again.

It was then, while he studied his heart's desire, that he noticed the waiting plate and flatware on the table next to her. Was the vacant seat and place setting meant for him? he wondered as his spirit soared. The gentle German family had become so dear to him, and every fiber of his being wanted to have the chance to become a part of it. But was that possible? Could he join them without putting them into Fetch's sights?

Besieged by question after question, Peter backed away from the doorway and leaned against the chest of drawers behind him. How was he going to win against the devious foreman? And how was he going to keep Daven and Anna and her family safe? As if answering, Doctor Spreyer's baritone voice drifted into the office and saturated the room with the Psalm he was reading. Listening to the accented rendition, Peter realized that the doctor was reading from an English Bible, not the family's German Bible that they had used in church. Warmed by the thoughtfulness of the gesture, Peter found himself drawn to the text even more, and he closed his eyes as it filled his ears.

"...though I walk in the midst of trouble, Thou wilt revive me: Thou shalt stretch forth Thine hand against the wrath of mine enemies, and Thy right hand shall save me..."

As Peter silently repeated the words, a whole new barrage of questions began to beat on his skull, and with a tired but determined resolve, he pulled the office door fully open and stepped into the kitchen. "Good morning, everyone," he offered as he approached the table.

"Guten Morgen!" the doctor announced, pointing to the empty chair next to Anna. "Sit down, my boy...there's plenty to eat."

Now knowing that the place setting was indeed meant for him, Peter sat and nodded in thanks to both God and the doctor. "Thank you...very much."

"Are you feeling better, Peter?" Anna asked as she passed him the meat-filled dish.

"Yes...much," he returned, almost forgetting why he had spent the night in the office. "I appreciate everything you did for me, Doctor...usually, my really bad headaches hang on for days."

"You're quite welcome."

"I, um, I heard what you were reading just a minute ago," Peter continued, sliding a piece of meat onto his plate. "Is it true? Can God really take care of Fetch and preserve us at the same time?"

Doctor Spreyer nodded and poured some of the steaming coffee into Peter's cup. "Absolutely."

"And will He make it possible for me to stay in Sandorville as I want?"

"I don't know…you need to talk to Him about that."

"And then what?"

"And then, if it's His will, He'll make it possible for you to stay."

"If it's His will? Then what's the use of talking it over with Him?"

"Pay-ter, the Lord is very generous," Doctor Spreyer replied, patting his Bible. "He gives us the freedom to blaze our own trails—and that's why we must talk to Him…to get His guidance about the way we should go…and if we choose according to His will, our path will be richly blessed."

"And what if we choose to go the wrong way?"

"God can still make good happen from bad choices…our lives may take a new direction, or we may have to endure a bumpy detour…but He'll somehow get us back to the route that He intended for us—especially if He needs us to accomplish something specific."

And that, Peter silently admitted, was exactly where he had been—on a detour, aimlessly trying to get somewhere that he probably shouldn't be going to in the first place. It had been years…and years…since he had consulted God before making a decision—he had just blindly plowed through life on his own. What blessings had he missed while on his bypass? he wondered. And was he now on the path that would be richly blessed? Maybe, it was time, he told himself. Maybe, it was time for him to allow Jesus to pilot his rudder.

Realizing that he had all but forgotten Anna and her mother, Peter smiled sheepishly and started to fill his plate with the bounty set on the table. "I apologize, ladies…I didn't mean to dominate the conversation."

Anna grinned and gently touched Peter's arm. "Don't worry about us…it's good to hear you ask questions about the Lord, rather than, uh…"

Peter chuckled while Anna, apparently, searched for a euphemism for his stubborn refusal to discuss the Almighty. "Rather than turning a deaf ear?" he teased.

"Those are your words, not mine," she returned with a laugh. Then, handing him the boiled eggs, she asked breathlessly. "Then you're planning on staying in Sandorville?"

Glancing at Anna, then her mother, then the doctor, Peter nodded. "I'd like to...I'd like the chance for both Daven and me to be able to stay in town—and be free from Quentin Fetch."

"Then that's what we'll pray for too," the doctor put in.

"But how will I know if it's what God wants?" Peter asked, warmed by the Spreyers' support.

Doctor Spreyer closed his Bible and smiled. "He'll let you know...in His time."

Anna bobbed her head in agreement, then pointed at Peter's cup of coffee. "Would you like some sugar?"

Peter answered with a nod, and as Anna rose, he stood and watched while she stepped over to the cupboards and grasped the sugar bowl. Maybe, it was the blush of the morning light...or maybe, it was Anna's simply decorated dress of blue...or maybe, it was her stunning, slim figure, which the cotton dress seemed to enjoy hugging...whatever it was, his sweetheart had never looked lovelier. And, having seen the kindness and gentleness that dwelled within her soul, he knew that he wanted to walk his chosen path with her at his side. Of all the women he had pursued, only Anna reached out to help lighten his burdens—the others had just added to them.

As the morning meal continued, Peter listened to and occasionally joined in with the Spreyers' lively discussions about the rain that had fallen during the night...and about Marion and Michael's departure for Grand Rapids...and about where the doctor's calls would take him. But, as much as he tried, Peter couldn't stop his thoughts from repeatedly drifting to his brother's recently barbered hair...and all that Daven had endured...

"Pay-ter?"

Shaking himself from his thoughts, Peter stared at the doctor. "I'm sorry, Sir...I didn't hear what you said."

"I have an early call in town…would you like to ride in with me?" the doctor repeated.

"Yes, I would…I need to talk to Karl. I keep losing my temper with him, and it's only making things worse."

"We can leave anytime you're ready," Doctor Spreyer said, pushing his scraped-clean plate toward the middle of the table.

Slowly, Peter wiped his mouth with his napkin. There would never be a better time to make his request, he told himself…but that fact still didn't stop his dread. "I need to ask you something first."

"Ja?"

"Actually, it's a…a question for…all three of you," Peter stammered as he absently fingered some spilled sugar into a neat little pile.

"What is it, Peter?" Anna asked, placing a warm hand on his.

"I thought about this all yesterday—as much as that headache would let me—and I didn't want to have to ask…I thought I could handle it myself… but…but I can't. I…"

Anna's grip tightened around his fingers. "What do you need?"

"Help," he murmured with a hard swallow. "I've got to talk to my brother… but it's too risky to meet where we used to."

"What can we do to help?" Doctor Spreyer asked.

Brushing aside his pile of sugar, Peter inhaled deeply. "I'd like to meet him here…in your barn or maybe your office."

"Well, of course you can—"

"No Sir, you don't understand…it could be very dangerous, for all of you, if Fetch ever found out that—" Stopping in mid-sentence, Peter closed his eyes and shook his head. It had taken far too long for him to admit that he needed help, but was endangering the Spreyers the best way to get that help?

"We will help you."

Immediately, Peter's eyes sprang open, and he looked at the source of the words—it was the first time that Anna's mother had ever spoken directly to him.

"Do you realize what could happen?"

Mrs. Spreyer nodded.

"Now, since that is settled, tell us what we can do," Doctor Spreyer announced.

"You don't have to do anything—just let us meet here on...with the Rheinhardts' reception, it's going to have to be Saturday."

"Will it be okay to wait until then?"

"It should be," Peter returned with a nod. "The project Daven's working on is due for delivery on Monday...they'd be stupid to do anything before then...they know, as well as I do, that no one around here has the talent to finish Daven's work...except maybe Karl."

"But how will he know to come here?" the doctor questioned.

"That'll be a little trickier...I'm going to the factory today, and I'll try to get word to Daven...somehow."

"Why not let me talk to him?" Doctor Spreyer volunteered, then downed the last of his coffee. "I occasionally stop in at the factory to see if anyone needs my services...Herr Fetch doesn't like the visits, but he's used to them—he wouldn't suspect anything."

Peter shook his head. "No...I think it should be me."

"It would be easier for me to—"

"I know it would," Peter sighed. "But let me try first...Daven doesn't know you—he might think that it's just one of Fetch's tricks...but if I can't get to him, then I'll need you to go...you'll be the only way I can get word to him."

"All right," the doctor agreed. "Just let me know if you need me."

"Before you leave, Pay-ter, I want you to come with me," Mrs. Spreyer declared, using the table to help her stand.

By Anna's wide-eyed expression and her hand's abrupt retreat from his, Peter guessed that the request was a surprise for her too. Rising from the table, Peter raised a quizzical eyebrow and looked at the doctor for an explanation, but only a shrug answered him. His heart pumping with nervousness, Peter walked over to Mrs. Spreyer, and after slipping her hand around his waiting arm, the frail woman voicelessly guided him out of the kitchen, down the hall, and into the front corner room on their left.

Having only glanced into the room previously, Peter now surveyed the interior of the light and airy chamber—which was in complete contrast to the somber, velvet-curtained parlor across the hall from it. The little room's two outside walls consisted more of glass than of wood and were bordered by the front and side verandas. All six of the tall and narrow windows were propped wide-open with notched pieces of wood, and in the corner, where the two outside walls met, sat a chair covered with crushed velvet and cat hair—obviously, a favorite perch for the animals. Suddenly, a wild gust of wind blew in through the front windows, but it immediately settled into a gentle breeze—almost as if it wanted to linger in the tranquillity of the chamber.

As he and Mrs. Spreyer strolled farther into the room, Peter noticed a small multicolored table sitting opposite the furry chair. Hundreds of paint dabs and accidental brushstrokes blended the little table into the painted canvases that leaned against it, and next to those stood an equally well-used easel.

"I have been working on a new painting," Mrs. Spreyer offered, pointing to the easel. "What do you think of it?"

Realizing that he had been allowed into the older woman's personal sanctuary, Peter felt both honored and awkward, and he carefully moved over to the fur-covered chair and gazed at the canvas clamped onto the easel. "Wow," he murmured as his attention locked onto the image that had been so carefully brushstroked that it looked alive. "I've never seen Anna look more beautiful."

"Ja, Ah-na is very beautiful."

Peter turned and half-smiled. As frail as the woman was, a strong determination still illuminated her face. "Ah-na," he repeated, echoing the German pronunciation of Anna's name.

"You knew, in the beginning, that I didn't approve of you seeing my daughter, didn't you?"

At first, Peter's mind raced to decipher Irene Spreyer's heavily German-accented words, then, as it did, the bluntness of her question rattled him to the core. "Yes," he murmured, taking hope in her past tense 'didn't.'

"Do you know why?"

"The fact that she's eight years younger than me?" Peter guessed with a shrug.

Mrs. Spreyer shook her head. "No...I didn't know where you were in your walk with the Lord."

"And now?"

"God's told me what I needed to know...and that's why I brought you in here."

Still not completely understanding, Peter nodded.

"Look at the painting," she began.

As Mrs. Spreyer tried to quiet a sudden bout of coughing, Peter studied the portrait of his sweetheart. In it, Anna wore an elegant dress of pink and gold brocade, and her hair, which was intermingled with pink flowers, flowed down her neck in loops and curls. The same tenderness that radiated from Anna herself shined in her brushstroked features, and her eyes...her eyes brought the painting to life. The only fault Peter could see was that the picture was off-centered...as if there should be another person behind Anna.

"Go close—very close," Mrs. Spreyer instructed.

Baffled by the request, Peter stepped forward.

"Do you see that tiny speck of white in the eyes?" she asked. "When you are that close, it seems so unimportant, doesn't it? It just gets lost in the broad strokes of all those other colors."

"Yes Ma'am."

"Now, come here."

Again, following the puzzling directions, Peter moved back to where Irene Spreyer stood.

"Now, look again...you can see that the white dab is really the reflection in the eyes...what do you think about that speck now?"

Becoming more and more confused, Peter brushed at his mustache with his finger. "It's a…a wonderful touch…without it, the whole painting would be so…so vacant."

Mrs. Spreyer smiled and patted his arm. "Ah! You understand!"

"No, I don't. Why…why are you showing me this?"

"So you will remember."

Figuring that the reason for his painting lesson was lost somewhere within their language gap, Peter nodded again. "It'll be very hard to forget this portrait."

Mrs. Spreyer coughed again, then said with a brilliant smile, "There is room for someone else in the painting."

"Yes, I noticed that."

"Like you."

Peter's heart began to pound at the unexpected blessing. "Would you like it to be me?"

"I would enjoy painting you with Anna, very much."

Standing once again in the middle of Fetch's office, Daven tried to calm his racing pulse. What had he done this time, he wondered, to be summoned into the foreman's lair?

"I hear you and Averill are havin' some rather chummy talks," Fetch announced, walking toward Daven and stopping only an arm's length away.

The statement hit Daven like a fist—Jaxson had been right…everything, somehow, got back to Fetch. Then, as both Leland Bryce and Frank Hallam entered the office from the outside—and closed the door behind them—Daven's apprehension spread. What did the foreman know? he silently questioned. And what were Bryce and Hallam going to do to him now? Taking solace in the fact that the two windows were still open and unshuttered, Daven peered into Fetch's eyes and tried to sound as nonchalant as he could. "I suppose we have."

"So what do ya talk about?" the barrel-chested foreman growled as he inched closer and closer to Daven.

"Just…just stuff.

"What stuff?!" Fetch barked.

As if by an unseen cue, Hallam and Bryce stepped next to the foreman, hedging Daven in on both the right and left sides.

Overwhelmed by claustrophobia, Daven backed up—but unfortunately, for every step he took backward, his three opponents took one forward. Then his heels hit the wall.

"What stuff?!"

"Just stuff."

Without warning, Fetch thrust out his thick arm and grabbed Daven around the neck. "What have you two been plannin'?!" the big man shouted as he pulled Daven forward, then slammed him back against the wooden paneling.

His lungs desperate for air, Daven clawed at the meaty fingers encircling his windpipe—but the only thing his fighting accomplished was making the foreman squeeze even harder.

"What do you and Averill talk about?!"

Again, the handhold tightened and Daven's air supply diminished to almost nothing—and with the suffocation came panic. "God!" Daven finally choked out, half in answer, half in appeal.

Slowly, the stranglehold slackened a bit, and Daven wheezed in a much-needed breath.

"Whatd'ya mean?!" the foreman demanded.

"We just…talk…about God," he rasped, still trying to catch his breath.

"You sure ya weren't talkin' about leavin'…runnin' out on us?"

A chill of fear shivered through Daven. How did Fetch know?

"Well?!"

"No Sir…nothing…like that," Daven offered, praying that the foreman couldn't feel the lie as it pulsed through his throat.

Once more, the foreman's handvise constricted. "You know what I'd do if you tried sneakin' out on your debts?"

"Kill…kill me?"

Fetch bellowed out a laugh, then looked at his henchmen, who joined in with their boss's merriment. "Not quite...now, if Averill took off, him I'd kill," Fetch returned with a chuckle. "But you...you'd prob'ly get those talented hands of yours so broken up that you'd never carve again...understand?"

Balling his hands into fists, Daven tried to blink away the tears of terror that had formed against his will. Unfortunately, Fetch had hit upon one of his greatest fears...losing his craft. "Yes Sir," Daven coughed out as the big man's fingers wrapped tighter yet around his neck.

"So it would prob'ly be a good idea for ya to just keep your mind on that writin' desk, huh?"

"Yes Sir."

"And, maybe, you shouldn't talk to Averill so much."

"But...but how can we get...the desk done if...if we can't—"

"I think you can finish it on your own—don't you?"

Suddenly, a barely audible pounding sounded on the door leading to the factory.

Mumbling out a curse, Fetch glanced at his henchmen, then tilted his head toward the door. "Well, since you have a whole desk to get done by yourself," he announced, finally releasing Daven, "maybe you should just get back to work."

As the muffled pounding on the door came again—this time longer and louder—Daven inhaled deeply and massaged his throbbing throat. "Can I...finish my lunch first...Sir?"

No response came from the foreman, but by his expression, Daven knew the answer was 'no.'

Rolling his watch chain between his fingers, Peter inwardly smiled as he entered the factory's front yard—so far, everything was going in his favor. Not only had he smoothed out the rift with Karl, but his 'chance' arrival at the factory had been timed perfectly—the men were having lunch, and Fetch was nowhere in sight. As he ambled through the yard and scanned the faces of the workers as they wolfed down their noontime-meals, Peter's hopes suddenly began to sink—Daven was not among the group outside. Then, spotting Jaxson, he meandered over to the fence.

"Mr. Averill," Peter said as he neared, "it's good to see you again."

Jaxson looked up and wiped his sleeve across his mouth. "Fetch has him in his office," he whispered.

The statement slammed against Peter, taking his breath away. "What?"

"Fetch's got him."

How did Jaxson know his purpose? Peter wondered as apprehension welled up inside him. Did the man suspect that there was a connection between him and Daven? Then, as the meaning of Jaxson's words crystallized in his head, his concern shifted entirely to his brother. With a tip of his hat and a silent 'thank you,' Peter circled, and forcing himself to keep a nonchalant pace, he walked through the yard, entered the building, and headed straight for Fetch's office. Without hesitation, he tried the latch on the heavy wooden door—figuring that he could come up with some excuse for barging in. But the handle refused to move, and in desperation, he pounded on the rough-hewn door...then again, harder.

Finally, the door swept open.

"What do you want!" Bryce sneered as he stood in the doorway, blocking the entrance.

Ignoring the challenge, Peter shouldered his way past the dark-haired man and stepped into the office—and his jaw immediately clenched. His brother was present and thankfully seemed all right, but he was also surrounded by Fetch and Hallam, who, like Bryce, were none too happy at the interruption.

"Leighton, I thought you were told to stop interfering with my work!" Fetch demanded.

Daven, look at me! Peter silently urged. Please, look at me. But his brother just rubbed his neck and stared at the floor. Turning his attention to Fetch, Peter surveyed the big man's granite expression, then he offered with a nod, "It was suggested that I stop interfering."

"Then why are you here?"

"It was only suggested." As Peter heard the words come out of his mouth and remembered where he had heard them before, he choked back a grin. Only a few days ago, his brother had used the same flippant statement when questioned about getting his hair cut.

Obviously, Daven, too, recognized the familiar phrase, and he raised his head up—and instantly, Peter's heart fell into his stomach. His brother's bruises had intensified in color and were now coupled with fresh marks on his neck.

At that moment, after seeing his sibling's battered face, Peter wanted to give up—their mission wasn't worth the misery Daven was going through. But then a subtle smirk formed on his brother's face, and reluctantly, Peter decided to continue with the fight.

"So what do you want, Leighton?" Fetch grumbled as he scraped a match with his thumbnail and held the flame up to a new cigar.

Peter's jaw clamped down tighter. In his concern for his brother's well-being, he had completely forgotten to concoct an excuse for his intrusion. "I, uh, I came to…to talk to Mr. Hallam."

Frank Hallam's mouth fell open. "Me?"

"What for?" Bryce demanded as he moved next to Peter.

"That's between Mr. Hallam and me."

Tossing his spent match at the spittoon, Fetch pointed his cigar at Daven. "You! Get back to work."

As he circled and headed for the door, Daven flashed Peter an almost indiscernible wink, then, massaging his throat once again, he left the office.

Although he was relieved to see the sparkle return to his brother's tired light-blue eyes, concern still jabbed at Peter, and he began to finger his watch chain. There would be no chance for him to get Daven alone now—which meant Doctor Spreyer would have to become their go-between.

"Shall we talk outside, Mr. Hallam?" Peter asked, motioning to the outside door—and wishing that he had some idea of what he was going to say to the man.

Stepping forward, Hallam hesitated, then turned back and peered at this boss. "Is it okay?"

Fetch shrugged and stuffed his cigar between his teeth.

"Whatd'ya think Leighton's up to now?" Bryce asked after Hallam and Peter exited the office.

"I dunno," the foreman mused rubbing his chin.

"Leighton's gettin' awful nervy...I think we'd be better off if he weren't around no more."

"I told you no!"

"But he's gotta be gettin' close to figuring everythin' out," Bryce returned, crossing his arms and spitting a wad of tobacco juice on the floor.

"So? Even if he does—nobody's gunna back him up. Not even the old man will be on his side...once I'm done."

"But—"

"Bryce, after all I've done to make this company mine, I ain't about to let Mr. highfalutin Leighton ruin everything...you can have your fun with him—but not right now."

Growling out a long exhale, Bryce plopped down on the edge of the desk. "So we're just supposed to stand around while he gets closer and closer?"

"Let me worry about Leighton, will ya? Besides, we've got somethin' else to take care of that's more pressin'."

Instantly, Bryce straightened up and a devilish grin formed on his face. "Averill?"

"Averill," Fetch replied with a wicked smirk and a puff on his cigar.

As Peter walked over to a stump behind the factory, he rubbed his thumb over his fingertips and searched for something to say to the blonde-haired man behind him.

Just think of something…anything…Peter hollered inwardly—but nothing came to mind. Lord, what reason can I give to Hallam for calling this meeting? he wondered, looking upward.

"Whatd'ya want to talk to me about, Mr. Leighton?"

Peter immediately raised an eyebrow at the question—and at the hint of respect in Frank Hallam's voice. "Well, as you may know, Mr. Hallam," he began as they halted next to the stump, "we are thinking of expanding our current line of furniture to include some more elaborate pieces."

"Yeah…so?"

"So," Peter continued as an idea finally started to form in his head, "with the added stock, we're going to need additional sales help."

"What's that got to do with me?"

"We'd like you to consider becoming a salesman," Peter declared, hoping that the offer sounded legitimate.

Amazement and confusion swept over Hallam's features, and he ran an unsteady hand through his blonde hair. "A what?"

"A salesman—to help sell the new pieces."

"But why me?"

"Well, I figured that a man in your position would know the furniture business quite well and could answer any questions the customers might have…what do you think?"

"A salesman, huh?" Hallam pondered as he put his foot on the tree stump and rested his forearms on his knee. "I might be interested…but I still don't know why you're askin' me…you know that…that I'm loyal to Mr. Fetch."

Peter nodded, surprised at the man's candor. "Yes, I do."

"Then why're you askin'? You think I'm stupid enough to gum up what I've got?"

"I don't really know what you're stupid enough to do, Hallam…but I do know, if you sit with garbage, you'll eventually smell like garbage."

His face turning to stone, Hallam stood up straight and glared at Peter. "What're you tryin' to say?"

"I'm telling you that here's your chance to get up and leave that garbage behind…if you want to."

Hallam's gruff expression slowly melted, and he gazed at Peter with wearisome eyes. "It ain't that easy," he muttered under his breath as he dabbed at the drops of sweat on his forehead with his sleeve. "And it ain't like I haven't tried before." Then, as if he remembered something that he had momentarily forgotten, Hallam vehemently shook his head. "I like what I do here!" he announced with a sneer and a raised fist. "So you can keep your idiot sales job!"

"Why don't you just think about it for a few days?" Peter persisted, almost becoming lost in the false offer himself.

"No!"

As Peter studied Frank Hallam—and the flicker of hope that glowed in the man's eyes—he began to regret his fictitious proposal, and he also found himself wondering what kind of man Hallam would be without Fetch as his puppeteer.

Sitting at one of the tables in the Rheinhardt Showroom, Peter drummed his fingers on the tabletop and absently stared at the pieces of furniture that surrounded him. If only he could concentrate, he groaned inwardly. If only he could focus on just one of the problems beating against his skull. But, no matter how hard he tried, his thoughts refused to be corralled, and all the worrisome issues continued to charge at him simultaneously, making it impossible to think.

"Pay-ter?"

Startled, Peter jerked upright and stared at the friendly bearded face opposite him. "Doctor Sprey…Otto, I didn't even hear you come in."

"I was curious if you got a chance to…" the doctor started, then his voice trailed off as he scanned the showroom's interior. "Are we alone?"

Peter half-smiled, grateful for the man's discretion. "Yes Sir," he answered and gestured toward the chair opposite him.

"So did you get to see your brother?" Doctor Spreyer inquired, settling onto the seat.

"I saw him—but I didn't get to talk to him," Peter replied as he slipped his pocketwatch from his waistcoat, clicked open the cover, and stared incredulously at the positions of the hands. "Man alive! I didn't realize it was so late." Pushing himself from his chair, Peter marched to the front of the showroom and bolted the door, then, moving to the window, he turned the wooden sign to read 'closed' for those passing by on the sidewalk.

"Are you going to make another attempt to see Daven?"

Peter let out a deep breath and shook his head. "It's no use," he answered as he meandered back to the table and collapsed onto his chair. "Fetch and his jackals watch me like prey while I'm there."

"Do you want me to try?"

"If you're still willing."

"Of course, I'm still willing...I'll stop in at the factory Saturday morning."

"Thank you," Peter returned. Then, as a brand-new dilemma rushed at him, he added quietly, "If you do get a chance to speak to Daven, you probably shouldn't mention my name at all...I just don't want Fetch to get wind of why you're there."

"You don't have to worry about that...when I make my visits to the factory, I usually go on Saturdays...Herr Fetch won't think anything's out of the ordinary."

Thinking once again of his brother's predicament—a predicament that Daven should have never been forced into in the first place—Peter interlaced his fingers and slouched down in his seat. If only he hadn't involved his brother in this mess...if only...

"What's wrong, Pay-ter...do you have another headache?"

"No," he answered, meeting the doctor's concerned stare. "I was just thinking that I...that I wish I could check on Daven tomorrow—just to make sure he's okay...Karl asked me to watch things here, so he and the bookkeeper could get things ready for the reception...I'm not going to get a chance to—"

"Pay-ter, you're holding on much too tight…you need to release your brother into God's care."

"I know. I just want Daven to know that I'm still here…that I'm working things out."

"And the Lord's telling you the same," Doctor Spreyer returned, placing his elbows on the table and leaning forward. "Now, tell me about your brother, so I'll know who I'm looking for."

Trying to take the doctor's advice, Peter nodded and blew out a long breath. "Well, he's tall and has long sandy—" Instantly, Peter's jaw clenched down tight as he caught his mistake…so much had changed in such a brief amount of time. "Uh, short sandy hair…and he has bruises on the left side of his face." Then, noticing the doctor's dubious expression, Peter added with a smile, "Don't worry, you'll know him right off…when you see two of the palest-blue eyes you've ever seen, you'll know you've found Daven."

With a groan of disgust, Daven plopped down on the assembly room floor and, for a second time, fished through his toolbox. But it just wasn't there—his best fine chisel was missing…again. And he knew exactly where it was—or at least who took it. Slamming the toolbox's cover shut, Daven massaged his left hand and shook his head. Why does he do this? he wondered, knowing he wouldn't get an answer. No matter how hard he tried, he just couldn't understand Leland Bryce's odd game of stealing and hiding his tools. But now, it was even more exasperating…it was Friday already. He should be polishing—not still carving.

Rising to his feet, Daven brushed the sawdust and wood shavings from his clothes. If only he could always keep his toolbox with him—then Bryce couldn't play his game of hide-and-seek—but Fetch refused to allow the tools to leave the factory. And the reason for that command was easy enough to figure out…he would never leave without his gouges or his chisels or his father's carving—and Fetch knew it too.

"All right, Bryce," Daven muttered as he moved to the stairs and descended, "Ready or not..."

Instantly overwhelmed by the din and dust of the ground floor, Daven stopped on the bottom step and searched for...

"There you are," he said, spotting his dark-haired nemesis. Then, as he continued to watch the scene in front of him, a cold chill abruptly rippled down his spine. Bryce, who rarely interacted with the workers, stood in front of one of the lathes and was having an unusually jovial conversation...with Jaxson. Unsure if he should be concerned or not, Daven thrust himself off the stairs and rushed toward the unlikely duo, but while weaving in and out of the machines, another movement caught his attention. Standing only a few feet away from Jaxson was Josh Clayton—a minor Fetch confederate—who was sweeping a long piece of maple into a backswing. What's going on? Daven asked himself as Bryce stepped away from the lathe and Clayton started to swing the heavy board forward.

Suddenly, as if someone had whispered the play's ending in his ear, the conspiracy became all too clear...the blow from Clayton would strike Jaxson across the chest and send him backward—into the lathe's circling power belt.

"Jaxson! Get down!" Daven yelled, but he was mute next to the screeching saws. And, as the thought of running over and pulling his friend out of harm's way shot through his mind, he realized that he already was. "Jaxson! Down! Get down!" he shouted, getting closer and closer. "Jaxson, get down!"

Finally, his friend heard him and dropped to the floor just as the piece of maple swooshed crosswise, knocking the lathe's power belt off its pulleys.

That was all Daven remembered...until a hand touched his shoulder and gently shook him.

"Daven?"

The name echoed inside his head, the smell of cut wood filled his lungs, and all he could see was a forest of blurry boots.

"Daven?"

Reaching up, Daven brushed a hand across his sweat-drenched face. Where was he? he wondered as a cacophony of disjointed voices floated over him.

"Daven?"

Slowly, the confusion faded and he became painfully aware that he was in the Rheinhardt Factory...and that he was lying on the floor...and that a sharp ache pulsated through his right temple. And, as he pulled his hand in front of his eyes, he realized one other horrible fact—it wasn't perspiration trickling over his features...it was blood.

"Averill!" he heard Fetch snarl. "Take him to the doctor, and get him back here fast!"

Daven was then yanked to his feet, causing the river of red drops to fall from his face and splatter onto his clothes, his boots, and the sawdust at his feet.

"The rest of you get back to work!" the foreman continued as he shoved the idle men around him into action. "And you two!" he bellowed, pointing at Bryce and Josh Clayton. "Get into my office—now!"

His head still swimming, Daven felt himself being tugged toward the factory door and out onto the loading platform. As the bright daylight surged over him, so did a wave of light-headedness. Yanking away from Jaxson, he lowered himself onto the platform's steps and wiped at the blood streaming down his face.

"Here," Jaxson said as he removed his vest, crumpled it into a ball, and placed it against Daven's temple.

"What...what happened?" Daven murmured, pressing the garment firmly to his head. "I don't even remember falling."

"You didn't fall," Jaxson returned with a sarcastic lilt. "Think you can walk now?"

"Yeah, I guess...but you better get back in there. You'll get in trouble for helping me."

"Fetch told me to help ya," Jaxson explained as he squatted on the steps and used the stoop's railing to pull himself and Daven erect. "Besides, he's too busy yellin' at Bryce and Clayton for hittin' you instead of me."

Barely able to make his legs move, Daven held onto his friend and allowed himself to be practically dragged out of the factory's yard. "What...what do you mean, hitting me?"

"I mean, you saved my hide again. I never even saw that board comin'...if you hadn't yelled for me to get down..."

"I remember seeing you duck...but not much else."

"Well, when Clayton missed me, he hit the lathe's belt instead...that board just flew out of ol' Clayton's hands and shot back toward you...clipped ya pretty good too."

"Oh...where are we going?"

"To see the doctor."

"The doctor!" Daven exclaimed, stopping in mid-stride. "I can't afford a doctor."

"This one you can...he's helped a lot of us for free," Jaxson said, tugging on his friend's arm. "I want ya to promise me somethin', Helpful."

"What's that?"

"Next time, have 'em hit ya someplace different than your face, huh?"

Daven smiled at his friend's attempt to cheer him, but underneath the humor lay the crushing fact that there probably would be a next time.

As she stood next to the kitchen table and snapped off the ends of some green beans in preparation for her parents' supper, Anna couldn't stop herself from staring at the cuckoo clock on the wall. With only hours until the Rheinhardt reception, she was finding it harder and harder to wait. She had already finished getting ready to go. All that was left was to change into her new dress. But it wasn't the reception itself that brought such delight—it was the thought of spending the evening with Peter. After their brief conversation—and kiss—the night before, she finally knew how he felt about her. And that knowledge deepened the feelings she had for him.

"Excuse me, Miss."

The unexpected voice yanked Anna from her reverie, and dropping the bean she was holding, she spun around. "Yes?" she called as she moved to the screen door and peered at the two men standing on the back porch.

"My friend has to see Doc Spreyer...is he here?" the first man asked.

Gazing at the tall black man and his obviously injured friend, Anna bit at her lower lip. She knew they needed help, and her heart mourned for them, but there was also a hard-and-fast rule in the Spreyer household—a rule she was told never to break. "No, I'm sorry, he was called to an emergency...you'll have to go to the hospital."

"But...but that's so far away," the dark-skinned man moaned. "He's hurt bad."

Then the second man removed the makeshift bandage he held against his face and looked up, causing Anna to draw in a quick breath of surprise. There was no mistaking those sky-blue eyes—it was the same handsome young man that had bumped into her outside the dry goods store. "Oh, my!" she exclaimed, partly from amazement at meeting the azure-eyed stranger again and partly from horror at seeing the gash on his temple and the bruises on his face. "Please come in," she said compassionately as she opened the screen door.

"We, uh, we keep running into each other, huh?" the injured young man offered as he and his friend stepped inside the kitchen.

"Yes, we do...only you weren't bleeding then, Mr....?"

"Ashby."

"Mr. Ashby, if you'll come into my father's office, I'll see what I can do," Anna volunteered, moving over to the office door and pushing it open. Then, following the two men inside, she pointed to a chair near one of the windows. "Over there, please...the light's better."

"Jaxson, you'd better get back to the factory," the young man muttered as his friend lowered him onto the designated seat.

"I ain't leavin' ya, Helpful."

"Are you two from the Rheinhardt Factory?" she asked, quite sure she already knew the answer.

"Yes, we are," the blue-eyed man replied. "And he should really get back there."

"I told ya…I ain't leavin' ya."

Warmed by the men's camaraderie, Anna grabbed an empty pitcher from a shelf and handed it to her patient's faithful friend. "Would you please fill this up…I'm sorry, I don't know your name either."

"Jaxson Averill, Ma'am."

"Mr. Averill, would you please fill this up with some water…there's a pump at the dry sink in the kitchen."

"Yes Ma'am."

Sliding a tall table next to her patient, Anna reached into the cabinet above her and removed a bowl and some towels. "What happened, Mr. Ashby?" she asked as she placed the items on the table.

"An accident."

"It looks as though you've had quite a few accidents lately," she said, gesturing toward the left side of his face.

"I suppose I have."

Carefully, Anna examined the wound above her patient's eye, and as she did, concern for Peter's brother suddenly filled her mind—Daven was, most likely, facing the same kind of mistreatment.

"Here's the water, Ma'am," Jaxson announced from behind her.

"Thank you," Anna replied as she took the pitcher and filled the bowl on the table. "I'm going to clean off some of the blood, Mr. Ashby, so I can see your injuries better…all right?" Then, without waiting for a response, Anna pressed one of the towels into the bowl, wrung out the extra water, and began tenderly wiping at the deep scrapes on her patient's face. Noticing his discomfort, Anna tried to fight the tears forming in her eyes and the rage welling up inside her. She knew it wasn't fair, but she found herself growing angrier and angrier with Karl Rheinhardt—and with Peter. Karl should have been more vigilant with his factory, she declared wordlessly, and Peter should have never placed himself or his brother within Quentin Fetch's reach.

"How bad is it, Miss?" her patient inquired, intently gazing up at her with his azure orbs.

Anna rinsed out the towel and wiped away a tear with her cuff. "You have quite a few scrapes that extend from your eyebrow back into your hairline, but there's one on the forehead here," she returned, touching him with the towel, "that is very deep and—"

Flinching in pain, he grasped her hand and pushed it away.

"I'm sorry, Mr. Ashby," she cooed sympathetically. "It's a very deep laceration...it'll need to be stitched closed."

"Will it scar?"

"Probably...I can do it or you can wait for my father—but it still needs to be done."

"No, I can't wait that long...go ahead and sew it up, Miss Spreyer."

As she walked over to her father's glass-fronted cabinets, Anna nodded at Jaxson, who sat on the first bed. She knew her father would reprimand her for allowing two strangers into the house when he wasn't home, but for some reason, she trusted these two—especially the young man with the crystal eyes. There was just something so familiar about him. She had sensed it when he plowed into her outside the dry goods store, and the feeling was the same now. It was as if a long-lost relative had come home.

Gathering the items she needed from the cabinets, Anna moved back to her patient. "You have some slivers of wood mixed in with your scratches, Mr. Ashby," she explained as she deposited the supplies onto the table. "I'm going to have to remove them also."

He nodded and braced himself for the hurt she was about to inflict upon him.

"You're very fortunate," Anna offered, hoping to distract her patient as she grabbed a needle and a pair of tweezers. "If this cut had been any lower, you probably would have lost your sight on this side."

"Thank goodness the Lord had His angels pull me away just in time, huh?" he murmured.

Anna smiled and looked at him, but his vivid eyes were closed. Maybe that was it, she told herself as she quickly and carefully removed the splinters and stitched closed the still weeping gash above his eye. Maybe, it was his Christian spirit that made him familiar to her. Finally finishing her suturing, Anna nodded at her handiwork. Her sisters, for once, might have been right—she would make a fine nurse.

"Is that it?" he whispered as his eyelids fluttered open.

"That's it…give me a moment to clean up, then I'll bandage the wound."

"That's all right, Miss…we need to get back to work."

Anna shook her head and pressed her patient back onto his chair. "You are not leaving until I get something to keep those stitches clean…I'll be right back."

Daven grinned at the firm but sweet-tempered remark, then, as the doctor's daughter left the office and softly clicked the door shut behind her, he stood, turned, and looked into the oval mirror hanging on the wall behind him. "Man alive!" he gasped as he moved his head around and viewed his injury from different angles. Suddenly unable to stomach his reflection any longer, Daven closed his eyes, hoping that the swollen slash would just disappear. But it didn't, and he moaned as he once again studied the permanent change to his features. He would never look the same…never. It wasn't that he ever used his looks to gain an advantage, but he knew they did bring him certain favors, and he had gotten used to that. Now…now, he'd have to learn to live without the benefits of that symmetry.

"I'm sorry, Helpful," Jaxson announced as Daven made his examination. "You should've just let them hit me."

Circling, Daven scrutinized his friend. "I'll get used to this," he replied, pointing to his forehead. "But it'd be a lot harder to get used to not having you around."

Jaxson shook his head. "Well, you're gunna have to…remember? I'm leavin' tonight."

"You're still going to leave? Even when everything could be over soon?"

"You want me to stick around and give 'em another chance to kill me?!"

"Well, leaving is giving them an even better chance—and a reason."

"A reason?!" Jaxson snapped as he jumped to his feet. "What're you thinkin', Helpful? That they set up this accident just because? They had a reason."

"What reason? They already separated us...why'd they try to hurt you?"

"I dunno...maybe they found out that I was plannin' on leaving."

Daven frowned and staggered over to his friend. "I didn't tell them anything...believe me, I didn't."

Glancing at Daven's stitches, Jaxson nodded. "I believe ya, Helpful."

"Please, don't leave...we can make sure that they don't try anything like this again—at least for awhile."

"How?"

"We'll use this as an excuse," Daven answered as he fingered his stitches. "I'm not going to be able to move as fast with this pounding in my head...I might not get that stupid desk polished for Monday—unless they let you help me again."

"You think they'll believe that?"

"They'd better...it's the truth."

Reaching out, Jaxson placed a hand on Daven's shoulder. "I'm obliged for what you did...and I'm sorry 'bout the scar."

Daven shrugged. "It's all right."

"Hey, with them eyes of yours, nobody's ever gunna notice it anyhow."

From where he stood, Daven circled and cast another look into the mirror. Jaxson's words may have been comforting...but they weren't true. "I don't know," he offered as he considered his scarred reflection. "Maybe it'll end up making me look mysterious, huh?"

"Yeah, maybe."

"So will you stay?"

Jaxson sighed and bobbed his head. "I s'pose...somebody's gunna have to take care of ya and make sure ya don't get into any more accidents."

Daven chuckled, then his smile slowly faded—the statement could have just as easily been said by Peter. For so long, he had resented his brother's firm hand, but now, he realized just how much care and protection that hand had provided—and he missed it. "When we get back, I'll tell Fetch that—" Daven started, but he immediately stopped as the door swung open and the doctor's daughter reentered.

"I'm sorry that took me so long, Mr. Ashby."

"That's all right, Miss," he said, returning to his chair.

"I remembered that we had some soft cotton upstairs...I thought it would make some nice bandages for you."

As she wrapped his head and covered his wound, Daven studied the doctor's pretty, dovelike daughter. Her beauty, her touch, and her soul had a strong gentleness, which made her both delightful and desirable. Then Daven's thoughts drifted to Ivy...he really liked Ivy—but this girl would be the one Peter would approve of.

"How does that feel, Mr. Ashby?"

"That's fine...thank you, Miss Spreyer."

"It's important to keep the wound clean," she explained, removing some more fabric pieces from her apron pocket. "Take these so you can change the bandage."

Daven nodded and stuffed the material into his shirt.

"Now, my father should really take a look at you too...I'll have him come to the factory as soon as he can, all right?"

Rubbing his eyes, Daven released a long breath. "Sure."

"Would you like some laudanum for the pain?"

"No Miss...I've got too much to get done tonight."

Taking a few steps backward, she stared into his eyes. "Tonight?"

"Yeah."

"But you need time to heal."

"I can't...I've got a project that I have to—"

"We gotta go, Helpful," Jaxson interrupted loudly, dashing over to Daven.

As he glanced up at his friend, Daven gritted his teeth. He had said much, much more than he should have—obviously, his head wound was dulling his wariness. The doctor's golden-haired daughter seemed trustworthy, but he had to remember that Quentin Fetch's reach was long and deadly.

"We have to go," Daven agreed and unsteadily rose to his feet. "How...how much do I owe you for your help, Miss Spreyer?"

"Nothing, Mr. Ashby...just a promise that you'll be careful and not have any more accidents."

Daven grinned weakly. "I'll try my best."

⊱ Nine ⊰

As Peter stepped onto the Spreyers' front porch, he heard something that was completely unfamiliar. The doctor, who was somewhere in the house, was bellowing in German—which, in itself, was not unusual—but now, the baritone voice was laced with irritation and impatience. Wishing he knew even a few words of the language, Peter knocked on the screen door. Then again—louder. Finally, a red-faced Doctor Spreyer appeared on the other side of the door and pushed it open.

"Good evening, Sir," Peter offered tentatively as he entered.

The doctor scowled but said nothing as he shoved the screen shut.

Frowning in bewilderment, Peter hung his hat on the stand in the entranceway, and as he did, he noticed another irregularity—the air inside the big farmhouse was saturated with anger.

Suddenly, the doctor blasted out another German tirade.

At first, only silence answered him. Then came a slam from a drawer. And, finally, Anna shouted from the kitchen, "The hospital was too far—he was hurt."

The doctor spouted off again, and although he wasn't positive, Peter thought he heard his name among the unknown words.

Immediately, Anna appeared in the kitchen doorway with her hands on her hips. "He needed my help, Papa—I just couldn't turn them away."

"It wasn't safe to let them in when only you and Mama were home," the doctor barked from the entranceway.

Anna slowly walked to the front of the house, her countenance darkened with outrage. "Papa, he could barely stand upright—he was in no condition to cause problems." Then, turning her attention to Peter, Anna's eyes narrowed. "And I'm not going to that reception, that's for sure!"

Shocked by the harshness in Anna's voice and her renouncement, Peter tried to stutter out a response, but she quickly spun around and stomped up the stairs.

His mouth falling open, Peter peered at the doctor for some sort of explanation. "Is she angry with you or with me?"

Doctor Spreyer let out a deep breath and moved to the bottom of the stairs. Once more, he called out in German, but this time, his voice was less ferocious.

All was quiet for a few agonizing minutes, then Anna walked back downstairs.

A smile parted Peter's lips as he watched her descend, but it quickly faded when he noticed the fury still burning within her eyes.

"I'm angry with Papa—and you," she announced.

"Why? What did I—"

"And I'm not going tonight."

"What did I do?"

Anna inhaled deeply and her shoulders relaxed as she stared into Peter's eyes. "I'm not really angry with you."

Peter's brow furrowed—although relieved by the confession, he was now even more confused.

"There was an accident at the factory," the doctor explained.

"An accident!" Anna echoed with sarcasm.

"One of the workers was hit with a piece of lumber," Doctor Spreyer continued, ignoring his daughter's remark. "He was brought here and Anna sutured the wound." Then, he firmly added, "Even though she knows she is not supposed to allow strange men into the house when I'm not at home."

"Papa, you wouldn't say that if you saw what they did to his face…poor Mr. Ashby will carry that scar around for the rest of his life."

"What?!" Peter gasped as every fiber inside him constricted with alarm. "What was the worker's name?"

"Mr. Ashby."

"Oh, no…no," Peter moaned as the thought of a scar marring his brother's handsome face slugged him in the gut.

"What's wrong?" both Doctor Spreyer and Anna called out simultaneously.

Unable to answer and running a quivering hand through his hair, Peter staggered into the parlor. Why didn't he get Daven away from Fetch when he had the chance? he inwardly groaned. Now…now, it was too late—his brother was permanently scarred.

"Peter, what's wrong?!" Anna begged, following after him and grabbing his arm.

Pulling away, he sank onto the sofa and held his head in his hands.

"Peter?"

"The man you treated was Daven," he answered in a hoarse whisper.

Anna gulped and dropped to her knees in front of him. "No…no, he couldn't be…he…he didn't look anything like you."

Lifting his head, Peter gazed at Anna's distressed features, then he sadly shook his head. "He's my stepbrother, Anna…we look nothing alike."

Her eyes widening in horror, Anna grasped both his hands in hers. "Oh, my goodness, Peter…I…I forgot."

"It's all—"

"You never told me his surname," she went on as the tears began to roll down her cheeks. "And you never told me what he looked like…except that he had long hair."

"Anna, it's all ri—"

"This man had short hair…maybe, it wasn't Daven."

Peter shook his head again. "He got it cut a few days ago."

"But—"

"If he had crystal-blue eyes, it was Daven."

Anna averted her gaze, which spoke more loudly than words—the patient had definitely been his brother.

"Peter, I'm so sorry," she went on. "He seemed familiar somehow, but it never occurred to me that he might be Daven."

Brushing away her tears, Peter half-smiled. "It's all right…sometimes, I even forget that he's a stepbrother…how…how badly was he hurt?"

"He has a deep gash, here," she said, touching Peter's forehead just above the right eye. "It'll heal…but with a scar."

Peter closed his eyes and tried to picture his brother with the disfigurement. "He'll never forgive me," he murmured, not even realizing that he spoke aloud.

"I'm sure he doesn't blame you."

"Well, he should," Peter returned as his eyelids snapped open. "I involved him in this whole mess," he continued, pushing himself from the sofa. "I have to get him out—now." And, with his statement, Peter marched to the parlor's doorway—and right into Doctor Spreyer, who was blocking the exit.

"Nein…you're not leaving…not in your current frame of mind."

In his heart, Peter knew the doctor was right…he wasn't thinking clearly. But, at the moment, his only concern was his brother's safety. "I have to do something…I have to see him," he replied, still trying to get around the doctor's blockade.

"Tomorrow, Pay-ter."

With a hopeless sigh, Peter quit his maneuvering and, instead, peered at the doctor's kind, sympathetic expression. "But what if they won't let Daven leave the factory?"

"He'll be able to leave," Doctor Spreyer replied confidently.

"How do you know?"

"Herr Fetch can't refuse—not if I tell him that Daven must come here, so I can check his wound for any signs of infection."

"After I finished with his stitches," Anna put in, joining the two men at the door, "I told Daven that Papa would want to check on him."

"You'll have your brother back," the doctor announced with a nod. "But you'll have to wait until tomorrow."

Resignedly, Peter bobbed his head in agreement, then he leaned against the doorjamb. He was grateful for the doctor's encouraging words, but they did nothing to quell the sharp jabs of guilt in his gut. Glancing at Anna, Peter smiled slightly. "So now you know Daven."

"I'm so sorry, Peter...if I had—"

"No, I didn't mean it that way...I just meant that I'm glad you got to know him as a person—instead of as my little brother."

For a moment, no one spoke, then, in the silence, seven 'cuckoos' sounded from the clock in the kitchen.

"It's okay if you don't want to go to the reception tonight," Peter said, stroking Anna's arm. "But I have to...Karl's salesman is going to be there...and if I can ask the right questions, maybe I can piece everything together—and be done with this whole disaster."

"No, Peter, I want to go...to be there for you," she returned. "I just have to change."

As Anna left the parlor and headed for the stairs, Peter aimlessly ambled over to one of the windows and peered at the gloominess forming outside. "Looks as though we're in for some more rain," he offered absently.

"Daven will be fine," Doctor Spreyer replied, joining him at the window.

Glancing sideward at the doctor, Peter shook his head, trying to hide his uncertainty. "He's all the family I have."

"No, Pay-ter, your family now includes us...so you don't have to do all the worrying yourself."

Peter grinned at the insightful statement—worry was definitely vying for his attention, along with guilt and doubt.

"If it is going to rain," the doctor put in, "you should probably borrow my carriage...it'll offer a little more protection than—"

"Oh, the rain won't be a problem—with that," Peter declared, gesturing toward the window. "Karl didn't want me coming in a rented carriage, so he loaned me his coach and driver for the night."

"Impressive," Doctor Spreyer returned with a nod as he gazed at the carriage waiting in the street.

Continuing with their now trivial discussion, the two men whiled away the time—until Anna appeared in the parlor doorway wearing a gold-and-pink brocaded dress. Then the conversation abruptly ended, and Peter let out a deep breath. It was amazing. Anna looked just like her portrait...the same creamy complexion...the same pink gown...the same flowered cascade of looped curls. But, as beautiful as the painting was, it paled against the real image.

"You'll outshine every woman at the reception," Peter declared, walking over to her and taking her gloved hand.

Anna blushed and smiled, then, glancing at her father, she offered, "I'm sorry, Papa, for losing my temper earlier."

Stepping next to his daughter, the doctor gently kissed her on the forehead. "As am I."

"And I apologize to you too," she said, gazing at Peter. "I was angry with the circumstances—not you...it's just so hard to see what those factory men go through...and then they're forced to go back to work without any time to heal."

Instantly, Peter's brow crinkled in consternation. "What do you mean?"

"Daven said he had to go back to work—tonight."

Peter's jaw clenched at the answer. "They must be pushing him to get the desk done," he muttered under his breath as he lost all desire to be associated with the Rheinhardt Furniture Factory.

Arm in arm, Peter and Anna walked through the rose-and-vine-decorated arched doorway and entered the Rheinhardt ballroom. Quickly surveying face after face, Peter searched for his employer—then he finally found him, Mrs.

Rheinhardt, and Lori standing together in front of a mammoth stained-glass bay window at the far end of the room.

"There's Karl," Peter whispered to Anna while pointing toward the window. "Remember not to say anything about my brother."

Anna patted his arm and smiled as amusement glittered in her eyes. "I won't say anything."

"Are you ready to meet our hosts?"

Her grin widening, Anna nodded. "You can stop worrying," she said with a light titter. "I'll hold my tongue and be civil."

Realizing that Anna had misunderstood his comment, Peter shook his head. "No, I wasn't referring to that…you see, I'm never ready to talk to that one," he explained as he pointed to Lori Rheinhardt.

"Is that Lorelei?"

"Yes."

"Any advice?"

"For dealing with Lori?" he replied with a shrug. "Just keep smiling."

As they edged their way around the waltzing dancers, Peter examined the elegant ballroom, which was a recent addition to the Rheinhardt mansion. Set into the walls, at ten-foot intervals, were massive Greek-style columns, and between those were brass-framed mirrors that had been decorated for the reception with fresh rose-and-vine garlands. A domed ceiling, accented with carved wooden roses, topped the magnificent room, and a highly polished walnut floor that was adorned with multitonal, wooden inlaid designs gave the guests a regal footing as they waltzed to and fro. It was an impressive ballroom, Peter admitted silently, but there was something keeping it from being truly grand…something cold and unfriendly.

Suddenly, Anna's grip tightened around his arm, and Peter's attention was drawn to an army of strangers, which was quickly moving toward them and clamoring as if he were a long-lost friend. Knowing that he'd probably regret not maneuvering around the throng, Peter pasted a wide smile on his face, patted Anna's fingers, and waited for the inevitable. Then, as the army arrived, it formed a makeshift line, allowing each person to individually approach him, shake his hand, and tell him how good it was to see him again. Irked by the mock familiarity, Peter continued to grin and greet, until, finally, the last person passed by.

"How do you know all those people?" Anna asked, peering at him in amazement. "I've lived in Sandorville for years, and I don't know half of them."

"I don't know any of them."

"But they act as if—"

"Acting is exactly what they were doing," he returned. "I think they're more impressed by the fact that I'm Karl's assistant, than by me."

As they started once again to make their way toward the bay window, Peter glimpsed himself and Anna in one of the decorated mirrors. Slowing to study the reflection, he nodded slightly in approval—it was an image he hoped he would see again and again. Then, as his gaze lingered on the mirror, Peter realized that he was not the only one who was getting attention. Many of the men behind them were admiring Anna, causing a mixture of pride and jealousy to well up inside him.

Pulling himself from the enjoyable yet worrisome mirrored reflections, Peter glanced at Anna. "When I finally get the chance to meet Karl's salesman, I'll need to talk with him alone," he explained.

"I understand."

Peter bobbed his head in thanks. But, as he watched the other men steadily stare at his sweetheart, he became very uneasy about leaving her unescorted.

"Hello, Peter!" Karl announced as they neared, "I was beginning to think that you weren't going to show up either."

Grateful that Lorelei was busy talking with another guest, Peter guided Anna toward his employer. "Either, Sir?" he questioned, noticing the older man's sullen expression. "Who didn't show up?"

Karl cast a chary glance at his wife, who was standing next to him. "My brother-in-law…he telegraphed earlier…he's ill and won't be able to make it tonight."

"I'm sorry to hear that, Sir."

"He also asked if I would oversee the construction of his factory until he gets back on his feet."

"Really?" Peter returned. "He must be quite sick then."

The older man nodded and wrapped an arm around his full-figured wife. "I'm afraid so."

Suddenly noticing Karl's and Mrs. Rheinhardt's interest in Anna, Peter realized that he had neglected to offer any introductions. "Forgive me," he proclaimed. "I've forgotten my manners...Karl, Mrs. Rheinhardt, I'd like you to meet Miss Anna Spreyer...and, Anna, is this Mr. Karl Rheinhardt and his wife, Victoria."

"Miss Spreyer, I'm honored," Karl said as he took Anna's gloved hand and lightly kissed it.

"Thank you, Mr. Rheinhardt...how do you do, Mrs. Rheinhardt?"

"Just fine, Dear," Mrs. Rheinhardt returned. Then, eyeing Peter, she added, "I was beginning to think that you had left town."

"Why is that?"

"Because it's been over a week and I've barely seen you," she answered with a slight bite in her words.

"I know...I apologize...I've been very busy."

"And I can see why," Mrs. Rheinhardt returned as she switched her attention to Anna. "Spreyer...Spreyer...are you related to Doctor Otto Spreyer, Dear?"

"Yes, he's my father."

"Ah, is he now! And how are you enjoying the reception?"

"It's very nice," Anna replied. "The ballroom is beautiful."

"Thank you...my daughter designed the interior herself."

After hearing Mrs. Rheinhardt's statement, Peter studied the room once again. Maybe that was it, he remarked to himself. Maybe, it was Lori's touch that had made the ballroom so cold and uninviting.

"And the decorations are marvelous," Anna continued, pointing to the mirrors, "especially the flower garlands."

Mrs. Rheinhardt's face beamed with pride. "Aren't they wonderful? The servants and I put those together from the flowers in my garden...the rejects of course."

"The rejects?"

Karl chuckled. "You are looking at the town's reigning flower champion," he said with a touch of jesting in his voice. "My wife has won every season's flower show for the last four years."

"That's wonderful," Anna declared. "If these are your rejects, I can see why you're a winner."

"Why, thank you!" Mrs. Rheinhardt gushed, grinning from the praise. "My daughter and husband think the shows are a waste of time...are you planning on attending the summer show, Miss Spreyer?"

Anna shook her head. "No, I don't—"

"It's next Saturday...you just have to come and see my newest rose entry."

Again, Anna shook her head. "I...I just don't think I can...I help my father on Saturdays."

"But you must," Mrs. Rheinhardt pressed. "I'd be disappointed if you and Peter didn't come."

"Peter?" a sugary voice suddenly announced. "It is you! I thought I heard your name."

Cringing at the overly sweet greeting, Peter turned and faced Lori. "Hello, Lorelei."

"I'm so glad you came!" Lori trumpeted as she practically elbowed her mother out of the way.

"I hope you're enjoying your birthday," he offered, removing a small wrapped box from his frock coat. "Here's a little something for you."

"Oh, Peter, how thoughtful!" Lori returned as she took the gift, then, with a covert glimpse toward Anna, she kissed him on the cheek.

"It's just some rose water...your father said it was your favorite."

"It is," Lori purred as she glanced at Anna once more and caressed Peter's forearm. "But just having you here is present enough."

Immediately, Peter frowned at Lorelei's affectations—which he figured were more for Anna's annoyance than for his. He knew he needed to nip them in the bud as soon as he could, and there was one very easy way to do that. "Lori, I'd like you to meet Miss Anna Spreyer," he announced, stroking Anna's fingers, "my fiancee."

Lori's eyes widened at the declaration—as did Karl's and Mrs. Rheinhardt's. And Anna's grip tightened around his arm, but thankfully, Peter didn't see any change in her expression. He knew his statement had startled everyone—especially Anna, but he was quite sure that the almost scandalous announcement would put an end to Lori's baiting game. Then, glancing at Anna and giving her a slight wink, Peter reminded himself to apologize for the lie—which he now wished was the truth.

After a moment, Karl's surprise melted into disappointment, and that, eventually, transformed into a crooked grin. "My boy," he said, slapping Peter on the shoulder, "I couldn't have done any better if I had picked her out myself."

Stroking his mustache, Peter nodded—partially in thanks and partially in astonishment at his employer's quick acceptance that there would never be a Mrs. Lorelei Leighton.

"What a lovely dress," Lori blared at Anna, obviously trying to steal back some of the attention. "It's a copy of a Worth design, isn't it?"

Anna smiled. "No...Mr. Worth's designs just didn't fit the fabric, so we just created our own."

"We?"

"My mother and I."

"How interesting," Lori returned coldly. "Perhaps one day you and your mother can design a gown for me." And, without waiting for an answer, Lori circled and gestured toward a chubby red-haired man who was busy grabbing hors d'oeuvres from a servant's tray. "Sweety, would you come here please?"

Reluctantly, the man retreated from the now half-empty tray, and stuffing the morsels into his mouth, he dusted off his hands and walked over to Lori.

"Victor, would you be a dear and put this with my other gifts?" she cooed, handing him the package of rose water.

"Victor?" Peter echoed.

"Oh, that's right," Karl proclaimed. "You two haven't been introduced yet...Victor Kilian this is Peter Leighton. Peter...Victor."

A wide smile spread across Victor's face, revealing a mouthful of oversize teeth. "Welcome to the furniture business," he announced with a laugh. "I hope you're ready to jump right in...with all the orders I just brought back, it's going to get pretty hectic around here."

"None of that," Lori interrupted. "No furniture talk on my birthday."

Victor laughed again, and with a nod of apology, he walked over to a long table in front of the bay window and added Peter's gift to the mountain of birthday packages.

"Victor! Victor!" Lori suddenly shouted as if calling for a dog.

"Yes, Dearest?" the red-haired man puffed as he hurried back to Lorelei's side.

"Do you recognize the tune that's playing?"

Victor tilted his head and listened to the string quartet for a moment. "It's the one you made them keep practicing, isn't it?"

Lori's eyes narrowed and she hissed out a short breath. "It's my favorite—I wanted them to play it well."

"Yes, Dearest."

"So? Are you going to ask me to dance?"

His face lighting up with understanding, Victor held out his arm. "Would you care to dance, Dearest?"

With a chirp of mock surprise, Lori beamed. "How sweet of you to ask... yes, I would love to!"

Shaking his head in disbelief—and grateful that he had never been lured into becoming a lovesick suitor by Lorelei Rheinhardt's comely but toxic charms—Peter watched her and Victor disappear into the crowd of swirling dancers, then he stepped over to his employer. "We need to talk, Sir."

Karl nodded, turned toward his wife, and pointed to one of the mirrors. "Victoria, why don't you show Miss Spreyer one of your flower things—close up."

Now alone with the older man, Peter focused all his attention on the matter that had plagued him all day. "We need to speak to Victor about staying in town until Wednesday."

"Does it have to be tonight?" Karl muttered harshly. "Can't we talk about this tomorrow morning?"

"No, it has to be tonight," Peter returned. "I want to know if he's working for Fetch."

"That could still wait until tomor—"

"No!" Peter loudly cut in. Then, quieting his tone, he continued, "I want some idea of where Victor stands, because I'm pulling my brother out."

"Out? But we need him."

"I know it'll be harder to oust Fetch without him, but I'll think of something."

"But what about the tables," Karl replied, shaking his head.

"The tables?"

"He was going to make some samples, remember? So we could start manufacturing the pedestal tables."

Peter's jaw clenched in frustration—once again, his employer was lost in a haze of oblivion. "Karl, let's just worry about getting the factory out of Fetch's grasp for right now...okay?"

"I don't think we need to go that far, Peter."

"Pardon?"

"Quent's admitted that there are some disciplinary problems in the factory, but I don't think that's any reason to put him through the mill as you've been doing."

"What?! That man is dangerous, Karl."

The older man didn't voice a reply, but the rolling of his eyes and his expression of disgust said it all. Glancing at the stained-glass window behind him, Peter tried to conceal his aggravation. Somehow, the foreman had gained Karl's favor once again.

Lowering his gaze, Peter absently studied his freshly polished boots. If he was going to dethrone Fetch, he had to persuade his employer to have confidence in him—and him alone. It was possible, but it wasn't going to be kind. With a few carefully chosen phrases, Peter knew he could completely sway Karl to his side...yet he still hesitated. He detested himself for all the misery he had inflicted upon his stepfather—but that treatment would pale in comparison to what he could do to his employer...

"Karl, I...I want you to know how much I appreciate what you've done for me. I've really enjoyed working with you...I know we've had our differences, but that hasn't changed how I feel," Peter said, clenching his jaw tighter and hating what he was about to say. "I've felt as if I've been working with my father."

The older man's eyes started to water. "And I've felt as if I've been given one of my sons back."

"That's why I'm pushing for everything to come to an end—so you and I can get this factory straightened out and running smoothly again...as a father-and-son team."

Karl nodded and patted Peter on the shoulder. "All right, Son...we'll talk to Victor as soon as possible."

Peter forced a smile. Karl was now on his side, but the taste of victory was still bitter. "Good...now, if you'll excuse me, I'd like to dance with Anna."

"I don't blame you...she's stunning."

"Thank you...I think so too," Peter returned, then he wandered over to where Mrs. Rheinhardt and Anna stood admiring the rose-and-vine garlands. "Excuse me, ladies...I apologize for the interruption, but I was wondering if you would like to dance, Anna."

"Yes!" she cried, turning to face him.

Holding back a laugh, Peter grinned at Anna's emphatic response—obviously, she had grown weary of discussing flowers. "Please excuse us, Mrs. Rheinhardt."

"Oh, thank you," Anna sighed as she and Peter joined the other waltzing guests. "She's a nice woman, but all she could talk about was her prize roses... over and over."

Peter chuckled. "I didn't mean for you to get caught in the middle of this."

"It's all right—really...Mr. and Mrs. Rheinhardt are not what I expected— they seem quite nice...but their daughter..."

"I know," Peter replied quietly. "Lori has always been, uh, interesting to deal with."

"Is there something wrong?" Anna asked, gazing at him. "Didn't your talk with Mr. Rheinhardt go very well?"

"Why?"

"Well, you look...sad."

"No, it went very well," Peter returned with a shake of his head. "But I did something that I'm not very proud of."

"What?"

Peter hesitated while peering into Anna's hazel eyes—would the truth of his disgraceful act turn her against him? "I, uh, I told Karl that he was like a father to me...it wasn't the kindest thing to do, but it was the only way to get him to listen to me," he answered, trying to convince himself as well as Anna.

"Then you don't really feel that way?"

"No...he's been very good to me, but I've never thought of him as anything but my father's friend."

"And what about your other lie?" Anna asked, her eyes sparkling with mirth.

Peter smiled—he knew he'd have to face calling her his fiancee sooner or later. And, as if by cue, the quartet started playing a slower tune, giving him the chance to concentrate on his words. "Forgive me for that...but the only reason Lori was clinging to me was to irritate you, and I thought if I announced that we were engaged, she'd stop her theatrics...did, uh, did you mind me saying it?"

Anna shook her head as a blush covered her face.

Peter's heart jumped at the positive response, and he found himself opening his mouth to ask her to be his wife—then he swallowed back the proposal. It had only been a week—how could he be thinking of marriage? Daven was the impulsive one...not him.

Suddenly, Peter caught a quick glimpse of one of the guests dancing near him, and he drew in a quick breath. The man's long, flowing hair was unmistakable—it was Daven...no...no, it wasn't. Closing his eyes, he laughed.

"What is it, Peter?"

"Do you see that man?" he returned, tilting his head to the left. "There—the one with the long hair."

Anna nodded.

"For a minute, I thought it was my brother—with that long hair, the man reminded me of Daven. Well...reminded me of Daven before his hair was cut." And, as Peter continued to stare, he realized that the purple-gowned woman dancing with the long-haired stranger was Lori...and that meant Victor might be available for their much-needed talk. Surveying the ballroom, Peter smirked as he spotted the salesman, who had located another servant with a full tray of hors d'oeuvres. Now, all he had to do was find Karl...and with the thought came a light tap on his shoulder.

"Karl?" Peter asked with surprise as he and Anna immediately stopped dancing.

"Victor's free," the older man replied. "Why don't you go and speak with him, and I'll finish your dance with Miss Spreyer."

"But you should really be the one to ask him to stay in town, Sir."

Karl shook his head. "I want all the men to know that whether an order comes from me or you—it holds the same weight."

"Even Fetch?"

Glancing at Anna, Karl frowned. "We will discuss him another time."

As the older man took Anna's hands and waltzed off with her, Peter stood motionless in the middle of the dance floor. Apparently, he didn't accomplish as much as he thought—although he had succeeded in getting Karl to trust him, he still needed to figure out how to get his employer to see the real Quentin Fetch. Noticing that Victor had cleared the servant's tray of every morsel, Peter hurried over to the salesman—before the portly man went in search of more food.

"Mr. Kilian," Peter called.

"Hello," the salesman returned, brushing the crumbs from his fingers. "And, please, we're going to be working together much too closely to be so formal."

"All right...Victor."

"Quite a reception, isn't it?" the salesman murmured as he glanced around the ballroom.

"Yes, it is."

"Sure is a nice ending to a long trip," Victor continued, his attention fixating on a tray of appetizers.

"Then you wouldn't mind spending a few days in town?"

"Well, I, uh...why?"

"I was hoping you'd help me run an inventory at the factory," Peter replied as he watched for the salesman's reaction.

"An inventory? Quentin's really allowing that?"

"He doesn't have any choice," Peter snapped, becoming agitated at the reminder of Fetch's control. "I also wanted to discuss a selling strategy for a new table that we might be making...we should be through with everything by Wednesday...if that's okay?"

Pulling his gaze from the trayful of food, Victor peered at Peter and wiped at the perspiration rolling down his face. "Um…it's fine…but I do have a…a few things to take care of on Tuesday…out of town."

Peter's spirit soared. "Oh, well, I'm sure we can work around it…where do you need to go?"

"Uh, Crestfield."

Inwardly, Peter cheered at the revelation, and he wished Karl had been around to hear it also.

"What about Crestfield?"

Jumping at the question, Peter circled and looked at his employer, who now stood behind him—it was the second time the older man had appeared at exactly the right moment.

"I, uh, I need to go there on Tuesday to, uh, take care of some things…some personal things," Victor answered, tugging nervously at his starched collar.

With a faint smile of triumph on his lips, Peter nodded. He was both elated and somewhat sorry to see the somber grimace on his employer's face. Then Peter's grin disappeared. If Karl was here…who was with Anna? Moistening his lips, he quickly scanned the faces of the twirling guests. And, finally, he spotted her—dancing with the long-haired stranger.

"I hope this meeting isn't about furniture," Lori declared as she joined the men. Then, leaning over to whisper in Peter's ear, she added, "His name is James B. Wild—the third…he's rich…and powerful…and he was very interested in meeting Miss Spreyer…don't they make a cute couple?"

As an uncontrollable twinge of jealousy ran down his neck, Peter glowered at Lori. "Don't even start."

Lori giggled and hid her wicked grin with her fan. "I wouldn't worry too much about…well, well," she announced, interrupting herself and motioning toward the arched doorway, "look who's here."

Curbing his anger and annoyance, Peter looked in the direction of Lori's gesture—and his heart skipped a beat. It was Quentin Fetch—looking uncommonly pleasant in a high-buttoned black suit.

"Daughter," Karl warned loudly, "if you cause a scene, it'll be in tomorrow's Social Column."

"Oh, Father, give me a little credit, will you?" Lori sneered, rolling her eyes. Then, grabbing Victor's arm and pulling him onto the dance floor, she snipped, "I want to dance—now!"

"What was that all about?" Peter asked, completely bewildered by Lori's outburst.

Karl snorted. "Well, Lori and Quentin don't really get along very well anymore."

"Anymore?"

"He used to be one of Lori's beaus."

"What?!" Peter gasped, his brow furrowing with concern. "Why didn't you tell me that?!"

"Because it happened a very long time ago and it's over...both my son and I saw to that."

"I don't understand you, Karl," Peter returned, shaking his head. "You don't trust Fetch with your daughter, but you do trust him with your business?"

"Precisely," the older man retorted, his nose in the air. "Quentin has been a fine employee, but he isn't the right caliber of man for my daughter...I told you before that Lori always picks men who aren't right for her."

"So how did you split them up?"

"That was Marcus' idea...he offered an assistant's position to Quentin—if he gave up Lori."

"So, obviously, Fetch took the promotion."

"Yes, he did."

Peter shook his head again—something just wasn't right...Fetch was not the type of man to let such a slap in the face go unpunished. "And he didn't hold any grudges against you or Marcus? I mean, you both more or less told the guy that he wasn't good enough for Lori...didn't he get angry?"

"No, he didn't," Karl shot back. "That's the kind of man he is...he said he understood our uncertainty and that he was going to do whatever it took to raise himself up to our level."

Yes, Peter commented to himself, that was Fetch all right—the foreman was definitely not letting the slap go unpunished. Poor Karl...his employer truly believed Fetch was striving for self-improvement. But Peter could see exactly what the man was striving for—vengeance.

"The only ill feelings," Karl went on, "were on Lori's part...she hasn't spoken to Quentin since he chose the promotion over her."

Although still bothered by the situation, Peter was grateful for Karl's last statement—at least there was plenty of distance between Fetch and Lori's knowledge of Daven. "I still can't picture those two together," Peter remarked under his breath. "What attracted them to each other?"

Karl shrugged. "You know how fragile Lori is...I think she was looking for someone strong to take care of her."

Fragile? Peter echoed inwardly. He knew, firsthand, that Lori used her kitten act to disguise the mountain lion that really dwelled within her. No, Peter thought, what Lori saw in Fetch was a thirst for control that complemented her own.

"I still wish," Karl added with a sigh, "that Lori would find someone... like you."

"Karl..."

"I know," he returned, holding up his hand. "Don't worry. I think your Miss Spreyer is a wonderful girl...but I can't stop wishing."

"Well, what about Victor."

Karl smirked. "Yes...but...say, what about your brother?"

Peter glared at his employer. "No!" he emphatically returned, and getting tired of their current conversation, he decided to steer the discussion back to a more important issue. "You do recall hearing Victor say that he had to go to Crestfield, don't you?"

A nod was his only response.

"It proves that Victor's working with Fetch."

"It proves that he's going to Crestfield," the older man corrected.

Peter sighed in exasperation. "Karl, I don't see why—"

"I will be convinced of Victor's guilt on Tuesday," the older man cut in, "when we find out if he tries to locate your imaginary client—or not."

"And, when we go to the Hopewells' and see Daven's desk in their house, will you be convinced of Fetch's guilt too?"

"Yes…but only then," Karl growled in reply.

Hesitantly climbing the steps leading to the Spreyers' back door, Daven furtively glanced around and ran his fingers over the stitches on his forehead. Although he had been given permission to see the doctor, he still felt as if he were going to be walloped for…for something. As he stepped onto the porch and tried to quiet his grumbling stomach, Daven lightly knocked on the door-jamb. He appreciated the doctor's concern, but he would have preferred to take the wagon back to the boarding house, where he could get some food—even Everly's tasteless mounds were better than nothing at all. When no answer came in response to his knock, Daven raised his hand to rap once again, then, suddenly, the door swung open, and the doctor's pretty daughter appeared opposite him. The thought instantly passed through his mind that he should comment on how lovely she looked, but the marvelous aroma from the kitchen steered his thoughts in another direction—food.

"Hello, Daven," she offered. "Please come in."

"Um, your father was at the factory earlier," he explained as he entered the kitchen. "He said I should come."

"Yes, we've been expecting you."

Noticing an older woman sitting at the kitchen table, Daven removed his hat and brushed a hand through his hair to straighten it. The resemblance between the two women was unmistakable—and could mean only one thing. "How do you do, Mrs. Spreyer?" he greeted.

A stunning smile and a nod answered him.

Then, turning back to the daughter, Daven continued, "I'm sorry to bother you so close to your supper, Miss Spreyer."

"You're no bother," she returned. "Your wound looks better today."

"Think so?" he asked, fingering the stitches again.

"Just let it heal, Daven," she murmured as she gently pulled his hand away.

Daven knew she was right, and he now regretted discarding his last bandage. But it, like the others, had become so soiled with sweat, sawdust, and blood that it became unbearable to have around his head.

Suddenly, a chill ran down Daven's back, and he stared at the doctor's daughter. Yesterday, he had been Mr. Ashby…now, she was calling him by his first name—as if they were familiar friends.

Before he could question the change, she took his hat and motioned for him to follow. Passing by the doctor's office, she led him to the front of the house and finally stopped at the parlor door. The room's heavy velvet curtains had been pulled closed, and as his eyes adjusted to the darkness, he saw the outline of a man at the fireplace. At first, he thought it was the girl's father, but the figure was much taller and more sinewy than the doctor. Wondering what he had gotten himself into, Daven started to back up.

"It's all right," the doctor's daughter cooed as she tenderly took his arm and guided him into the parlor. Then, striking a match, she lit one of the gas lamps next to the doorway, and the man at the fireplace slowly turned around.

"Peter?" Daven gasped in surprise.

Another lamp was lit, brightening the room even more.

"Peter!" he repeated. And, pushed forward by joy and relief, he hurried to the hearth and tightly embraced his brother.

"It's good to see you," Peter said, returning the hug.

Savoring the comfort of being near his brother once again, Daven tightened his hold, then, reluctantly, he let go.

"I'm sorry about what they've done to you, Dave," Peter offered, staring at all his injuries. "I'm so sorry."

Daven's mouth fell open in bewilderment—the face and voice were definitely his brother's, but the words were not even close to something Peter would say. "You're what?"

"I'm sorry."

"I don't think you've ever said that to me."

"I know," Peter said with a nod. "I apologize for that too."

Confounded, Daven studied his brother's face—this was not the Peter he was used to. And, as he glanced around the Spreyers' parlor, he became even more confused. "How'd…how'd you know that I'd be here?"

"Because I arranged it," his brother returned, pointing toward the room's doorway.

Following the gesture, Daven circled and immediately recognized the bearded doctor standing next to his daughter.

"The Spreyers have offered to help us," Peter continued.

"I had no idea that you were Peter's brother when you were here yesterday," the daughter announced. "If I had known, I would have said something."

"That's okay, Miss Spreyer."

"Please, call me Anna," she returned as she moved into the parlor and grasped Peter's hand in hers.

Looking first at Anna, then at his brother, then back again, Daven smiled. He knew, right from the start, that Peter would approve of the doctor's daughter—and he began to wonder if she was the reason for his brother's new disposition. "That's all right, Anna…I didn't know that you were, uh, friends with Peter either."

"Are you hungry?" she asked.

"Very."

"Then I'll start getting supper ready."

"And, just to be safe," Doctor Spreyer put in, "I'll draw the kitchen curtains too."

"I appreciate it, Otto…thank you," Peter called as the doctor and his daughter left the parlor.

Instantly, Daven's eyebrows raised—not only was there a very noticeable change in his brother's demeanor, but Peter was also on a first name basis with the doctor. "Why close the curtains?" he asked.

"So no one can accidentally see us together."

"And why are you staring at me?"

"I barely recognized you the other day…I'm still not used to you with short hair."

Daven's eyes narrowed. "But you've always wanted it short."

"I know…forgive me, I shouldn't have pushed you into it."

Astonished by yet another apology, Daven shook his head. "You didn't—the heat did."

"You sure have taken a pounding."

"Yeah, but a lot of it's been my fault."

"Oh, come on," Peter exclaimed as he once again examined Daven's injuries. "How can any of this be your fault?"

"I, uh, haven't always used my head…and this," he said, pointing to his stitches, "was definitely my fault. They were aiming for Jaxson, and I just got in the way."

"Well, nothing else is going to happen to you—because you're not going back."

"I'm not what?"

"You're not going back to the factory…you're staying here with the Spreyers until I'm finished with Fetch."

Daven tried to scowl in return, but the movement pulled at his stitches and he relaxed his expression. "You mean you wouldn't mind if I quit in the middle?"

"Mind? I think you've endured quite enough."

Shaking his head, Daven meandered over to the sofa, slumped onto the seat, and looked up at his brother—his amazingly coolheaded brother. "But…but I haven't finished the desk yet…I'm still workin' on the polish."

"That's okay."

"But you said you needed the desk to trap Fetch...now, you may not be able to use it."

"Yes, we can."

"But—"

"Daven, I'm sure someone else in the factory can finish the polishing."

"I know...but what if my disappearance makes Fetch suspicious? Even if the desk gets done, he might hold off on delivering it."

"Then I'll figure out another way to catch him...don't worry."

But worry already gnawed at Daven, and he started to massage his left palm. He had promised Jaxson that everything would be different after Tuesday...that Fetch would lose his reign. Now, if that didn't happen, his friend might lose heart and go through with his escape plan—which, Daven was sure, would end in bloodshed...Jaxson's blood. "No," Daven sighed, "I'll see this thing to the end."

Pushing himself from the fireplace's hearth, Peter walked over to the sofa and peered at Daven with an expression of uneasiness, pride, and surprise. "What?"

"I'm going to finish the desk."

"No, you're not."

"Yes, I am, Peter."

"Daven, I understand that you want to be part of the decisions that affect you," Peter announced calmly but firmly as he crossed his arms. "But I won't go against my better judgment this time...you are staying here."

Daven swallowed hard. Apologies, consent to leave their mission, and now an 'I understand'—although perplexed by Peter's good-temperedness, Daven still applauded it. Yet he was quite sure that it would disappear after he voiced the announcement he knew he had to make...

"Peter, I can't stay here...I have to finish the desk...you see, I, uh, I told Jaxson about what...what we're trying to do...and I told him that...things were going to get better after Tuesday...I can't let him down," he stuttered out as he closed his eyes and waited for his brother's inevitable reprimand for not keeping their task a secret.

"I'll talk to him and explain it…you won't let him down," Peter returned, also taking a seat on the sofa.

Daven's eyes sprang open. "Did you hear what I said? Jaxson knows everything."

"I figured he might," his brother said with a shrug.

"You're not mad?"

"Are you mad that I told the Spreyers?"

Daven opened his mouth to speak, but not being able to think of a response, he just chuckled lightly—he still wasn't used to Peter's newfound calmness. And, as much as he wanted to remain within the safety of the doctor's house, he knew his disappearance from the factory would propel Fetch into a frenzy—and that anger would be taken out on one person…Jaxson. "Peter, you don't know Jaxson…if I don't go back, he'll try to escape from the factory…and they'll kill him—just like that Perryn guy."

"I'm not going to let you talk me—" Peter started to reply, but he stopped as Anna appeared in the parlor doorway.

"Everything's set," she announced sweetly. "You two can come and eat."

At the thought of having some food with taste, Daven jumped up from the sofa. And, purposefully ignoring his brother's partially spoken rebuttal, he followed Anna into the kitchen—where the doctor motioned for him to sit at the head of the table. As he settled into his place, Daven watched Peter lightly kiss Anna on the cheek, then hold her chair as she sat. Suddenly, Daven realized that his brother's life had changed during their separation—and he also realized that he was no longer Peter's only concern. Bowing his head for the meal's blessing, Daven considered what his life would be like away from Peter's authority. The thought intrigued him…and, at the same time, dismayed him.

"It's a simple supper," Anna declared, handing Daven a plate of still-warm bread. "I hope you like it."

Breathing in the bread's sweet scent, he sighed. "I'm sure I will."

As the platters of food were passed hand to hand, Daven crammed as much as he could onto his plate. Finally, after filling his dish to overflowing, he grabbed his fork, stabbed the tines into the aromatic stacks on his plate, and lifted the utensil to his mouth—only then did he remember his manners. Holding his fork just inches from his lips, Daven forced himself to wait until the doctor and Mrs. Spreyer had taken their first bites, then the meal's aroma overpowered him, and he started shoveling endless forkfuls into his mouth.

"Daven, slow down," Peter gently reprimanded.

Swallowing a mouthful, Daven glanced sheepishly at the others. "I'm sorry…I really do have better manners than this."

"We understand," Doctor Spreyer chuckled. "After a long day, I sometimes feel the same way…go ahead and enjoy. You can eat all night if you'd like."

"I'd like nothing more—but I have to be back at the factory by seven," Daven returned, gulping down some more food.

"Does Fetch have you working late again?" Peter asked.

"Not just me—everybody."

"Just what does he have to keep the men there that long?"

"Threats, Peter, he has threats," Daven returned bristling at the question. "Fetch'll take away whatever matters most to you—a guy's belongings, his family, his life…" And, remembering his own personal threat, he added quietly, "His hands."

Immediately, the muscles in Peter's jaw tightened—which was never a good sign. Fortunately, his brother's anger didn't seem to be directed at him this time.

"Did Fetch say he would hurt your hands?" Peter asked in a low rumble.

"Yeah."

"That's exactly why I don't want you going back…it's not safe for you."

"I told ya, Peter. I gotta go…I know it's safer for me to stay here…and believe me, I wanna stay. But I…I couldn't bear it if something happened to Jaxson because I…because I just gave up the fight."

"And what if I ordered you to stay?"

Daven snorted out a laugh. "Did that ever work before?"

Peter remained silent for a moment, then he took a deep breath and shook his head.

Impressed by the concession, Daven smiled. It was comforting to be treated as an equal member of the family—and it was even more comforting to know that his older brother's protective hand was still within reach…just in case.

"I know Fetch uses threats," Peter continued quietly. "And I know he follows through with them, but that's not what I was asking about before…I meant to ask, does Fetch really have enough of his own orders to keep the men busy through the evening?"

Daven nodded. "Yeah…Jaxson says he gets new orders every other day or so."

Putting his fork down, Peter leaned back in his chair. "Have you seen how Fetch gets the orders?"

"No, not really…but he does leave for a couple of hours—just about every day."

"Just him?"

"Yep. Ol' Hallam and Bryce are always around. So's everybody else," Daven answered as he scraped the last bits of food together on his plate.

"Would you like some more, Daven?" Anna asked, passing him a platter of meat.

Daven half-smiled. He had been so preoccupied with the meal and his conversation with Peter that he had forgotten about the Spreyers. "Yes, I would. Thank you," he replied, taking the dish and pushing the remaining meat onto his plate. Then, pulling his watch from his vest, he clicked open the cover, and after a few seconds of arithmetic, he sighed—time was going by too quickly.

"Then it has to be Fetch himself…" Peter murmured, while absently connecting the condensation drops on his lemonade glass.

"What has to be Herr Fetch?" the doctor inquired.

"What?" Peter muttered, coming out of his trance. "Oh, sorry. I was thinking out loud…you see, anything regarding Fetch's personal operation is sent through the mail—to a fictitious Samuel Kelly, in care of the Rheinhardt Factory…and somehow, those letters eventually get to Fetch," he finished, his brow furrowed in thought. "So it has to be Fetch picking them up."

"You mean someone at the post office is helping Mr. Fetch?" Anna asked incredulously.

"It's the only answer," Peter murmured, then he grunted. "But something's not right—there's still a piece missing…when I questioned the kid at the post office, his answers were very odd…I think I'll have another talk with him on Monday."

"So who sends the orders to this Samuel Kelly?" Daven inquired as he started to devour his second plateful.

"Karl's salesman."

"Karl's salesman is Fetch's salesman?" he returned through a mouthful of food. "I thought you weren't going to find that out until Tuesday."

"Well, after talking to the man last night, I'm convinced, but Karl isn't—yet…after Tuesday though, I'll have all the proof I need—and so will Karl."

"Will it really be over then?"

Peter bobbed his head. "When Karl and I see your desk sitting in the Hopewells' library, it will definitely be over…that is if you think you can get the desk done in time."

"I'll get it done…I'll spend all day tomorrow polishing, but I'll get it done."

"Tomorrow?"

Daven smirked. "I'll miss church—the first time ever."

"Fetch has the factory running on Sundays?"

"Every day…until eleven."

As Peter lowered his eyes and drifted back into thought, Daven turned to the Spreyers. "This is the best meal I've had in days…thank you, but I'm going to have to get back."

"Not until I take a look at that wound," Doctor Spreyer announced, rising from his chair. "Come into my office."

As Daven stood and pushed his napkin onto the table, he brushed against his fork, causing the utensil to fall to the floor.

Jerked from his contemplation by the fork's clatter, Peter peered at his brother, then at Doctor Spreyer. "What's wrong?"

"I'm going to apply some salve to his cut and put on a new bandage," the doctor explained.

Peter smiled and lightly patted Daven's arm. "Everything's going to fine, Little Brother...God has it all worked out."

Immediately, Daven's jaw dropped open in astonishment, and he stood motionless, as if his boots had been glued to the floorboards. He had never heard Peter use God's name—except as a curse. Then, glancing at Anna Spreyer, Daven grinned—she was definitely going to be very good for his brother.

As the doctor and Daven disappeared into the office and the door quietly closed, Anna clutched Peter's hand. "Daven's very sweet," she offered with a light squeeze.

"Yes, he is," Peter returned, rubbing his temple. "And he has a lot more strength and dedication than I ever gave him credit for."

Anna tightened her grasp. "It'll be over soon."

"Maybe very, very soon."

"What do you mean?"

A wide smile parted Peter's lips. "I mean, I'm going on a carriage ride with Karl tomorrow...and I don't think he's going to be very pleased with his foreman when he sees the factory open and running on a Sunday."

⊹⊱ Ten ⊰⊹

"Peter, where are we going?" Karl grumbled as their carriage bumped over East Lane's rutted dirt surface. "It's just too hot for a ride today."

"I told you, Sir...I have something I want you to see," Peter answered, moving his window curtain to the side so he could look out.

As he studied the passing landscape—and tried to ignore his employer's impatient glare—Peter wiped at the sweat rolling down his neck. He still couldn't decide which was worse—the heat or the tension inside the coach. Even the growing winds failed to cool the scorching uneasiness inside the curtained carriage. But the discomfort would be all worth it, Peter told himself, when Karl laid eyes on the factory.

Surreptitiously slipping his watch from his waistcoat pocket, Peter quietly clicked open the cover and checked the time. Seven-thirty. According to Daven, the factory would now be running full tilt and be filled with workers—on a Sunday evening...exactly the opposite of what Karl would expect to see.

Suddenly, the coach slowed, made a slight turn to the right, and rolled to a halt. With a relieved sigh, Peter glanced out the window again—they had reached Victoria Road. More of a driveway than even a byway, the little treeless road, named for Karl's wife, was unfortunately the one and only route to the Rheinhardt Factory. Hoping that they were far enough away to be inconspicuous yet close enough for his employer to see the activity inside the building, Peter pointed out the carriage window.

"What now?!" Karl demanded.

"This is what I wanted you to see."

With a grunt, the older man nudged his curtain aside and gazed out the window—then his face paled. "Why?" he asked unsteadily as he recoiled and peered at Peter. "Why did you bring me here…you know how I…I feel about being at the factory…"

"I know, Karl, but just look…I'm not asking you to go in—just look at the building."

"No, I…I can't…"

"Please?" Peter urged, wondering if the whole carriage ride had been for naught.

"Why?"

"Because it will answer a lot of questions."

With an agitated grunt, Karl reluctantly returned his attention to the factory, and as the older man's expression transformed from sorrow, into confusion, and then, lastly, into anger, Peter's spirit soared—albeit somewhat sadly.

"You see, Sir?" Peter murmured, knowing that he had to tread very lightly. "Fetch has been lying to you. He has been running your factory—and your workers—day and night for his own gain."

"Maybe…maybe, he's just behind schedule."

Peter shook his head in disbelief. "You know that's not true, Karl…you know, as well as I do, that there is no reason the factory should be running on a Sunday evening…Daven told me that he and the other men work every night. You have a lot of orders, but not enough to dictate that kind of timetable…right now, those men are working on Fetch's furniture…not yours."

"I guess…I guess you've been right all along," the older man moaned as he bowed his head.

"So are you finally convinced Fetch is guilty?" Peter asked, then, after hearing his own words, he reprimanded himself for the sarcasm that had accompanied them.

Karl nodded.

"Then let's go!" Peter announced, pushing the coach door open.

"What are you doing?!" Karl exclaimed as he grabbed Peter's arm and forced him back.

"I'm going to tell Fetch that he's through."

"No."

"Karl, you just finished telling me——"

"Now, who's not thinking?" the older man cut in. "Do you really expect to just walk into the factory, unarmed, tell Quentin that he's fired, and walk back out unscathed? You're the one who keeps telling me about how dangerous Quent is and about how many others he has on his side…wait until tomorrow. We can get a couple of patrolmen and confront him in the morning at his house—where he'll be alone."

As he listened to the older man's speech, a smile formed on Peter's face. His employer's logic and reasoning were not only correct but also incredibly shrewd. This was the Karl Rheinhardt that he remembered admiring—strong, alert, and ready for battle. "You're right, Sir."

"We'll meet tomorrow morning at my home at quarter to six," Karl announced as a fire lit up his eyes, "grab a patrolman or two—or even the Marshall—and head over to Quentin's house."

Peter breathed out a long exhale of satisfaction, then his eyes narrowed and he studied his employer. "Are you sure? You've retreated from this fight before…Sir."

"No, Son, I won't this time…I'm awake—for the first time in three years."

With a wide, contented grin, Peter grasped the still-open carriage door and pulled it closed. Finally, he inwardly cheered. Finally, everything was going according to his plan…the old Karl was back…Fetch's reign was on the verge of ending…and by morning, Daven would be safe at home.

"Quarter to six…I'm looking forward to it," Peter declared as he pounded on the roof and signaled the coachman to start the drive back to town.

"It's fine the way it is," Fetch growled. "I want it loaded on a wagon tonight."

Daven glanced at the carved writing desk that he had grown to hate. So much of his time, muscle, and sweat had gone into it—the last thing he wanted was for it to go to its buyer incomplete. "I'd still like to apply a few more coats of polish," he explained, praying that his persistence wouldn't result in new injuries to his exhausted body.

"It looks good to me," Hallam put in. "You did a good job—considerin'… don't you think so, Bryce?"

Squatting next to the desk, Leland Bryce studied the carved accents as he caressed the deep grooves with his index finger. "It could use some improvement," he replied as he chewed on a wad of tobacco. "But I reckon it'll do…hey, what in Sam Hill is this?" he demanded, pointing to the lower right-hand side.

Daven tensed—apparently Bryce was much more sharp-eyed than he appeared. "Those are my initials."

"Take 'em off," the dark-haired man ordered as he stood up.

"No," Daven returned, his back stiffening. "I carve it—I sign it."

"Take 'em off! Or I'll—"

"Forget about it, Bryce," Fetch interrupted. "There's no time and it'll wreck the polish anyway."

Sneering at the foreman—and at the obvious lack of support—Bryce spit a glob of tobacco juice on the floor, then stomped over to one of the windows.

Ignoring the hostility, Fetch turned to Hallam and gestured at the writing desk. "Make sure you burn the 'R' somewhere on it before you load—"

"Mr. Fetch, come here…hurry!" Bryce yelled from the window.

Cursing under his breath, the foreman jogged over to the dark-haired man. "What?!"

"There…see it?" Bryce shouted, pointing toward Victoria Road. "That coach that's leaving…I swear that's one of Mr. Rheinhardt's."

"The old man would never come here."

"No…but somebody else would," Bryce returned. "I saw a black-haired man pull the carriage door closed."

"Leighton!" Fetch snarled as he pushed his face up to the glass and swore. "I should've let you kill him when you wanted to."

Instantly, a shiver shot through Daven, and trying to hide his shaking limbs, he lowered himself to the floor and started fiddling with the carving on the desk.

"So what do we do now?" Hallam asked, joining his boss and Bryce at the window.

Crimson-faced, Fetch peered at his blonde-haired assistant, then he looked Bryce in the eyes. "Leighton's gotta have an accident—tonight," he hissed, "before he ruins everything."

Even though the foreman spoke in a whisper, Daven heard the words as clearly as if they had been spoken directly to him. Glancing around, he swallowed hard. He had to warn Peter—he had to make sure his brother stayed safe. But how, God? he silently asked. How can I get word to him? Then, as he spotted his toolbox, the answer came to him, and keeping a watchful eye on the trio at the window, Daven noiselessly slid over to the box, grabbed a gouge, and crawled back to the desk.

"I don't think killin' Leighton's gunna help," Hallam declared in a hushed tone. "He's prob'ly on his way to see Mr. Rheinhardt right now."

"We ain't gotta worry about the old man," Fetch replied. "You keep forgettin' about the ace I have up my sleeve."

Making sure the three men were still immersed in their discussion, Daven lightly touched his carved initials on the desk, then, tightly clenching the gouge, he scraped the tool across his left palm. Immediately, a stream of blood flowed across his hand and dripped onto the floor, and with a genuine gasp of pain, Daven dropped the tool onto the freshly stained floorboards.

"What'd you do?" Hallam announced as he and Fetch stepped over to the desk.

"I...I was going to get rid of my initials as Mr. Bryce ordered," Daven answered and held out his bleeding hand. "But the gouge slipped."

With a grimace of annoyance and anger, Fetch examined the wound. "Serves ya right...I told ya before to forget about it...it's just gunna wreck the polish!"

"Yes Sir...I'm sorry...may I go to Everly's and have Ivy take care of this?"

Fetch breathed out deeply, then, with a flip of his hand, he motioned toward the staircase. "Go...get outta my sight—before I cut ya even worse," he bellowed as he returned to Bryce and the window.

Grateful for the dismissal, Daven started to leave, but Hallam quickly moved in front of him, blocking his exit.

"Yes Sir?" Daven inquired as his heart thumped against his chest.

At first, the blonde-haired man said nothing, he just looked from Daven's bloody palm, to Fetch, and back again. Then, without warning, he began to chuckle. "Well, I'll be..."

"What?!" Fetch barked, turning away from his discussion with Bryce.

"Uh? Oh, nothing, Sir," Hallam replied with a crooked smile.

As Daven Ashby rushed down the stairs, Quentin Fetch mentally questioned his blonde-haired employee's slightly amused smirk, then, scratching at the stubble on his chin, he shrugged off the matter—he had a much more important issue to deal with. Pushing all concerns—save one—from his thoughts, the foreman pivoted on his heel and stared into the cold black eyes of the only man he fully trusted. "Bryce, I want you to do whatever you have to...just find Leighton...check the showroom and his office first, then the hotel...just get rid of him—tonight."

A sly smile formed on the dark-haired man's face. "You can count on me, Mr. Fetch."

"I'm sorry," Peter offered as the coach crawled to a stop.

"Why are you sorry?" Karl asked. "You were right."

"I'm sorry that Fetch took advantage of your trust."

"Me too," the older man replied, slowly nodding his head. "But I thank God that you're as pigheaded as you are…I would have never known the truth otherwise."

A smile instantly parted Peter's lips—rarely did anyone compliment his stubbornness. "Until tomorrow," he said, unlatching the carriage door and stepping onto the street in front of the Spreyers' house.

"I'll be waiting…quarter to six!"

Sobered yet invigorated by the thought of the early morning task, Peter watched his employer's coach rumble down Highview Street. Then, suddenly feeling a hand on his shoulder, his gut knotted, and fearing that Fetch was still one step ahead of him, he whipped around—and thankfully came face-to-face with Doctor Spreyer.

"I didn't mean to startle you, my boy," the doctor chuckled. "I called to you, but you must not have heard."

Peter shook his head. "No Sir, I didn't," he answered, trying to calm his racing heart.

"Did you accomplish what you wanted to with Herr Rheinhardt?"

Reminded of his earlier success, Peter grinned. "Even more than I had hoped for…one glance was all it took—all the reasoning and persuasion in the world would have never accomplished what that one glance did…within seconds, Karl snapped out of his apathy."

"Wunderbar!" the doctor exclaimed with a slap on Peter's back. "Then it's over?"

Peter's smile weakened—as did his enthusiasm. "Well, after tomorrow morning it will be…that's when we're going to confront Fetch at his home."

Doctor Spreyer nodded. "You'll be in our prayers."

"Thank you…that's good to know."

"Why don't we go in and tell Anna and Mama the good news? They've been fretting all day."

Peter nodded and started up the wooden walkway, then, as he reached the stoop, he paused and considered the doctor's phrasing. It wasn't 'Mrs. Spreyer,' 'my wife,' or even 'Irene.' It was 'Mama'—as if he were already a member of the family. Maybe, Peter thought. Maybe, it was time…

"Otto, I'd like to ask you something," he began as they slowly ascended the porch steps.

"Ja?"

Once again, Peter's pulse started to race—but this time, for an entirely different reason. Even though he was ready to make his announcement, he wasn't so sure the doctor was ready to hear it. "I'd…I'd like your permission to…to court Anna."

Doctor Spreyer leaned on the post next to the steps and stroked his beard. "I thought you already were."

"Well, yes, I am…but I'd like to make it more…permanent."

"What are you really asking me, Pay-ter?"

Mustering all his courage, Peter took a deep breath and offered the words he knew he had wanted to say ever since the Rheinhardts' reception. "I'd like your permission to ask Anna for her hand in marriage."

Silence.

"I realize that this is very sudden…"

More silence.

"And I also realize that it's only been a week since I met her…"

The doctor crossed his arms. "Ja," he grunted—then a smile broke the stern expression on his face. "But it has been a very long week."

"Yes, it has."

"Well, Pay-ter, I have to tell you," Doctor Spreyer said, sliding his thumbs behind his suspenders and rocking back on his heels, "Mama and I discussed this very subject after you and Anna left for the reception the other night."

Peter tried to swallow the lump in his throat as he fingered his watch chain. "And?"

"And…we believe the engagement should be at least one year."

Peter grinned in relief as a radiant smile spread across the doctor's countenance.

As if she knew the conversation was about her, Anna suddenly appeared on the other side of the screen door.

"Hello!" Peter exclaimed as he stepped over to the door and pulled it open for her. "We were just—" Then, noticing the cloud of concern hovering over her, his excitement waned. "What's wrong?"

"Daven's in the kitchen," she answered in a whisper. "He ran all the way from the factory to get here."

Worry instantly doused what was left of Peter's joyful mood, and without a word, he darted past Anna, down the hall, and into the kitchen. Tossing his hat onto the table, he rushed over to his brother, who was standing next to the dry sink with Mrs. Spreyer. "Daven, what happened?"

"It's nothing to worry about," Daven replied as he held up his left hand and revealed a new injury.

"Why?! Why'd they do this?!"

"They didn't."

Gently drawing Daven's hand back toward the wash basin, Mrs. Spreyer began to rinse the sawdust and dried blood from the wound.

"Why did they hurt your hand?" Peter tried again.

"They didn't," Daven countered. Then, nodding at Anna and the doctor as they entered the kitchen, he added, "I hurt it so I could have a reason to leave the factory…I didn't know how else to get word to you."

Scenario after scenario—all of them concerning Fetch and his brother and what would happen if the foreman found out who Daven really was—flashed through Peter's mind. "Aw, Daven, coming here was…was just plain foolhardy… we can't be seen together," he groaned, trying to push the dreaded scenarios from his head.

"Oh, yeah? Well, it was even more foolhardy for you to come to the factory tonight!" Daven shouted as he yanked his hand away from Mrs. Spreyer and faced his brother. "Fetch saw the carriage—and you."

"Oh," Peter murmured, rubbing his forehead and silently condemning the barren and treeless Victoria Road.

"And I didn't know you were here," his brother continued, simmering. "I only wanted to leave a message with the Spreyers…Fetch is makin' plans to kill you—sometime tonight."

Peter glanced at Anna, then at the doctor, Mrs. Spreyer, and his brother. Deep within his heart, he always knew that Fetch's animosity toward him could turn deadly, but he never really allowed himself to dwell on the subject…not until now…not until he gazed at the four panic-stricken faces around him. "Did they say anything about seeing Karl?" he asked as he tried to distract them all from the death threat.

Daven's brow crinkled in confusion as if he were attempting to decipher an unknown language. "What?"

"Did they think Karl was with me?"

"I, uh, no…no, I don't think so…they talked about wanting to get rid of you before you ruined everything."

"Good…good."

"Peter, did you hear what I said?" Daven asked, his voice quivering. "Fetch said you had to have an accident."

"I heard you," he returned, hoping to hide the uneasiness that pulsated through him. "All that matters is that they don't know that Karl saw them too."

"That's all that matters?!" Daven yelled indignantly, then, pushing Peter aside, he stormed out of the kitchen and onto the back porch, slamming the screen door behind him.

Realizing that his nonchalance was the cause for his brother's outburst, Peter's jaw immediately clenched in regret. After tomorrow, he told himself...after Fetch was removed from power...after it was all over...then he'd make amends.

"Go after him!" Mrs. Spreyer exclaimed. "Don't let it end like this."

With a pang of guilt and surprise, Peter circled and stared at Irene Spreyer—he had never heard her speak so sharply.

"He's afraid of losing you," she added. "Now go!"

Shoved out the door by the distress in her voice, Peter hurried after his brother. "Daven!" he called in a hushed voice as he ran into the backyard. "Daven...Daven." Finally catching up, Peter reached out and grabbed his brother's arm. "Wait."

"Why?" Daven fumed, yanking himself free. "If you don't care that you're in danger, then neither do I."

After surveying the area for any lookers-on and eavesdroppers, Peter led his brother over to the Spreyers' barn. "I'm sorry...I didn't mean to make light of the situation."

Daven sighed and shook his head. "I need you, Peter...don't you know that?"

Startled by the revelation, Peter stepped back and leaned against the barn door. "I need you too."

"No...not as much as I need you."

Peter nodded—even though he still believed the reverse was true. He had experienced so many losses in his life...taking care of his brother was the only thing that kept him from giving up completely. "I know taking that carriage ride tonight was a risk," he offered, intentionally derailing the conversation. "But it was definitely worth it."

"What do you mean?"

"Karl finally saw Fetch for the liar he is."

"And?"

"And, tomorrow morning, Karl and I and some patrolmen are going to confront Fetch at his house."

Daven shook his head again. "I think Fetch has a patrolman on his side...I don't like this—it's getting too dangerous for you."

The statement caused an instant and uncontrollable grin to appear on Peter's face—it was as if he were having a conversation with himself.

"It's not funny, Peter!"

"I know...but you sounded like me just then."

"I did?" Daven asked with mock concern. Then, lightly jabbing Peter with his elbow, he added, "That's a scary thought."

As Peter answered with a quiet laugh, a strong breeze circled around them, and after rifling through their jackets, it drifted away. Looking skyward, Peter watched for a moment as a thick curtain of clouds started to darken the sky. "Rain's coming," he said absently.

"Uh huh."

"I'll be careful," Peter put in, his attention refocused on his brother. "And you do the same."

Daven's expression once more filled with apprehension. "Okay."

"Don't worry—everything will be different tomorrow."

"I'd say everything's different now," Daven returned, motioning toward the Spreyers' back porch and to the trio huddled on the stoop.

"Uh, yes," Peter murmured, "I guess it is."

A glint shined in Daven's bright-blue eyes and he smiled. "I like her...I like 'em all."

"Them," Peter corrected, then he clamped his jaw shut. "Sorry."

Daven's grin widened. "It's all right," he said. "I should go...it's a long walk back to Everly's."

"Why don't you just stay here...it'll be over in the morning anyway."

"No, Fetch may get cagey."

Peter bobbed his head in agreement, and pulling his brother toward him, he gave Daven a tight hug. "Just be care—"

"Careful—I know." With that and a wink, Daven turned and headed toward the street.

As he watched his brother disappear into the fading twilight, Peter once again felt a hand on his shoulder. But, this time, he recognized the soft, gentle touch and the sweet perfume of violets that accompanied it. "It's hard to believe," he muttered as he wrapped his arm around Anna's waist. "It's just not right."

"What is?"

"It was just a few days ago that I complained to Karl that Daven never seemed to have any concerns...now, he has too many."

"He's not the only one with concerns," Anna put in, patting Peter on the chest. "Papa, Mama, and I want you to stay here tonight...it'll be safer than your hotel."

Shaking his head, Peter turned slightly and faced his sweetheart. "Safer for me...but not for you and your family."

"But—"

"I'm going to put myself and Daven into God's hands tonight," he proclaimed as he fingered the curls on Anna's forehead. "It's all I can do...but I'll stop by early in the morning, before I go to Karl's, to let you know that I'm all right...okay?"

Averting her gaze, she nodded.

Gently, Peter grasped Anna's chin and lifted her head up. Then, as he gazed into her worried-filled eyes, he whispered, "I love you." And, drawing her even closer, he kissed her passionately, savoring the sweetness of her lips...possibly for the last time.

Leland Bryce urged his horse into the factory's yard while desperately searching in the near-dark for his boss. Then, spotting the foreman's silhouette on the loading platform, he dismounted, rushed over to the building, and bounded up the steps.

"You take care of Leighton?" Fetch asked, spitting a wad of tobacco juice on the ground.

Bryce stared at the brown stain—which told him more than he really wanted to know…his boss, who rarely chewed tobacco, was extremely irritated.

"Well?!"

"Not yet," he answered, knowing that his report would only darken the foreman's mood. "But I did find somethin' else."

Fetch squinted and crossed his arms. "I'm only int'rested in hearin' that Leighton's dead."

"Well, I think you're gunna want to hear this too."

No response.

"I didn't find Leighton at his hotel, so I broke into the showroom and went up to the office that he's usin'…then I checked Rheinhardt's office…and you know what I saw in there?"

Fetch spit again.

Figuring that his boss was not in the right frame of mind for a guessing game, Bryce answered his own question. "I saw three pieces of furniture with Ashby's initials carved into 'em."

Fetch wiped his sleeve across his mouth. "You sure?"

Bryce nodded. "Uh huh."

"That is int'resting…the old man doesn't allow any furniture into his office unless he knows the carver," Fetch said, scratching the stubble on his chin. "I better talk to my ace and see what's goin' on…while I'm doin' that, I want ya to stay here and help Hallam load that desk onto a wagon."

"But what about Leighton?"

"Forget about him—for now."

"But—"

"Just do what I say…I wanna get some answers about Ashby first, then we'll take care of Leighton."

Sitting on a large ruffle-covered chair, Quentin Fetch leaned back and stretched out his legs. Then, with an impatient grunt, he pushed himself upright, placed his elbows on his knees, and rested his chin on his folded hands. Why was it taking so long? he inwardly questioned as he glanced around the shadowy, gaslit sitting room. Switching positions on his petticoated seat once again, he cursed. He hated the Rheinhardt guest house—it always felt as if he were inside a millinery.

"It's late…what's going on?"

Looking first at the tall clock in the corner, then at the voice's source, Fetch smirked. "What took ya so long…I signaled a long time ago."

"And it was only by chance that the maid saw the signal when she was turning down the bed…you took quite a gamble coming here at this hour."

"I had to see ya," the foreman explained, rising from his frilly chair.

"Oh? Couldn't wait for our usual time, huh?" Lorelei Rheinhardt cooed as she rushed forward, wrapped her arms around him, and firmly pressed her lips against his. Instantly and with a grimace, she shoved him away. "I thought I asked you to stop chewing that awful muck. Those cigars are bad enough to—"

"I'm not here for that, Lori," he cut in.

"Good…because your mouth tastes like a spit—"

"We've got trouble."

"Can't it wait until the morning? My parents might—"

"No, it can't," he snapped. "Your father has some furniture in his office that was carved by a kid named Daven Ashby…you know him?"

A coy smile spread across her face. "I may…are you jealous?"

"I'm not playin'!" Fetch sneered as he roughly grabbed her shoulders and shook her. "Do you know this kid?"

Lori's grin disappeared and she stared into the foreman's gray eyes. "You're hurting me, Quent."

"Do you know him?!" he shouted, loosening his grip slightly. "Ashby. Daven Ashby. Tall, good-lookin' kid with light hair and pale eyes."

Normally, Lori would have continued with her teasing, especially after the description she was given. But something in Quentin's eyes—something she had never seen before—told her to take the question seriously. "Ashby...Ashby..." she repeated, trying to recall the name. "No, I don't know him."

Fetch cursed under his breath. "You sure?"

"Yes!"

Releasing his hold, the foreman swore again and turned toward the window.

"What's going on, Quent?"

"Leighton knows."

"Knows what?"

"He knows that I've been runnin' the factory and workin' the men when I shouldn't be," he answered, circling back to face her.

"How does he know?"

"He was in a rig that drove by the factory tonight...Leighton knows what we're doin', Lori...we gotta stop him before he convinces your old...your father to get rid of me."

Lori paled and sank onto the ruffled chair. "Oh, no!"

"What?"

"My father and Peter went for a ride earlier...Peter said he wanted to show Father something."

Fetch bellowed out a curse, and reaching down to the table next to him, he grabbed a vase of flowers and whipped it at the wall.

Annoyed, Lori stood and placed her hands on her hips. "Throwing flowers isn't the answer, Love," she announced harshly. "There must be something we can do to fix all this."

"Yeah, there is...kill Leighton."

Lori rolled her eyes. "I need solutions—not jokes," she declared, and ignoring a mumbled response from the foreman, she started to pace. She needed to think of something...

"How's this for a solution," Fetch proclaimed, scratching the stubble on his chin. "Tell your father everything."

Unfurling her hair from the braided knot at the back of her neck, Lori shook her head. "I don't think he's ready to hear the truth…"

Lori knew her father adored her, but to him, she would always be a useless female. It didn't matter that she was a capable manager—more capable than any of her brothers had ever been. And it didn't matter that she was the only heir left in the family. But it did matter that she was a woman. It was that reality that blocked her rightful acceptance into the family business—and forced her to prove that she could govern as well as any man. She never liked sneaking furniture orders in and out of the factory, but it demonstrated that she could handle the business and make a good profit doing it.

"You ain't got a choice…you gotta tell him," the foreman countered. "Leighton knows something's goin' on—and now, so does your father."

"But—"

"Just tell him, Woman! Tell him about the extra orders…and that I've been helpin' ya…and that you wanna be boss…then tell him that you did it all for him and the company."

"Oh, Quent, I can't say—"

"If you don't, Leighton will end up with the factory."

Lori bristled as she considered Quentin's words. She just couldn't let Peter Leighton take her place—her rightful place—without a fight. "I can try…but Peter's gotten awfully good at pulling Father's opinion back to his side."

Fetch shrugged. "Just do your little girl act…your pa can't resist that."

Her expression softening, Lori pouted her lips and sauntered over to Quentin. "And neither can you, Love," she whispered. Then, as she brushed her hand through his hair, an addendum crept into her thoughts. "Maybe, I can try to use a little charm on our dear Peter too…and persuade him to stop working against us."

"Well, if somethin' ain't done, he'll end up ridin' me out of town on a rail," Fetch returned, caressing her face. "Just don't go usin' up ever'thing on Leighton—save some of it for me."

Lori smiled. The last thing she wanted was to lose Quentin Fetch—he was the only man who had ever treated her as an equal. "I'm sorry you got dragged into this, Quent," she purred. "It's all Peter's fault—he's messed everything up...he should've just stayed in Bradlee..." Suddenly, as her mind focused on Peter Leighton's home town, a name flashed through her head. "You said Daven Ashby, didn't you?"

Fetch's eyes opened wide. "Yeah...who is he?"

"I couldn't place the name before because—"

"Who is he?!" Fetch hollered, tightly grabbing her wrists.

"Quent, you're hurt—"

"Who is he?!"

"Peter's stepbrother."

"His what?!"

"Daven Ashby is the name of Peter's stepbrother."

"Stepbrother?!" Fetch barked as a mask of rage blanketed his features. "Then Leighton knows everything...absolutely everything!" he roared as he shoved Lori backward, causing her to lose her balance and fall onto the ruffled chair.

"Quent, what's...what's gotten into you?" she wailed, half in anger, half in fear. She knew Quentin Fetch had a temper, but never before had she seen the sinister expression that now darkened his face.

"It ain't gunna happen again," he growled. "I'm not gunna lose what I've worked so hard to get!"

Lori righted herself on the chair. "You mean what we've worked so hard to get, don't you?"

"No—I don't."

Staring in bewilderment at the foreman, Lori frowned—his wild eruption just didn't make sense. She was the one who would lose the most...her father's trust...the chance to take control of the business...the man she loved. Quentin, on the other hand, would just lose his job...

"Do whatever it takes, but get your father back on our side," Fetch seethed as he pivoted on his heel and headed for the doorway.

"Wait!" she called pushing herself up. "Where are you going?!"

"To make Peter Leighton sorry he ever came to Sandorville!"

"What do you mean? Wait!"

But he was already out the door.

As Frank Hallam entered his boss's office, he could almost see the enmity hanging in the air. "What's going on?" he asked as he leaned against the door to close it.

Fetch glowered at him, then pulled a revolver from his desk drawer.

"What's going on?" he repeated, this time addressing Bryce, who stood next to the foreman.

"Mr. Fetch just found out that Ashby is really Leighton's stepbrother."

"Stepbrother, huh?" Hallam murmured with a surprised lilt—even though he wasn't really surprised by the news.

"It all makes sense now," Fetch snarled as he checked to make sure the pistol was loaded. "Leighton always seemed to know what we were doin'—now, we know why."

Hallam looked at the revolver, then at his ruddy-faced boss. The reasoning was most likely correct, but he still had to try to create even an ounce of doubt. "Bein' related doesn't prove that Ashby's been tellin' Leighton stuff."

Bryce snorted out a laugh of both shock and contempt. "Just how stupid are you, Hallam?! Actin' like they didn't know each other...of course, he's been tellin' Leighton stuff."

Fetch nodded in agreement while stuffing the pistol into a holster. "Lori could've convinced the old man that we were just makin' furniture on the side to help her...but because of Ashby, Leighton knows the whole truth...he knows I ain't payin' the men...he knows about my loans...he knows about Everly's..."

"So whatd'ya gunna do?" Hallam asked, already knowing the answer.

302 of Nancy Feldbush

"I'm gunna kill 'em both."

"What good will that do?"

"What good will it do?!" Fetch returned with a curse. "It'll get rid of our little tattletale…and it'll send Leighton—and his proof—to a well-deserved grave…and it'll prob'ly make the old man loonier than he already is…and best of all, it'll make me very happy…that's what good it'll do."

Bryce nodded emphatically. "Any more stupid questions, Hallam?"

"No."

"Then let's get going," Fetch thundered. "Hallam, get some horses and lanterns…we'll start with Leighton."

"No."

"What do you mean 'no'?!" Bryce and Fetch bellowed in tandem.

"I don't want any part of this."

Instantly, a ghostly silence gushed into the room.

"You!" Bryce hissed, finally breaking the stillness. "You've been diff'rent ever since Leighton asked ya to be a salesman," he continued, pointing his finger at Hallam. "You workin' for him now?"

"No."

"Then what're ya bellyachin' about?" Fetch asked, spitting a wad of tobacco juice onto the floor.

"I just don't wanna be a part of it this time," Hallam answered with a shrug.

"You'll go back to bein' one of them again," Fetch sneered as he gestured toward the heavy wooden door that led to the factory. "No more favors…no more money…you'll be on your own hook."

"I know."

"And you'll die—just like the rest of the mudsills—if ya tell anybody 'bout what goes on here."

"I know that too."

"You're an idiot, Hallam!" Fetch snorted as he slammed his fist on the desk. "Do you know what you're givin' up?"

"Forget him," Bryce announced arrogantly. "I know who I can get to replace him…somebody who won't turn yella."

Ignoring his coworker's comment, Hallam stared at his boss. "Yes, Mr. Fetch, I know exactly what I'm givin' up."

As Daven walked into Everly's front yard, a light rain began to splatter on the ground around him. Hoping that the cool drops would chase away the fatigue that haunted him, Daven closed his eyes, lifted his face upward, and tried over and over to gather his scattered thoughts so he could concentrate on talking with God—but his tired mind just would not obey.

Suddenly and mixed with the rain, he heard the rustle of footsteps. As his heart began to gallop, Daven forced his eyelids open and he scanned the darkness. At first, nothing appeared, then, through the glow of the restaurant windows, he saw a petite silhouette rushing toward him.

"Ivy," he breathed out in relief.

Without a word, Ivy threw her arms around his neck and pulled herself up to kiss him on the lips.

Gently pushing her away, Daven smiled. "Whatever happened to 'hello'?"

"That was 'hello,'" she beamed. "What've ya been up to? This is the second night you've missed supper."

"Mr. Fetch wanted me to stay tonight and finish something."

"You sure you're not carryin' on with somebody else?"

Daven grunted out a chuckle. "Nope, there's no one but you," he returned, putting his arm around her.

"Well, that's good," Ivy announced. "I'd have to fix the girl's flint otherwise… come on," she continued, dragging him toward the restaurant. "I saved ya some food…I was gunna take it up to your room, so it'd be there for ya when ya got home…but now, ya can come in and eat."

"Thanks, Ivy, but I got something I—"

"Hey, not that I'm complainin', but why are ya here? The wagon's not due for a couple of hours."

"I, uh, I finished the...my project, so Fetch said I could leave."

"Well, come on then...it'll be real cozy—just you and me."

At first, Daven resisted, but hunger won the battle, and he allowed Ivy to pull him into the building.

"You can sit there," she said, motioning at a large table by the door. "I'll be right back."

As Ivy disappeared into the kitchen, Daven slumped onto a chair and surveyed the dimly lit dining room. By sunrise, it would be over, he reassured himself. He would be released from Fetch's hold and would never have to return to Everly's restaurant or his cramped, stifling room in the boarding house. He would be free—finally. But then what? he wondered. Now that his brother had...had other commitments—where did that leave him?

Shoving the kitchen door open with her hip, Ivy reentered the room with a plate in one hand and a glass of water in the other. "It's kinda cold," she declared as she sashayed over to Daven and placed the dish of lumpy food in front of him. "But at least it's something."

"Thanks, Ivy...I hope you're not going to get into trouble for this."

Bending over to set the glass on the table, Ivy pressed herself against him. "Oh, I'm sure I will—but you're worth it," she cooed, wriggling even closer.

Having no other choice but to stare at Ivy's voluptuous chest, Daven noticed something new hanging around her neck. "Pretty necklace," he offered as she slid onto the chair opposite him.

Ivy held up the piece of jewelry so he could see it better. "I made it," she proudly proclaimed.

Leaning across the table, Daven studied the crafted necklace. The delicate, beaded chain was made from braided...

"Is that hair?" he asked, amazed that anything so fine could be worked with at all.

Ivy nodded and her eyes began to dance. "Yep. I used mine for the chain…"

"Huh," Daven grunted, stuffing a forkful of potatoes into his mouth.

"And I used your hair for the beads."

Startled by the statement, Daven accidentally swallowed his unchewed potatoes. "You…you used…what?" he choked out between coughs.

"I made the beads from your hair…I saved some the day I cut it," Ivy replied, stroking the necklace.

With a half-smile, Daven once again leaned over the table and examined the woven keepsake more closely. Ivy had created tiny hollow beads, then masterfully worked them into the braided chain—her skill was admirable. "You're very good," he offered, settling back down on his chair.

"Would you like to find out just how good?"

Shaking his head at Ivy's brashness, Daven grabbed for his glass of water, but the movement pulled at his forgotten cut and tore open the newly formed scab. Flinching, Daven looked at his palm as the bleeding started again.

"Sakes alive!" Ivy exclaimed. "What'd they do to you now?"

"It's okay…one of my tools just slipped."

"I better get somethin' to wrap it," she cried, jumping up from the table.

"Wait…" he called, but she had already vanished through the kitchen door.

As Daven skewered a badly burned piece of chicken with his fork, the restaurant's front door creaked open just far enough to disturb the rusted chimes that hung over it. Looking up at the ajar door, Daven's pulse began to race, but no one entered and nothing passed over the threshold—except the rain. Figuring that it was just the faulty latch, Daven shoved the forkful of meat into his mouth, pushed himself from the table, and stepped over to close the door—and as he did, he came face-to-face with Quentin Fetch.

For what seemed like hours, the big foreman just stood in the partially opened entrance, then, he pushed the door back and entered, followed closely by Leland Bryce, of course, and…Josh Clayton? As he hurriedly chewed and swallowed his mouthful, Daven studied the man who stood in Frank Hallam's usual place. Clayton had been just another pawn when he tried to heave Jaxson into the power belt at the factory—now, he was one of Fetch's highest-ranking henchman. What had happened, Daven wondered, to make the foreman change his guards?

The question was immediately forgotten as Fetch thrust out his powerful arm and shoved Daven backward into the middle of the dining room. As he peered at the foreman's drenched, hatred-twisted expression, Daven's heart skipped a beat, then another. He had never seen the big man look so...so deadly. "Mr....Mr. Fetch," he stuttered, trying to catch his breath.

"So did ya talk to your brother tonight?" the foreman wheezed out between clenched teeth.

Daven's body started to shake, and automatically, he reached over to massage his left palm—but his new injury made the habit impossible. "I...I don't know what...what you're talking about," he tried as his nervousness grew tenfold.

"Did ya go and tell Peter Leighton—your stepbrother—'bout our plans?" Fetch asked, moving closer to Daven. "Like you've been doin' from the first day."

Daven backed up a step and another, but he froze in place as he watched the foreman pull out a revolver. At that moment, as he glimpsed the raw fury in Fetch's eyes, Daven guessed that he would not live to see Monday's sunrise. His thoughts immediately darted to Ivy, then to Jaxson, then to his brother and finally settled on his only source of comfort—God. Silently, Daven offered up a prayer that the Lord keep him—not necessarily from getting shot—but just keep him.

"Where's your brother?!" Fetch demanded, punctuating each word with a wave of the pistol.

Suddenly, a strange stillness poured over Daven, which he fought against with all his strength—in his present situation, he should be terrified or angry or spiteful...anything but calm.

"Where's your brother?!" Fetch barked with a curse as he forced down the hammer on his pistol.

Realizing that Peter must still be safely at the Spreyers' and that the foreman had no idea of his brother's whereabouts, Daven just shrugged. "I can't tell you," he returned, and noticing how much his calmness irked Fetch, he stopped fighting the peace that had filled his spirit.

The foreman's face darkened, and lifting the revolver, he pointed it at Daven's chest.

"No!" Ivy shrieked as she reentered the dining room and ran over to the foursome. "No, don't...not him too," she pleaded, placing herself between Daven and Fetch.

"Get her outta there!" Fetch bellowed, motioning at Bryce.

The dark-haired man immediately marched over to Ivy and yanked her away from Daven.

"No!" she screamed. Then, giving Bryce a hard bite on the back of his hand, Ivy pulled herself free and rushed over to the foreman. "Please, don't! I...I love him."

Dragging Ivy away again, Bryce laughed. "Yeah, him and every other man you can get your claws into."

Ivy's eyes opened wide and she slapped the dark-haired man across the face, causing him to release his hold once more. Darting back toward Fetch, Ivy tugged at the big man's arm as tears fell from her eyes. "Don't do this," she begged. "Don't do this to him...or to me."

Fetch swore. "Maybe you can keep hold of her," he said, pushing Ivy over to Clayton. "You don't understand, Girl," the foreman continued. "Ashby here is Leighton's stepbrother, and they've been workin' together to get rid of me."

Ivy cackled out a humorless laugh. "Who told you that lie?" she demanded as she fought against Clayton's grip.

"Lori—and it ain't no lie...she knows 'em both," Fetch growled, waving the pistol at Daven. "Ashby's been tellin' his brother all about what I do at the factory."

Still trying to jerk her arm out of Clayton's grasp, Ivy glared at the barrel-chested foreman. "So? It's no different than what I do for you!"

Ivy's statement wrenched Daven away from attempting to place the name 'Lori,' and wide-eyed, he looked at the tiny, flaxen-haired girl—but she wouldn't meet his gaze. "What?" Daven gasped, not even realizing that he said the question aloud.

Fetch snickered. "Pretty funny, huh? You really work for Leighton, and Ivy really works for me."

Instantly, Jaxson's warnings crept back into Daven's head. His friend had told him that it wasn't safe talking to people and that word always seemed to get back to Fetch—and this was how. None of the men would have ever guessed that sassy, little Ivy was the foreman's ears and eyes.

"Why, Ivy, why?" Daven asked as he digested what he had just learned.

Ivy lifted her head and looked into his eyes. "Do ya remember askin' me if I had anybody to help me outta this mess?"

Daven nodded. "You said you had an uncle, but that he wouldn't help you."

"Nope, he won't help me at all," she muttered as her eyes narrowed and focused on Fetch. "He won't help me 'cause then he'd lose his snitch."

As he looked from Ivy's tear-stained face to Fetch's smug grin, Daven's heart filled with sympathy for the girl. He knew how painful it was working for Fetch—and he could only guess what kind of life Ivy had as the man's niece. And, with that thought, Daven thanked God for giving him Peter—overprotective, dogmatic, marvelous Peter—as his guardian.

"Last chance, Ashby," the foreman sneered. "Where's your brother?"

Daven shook his head slightly...then everything seemed to happen at once. The revolver exploded—twice...Ivy screamed and screamed...the searing bullets tore into his body and pushed him into the empty tables behind him...he hit the floor—hard—and everything darkened...then Jesus touched him...

Using the light from the factory, Jaxson inspected the ropes and tarpaulin that held the crated mahogany writing desk safely in the wagon bed. He still believed that it was a bad idea to load the desk onto the wagon already, especially when the chance of another rainstorm was so great. But Hallam was handing out the orders, and he wasn't about to argue. As he checked the ropes a final time, Jaxson sighed—it was the first time he actually wanted to return to Everly's Boarding House. He had hated leaving his friend at the factory during the supper break, but Fetch insisted that Daven stay and finish the desk—alone. From there, the evening had become just a blur of troubling events, and Jaxson yearned to return home, so he could talk to his friend and put all the puzzling pieces together.

As he absently kicked at the muddy dirt on the wagon's back-right wheel, Jaxson shook his head. No matter how hard he tried, all he could see was his friend's newest injury. Yet it was more than the damaged palm that bothered him—it was also the panic that had been in Daven's eyes. What had happened? Jaxson wondered. He had tried to find out...he had begged his friend to tell him what was wrong, but he received only 'I'll tell you later' as an answer. Now, it felt as if later would never come...

Leaning against the wagon, Jaxson stared into the darkness, and he couldn't help but laugh at himself. He had been so annoyed, at first, with Daven's attempts at friendship. For some reason, the kid had taken a liking to him—but the fondness wasn't mutual. Daven's charitable disposition and good-natured attitude were irritating enough, but somewhere along the way, they had also become reminders. With a long exhale, Jaxson gritted his teeth—they had become unbearable reminders of what had died within himself so very long ago. But, thankfully, Daven never gave up and eventually dragged him from the mire. With that thought, Jaxson laughed. Whether he wanted one or not, he now had a friend...a friend whose well-being dominated his every thought.

"You done yet?"

Coming out of his reverie, Jaxson looked at Hallam, who stood in the factory's doorway. "Yes Sir."

The blonde-haired man looked from the loaded wagon, to Jaxson, then to the darkened cloud-filled sky. "Ya might as well just wait for the wagon to take ya back to Everly's...I ain't got nothin' else for ya."

As Hallam turned and disappeared into the factory, Jaxson rubbed his hand over his face—the puzzle kept growing more and more confusing. It wasn't typical for Frank Hallam to be generous. And it was even more unusual for the man to remain at the factory, especially when Fetch, Bryce, and Josh Clayton had departed together—obviously on business.

It was then, in the somber darkness, that Jaxson spotted a flicker of light coming toward the factory. Was it the wagon? he wondered. No, it couldn't be—the boarding house wagon could be heard for miles as it bumped along Victoria Road. No, this was the glimmer of a single lantern, and as the light drew closer, Jaxson's thoughts congregated on one subject—Daven. Suddenly, he found himself walking toward the bobbing glow, then he stopped.

"Ivy?" Jaxson questioned in a whisper.

"Oh, Jaxson!" she whimpered as she ran up to him, holding the lantern in one hand and a small satchel in the other. "They shot him!"

"Shot who?"

"Daven...they shot Daven."

The words knocked Jaxson backward as if he had been slugged in the face. "No," he moaned, but as he stared at the tears running down Ivy's cheeks, he knew it was true. At least now, he understood one of the odd events that had taken place earlier—now, he knew why Fetch had left with a pistol hanging from his belt. "But...but why?"

Holding tightly onto the lantern handle, Ivy lifted the lamp up to her face and wiped at her tears with the back of her hand. "They found out...that he's Peter Leighton's brother...and that the two of them been workin' together."

Jaxson's mouth fell open. "How?"

"And Mr. Fetch shot him," she cried, slowly swaying back and forth. "You gotta go find Daven—before it's too late."

"Then...then he's still alive?"

Ivy shrugged and brushed at her tears again. "He was when they left...they were going to leave him somewhere along the South Pine River."

Jaxson closed his eyes. The South Pine. It was so far and it would take so long to get there without a horse. With a fearful glance toward the factory, Jaxson shivered. He knew he would never get permission to go search for Daven, and if he left anyway, he would probably end up getting a bullet aimed at him too. He would end up losing everything...the money he had worked so hard to collect...his chance to escape...his life...

Slowly, Jaxson's eyelids fluttered open, and he shrugged off the cloak of trepidation that had wrapped itself around his shoulders. It was time to decide what was more important to him—his own life or his friend's.

"I'm gunna need help, Ivy," Jaxson finally breathed out. "You'll have to—"

"No, I can't," she returned, holding up her satchel. "I'm leaving town—tonight...now."

"I thought you cared for Daven!"

"I do! But, even if he's alive, I could never face him again," she murmured, bowing her head. "What he must think of me now..."

"Ivy, that's no reason to leave...you have to stay and help me."

"I just can't!" she screamed. "Don't you understand? I just can't do what my uncle wants anymore...not after this!"

Jaxson shook his head. Their argument was accomplishing only one thing—wasting precious searching time. "What's your uncle got to do with this?"

She lowered her gaze. "Everything...Quentin Fetch is my uncle."

Jaxson swore as the true meaning of Ivy's revelation hit him. "Your uncle?! I should've known it was you...ever'body trusted you...includin' Travis Perryn... you told Fetch about Travis' plans, didn't ya? Did ya betray Daven too?!"

Ivy dropped the valise she was carrying and slapped Jaxson's cheek. "Travis promised to take me with him, and when he didn't, yes, I told my uncle about his escape...but I didn't think he'd kill Travis...I didn't want that."

"And what about Daven?"

"I never knew about him and Peter Leighton bein' brothers."

"Then how'd Fetch find out?"

"Lori Rheinhardt."

Dumbfounded by the sudden turn in the conversation, Jaxson's brow wrinkled in confusion. "Lori Rheinhardt? How'd...how did—"

"Her and my uncle are partners...all the way partners."

With a final curse, Jaxson yanked the lantern from Ivy's grasp and headed for the South Pine River.

⊰Eleven⊱

It was hopeless, Jaxson inwardly commented as he tramped along the riverbank—absolutely hopeless. Without warning, the rain-soaked ground relinquished its support, and he slid down the embankment into the mucky riverbed. He was never going to find Daven, he told himself—not alive anyway...not after so many hours...

Lifting the lantern above his head, Jaxson surveyed the area, trying to find the best place to climb out of the deep trench. Then he spotted it—only a few feet away. A tree, which had obviously grown tired of standing on the river's edge, leaned over the gully, almost touching the ground on the opposite bank. Immediately, Jaxson headed over to the tree, and hanging his lantern on a branch, he pulled himself out of the riverbed. Balancing on the huge trunk, he grabbed the lamp and maneuvered his way onto the embankment.

He knew, in his head, that he should just give up—but the feeling that Daven was near poked at his heart, and he started his search again. With a look skyward, Jaxson's shoulders slumped in disappointment—dawn was still hours away. Even the clouds were against him—blocking the light the moon could have offered. Lord, how am I going to find him? he silently asked.

As his attention refocused on his trek, Jaxson saw a huge dark shadow forming in front of him. With a hard swallow, he raised the lantern up, then released a grunt of relief—he had reached the mammoth boulder that marked the little river's turn southward. Walking over to the rock and using the dim glow from the lantern, Jaxson surveyed the area—and no matter how hard he tried, he couldn't stop his thoughts from drifting to Travis Perryn. It was at the big boulder—at least that was the rumor—that Fetch had waited to ambush poor Travis.

As he bowed his head in despair and stared blankly at the mud, Jaxson slowly realized that he and the boulder were surrounded by scores of fresh hoof and boot prints. Someone had been here—recently. With renewed hope, Jaxson waved the lantern about, calling Daven's name over and over. Then, cautiously, he moved to the river's edge, and holding the lantern out, he scanned the area below him.

"Daven!" Jaxson shouted as he saw his friend lying facedown at the river's edge. Jumping into the little ravine, he set the lantern next to him and carefully turned Daven over—and his happiness immediately withered. His friend's shirt and vest were drenched with blood and mud, and two bullet wounds, one high on the chest and one low, were clearly visible. As he lowered his ear to Daven's heart, Jaxson closed his eyes and silently prayed that he'd hear something.

There! he hollered to himself. He heard a beat—there was still a chance! "Daven?" he called. "Daven, it's Jaxson." Lifting his friend's head, Jaxson cupped his hand, dipped it into the river, and brought the water to Daven's lips. Nothing happened and he tried again...and again.

Then his friend moved.

"Come on, Helpful," Jaxson urged, raising up a fourth handful of water.

Slowly, the pale-blue eyes opened.

Elated, Jaxson slipped his arm under Daven's back and lifted his friend to a sitting position. "You're gunna be okay, Helpful...I'm gunna get ya outta here. We'll cut through the Manvil farm and get to Doc Spreyer's real fast...okay?" Jaxson explained, trying to reassure his friend—and himself. Then, using all his strength, Jaxson started to pull Daven to his feet, but stopped when his friend cried out in pain.

"Wait..." Daven choked out in a hoarse whisper.

Reluctantly, Jaxson eased his friend back down. "We gotta try again, Helpful."

Daven mouthed a few inaudible words while fumbling with his watch chain.

"What do you need?"

"Watch..."

Reaching into Daven's vest pocket, Jaxson removed the pocketwatch. "Here," he said, and as he placed the timepiece in his friend's hand, fear suddenly grabbed at Jaxson's neck and raised the hairs on the back of his skull—Daven was so cold.

"No...give...Peter..."

Immediately, Jaxson's eyes started to water. He wanted to tell his friend that the bequeathal was unnecessary...that everything was going to be okay...that he would see his brother soon. But all Jaxson could do was nod and stuff the watch into his trouser pocket. "I'll make sure your brother gets it."

Daven smiled slightly. "Take...care...of him."

Blinking back his tears, Jaxson nodded again. "I will...I promise."

"Tell him...I...love..." Daven murmured, his voice fading.

"I'll tell him."

Knowing that there was very little time left, Jaxson again shoved his arms around his friend, and this time, he didn't stop moving until he had Daven over his shoulder. Then, grasping the lantern, he started to trudge through the mud—knowing that his only hope of getting out of the riverbed with his friend was the fallen tree he had used earlier.

Clang. Clang. Clang.

Anna jerked instantly awake at the sound of the emergency bell at the kitchen door. And, as thoughts of Peter—and the threat against his life—filled her head, she threw off her sheets and sprang from her bed. Quickly slipping a wrapper over her night robe, Anna ran into the hall just in time to see her father and the flicker of his candle descend the stairs. With her heart thumping against her chest, she rushed down the staircase and into the kitchen, and as her father opened the back door, Anna grabbed another candle and some matches from the pantry shelves.

"My friend's...been shot. Help him...please," the person at the door begged breathlessly.

Anna immediately recognized the voice, and the words 'my friend' ripped through her body. Trying to calm her shaking hands, she lit her candle, then, as she turned, she saw Jaxson Averill in the middle of their kitchen—with a man slung over his shoulder.

"Bring him into my office," Doctor Spreyer bellowed, rushing into the room.

Jaxson followed the doctor inside, and Anna followed after them—all the while praying that she was wrong about the identity of the injured 'friend.'

"On the table," Doctor Spreyer ordered as he headed to his cabinets.

"This way," Anna urged while dashing in front of Jaxson so her candle could light the way. "Put him down here," she said, pointing to a tall and narrow table against the wall.

As Jaxson carefully shrugged his friend off his shoulder and onto the table, Anna placed her candlestick on the windowsill and quickly grabbed some towels. Then, turning back toward the table, her heart sank as she peered at the face of the injured man. "Oh, no," she moaned as she started to wipe the mud from Daven's face.

With his stethoscope and a few other utensils in his hands, the doctor hurried over to the table, elbowed a soaked and stunned Jaxson out of the way, and froze for a heartbeat as he, too, recognized his patient. Setting his tools on the table, Doctor Spreyer grabbed his stethoscope and placed it on Daven's chest.

For a few moments, no sound could be heard—except for the doctor's movements as he made his examination. Then, trying to hold back her tears, Anna whispered, "I'll get some lamps, Papa...you'll...you'll need more light than this for...for surgery."

"Ach...nein...surgery isn't going to help," the doctor murmured as he laid his hand over Daven's eyes and closed the powdery-blue gems...for the last time.

Jaxson watched in silence as Mrs. Spreyer filled the cup in front of him with coffee, then she patted him on the shoulder. Not quite knowing why he had been invited to stay with the doctor's family, Jaxson nodded his thanks, grasped the earthenware cup with both hands, and took a sip of the hot liquid. Maybe, it was all just a terrible dream, he reasoned. But, as he scanned the mournful faces around him, he knew it wasn't a dream—it was a real-life nightmare.

"Peter will be here soon," Anna whispered, her voice shaking. "He said he was going to stop by this morning before he went to…"

"I'll tell him," the doctor said, tenderly grasping his daughter's hand.

"No, it's something I should do," she returned as her tears started to fall once again. "I want Peter to know that…that he's not alone…that his family is here for him."

Suddenly, a cloud of confusion parted, and Jaxson started to understand why the Spreyers had befriended him…and why they were hurting as much as he was. They knew Peter Leighton, and from their conversation, Jaxson guessed that they also knew Peter and Daven were brothers. Taking another swallow of his coffee, he shook his head. Daven had never mentioned knowing the Spreyers—but then there was a lot about his friend that he never got the chance to know…

"Oh, poor Peter," Anna moaned. "Why did this have to happen?"

Irene Spreyer stroked her daughter's cheek. "I don't know why, Liebchen. And we may never know why God allowed it to happen…we just have to trust Him and His decisions."

"But Peter's faith is just starting to bloom again. What is going to happen to that faith now? And what can I do so he doesn't turn away from God?"

"You can pray for him," her mother returned softly. "But this is Pay-ter's crossroads, Liebchen…he and the Lord must work it out."

"I know, but this is going to be so hard…Peter's already lost so much."

"Ja," the doctor agreed. "But there is a reason and a purpose for this dark time…we'll just have to pray that Pay-ter runs to the Lord for comfort, instead of shaking his fist at Him."

Anna nodded as a knock sounded at the front door. Rising from her chair, she took a deep breath, then another. She had to be strong, she told herself as she reluctantly headed to the front of the house. She needed to be the support that Peter could lean on. Brushing the tears from her eyes, Anna grabbed the latch and slowly opened the inside door.

"Anna," Peter whispered from the other side of the screen, "I'm running late, but I wanted to stop and let—"

As Anna pushed the screen door open and the morning light illuminated her face—her tear-swollen, so very sad face—Peter cut himself off in mid-sentence. "What…what's wrong?" he asked as a wintry foreboding clutched his throat.

"Oh, Peter…"

Panic-stricken, Peter stepped inside the entranceway and gently grasped Anna's shoulders. "Anna, what's wrong…what's happened?"

His only answer was the tears rolling down her cheeks.

Another chill raced through him, causing the hairs on the back of his neck to stand on end. "Are you all right? Your mother and father?"

"We're okay…it's Daven."

"Daven?" he repeated, suddenly unable to catch his breath. "What…what happened?"

"He was shot."

The word echoed inside his head. "Where is he?"

"In Papa's office, but…"

Backing away from Anna, Peter turned and started to run down the hall.

"No, Peter! Wait!" she called, rushing after him. "There's something you have to know."

Peter stopped and stiffened as if ice water had been poured over him, and he circled to face her.

"I'm so sorry, Peter…but Daven died—"

"No! Don't you dare tell me that!" he shouted, emphasizing each word with a pointed finger. "Don't you dare tell me that my brother's dead!"

With his eyes ablaze with anger and anguish, Peter sprinted toward the doctor's office, and ignoring the sympathetic faces and pleas from those in the kitchen, he darted into the room—and panicked upon seeing a bloodstained sheet covering a lifeless body. Rushing over to the table, Peter yanked back sheet—and gasped as he beheld his brother's ashen, unmoving features.

"No!!" he screamed, slamming his fist on the table. "No!"

Then, as his tears started to fall onto Daven's bruised face, Peter pulled his brother toward him. "No, Dave, no," he cried, hugging him even tighter. "What am I going to do without you? This is all my fault…I should have never asked you to…" Choked by his own sobs, Peter fell silent and just held his brother while slowly rocking back and forth.

Anna gazed at Peter's back as he stood in the kitchen's outside doorway and blankly stared at the bright morning sky. She desperately wanted to chase away the guilt that had perched itself like a demon on his shoulder and which constantly prodded him—telling him that he was to blame for Daven's death. Slowly, Anna approached Peter from behind and wrapped her arms around him—and as they stood in silence, she felt a chill run through him. She had already urged him twice to come out of the cool morning air, but he refused. Nor would he don his frock coat and vest, which he had discarded after noticing that they had been stained with Daven's blood.

"Peter, please come inside," Anna tried again, gently stroking his arm.

He finally yielded and let her guide him to the kitchen table. Slumping onto one of the chairs, Peter wearily looked from Anna, to the doctor, to Jaxson, and finally, to Mrs. Spreyer.

"You knew he was going to die, didn't you?" he asked Anna's mother.

Mrs. Spreyer shook her head. "No."

"Yes, you did," he pushed. "That's why you had me go after him last night. You said, 'don't let it end like this'—you knew."

"No, Pay-ter, I just knew that you couldn't let the conversation end with anger."

At her response, Peter lowered his eyes and started massaging his left palm with his right-hand thumb. Then, realizing what he was doing, he shook his hands and curled them into fists—somehow, he had inherited his brother's nervous habit.

"We can take care of the arrangements for you, Pay-ter—if you'd like," Mrs. Spreyer offered.

"No, I'll take care of Daven," Peter murmured, "as I should have been doing right along."

"Pay-ter," Doctor Spreyer put in quietly, "you must stop blaming yourself."

"Why? It was my fault—and God's…I put Daven into His hands last night, and this is how He takes care of him!"

"God was there with Daven…the Lord may not have protected Daven the way you wanted Him to—but He was there."

"If He was there, He should have done something to save my brother," Peter said as he rose from his chair and started to pace. "The truth is—God just let me down again."

Standing up, Doctor Spreyer moved toward the dry sink and intercepted Peter's meandering path. "Are you angry with the Lord for taking Daven home?" he asked, placing his hands on Peter's shoulders. "Or for taking him away from you?"

Peter peered deeply into the doctor's eyes. "Both," he answered, then he pulled away and returned to his pacing. "No…I guess I don't blame God for taking Daven away from me—I failed to take care of him…I should have never waited to get the Marshall…I should have never let Daven leave last night…and I should have never involved him in the first place…this wouldn't have happened if I had—"

"The Lord called Daven," Anna tried. "It was his time."

"His time?! He was your age, Anna!" Peter exclaimed. "He should have had more time…he should have had the chance to…to accomplish something."

"But he did. Daven touched all the lives he was supposed to…so he was called home."

With all his might, Peter fought the urge to scream. He wanted, so badly, to shout at the Spreyers to just shut up and leave him alone…but he couldn't do that—they were the closest thing to a family that he had now. There was no one else. Then, as his thoughts strayed to his brother, Peter's eyes started to water. "I just don't see it that way," he said, blinking the tears away.

"Don't you remember Anna's portrait that I showed you?" Mrs. Spreyer asked as she fought against an attack of coughing. "Don't you remember the white speck?"

"I don't really need a painting lesson right now," Peter hissed between clenched teeth.

"The white speck…the reflection in the eyes…do you remember it?" she persisted.

"I remember. But I don't see what that has to do with—"

"When you were up close to the painting," Mrs. Spreyer cut in, "the white reflection seemed so tiny and to serve no purpose, correct?"

"Yes," he moaned, wishing that she would just stop talking.

"But, when you looked at that dot from far away, you saw how important it was," she went on, her voice becoming hoarse. "You said yourself that without that little white speck the painting would be vacant—that it wouldn't have any sparkle...that speck is..." Mrs. Spreyer tried to continue, but another coughing bout interrupted her.

"That speck is Daven," the doctor offered. "You're looking at your brother from up close—it's God who sees the complete painting. To you, Daven's contribution may have seemed too small and to serve no purpose—but from the Lord's perspective, it was a very, very important part of the portrait...he is the sparkle in our life's picture."

Peter stood speechless. He understood the explanation—he even believed it—but it still didn't take away the pain...or the guilt...or the anger...

A sudden cuckoo from the kitchen's clock pulled Peter from his rumination and told him, with every sound, that he should have been at Karl's house over an hour ago. He knew he should go and finish the job that had brought him to Sandorville—and that his brother had died for—but he just couldn't move. Leaning against the kitchen counter, Peter haphazardly reviewed the events leading up to the loss that pierced him to the core—then his mind caught on a barb he hadn't seen before. "Why did this happen?" he asked as his thoughts remained with the vital point that had snagged him.

"Oh, Peter..." Anna soothed, rising from her chair.

"No. Why did they kill him? As of last night, we had the advantage...and how did Daven get here?" Peter questioned, his voice rising along with his frustration. "What happened last night?!"

"I brought him," Jaxson offered quietly.

As he studied his brother's friend, Peter finally noticed that Jaxson was even more mud-covered than Daven had been—and that the man's shirt was discolored with blood.

"Do you know what happened?"

Jaxson shrugged. "Some of it."

"Tell me."

"Well, they let Helpful, uh, Daven go early 'cause he hurt his hand."

Peter nodded. "I know about that part."

"A lot later," Jaxson continued, "Ivy came out to the factory."

"Who's Ivy?"

"A girl who works at Everly's…she told me that Fetch shot Daven and that they dumped…that they took him to the South Pine…that's when I went to look for him," he answered. Then, after wiping a sleeve across his watering eyes, Jaxson reached into his pocket. "Here," he added, holding Daven's watch by the chain.

As the timepiece pendulumed back and forth, Peter's features stiffened, and with a shaking hand, he reached out and grasped his brother's treasured pocketwatch. "Oh…oh, no," he moaned as shame and sorrow started to pound at his temples. "It's all my fault." Tightly clutching the watch in his palm, Peter raised his fist and brushed at the tears rolling down his face.

"Daven said to tell ya that—"

"Daven said?" Peter cut in, shuddering at the words. "He was alive when you found him?"

Jaxson nodded. "Yeah…he told me to give ya the watch and to tell ya that he loved ya too…I tried to get him here as fast as…"

Peter didn't hear the rest. All he could hear was remorse beating against his skull. Although he had loved his brother very much—he had never voiced that emotion to Daven. Turning his back to the others, Peter stared at the watch in his hand, but it soon blurred as his eyes filled with tears.

It wasn't supposed to have ended this way…it just wasn't part of the plan. Rubbing the moisture from his eyes, Peter recalled the map he had written for his life. Instantly, despair clutched his throat…now, he'd have to rewrite his future again—and this time without Daven. Looking once more at the timepiece, Peter shook his head as he imagined his brother's horrible, pain-filled last hours. He, not Jaxson, should have been there for Daven.

Feeling Anna's hand on his arm, Peter circled back around and slipped the watch into his trouser pocket.

"Come sit down," Anna urged, gently tugging on his forearm.

Peter shook his head and peered at Jaxson. At least, he told himself, Daven didn't die alone. "Did you say that Fetch shot him?"

Jaxson nodded.

"Do you know why?"

"Yeah...he found out that Daven and you were workin' together."

The muscles in Peter's jaw tightened. "Oh, no...they must have...they must have seen us when we were talking out by the barn last night...I should have never—"

"No," Jaxson cut in, standing up. "Ivy said that Miss Rheinhardt told Fetch that you two were brothers."

"Miss Rheinhardt?" Peter echoed in disbelief.

"Uh huh."

Peter massaged his aching temples. Why didn't he have Daven use an alias? Why? He knew that Lori could inadvertently reveal who his brother really was—he even voiced that fear on the day he arrived. Lori didn't know Daven's face, but she knew his name...if only he had given his brother a pseudonym...

"I wonder how she ended up telling him," Peter murmured, not even realizing that he spoke the words aloud. "Karl told me that Lorelei and Fetch didn't exactly enjoy each other's company anymore."

"That ain't true," Jaxson replied. "Ivy said Fetch and Miss Rheinhardt are..." Letting his sentence fade into silence, Jaxson glanced at Anna and her mother, then he continued in a whisper. "They are bedfellows—day and night bedfellows."

"What?!" Peter gasped, feeling as if Jaxson had just sliced him with a knife.

It was Lori! She was the missing piece in his puzzle. She, somehow, bridged the gaps between the salesman, the letters addressed to the fictitious Samuel Kelly, Henry at the post office, and Fetch. And that meant she was also a part of the whole plan to steal the factory away from Karl. Peter shook his head, disgusted with himself. It had never occurred to him that Lorelei might be involved in the scheme or that she was the one charming Karl into letting go of the reins.

Now, it all made sense…now, he understood why she had despised him and his new position within the company. Suddenly, Peter's simmering rage started to boil. "If you'll all excuse me," he announced, moving toward the back door, "I have a couple of necks to wring."

"Nein, Pay-ter!" the doctor exclaimed, rushing over to the screen door to block Peter's exit. "Go to the Marshall instead."

"Please, listen to Papa!" Anna begged as she joined her father at the door. "Revenge isn't the answer…it'll only get you killed too."

Peering at the two distressed faces in front of him, Peter exhaled. Somewhere, deep inside his heart, he knew they were right, but he couldn't fight the fermenting anger and grief that was prodding him forward. Without answering, he squeezed between the human blockade, dashed off the porch, and bolted for the barn—and the doctor's carriage. Then, noticing someone at his heels, Peter stopped and turned around. "Go back into the house, Jaxson!" he hollered. "You're not going to change my mind!"

"Don't plan to…I'm goin' with ya."

"This isn't your fight."

"Yeah, it is," Jaxson returned. "I got a promise to keep."

Lori Rheinhardt lounged at the dining room table and studied the Social Column's report of her birthday reception. Even though she had practically memorized the two-day-old story, she still couldn't stop herself from rereading it once more.

"Aren't you tired of that article yet?"

Startled, Lori glanced up. "Father?" she asked in surprise. It had been a long time since she had seen her father up and dressed before eight in the morning.

"Where's your mother?" he asked, pointing to the empty place at the table.

"In the garden."

"At this hour?"

"The flower show is in a few days, Father."

Karl held up his hand. "Say no more."

"Do you want me to have the cook make you something for breakfast?"

Sinking onto the chair at the head of the table, Karl sighed. "No, thank you. I'm fine."

"Why are you up so early, Father?"

"Peter was supposed to meet me here—quite awhile ago," he said, glancing at the clock sitting on the sideboard. "We had something to take care of regarding the factory."

Lori took a deep breath—Quentin was right. If she was going to remain the only beneficiary to her father's company, she had to tell him about the extra pieces of furniture that were being made in the factory...she had to tell him about her involvement...and she had to get him to stop trusting Peter Leighton. But how?

"Oh?" she purred in a sugary voice. "What's wrong?"

"It's nothing you have to worry about."

"But I'd like to help."

"Peter and I can handle it, Lorelei."

"But—"

"It's a company matter," Karl cut in crisply, "so it's none of your business."

Lori's lips stiffened. The kitten act wasn't working, and she knew it was time to finally stand up to her father—no matter what damage it did.

"It is my business, Father," Lori announced, pushing the newspaper aside. "I have as much right to be a part of Rheinhardt Furniture as my brothers did...and more right than Peter Leighton has."

"Daughter, this is not the time," Karl returned as he stood and walked into the solarium.

Growling under her breath, Lori shook her head. She hated the name 'Daughter'—it was a constant reminder of her 'defect.' And it told her that she was losing her battle already. Sliding her chair back, Lori rose and followed after her father.

"This is the time," she proclaimed as she entered the sun parlor, "especially if you and Peter were planning to confront Quentin about the furniture that he's making on the side."

Slowly, Karl turned from the large window overlooking the garden. "What?"

"Is that why Peter was coming here? So you two could go see Quentin?"

His brow creasing in confusion, Karl just nodded.

"Well, you're blaming the wrong person."

"We know Victor's involved too."

Lori stomped her foot on the floorboards. "No! I'm the one who's responsible."

Karl laughed. "I know you have a certain attachment to Quentin because he's one of your old beaus, but for you to try to take responsibility for what's going on is ridiculous," he returned, circling back to look at the garden.

Lori's eyes widened with rage, and rushing over to the window, she grabbed her father by the arm and spun him around to face her. "It is not ridiculous!" she seethed. "You have become so...so melancholy since Marcus was killed...and you let Rheinhardt Furniture just drift away from you."

Karl glanced at his daughter's hand as it clutched his forearm, then at her flushed features. "I...I know...that's why I called Peter in."

Lori screamed. "Why? Why didn't you think of me?"

The older man chuckled and, one by one, peeled Lori's fingers from his arm.

Her father's laughter—and the leech-like removal of her grasp—intensified Lori's rage. "Why didn't you ask me for help? Is it because I'm not one of your precious male heirs?" she demanded. "Well, Father, I have a bit of news for you...I have a rightful place in this family's company—I plan to take it."

"But you don't know anything about—"

"About how to run a furniture business?" she cut in. "I know everything... I've been doing it ever since Marcus died."

"Been doing what?"

"Running a business."

Karl grunted and stroked the side of her face as if he were trying to calm a lunatic's rantings. "Lorelei..."

Bristling at her father's patronizing tone, Lori averted her gaze and shook her head. How was she ever going to unbolt his prejudiced, bullheaded, closed mind? she wondered. How was she going to make him listen to her? Her kitten act had failed, and she was scorned as a lioness...what could she do now?

"Father, I know that you're disappointed by the fact that I'm female," she offered, hoping that her newest stratagem would work, "but I'm the only child you have left. And I also know that you've enjoyed having Peter Leighton close by—but he's not family. He's just the son of a man you met in the war. He's really a stranger...a stranger that you've seen just a couple of times in the past few years—and only then because he needed money."

"Lorelei, Peter's not like that."

"I know you think highly of him, Father, but you really know nothing about him."

Silence.

Unsure if she had made any progress in prying open her father's opinions, Lori moistened her suddenly dry lips and offered, "You've never given me the chance to become a part of our company."

"Lorelei, you're just not equipped to deal with—"

"Why?! Because I'm a woman?!" she interrupted, her fury renewed. "For your information, Father, I am equipped to run Rheinhardt Furniture, and your attitude has forced me to prove it to you."

Again, no reply.

Drawing in a deep breath, Lori stared at her father's stony countenance. She had no idea if he was about to hug her or strike her, but either way, she was already too far down a forbidden road to stop now...she might as well see what was at the end...

"I asked Victor and Quentin to help me show you that I was more than capable of becoming involved in the factory, so whatever you do, don't put any of the blame—or the credit—on them. It was all me...Victor has been gathering special furniture orders and sending them to me. They're orders for the carved pieces that you're so against creating—but that our company can make so beautifully."

"And who's Samuel Kelly?"

Lori flinched at the question, realizing that Peter and her father had managed to find out quite a lot about her venture. "I'm Samuel Kelly...Victor addresses the orders to Samuel Kelly, and little Henry at the post office puts them aside for me. Henry thinks they're a coded message from a beau that you don't approve of, and he just loves helping me...anyway, I pick up the orders and get Quentin started on filling them…I take care of ordering the wood, billing the customers, taking care of the books…"

Karl's eyes grew wide and his features stiffened. "All behind my back?!"

"Yes—because you forced me to. I had to show you that I could do it."

Karl ran his hand through his silvery hair and plopped down onto one of the rattan chairs facing the garden. "How…how could you be a part of this…this scheme?"

"It was never meant to hurt you, Father."

A snort answered her.

Wondering if her father had been silenced by rage, disappointment, revulsion, or indulgence, Lori turned and gazed out the window. "How did you find out? Both Victor and Quent told me that they said nothing to you."

"I, uh, I got a letter from Mrs. Hopewell," Karl murmured.

"Mrs. Hopewell? How? How did you get it?"

"She sent it to me—the owner—not to your Samuel Kelly…she told me all about the wonderful carved cabinet that my company made for her…that's when I knew something was wrong—and I sent for Peter…since then, he and his brother have been trying to find out who's been stealing from me."

As she listened to her father's words and heard his wounded tone, Lori circled and lowered herself onto the floor by his chair. "No, not stealing…all the money I've made is in the bank, except for Victor's and Quentin's share of it—and it's all yours. I never wanted it…I only wanted you to accept me as you did the boys," she said, then she put a pout on her face and lowered her head onto his knee. "But now, you hate me…"

Karl caressed her hair. "No…"

Looking up, Lori forced tears to fall from her eyes. "Then you forgive me?"

"I don't know why you did this…but we'll make things right…somehow," Karl muttered.

Lori stifled a cheer. At least the most difficult part—getting back into her father's favor—was now over.

"But why?" Karl continued. "Why did you need to take advantage of the men?"

Before Lori could answer, a loud pounding sounded on the front door, followed by someone yelling "Where is she?!"

And, suddenly, Peter Leighton burst into the solarium.

"I tried to stop him, Mr. Rheinhardt," the butler angrily puffed from the doorway. "But he just—"

"It's all right, Kenley," Karl announced with a wave of his hand, dismissing the servant.

Lori rolled her eyes and pushed herself from the floor. Peter Leighton! His interference never ended. Then, as she studied the wild-eyed, disheveled, and obviously distressed Peter and the bloodstained man standing next to him, Lori realized that something was terribly amiss, and her pulse began to quicken.

"You! You're working with Fetch!" Peter snarled and pointed at her. "You've been in on his whole operation from the start!"

"It's all right," Karl said, rising. "Lori explained it all to me."

"It's all right?!" Peter exclaimed with a loud curse. "Last night, she told Fetch that Daven was my stepbrother!"

As everyone's eyes fell on Lori, she backed up a step. "So?" she snipped, bewildered by the sudden animosity. "Quent said there was some furniture in Father's office that was carved by a kid named Daven Ashby, and he asked me if I knew him."

Peter instantly paled and the anger in his eyes melted into sorrow. "Fetch must have recognized Daven's work," he moaned, gazing at Karl.

"The truth is out now," the older man declared with a shrug. "What difference does it make?"

"The difference between life and death," Peter choked out, his voice breaking. "Namely, my brother's…Fetch killed Daven last night."

Lori laughed at Peter's pathetic and conspicuous attempt to lure her father away from her once again. "That's not true! Why would you make up such a horrible lie?"

"Would you like to see the truth, Lori? Daven's body is still at the doctor's house."

As Lori studied Peter's anguished expression and remembered Quentin's odd and barbarous behavior from their meeting the night before, her confidence began to fade. "What makes you think that Quent had anything to do with your brother's death?"

"Because Daven's been working in the factory—as the carver."

Her brow furrowing in puzzlement, Lori shook her head. "What are you talking about? The carver's a man named Travis Perryn."

Peter grunted. "Seems your precious Quentin hasn't been keeping you very well informed of the goings-on…Fetch got rid of Travis a long time ago…in fact, he killed him too."

"That's not…"

"And he replaced Travis with my brother."

Without warning, her father's words—words she had ignored during their battle—came crashing back into Lori's thoughts…

'That's when I knew something was wrong—and I sent for Peter…since then, he and his brother have been trying to find out who's been stealing from me.'

"This doesn't make any sense," Lori murmured. "Even if Daven was working in the factory, why would Quentin—"

"Kill him?" Peter interrupted. "Because Daven knew, firsthand, about your operation at the factory and how you're treating the men…and he told me…and I told your father."

Guessing that Peter's reasoning had been clouded by the shock of losing his brother, Lori looked to her father for a coherent explanation. "What does he mean…how we're 'treating the men'?"

"He's talking about what Daven went through while he was at the factory," her father answered.

"What did he go through?!"

"Quit the game, Lori!" Peter hollered. "We know all your tactics…forcing the men to work for absolutely nothing…threatening them if they try to leave…beating them if they—"

"You're insane, Peter Leighton!" she shrieked. "Those men are paid—and paid well—no matter whose order they're working on…I made sure of that!"

"They are not paid at all—Fetch keeps their wages."

As the dark-skinned stranger next to Peter nodded his head in agreement, realization and humiliation washed over Lori. Quentin had used her! The manipulator was now the one being manipulated. Turning sideward, Lori faced her father. "If Quent is doing that, he's doing it on his own." Then she glanced at Peter. "I didn't know Quentin had plans to kill Daven."

Peter winced at the reminder of his brother's death. "I can't believe this! How could both of you have been so blind?!"

Only silence answered him.

Staring at Karl and Lori in disbelief, Peter growled in frustration and anguish, and as the noiselessness started to suffocate him, his anger toward Fetch condensed into one single thought. Turning on his heel, Peter bolted from the solarium, through the dining room, and back into the entranceway, then, as he ran for the front door, he came face-to-face with Jaxson.

"Move!" Peter barked, his eyes fixed on the door.

"You're not thinkin' right," Jaxson returned, grabbing Peter's arm.

"Fetch has to pay for what he did."

"He will—God'll see to that."

"God?" Peter fumed, yanking his arm away. "I trusted Him and look what happened! No more—I'm going to handle things now!"

"Fetch'll be waitin' for us! Don't ya know that?!"

"You don't have to come."

Jaxson frowned at Peter's remark. The same thought had occurred to him. He knew he should just walk out the door and keep going…but he couldn't. He couldn't leave—even though siding with Peter meant a probable end to his life. "I'm still goin' with ya."

Peter's brow furrowed. "Why?"

Why? Jaxson repeated inwardly. Why? He couldn't really explain it. The promise he had made to Daven was only half of the reason for his new loyalty— the other half was Peter himself. As he stared at his new ally, Jaxson realized that there was very little in common between the two stepbrothers, except for the same headstrong trueheartedness…he had admired that quality in Daven—and now, he admired it in Peter.

"Let's go," Jaxson announced as he pulled open the Rheinhardts' front door.

As the coach carrying both him and Jaxson sped into the factory's yard, Peter quickly pulled in the reins, then, jumping from the still-rolling carriage, he darted up the steps, across the platform, and into the building.

"Fetch! Fetch, where are you?!" he shouted—but the roar of the machines smothered his words.

Running through the factory and ignoring the bewildered and questioning workers, Peter hollered for his brother's killer as he pushed at the overhead levers and disconnected the saws and lathes from their power source.

"I'm right here."

Instantly, Peter whipped around and sprinted toward the source of the gruff voice.

"What's the matter, Leighton?" the big man asked as he puffed on a freshly lit cigar. "Did ya lose somethin'?"

The question struck Peter as hard as a fist, and halting in mid-stride, he reached out to grab the foreman's neck—but immediately stopped when Bryce and another man appeared behind their employer.

"Odds ain't too good, are they, Leighton?" the big man teased as seven more men joined his group.

Peter swallowed hard and glanced at Jaxson and the rest of the workers— who stood as far away from the impending bloodshed as they could. Slowly, Peter's heart sank. He was just one man against the ten that stood in front of him—then his hopes were hit with another blow as Frank Hallam walked over and boosted Fetch's number to eleven. As he studied the hopeless scene in front of him, all Peter could think of was his recent conversation with Jaxson…he had so confidently announced that he was 'going to handle things now.'

Yes, Peter thought, he had handled them all right—as usual, he had plowed ahead without consulting God…and now, only God could get him out of the mess he was in. Oh, Lord, Peter prayed silently, *I wouldn't blame You if You've closed Your ears to me...but if You're still listening...I need Your help...*

"You ready to join your brother?" Fetch announced.

The query infuriated Peter—as did the foreman's smug expression. "You had no right to kill Daven."

Fetch laughed again. "I had every right to get rid of that blue-eyed snake," he said, throwing his lit cigar to the floor.

"Your fight was with me...not my brother."

"That's right, Leighton, my fight's with you—and you're gunna suffer for what you've done," the foreman declared, removing a half-finished table leg from the lathe next to him. "Killin' your brother was just the beginnin' of the hurt I'm gunna make you feel."

Peter's strength instantly plunged as the foreman's words rang through his skull, and as he averted his gaze and bowed his head, he suddenly became aware of a low murmuring coming from the distant workers behind him. Then someone tugged at his left sleeve. Looking up, Peter gulped—it was Jaxson. And behind him stood a thin, wiry man who loudly spoke out in German. The foreign words flew past Peter's ears—and his understanding—all of them, except one...Daven's name. Peter nodded, although he wasn't quite sure what he was agreeing with.

"Mr. Leighton?"

The call drew Peter's attention back to Fetch's bunch, and he watched in stunned amazement as Frank Hallam stepped away from the foreman's side.

"I'm sorry about your brother," Hallam offered as he walked toward Peter. "I don't wanna sit with the garbage no more...can I join you?"

Unable to find any words to say, Peter just nodded.

"Hallam, you filthy snake!" Fetch barked. "Go ahead—and you can die with him too."

"I'll take care of my ol' buddy, don't you worry, Mr. Fetch," Bryce sneered as Hallam positioned himself next to Jaxson.

As the two factions formed and readied themselves for battle, the remaining abused workers started to come to life. Most of them, obviously not wanting any part of the approaching war, ran from the factory, but some moved behind

Peter. Fetch's eyes suddenly darted from side to side as he watched the odds grow against him. And, noticing the same, two of the men supporting the foreman withdrew, then rushed out the door—followed by two more.

"Odds ain't too good, are they, Fetch?" Peter asked, not being able to resist the taunt.

Fetch snorted out a curse as a drop of sweat rolled down his temple.

"Why not just give up right now?" Peter reasoned. "Your backers are leaving you—including Karl."

"I'll get him back to my way of thinkin'," the foreman snarled. "I always do."

"No, you didn't—Lori did…but I don't think she's going to be helping you anymore."

"Whatd'ya mean?" Fetch growled, his hands tightening around the oak table leg.

"Lori knows what you've done here, without her knowledge…and she's not very happy with you."

Fetch cursed. "You…you've destroyed everything!" he roared and wildly whipped the heavy table leg at Peter, who leaped backward just in time to watch the hunk of wood swoop harmlessly in front of him.

Using their leader's assault as a signal, Fetch's men sprang at Peter's supporters…and the war began.

Enraged by his failed strike, the foreman immediately swung the piece of oak again—and this time he didn't miss. The blow smacked Peter square in the chest and sent him to the floor. Trying to regain his breath, Peter glanced around from his new vantage point and saw dozens of boots and legs engaged in small scuffles throughout the building. Then his heart quivered as he spotted Fetch's cigar in the middle of the sawdust-covered floor—surrounded by a circle of red-orange flames.

"Oh, no…"

It was then, as he crawled toward the cigar in the hopes of extinguishing the burning embers, that Peter saw the blur of Fetch's table leg coming directly toward his head. Instinctively, he raised his right arm to stop the blow and protect his face, and as the wood hit, Peter heard something crack—then came an incredible jolt of pain. With a shout of agony, Peter drew his broken forearm to his chest, and grabbing onto the machine next to him, he tried to pull himself to his feet, but another jab from the oak leg knocked him back down. Again, Peter glanced at the cigar—the fire was dangerously creeping out in all directions, devouring and gaining strength from every scrap of wood and sawdust crumb in its path.

"Fetch, the building's on fire!" Peter tried.

Deaf to anything but his rage, the foreman continued to maniacally thrust and swing the table leg up and down and to and fro. The jabs forced Peter to remain on the floor, but through constant movement, he managed to avoid most of the strikes—which enraged the foreman even more.

Finally, a clear shot came for Peter, and he kicked at Fetch's left knee—again and again and again. Losing his balance, the big man finally collapsed and dropped the table leg. Dragging himself over to the piece of oak, Peter shoved the weapon out of reach—then he turned to check the fire's progress…and his eyes widened in horror. The quickly moving flames had already started to eat away at the center of the factory.

As he ran out of the flame-filled factory, Jaxson wiped at his eyes, trying to clear the film of smoke that blocked his vision. Squinting, he surveyed the yard and was relieved to see that many of Fetch's outnumbered and fleeing men had been overcome by his coworkers. But it was the faces that Jaxson didn't see that worried him—Fetch, Bryce, Hallam, and Peter were missing. Then he saw Frank Hallam near the corner of the building, rising from the ground.

"Hallam," Jaxson yelled, sprinting over to the blonde-haired man.

"Bryce got away," Hallam panted, wiping at the bloody cuts and welts on his face. "I tried to stop him, but that man always did fight like a panther."

Jaxson sighed in disappointment at the escape. "Well, at least he's out of our lives," he murmured. Then he and Hallam exchanged weary and worried glances—Leland Bryce was not the kind of man to let things end so easily. "Have you seen Peter?" Jaxson asked, glancing around the yard again.

"I don't think he got out."

A cloud of dread settled on Jaxson's shoulders as he surveyed the building—and the flames pushing themselves against the windows. Suddenly, all he could hear was Daven's plea...

'Take...care...of him.'

The words repeated themselves over and over inside his head, and Jaxson found himself walking toward the flame-infested structure.

"What are you doing?!" Hallam shouted, following after Jaxson.

"I'm gunna get my friend outta there."

"It's no use...the fire's spread too far."

"I gotta try."

"Then I'm goin' in with ya."

Jaxson stopped and shook his head. "No. I want you to stay put out here. If Fetch makes it outta the factory, I want him stopped...we can't let him get away too." After finishing his orders, Jaxson gazed at Hallam in silence. It had always been the blonde-haired man who barked out the commands. Now, within a few seconds, they had traded places—and Jaxson waited for the reaction to the switch.

Hallam's expression tensed, then he looked at the deteriorating building. "If you're going—go...I'll keep a lookout for Fetch."

"Fetch!" Peter yelled. "The building's on fire!"

"It was almost all mine!" the foreman bellowed as he threw a reckless and unsuccessful jab at Peter's face. "And you...you took it all away!"

Thrusting out his good arm, Peter smacked the big man in the jaw and forced him back. Then, as the smoke and flames licked at his heels, Peter rammed his boot into Fetch's injured knee. Instantly, the foreman fell to the ground, cursing and writhing in agony. Using the momentary respite, Peter tried to draw in a breath. "You've lost...Fetch," he said as he choked on the smoky air. "Give...up."

The big man scrambled to his feet and lunged at Peter. "Never!" he hollered, and with the vow, he threw an angry punch—which landed squarely on Peter's injured arm.

As a spasm of pain ripped through his body, Peter grabbed onto the machine next to him to steady himself, but as Fetch delivered another hard blow to the broken limb, Peter's legs buckled, and he dropped to the floor.

"I ain't...never...givin' up!" Fetch shouted as he grabbed Peter's throat and started to squeeze. "This...factory's mine...understand?"

Gasping for air, Peter pressed against the foreman's face with his good hand. "There is...no factory...look."

As Fetch turned and studied the fiery interior, his expression became as fierce as the flames.

"There's nothing...left, Fetch," Peter wheezed, coughing from both the stranglehold and the smoke. "It's over."

"It'll be over, Leighton, when you're dead," the foreman shouted. Then, hitting Peter in the arm a third time, the big man clambered to his feet and disappeared into the flames.

Clenching his teeth against the pain, Peter forced himself to sit up, and as he wiped the tears of hurt and smoke from his eyes, he caught a glimpse of the foreman—hobbling up the stairs to the burning second floor. There would be no escape up there, Peter told himself. Fetch was heading for certain death. Or was he? As his head filled with doubt, Peter started to fear that Daven's killer would, somehow, escape without being punished.

"Peter! Peter!"

As he labored to his feet, Peter stared at the smoke surrounding him, trying to find the source of the bodiless voice calling to him. "Jaxson?" he questioned, finally seeing a face in the haze.

"Come on," Jaxson yelled, trying to be heard over the roar of the fire. "We gotta get outta here."

"No...I can't let Fetch get away—he has to pay for what he did."

"He can't get away from God—he'll pay."

Shrugging off the words, Peter turned and hurried up the stairs to the second floor—but there was no sign of the foreman. Then, as the flames started to force him back down the steps, he heard something. Rushing to the middle of the room, Peter barely caught himself before he fell through a gaping hole in the floor—the only remaining element of the elevator that once hoisted the furniture up and down between the two floors. And there, hanging onto the edge of the hole by his fingertips, was Fetch—who had fallen into the opening.

It would be so easy, Peter thought—and so perfect. All he had to do was step on Fetch's hands, and his brother's killer would fall into the hungry flames below. No one would know...no one. Raising his boot, Peter placed his heel on the foreman's fingers...all he had to do was press down...

With a loud cuss, Peter moved his foot and stepped aside. Unfortunately, there were two who would always know the truth...himself and God. Clenching his jaw, Peter knelt next to the hole, hating every second of what he was doing.

"Fetch! Grab hold!" he called, reaching out with his left hand.

Both men resentfully stared at each other, then Fetch finally grasped Peter's waiting arm—and not quite knowing why he was doing it, Peter pulled with all his might, trying to drag his hefty nemesis to safety.

Without warning, the foreman's face contorted into a bitter snarl. And with the words "Now, it's over," Fetch yanked on Peter's arm—and they both plunged downward...

For a moment, all Peter could do was gasp for air and wonder what had happened. Then, as he blinked the smoke from his eyes and studied his surroundings, he understood all too well...

Below him was the red-hot ground floor—and the twisted, lifeless form of Quentin Fetch. And above was the crumbling second story.

Somehow, he had managed to grab onto the rim of the hole with his left hand—and now, he was the one dangling between the floors.

Glancing downward once more, Peter stared at the burning remains of his nemesis—the man had been right...it was indeed over. Then, as he sighed in relief, Peter's left hand slipped an inch. Automatically, he tried to reach out with his other hand to regain his hold—but his broken arm wouldn't move. And, despite the heat, a chill shot through him—with only one usable arm, there was no way to pull himself out...

Then his fingers slipped again.

Peter knew he had only a few seconds before his weakening grip would fail, and as he glanced at the violent fire below him, he choked out a humorless laugh—the rising flames would probably reach him even before that happened.

"Oh, Lord," he prayed aloud, "forgive me, please…forgive me for not appreciating the gifts you've given me…and for—"

In the middle of his petition, Peter's fingers went limp, and he felt himself fall…

Suddenly, his body jerked as something caught his wrist. Peering upward, Peter gasped in amazement—two dark-skinned hands were holding onto his good arm.

As burning timbers fell around him, Jaxson tugged and pulled and finally drew Peter from the hole. Then, picking up the uncharred end of a beam, he rammed the wood through one of the windows.

"The stairs are gone," Jaxson explained as he helped Peter up. "We gotta jump."

Peter bobbed his head in understanding and headed for the window, but as he neared, he caught sight of a familiar item and abruptly stopped. "Oh, Dave, I'm so sorry," Peter moaned as he watched the flames lap at his brother's toolbox.

"Peter! Peter, come on!"

Reluctantly, Peter hurried over to the window, then, looking at Jaxson, he smiled sadly. "I never thanked you for being my brother's fri—"

The rest of his statement was silenced as a part of the roof caved in and covered the opening in the middle of the floor. Both Jaxson and Peter spun around and studied the place where they had been just seconds before.

"You can thank me down there," Jaxson shouted, pointing to the ground.

Peter nodded, climbed onto the windowsill, and jumped. As he hit the ground, the jarring landing sent another spasm of pain through his arm, and he fell onto his side—just in time to see Jaxson descend next to him. Once again, he felt his friend's grip on his left arm, and they hurried to a spot far from the burning building.

"Thank you for being…my brother's friend…and mine," Peter panted as he and Jaxson collapsed onto the grass and coughed the smoke from their lungs.

"You're...welcome," Jaxson returned with a smile.

As they sat in silence, both men watched as the flames engulfed the entire second floor and edged their way to the outside of the wooden building—even the previous night's rain did nothing to slow the fire's steady advancement.

Finally, Peter's breathing became easier, but as his lungs cleared so did his thoughts, and the events of the last few hours beat upon his already aching head. "Oh, no..." he groaned as a horrible thought raced through his brain.

"What?"

Shoving his hand into his trouser pocket, Peter grunted in relief. Somehow, through everything, his brother's watch had remained safe. "I thought I had lost this too," he murmured, pulling the timepiece out.

"It'll be a good keepsake for ya," Jaxson offered, staring at the silvery memento.

Peter shook his head absently and clicked open the cover. No, he thought, it would never be a keepsake—it would always be a remembrance of his failure...and his loss.

"Daven's with Jesus, you know that, don't you?" Jaxson asked.

"And what about Fetch?"

"Him?" Jaxson answered with a shrug, "God's prob'ly dealin' with him right now."

"Yeah?" Peter wearily returned as he tilted his head to look at his friend. "And is he getting what he deserved?"

"We all gotta answer for what we do while we're here," Jaxson said, pointing to the ground.

"Do you really believe that?"

"Yep. For awhile I sorta forgot it, but I believe it. And I know that God's punishment is gunna be a lot harder than anything you could have done to Fetch."

Nodding, Peter looked back at the blazing factory. "Did the workers get out safely?"

"Yeah."

"What about the rest of Fetch's men?"

"When I went back in to get ya, our boys had 'em all just about rounded up...'cept Bryce, he got away."

Peter's jaw instantly clenched at the news, and he released a long, discouraged exhale.

"Don't worry," Jaxson continued. "Someday, Bryce'll have to talk face-to-face with God, just like Fetch."

"Peter?! Peter?!"

Upon hearing the sweet voice that he thought he would never hear again, Peter struggled to his feet. "Here," he called.

Anna waved in return, and followed by her father, she feverishly maneuvered her way through the crowd gathering around the dying factory. "Thank God, you're alive," she shouted as she neared, then she threw her arms around Peter's neck and kissed him firmly on the lips.

Even though he enjoyed Anna's boldness and her kiss, the embrace pushed against his arm, and Peter pulled away shuddering with pain.

"Oh, my goodness!" Anna exclaimed, staring at his swollen, bloody arm. "Papa!"

Winded from his run, Doctor Spreyer panted as he joined them and proceeded to rip off what was left of Peter's sleeve.

"I think it's broken," Peter offered.

The doctor chuckled, still out of breath. "I think that's…putting it mildly, Son."

At the word 'Son,' Peter smiled at the doctor, whom he already considered family…then he looked at Jaxson, his new friend, whose loyalty seemed to have no bounds…then Peter gazed at Anna, the woman he loved and cherished, and he wrapped his good arm around her waist, drawing her close…then his thoughts drifted to his brother, whom he sorely missed. He had never realized it, but he had been given some very special gifts. Recalling his prayer spoken while he dangled between life and death, Peter promised himself to try to cherish all that he had been given, and lifting his eyes upward, he thanked God.

The End

Born and raised in Michigan, Nancy Feldbush has always approached life with a creative flair, which can be seen in just about everything she authors. And, having worked as an Art Director, a Graphic Designer, a Copy Editor, and a Copywriter, she knows firsthand how thrilling and trying it is to transform ideas into reality. So far, her greatest accomplishments in bringing her creativity to life are her two novels, *To Repay A Debt* and *To Rebuild A Life*.

Writing, or wordsmithing as Nancy calls it, is one of the most pleasurable challenges that she has ever faced. To shape words together, then reform and chisel away at them until they make a reader sigh, or laugh, or shed a tear is her favorite way to spend time. And now, with the completion of her second book, Nancy prays that, God-willing, her hobby will become her next career.

Rivaling her joy of wordsmithing is her love of history—evident by the amount of research Nancy does for her books. Although she is captivated by the famous people of history, she is even more fascinated by the everyday individuals...the ones who toiled day by day to carve out a place for themselves—just as we do today. Mesmerized with the details of the past, Nancy can spend hours reading antique postcards and be amazed by the artwork, the author's choice of words, the strokes of the pen, and even the marks from the post office.

Surrounded by her dog and three cats, who produce the warmhearted atmosphere she needs to write, Nancy does her best to craft stories that combine her fondness of history, her faith, and her devotion to friends and family.

Moose Run™
Productions

A publisher of books that offer readers a wholesome and enjoyable respite.

Moose Run Productions publishes manuscripts of various genres that are decent, uplifting, and steeped in Christian values. If you would like a **free** copy of our catalog, please visit our Web site at moose-run.com or complete and send this form to: Moose Run Productions • 22010 Highview • Clinton Township, Michigan 48036.

Name _____

Address _____

City, State, Zip _____

E-mail (optional) _____